SOMETHING TANGLED
Something True

GIULIANA VICTORIA

Developmental Editing: Cynthia A. Rodriguez

Editing: Alexa at The Fiction Fix

Proofreading: Louise Murphy (Kat's Literary Services)

Cover Illustration: Adduani

Typography: Disturbed Valkyrie Designs

Formatting: Cynthia A. Rodriguez

Also by Giuliana Victoria

Philia Players Series

Quiver

Tremble

Quake

Shiver

Secret Trials Series

Resilient Love

Rosa Ranch Series

Something Tangled Something True

Standalones & Novellas

Mistletoe Misconduct

 Playlist

Ain't No Love In Oklahoma – Luke Combs
TEXAS HOLD 'EM – Beyoncé
Austin – Dasha
For Life – Kygo and Zak Abel feat. Nile Rodgers
you look like you love me – Ella Langley feat. Riley Green
Where the Wild Things Are – Luke Combs
JOLENE – Beyoncé
LEVII'S JEANS – Beyoncé feat. Post Malone
II MOST WANTED – Beyoncé feat. Miley Cyrus
A Bar Song – Shaboozey
Down Bad – Taylor Swift
Slow It Down - Benson Boone
Used To Be Young – Miley Cyrus
TEXAS HOLD 'EM (PONY UP REMIX) – Beyoncé
No Angels – Justin Timberlake
Dancing On My Own – Calum Scott
Jealous – Labrinth
Waves – Dean Lewis
Falling – Harry Styles
September Song – JP Cooper
Roots – Calum Scott
Funeral – Teddy Swims
Natural Disaster – Zac Brown Band
She'll Be OK – 4Fargo
Pony – Ginuwine
Lo Que Pasó, Pasó – Daddy Yankee
Rosa la Peligrosa – Alexander Abreu and Havana D'Primera
La Vida Es Un Carnaval – Celia Cruz
La Gozadera – Gente De Zona feat. Marc Anthony

Lloraras – Dimension Latina and Oscar D'Leon
Pedro Navaja – Willie Colón and Rubén Blades
MY ROSE – Beyoncé
Promise – Romeo Santos feat. USHER
Deja Vu – Prince Royce and Shakira
ADMV – Maluma
Rojo – J Balvin
Turn off the Lights – LA INDIA
Bailando Bachata – Chayanne
Dos Locos – Monchy y Alexandra
Stand by Me – Prince Royce

Signature Fragrances

Lola Lima: *XERJOFF Naxos Eau de Parfum*

&

Ryder Lockhart: *Mancera Cedrat Boise Eau de Parfum*

This one is for every person who lost themselves trying to find their "why," and for the people who helped them make their way back home.

<3

Table of Cocktents

Pronunciation Guide

Lola Lima (Low-Luh LEE-Maa) – Female Protagonist
Bexaida (Bay-eye-Duh) – Lola's Mother
José (Ho-say) – Lola's Father
Mayte Avila (MY-teh Ah-Vee-Uh) – Lola's Best Friend
Penny – Mayte's Horse
Ewelina (Ev-eh-Lee-Nuh) – Lola's Friend (out of state)
Yanet (Jan-et) – Lola's Friend (out of state)
Johanna (Joe-AH-nuh) – Lola's Friend (out of state)
Karmella (Car-may-uh) – Lola's Friend (out of state)
Russ (Russ lol) – Lola's ex-fiancé
Ryder Maddox Lockhart (Rie-der Mad-ox Lock-hart) – Male Protagonist
Bee (Bee lol, again) – Ryder's Mother
Harlan (Har-len) – Ryder's Father
Ezekiel (Ez-eek-ee-al) – Ryder's Younger Brother
Asier (AEZIY-er) – Ryder's Horse
Lemmon Meringue (Lemon Mer-ang) – Ryder's Ex-wife

Ryde or Dye Book Club

Levi (LEE-vy)
Rhett (Ret)
Callaway (Cal-away)
Wyatt (Why-et)
Teddy (Ted-ee)

Content Warnings

- Mentions of domestic violence (not between MCs)
- Verbal abuse and gaslighting (not between MCs)
- Death of a friend in young adulthood
- On-page panic attacks and night terrors
- Chronic pain
- Biologic injections for the treatment of Rheumatoid Arthritis (needles)
- Stalking
- Blood and gore (minimal)
- Gun violence
- On-page therapy
- Bexaida's chancla

Foreword

If you've read any of my works before, you'll realize pretty quickly that this series is the start of something totally new for me. Everything from the small town to the campy vibes, suspenseful undertone, slow burn, and emphasis on flashbacks is newer for me. You're still in for a man-obsessed, tons of yearning, pining, and an all-around good time, in my opinion.

It's my hope that you (the reader) enjoy a blend of close friendships, healing relationships of all kinds, diversity in many beautiful varieties, a couple with open communication, some laugh-out-loud, over-the-top moments, and an overall cozy read.

With that said, thank you for taking a chance on me and my writing.

In regards to the Latine representation in this book, I want to bring light to the fact that in the real world, Lola's struggles with finding her footing would be even more difficult to overcome as a result of racism, prejudice, social injustice, systematic issues, and a million other things because our world does not cater to those who are different from the mediocre white men governing the United States. While this is mentioned in different ways throughout this story, I also lean heavily into the small town with a huge emphasis on found family within that town. This means that the teeny tiny community they reside in is filled with people Lola grew up with, who love, care for, and adore her, so her transition there is easier than it would be elsewhere. My intention in this was not to lessen the very real struggles that the Latine community and other BIPOC experience. My hope is that while this book is based in fiction, I've tried to find a balance between portraying some of the struggles Lola might face if she were to exist in reality, while also putting an emphasis on her hard work and determination.

It's an honor that I'm able to write these stories, and that's something I don't take for granted. I'm privileged to have worked with sensitivity readers who were not only an integral part of the creation of this book, but for them to trust me enough to share their thoughts with me and encourage me to write this story. It wouldn't feel right for me to write books with a fully white cast because not only do I believe BIPOC should exist in all things, but I am so unbelievably blessed to be surrounded by friends and family from incredibly diverse backgrounds. As such, I want to point out that this is not a BIPOC romance. It is a book with BIPOC characters, but not a BIPOC book written by a BIPOC author. I ask that, whether you enjoy this book or not, please check out some of the authors I've included on the next page, as you'll never read more accurate or authentic representation than you will from the authors with that lived experience. The pure, raw talent of each of these authors is something I think you'd all enjoy immensely, and I can't recommend them enough.

BIPOC Authors

BIPOC Authors I Adore & You Should Check Out:

A.E. Valdez
AJ Alexander
Allie Shante
Amber V. Nicole
Ambar Cordova
Amy Oliviera
Anna P.
Annika Sharma
Ava Rani
Britney S. Lewis
BriAnn Danae
Catharina Maura
Cynthia A. Rodriguez
Danica Nava
Danielle Brooks
Deanna Grey
Esha Patel
Evelyn Leigh
Georgia K. Boone
Goddess A. Brouette
H.M. Wolfe
I.B. Solís
Jade Hernández/Aleera Ceres
Jada West
Janiah Benitez
Janisha Boswell

J.J. Greenaway
J.S. Jasper
Kanitha P.
Kennedy Ryan
Kristina Forest
L.M. Ramirez
Layna James
Leigh Carron
Lillier Eros
Marie Maravilla
Miah Onsha
Mikayla Hornedo
MK Owens
N.J. Weeks
Natalie Caña
Natasha Bishop
Nelle Nikole
Nisha J Tuli
Nisha Sharma
N.M. Patel
Nouha Jullienne
Nuhaa Bardien
Oona Arlo
Ophelia Reign
Parveen B.
Riss M. Neilson
Ruby Rana
Shilo Kino
Siren Crow
Sophie Thomas
Soraya Nadia Bouazzaoui
Talia Hibbert
Tay Mo'Nae
Tember Sapphire

BIPOC AUTHORS I ADORE & YOU SHOULD CHECK OUT:

Uzma Jalaluddin
Vai Denton
Vaishnavi Patel
Varsha Chitnis

Lola

Chapter One

HOPE IS A GOOD BREAKFAST BUT A POOR SUPPER

SATURDAY, APRIL 19

"*LEVANTA ESE CULO YA!*" Mayte shouts, waking me from my unnecessarily short nap. She's crammed a million activities into a single day—not to mention the several minutes when I feared for my life white water rafting—and she won't allow me the pleasure of an hour-long nap?

I can't help but groan. "Just five more minutes," I plead with her, but it's futile.

"Nope. We only have one night to do this right, and you've already wasted an hour of it sleeping. Get your perky ass up and get ready."

I drag myself out of bed, and Mayte proceeds to spend the next hour and a half doing my makeup and hair, dressing me up like a doll. Considering I've been left in the dark about this entire kidnapping—I mean, *bachelorette party*—Mayte had to pack for me.

Once we're all ready, I'm ushered into the living room, where Mayte and Karmella spent their dedicated nap time decorating the archway in our BnB.

"Aww, this looks super cute. Thank you, guys," I tell them,

my eyes welling with tears at the time and thought they put into this weekend.

"Stop crying and come stand over here for a picture," Mayte tells me, setting her phone up on a plant she grabbed from the porch to use as a tripod.

I stand with all my favorite women under a giant banner that reads, "Miss to Mrs With All My Bitches."

"Okay, just one more!" Yanet yells at us, running from her phone to jump into the photo. She fluffs her hair before shooting a wide grin at the camera. A blinding flash goes off, and a honk comes from outside.

"Our ride is here," Mayte declares, leading us outside and into the car after double-checking the license plate, making the poor guy show her his ID, and then checking every door latch to ensure the child safety locks aren't on. *Better safe than sorry.* Though this behavior has definitely become more apparent since she had my niece.

We pile into the SUV, the backs of my thighs sticking to the leather seats, my friends and I stuck like sardines in a tin. Our driver has a nineties hits radio station playing low enough that we're able to continue talking.

We arrive at the club, a tall building in the middle of a strip of similar ones. There's a rooftop terrace I can see from the street, and a line of people wraps around the corner.

We make our way to the back of the line, my feet aching in my strappy red heels as we wade through the crowd. Half an hour passes, with Ewelina repeatedly telling Karmella to quit bitching, and my fiancé has called so many times Mayte threatened to toss my phone under the wheel of the next moving car she sees before we finally approach the bouncer. He lets us in without a hassle, and we're admitted for free thanks to my bride's sash.

"The wait was worth it, eh?" Mayte asks, wriggling her dark brows at me as we make our way into a multilevel club, Latin music on one floor, rap and R&B on the others.

"It's perfect." I smile at her, and for the first time today, I don't feel like I'm lying.

We spend the next couple of hours dancing. My joints ache as we move, but the alcohol numbs some of the pain. Eventually, we close this place down at 2 a.m., hobbling down the street in search of our rideshare.

"Don't worry, I booked our ride so we won't have to wait forever," Mayte tells us. Thank God *one* of us can plan ahead.

As we wait on the sidewalk, my mind a foggy, drunken mess, my phone rings loudly, the shrill sound stabbing my eardrums.

I fiddle with my phone before answering and pressing it to my ear.

"Lola, why are you answering the phone this late? You should be in bed." Russ's deep voice greets me, the bite in his tone sending a shiver of apprehension down my spine.

"It's my bachelorette party, Russ. I'm *allowed* to have fun," I tell him against my better judgment.

"Watch your tone with me, Lola. I'm sick of you living your life on whims and hope alone. You need to start acting like an adult. What would our parents think if they saw you looking like a two-bit floozy tomorrow after a drunken night without me?"

I turn away from my friends, unwilling to deal with their heavy stares and prying ears on top of Russ berating me. It's just too much.

I focus my attention on the nasty cement wall in front of me, trash and gum plastered to it like a mural. "Are you going to answer me or not?" he snaps over the line.

It takes a long moment of silence for me to gather my wits before I drag in a ragged breath. "My parents would think I was having fun with my friends and would be *happy* for me. As for your parents, I don't really care what they think."

"Excuse me?" he spits. "My parents, the people you're so intent on disrespecting, have been nothing but good to you.

Don't forget that the money I've put away to go toward *your* health insurance directly takes from them."

"Why is everything about money with you people?" The words fall from my mouth without thought as my frustration climbs to new heights. Russ started his company from the ground up. When we first met, the man was as broke as I was. His behavior is practically the Hollywood sign, reminding me how money corrupts those with fragile egos.

"You people?" he seethes. "Are you fucking kidding me? *You* are about to *marry* me. From the sounds of it, all you want is to be like *us people*."

When Russ was a quiet nerd with nothing but pocket change and a small startup company, I had wanted to be a part of his family. Now though? I'm not so sure.

When he gets like this, it's hard not to think about how different my life would've been if Ryder and I had worked out. But we were young. I had so many plans for my future, and he was grieving, making our time together little more than stolen moments.

The press of my friends' eyes into my spine burns each of my vertebra as I stand with fire in my chest and a lump the size of Texas in my throat. "I have to go. I'll see you tomorrow," I croak out, a sudden wave of sadness hitting me like a punch to the gut.

I hang up without another word, silencing my phone as Mayte whispers, "Our ride share is here, Lols."

I blink back the tears threatening to overflow and spin on my heel, piling into the minivan that is our newest Uber.

"Where could we get some drinks at this hour?" Mayte muses from the front seat.

Our driver doesn't say anything; he only nods his chin in the direction of the largest strip club I've ever seen.

"Ooh, can you drop us off there?" Johanna asks, and he nods.

Once we pull up, our driver tells us, "They close late, and it can be hard to find a ride at this hour. I don't want you ladies getting stranded, so take my number and call me if you need a ride. I have an early drop-off at the airport, but I'll get you when I'm done."

"Oh my gosh, thank you so much. That's really thoughtful!" Karmella tells him, jotting down his number before we head inside. We pay the cashier for general admission, which, strangely, comes with tickets to a *buffet.*

"*Aseré,* this is the best brunch buffet I've ever seen in my life!" Karmella shouts over the music, her brown eyes bright. We make our way to the end of the buffet, where men in penguin tuxedos serve every breakfast item under the sun.

"It's weird, isn't it? At a strip club?" Yanet asks, but she grabs a plate anyway.

"And they don't have alcohol. They stopped serving at 2 a.m. like the clubs," Mayte grumbles beside me.

"Maybe that's *why* they offer brunch. Keeps people here longer, and maybe it decreases the rate of drunk drivers if people wait around and eat before they leave," Ewelina chimes in.

"That's a good point," Johanna says, pointing at the bacon for the man to pile onto her plate.

We all take seats in the black velvet chairs at the front of the stage. The dancers are dragging themselves through the motions, one of them spinning around the pole with her eyes barely open. It's a stark contrast to her rhinestone hot-pink bikini and holographic heels, but it's late, and I'm just impressed they're still moving at all.

We throw money at them anyway, enjoying our brunch.

A woman a few seats down from us catches my attention. The man with her gently rubs circles on the back of her arm, his eyes focused on her rather than the group of men in suits crowded around him at their round table.

I'm close enough to hear him whisper, "It's okay, baby. We can go home. Tonight was a lot."

She shakes her head. "I don't want to get in the way of your job."

So it's a work outing? I'm *all too* familiar with those.

"Your comfort is so much more important. Come on, let's get you home," he tells her, pressing a kiss to her temple and standing to announce their departure. A couple of the guys he's with make comments about him being "pussy whipped", but he brushes them off.

I guess *that's* what it's like to care more about your partner than you do about your career and the lowlifes you work with.

Too bad I wouldn't know anything about that.

And there it is again, that sour feeling in the pit of my stomach telling me something's just not right.

A hand rests on my thigh, fingers curling, giving me a tight squeeze. "Hey, *loca*. Everything okay?" Mayte asks me quietly.

I clench my eyes tightly shut and shake my head, finally ready to say what's on my mind, but a new song plays overhead, this one louder than the rest, and several dancers make their way out onto the stage.

Karmella, Johanna, Ewelina, and Yanet are in the front row now, dancing and cheering on the ladies trying to make a living. I can't help but smile. These women, no matter the physical distance between us, have always supported my goals. It never mattered how hard my body has tried to squash my dreams or how difficult opening my own studio has proven to be. They've always been in the background, cheering me on the same way they are the exhausted women on stage. It pulls my mind back to the present, and I can no longer get the words I had prepared to say out of my mouth. Instead, I shake myself out and give her a small smile I'm certain is anything but reassuring.

Mayte nods, turning her attention back to the dancers.

I've *officially* made my decision.

Lola

Chapter Two
COMIN' HOME

THE SUN POKES out from the horizon, illuminating the small BnB as we drag ourselves through the entrance.

I make my way to the shower, stripping as I wait for the water to heat. Once inside, a heavy sigh leaves my lungs at the warm water running over my aching muscles. I take far longer than necessary, doing my best to escape the thoughts dogpiling me.

If I leave him, how will I afford to live?

Will I ever dance again?

How would Karmella and Yanet feel about me leaving the studio?

Will I be letting them down after they took a chance on me?

Where will I go?

My muscles are still too tense by the time I climb out of the shower. My aching joints make it difficult to get over the lip of the tall tub, but I manage to grip the porcelain tight, swinging one leg over at a time.

After wrapping a towel around my waist, I glance around the tiny bubblegum-pink bathroom, and sag into myself. Damnit, I forgot a change of clothes.

I poke my head into the hall. "Could someone bring me something to change into?"

"One sec!" Mayte shouts, running to me ten seconds later with an oversized band-tee and black leggings in hand.

I don't bother asking how she grabbed them so quickly. I thank her and slip out of the bathroom with a heavy heart and anxiety rumbling in my gut.

The bathroom is at the end of the hall, and I pass the three empty bedrooms, my brows pinched as I listen for my usually rowdy friends, but I come up empty.

The five women are seated on the couch and loveseat, unspeaking as they stare at their phones, pick at their nails, and, in Ewelina's case, toss back another shot of vodka. I slump into the only open seat between Karmella and Mayte, clearing my throat loudly.

Their heads snap up, everyone's wide gazes set on me.

I can't keep my mouth shut any longer.

"I can't do this."

The room remains dead silent for an uncomfortable beat and, as Karmella would say, you could hear a cockroach fart.

"Can't do what?" Mayte asks, her words slow and hesitant.

"I can't marry him," I whisper, my lips trembling, hot tears flooding my vision. "It doesn't feel right. The pressure to go through with it has been suffocating, but I just can't," I admit, throwing my hands up in frustration. "He's made me feel like shit for longer than I realized, and every time I considered leaving him, he held it over my head that I need health insurance. But that's not a good enough reason to marry someone," I choke out, my tear-soaked lashes blurring my vision.

Mayte shakes her head emphatically. "No, that's not a good enough reason, especially if you don't love him. We'll find another way."

Johanna's eyes swing to me as she pins me to my seat with her wide stare. "As long as you're sure," she states.

Karmella blows out a long breath, clapping her hands on

her thighs. "Of course she's fucking sure! Have you met that *pendejo*? Yeah, *me neither!* Because he's been isolating her from anyone who could help her pull her head out of her ass. *Gracias a Dios!* Let's get the fuck out of here." She stands abruptly, my jaw hanging open at her statement. *She's right.* Russ never wanted my friends around, getting pissed when Mayte planned this bachelorette weekend without his approval. We certainly couldn't have anyone thinking he's an asshole, *now, could we?*

Karmella stomps through the living room, dragging the suitcases from the bedrooms, sweat beading on her forehead.

My head flinches back slightly. "What's going on here? How is everything already packed?"

"You really thought we were going to let you make the biggest mistake of your life by marrying a man who can't be bothered to meet your friends?" Yanet asks me.

"If you hadn't come to your senses alone, we were going to drag your ass back to Rosa Ranch," Mayte chimes in, and my head feels like it's about to explode with new information and lack of sleep.

Yanet moves from the worn-out loveseat, taking Karmella's place beside me as she gathers my hands in her lap. "Do you remember when you came to Fuego Fusion looking for a job?"

I bat away tears, choking on the ball of emotion stuck in my throat. "Of course. That day changed my life. Not only did I meet you and Karmella, but you gave me the opportunity to taste my dreams."

"Mhmm, and a year later, when you showed up an hour earlier than you were supposed to?" Yanet's brows are cinched, her eyes pleading for me to remember. As if I could ever forget. I'd arrived at the studio early, looking for an escape. Russ and I were having an argument about me moving in with him. I hadn't wanted to at the time, but he eventually beat me down until I felt there was no other option.

When I got to the studio, I didn't think anyone was there—the lights were off, and the front door was locked. I heard

Yanet and her husband, John, screaming at each other. I was terrified he was going to hurt her, but before I could step in, the yelling stopped, replaced by a loud thump and the shattering of glass I heard in my nightmares for months afterward.

"I remember," I whisper.

"You know, John wasn't always like that either. He's the one who helped me open the studio, worked tirelessly to figure out my permits and support my dreams. But when he shifted his focus to his own business and started making significantly more money than I ever could at the studio, that resentment changed him. It didn't happen all at once." She shakes her head. "It was a slow shift, so slow, I had time to acclimate to each change while constantly reminding myself of what a good man he had been at the beginning." She squeezes my hands, hot tears spilling down my cheeks. "It wasn't until he pushed me into that mirror and there was a *witness* to his abuse that I was able to crawl my way out from under him and *leave.*"

Mayte crouches beside us, flattening her palms over mine and Yanet's intertwined hands. "We love you *so* much, Lols," she whispers, her voice a broken plea. "We can't sit back and watch as we wait for Russ to do the same to you."

A choked sob leaves my mouth as I crumple against Yanet, her arms shooting out to wrap around me. Mayte runs a soothing hand up and down my spine as I let the tears fall. They spill out of me, hot and fast, tainted with the pieces of my soul I might never get back and the fear of what's to come.

The truck has been dead silent, save for Karmella and Yanet's loud ass snoring for the past four hours.

When the tires meet gravel, I know we've arrived, and apprehension floods my system. It's been years since I moved, leaving behind a life I'd thought I'd never want for myself, but now, the familiarity of this place has me wondering if I was wrong from the start.

There was a time when this was the place I'd felt most safe and loved, but then the boy I'd loved most had grown into a man. His grief too great to overcome the physical distance between us, forming an emotional valley that neither of us were equipped to handle. The thought alone has my heart beating a little faster and acid churning in my gut.

The girls stir in the backseat, and Mayte parks beyond the gate. We sit here in silence, taking in the acreage I grew up on.

My mood shifts, and a laugh bubbles out of me, with Mayte following suit, unable to contain herself.

Ewelina clamps a hand over her mouth, doing her best to hold it in, but Karmella's cackle results in the entire truck breaking out in a fit of laughter.

We're delirious, exhausted, and as the reality of what we've just done settles in, the laughter continues to grow.

"We did it." I chuckle, watching myself from somewhere outside of my own body, as if I'm floating above, disconnected from the moment, the world around me moving in slow motion.

"We really did," Mayte snorts between laughs, her eyes brimming with tears.

"You're a runaway bride!" Karmella shouts, officially breaking the dam that is Ewelina's mouth. She can't help but keel over in her seat, nearly hyperventilating with laughter.

Our bodies are shaking the truck until the last laugh makes it past our lips.

We sigh into the leather seats, unable to move.

Nothing about this is truly funny.

But sometimes, if you don't laugh, you'll cry. And I've already shed enough tears for that man.

Ryder

Chapter Three

GHOSTS OF THE PAST

WEDNESDAY, APRIL 23

"MY ROSE" by Beyoncé plays on the radio as I pull down the dirt road, finally back at the ranch.

Usually, on a Wednesday evening, I'd be tending to the cattle and making sure the ranch hands have everything stocked for the remainder of the week. Instead, I've spent the last few days on an impromptu fishing trip with no cell service, drowning my sorrows in self-help books and tacky music. I couldn't stand to be surrounded by my family as they talk about the wedding and try to show me photos of her, smiling, gorgeous, and happy.

Damn, maybe those self-help books aren't as helpful as I'd hoped.

I steer my thoughts away from Lola and focus on the crunch of my tires over the gravel, but the sound is drowned out by the ringing of my phone.

"Pops" flashes across the screen. I answer, putting him on speaker and turning down the radio.

"Hey, Pops. You need something? I'm almost at the gate," I tell him, prepared to turn around and get whatever he needs.

"No, no. Your old man is fine, son. I'm just glad I caught you. I, uh, well—"

This man is never at a loss for words, and now that he is, my anxiety is climbing.

"You mind tellin' me what you're gettin' at, please? You're worrying me."

"Well, I wanted to prepare you so when you got here, you weren't surprised to see —"

I'm not sure if he actually stopped speaking, or if it's the sudden buzzing in my ears that causes his words to fizzle out, but the moment my tires stop at the gate…

I see her.

Lola Lima is walking across my property, as gorgeous as ever. Hell, *more* gorgeous than ever, wearing a pair of cut-off denim shorts that hug her curves just right as she heads to one of the horse stables. Her long, dark curls are perfect ringlets hanging around her shoulders, swaying with every step. The sun glimmers off the dark strands, highlighting them to look like a halo. Her cheekbones shimmer in the last hours of daylight, and the sight of her makes my heart skip about a dozen beats before starting up again.

"Ryder? Ryder, did we lose connection?" Dad asks.

Shaking my head clear, I say, "No, sorry. I see her." Confusion mixes with apprehension as my mind runs a million miles a minute. "Why is she here?" I'm not upset about it, but I thought she was getting married over the weekend. *That* I'm crushed and furious over—not with her, but myself. "Wasn't she supposed to be off on her honeymoon?" Vitriol drips into the sentence uncontained, a raw bitterness slipping into my voice. The instant the words leave my mouth, regret stabs at me, twisting in my gut.

"She called it off." That's all he says, as if that answers anything.

"She called it off?" I ask in disbelief, repeating my father's words like they went straight in one ear and out the other. My jaw hangs and, despite myself, butterflies take flight in my gut as elation floods me.

For the first time in years, we're single at the same time.

"Yes, son. She said he wasn't right for her." I should be relieved to hear that confirmation, but it only makes my jaw tighten. "She called it off, and Mayte and the girls brought her here." He pauses for a beat, and it's a necessary reprieve for my racing mind. "She's gonna stay with us if that's alright with you. She's staying in her old room in her parents' cottage."

She's here. She's really *here.*

And if I'm not careful, I'll only push her further away. It's *my fault* there was ever any distance between us, after all.

"That's… Yeah, Pops, that's fine. I'll be inside soon," I tell him, not waiting for his response before ending the call.

I press the button for the electric gate, watching the motor whir to life, the belt moving in a smooth, methodical circle as the gate opens wide enough for me to pass. I drive slowly, avoiding kicking up too much dust, closing the gate behind me. My lungs protest as I suck in a breath so deep they might burst, blowing it out to lessen the suffocating weight pressing on my chest.

My fingers twitch with the desire to park by the stables and insist Lola give me even a moment of her attention, but if I come on too strong, she might spook. Her usual loose posture, the kind that tells anyone within a two-mile radius she's a dancer, her body ready to sway to the rhythm of any beat, is now the opposite. Her spine is ramrod straight, shoulders tucked back, chin jutted forward as she marches across the dusty land. Can she sense my gaze glued to her? It's like my eyes can't help but find her, from the moment I first saw her.

It only serves to remind me of the day we met, tugging me into a memory of a seven-year-old Lola stumbling out of her father's truck wearing a lilac dress covered in roses.

Her dark curls were frizzy, hanging loosely down her back. Wide brown eyes met mine, her chin ducked, cheeks turning pink as she held my gaze in her own.

"Lola!" Mayte shrieked, bolting down the porch steps of the ranch house, her feet glowing with each step thanks to the rainbow dinosaur light-up sneakers my mom had gotten her for Christmas the year before.

"Mayte!" Lola had screamed in return, her voice high-pitched and sweet, deliriously excited to see her friend. She took off toward Mayte's voice with a lingering glance in my direction.

A wide smile stretched my lips as I watched them embrace, my cheeks still flushed from her initial response to me. I'd known she was moving to the ranch with us because Mayte had moved here the year prior and spoke about Lola's arrival for months.

What I hadn't anticipated was how that pretty girl would become my best friend, and later, the one who got away.

Chapter Four

ROOTS

WEDNESDAY, APRIL 23

I SWEAR, I can feel his eyes burning into me as his truck stops at the gate. It takes everything in me to keep mine pinned straight ahead and not risk falling into his trance.

I *cannot* leave my fiancé at the altar one day and fall back into Ryder Lockhart's arms the next—no matter how big and muscular those arms are.

Jesus, Lola, stop it! You can't think about his arms. Eyes forward! Get to the damn stables.

Clearly, not much has changed since we last saw each other.

The pull to him is still there, same as always. Even after the dust had settled and we'd had the time to talk about all the reasons our breakup had made sense, it still hurts to know he'd married my childhood bully. It's an irrational thought considering I'd deliberately hidden the extent of her torment from him, but salt in the wound, all the same.

I release a sigh when I make it inside, grabbing one of the brushes off the wooden wall, where saddles and other equipment hang off rusted nails. Everything is in the same place it always was. I find where Penny, Mayte's Red Dun Quarter, stands at the last stall, her head hanging through the top of her door. She whinnies and chuffs the closer I get.

"Hey there, beautiful," I coo, unlatching the thick wooden stall door and leading her out.

She preens under my attention, much like she has every night since I've arrived.

I get to work, brushing her smooth, ruddy coat and preparing her for our nightly ride. I fully intend to make it a routine now that I'm here. At least, for as long as my body will allow.

Being at Rosa Ranch is surreal, like stepping into a place that should be familiar and comforting, yet enough has changed that it has me second-guessing myself. After Ryder and I had broken up, I'd been too busy to visit, and in the years after, I kept my visits as short as possible to avoid Lemmon's ire, but family dinners were unavoidable, and truthfully, I hadn't *wanted* to avoid him. He was my best friend for so long, and in the end, I'd failed him just as much as he'd disappointed me. Knowing I'm likely here to stay is a strange reality. It's the place I spent most of my childhood, learning to care for the rescue animals, milk the cattle, tend to the landscaping, and everything in between. It's where I met some of my very best friends, snuck out of the house, and got absolutely lost in the freedom of my youth. When I moved after graduating high school, I'd always hoped I'd come back someday, but I had no idea it would be under these circumstances.

I don't have a clue how I'm going to make any of this work. So much has changed since I've been gone, and somehow, not enough. The town is still overflowing with the same hardworking, kind, and generous people I once knew. All of them are complete gossips, so I'm sure they know I'm here by now.

The ranch is still littered with memories of the past, of what I might've had if I'd stayed.

My unfortunate reality is, there's no way to tell how my life would've panned out if I had stuck around. These days, it feels like a black cloud constantly looms over me, waiting for me to trip up or fail at the next thing. Maybe this time, I can learn to not do everything on my own. I can get my life back and do the things that bring me joy. I don't have to do what makes me feel like I'm stuck in a revolving door of degradation, pleading, and an inevitable return to loathing and self-hatred. Wash, rinse, repeat.

Russ really *was* the worst, huh?

I'm still shocked that, after my parents packed up my things and hauled ass out of the city, Russ hasn't tried to contact me. He's been eerily silent about this whole situation, and it makes me wonder if his family was just glad to have me gone from his life, no longer bringing their precious white-collar son into the mix of my artistic passions.

His mother had once described my aspirations as "childish dreams" I hadn't given up on and made sure I knew that: "The term starving artist is a stereotype for a reason, dear. If you don't give up on these fantasies of yours, you'll wind up starving with the rest of them. Russ can only subsidize you for so long." Truly, such big words for a woman who raised her child on meals from the local food pantry and worked three jobs to get him into college.

He had a beautiful childhood from what I know, but it isn't about what you have in materialistic things—it's about *who* you have. His mother seems to have forgotten that.

It wasn't until Russ got into "trading stocks," if that's really what he was doing, that she suddenly had fur coats and a stick so far up her ass, you could call her a flagpole. Some days, it's hard to believe I ever liked his family, let alone him.

I focus my attention on Penny, trying not to dwell too much on the past and look forward to the future. I get her saddle on, and we head outside. Penny's a gentle horse. She doesn't spook easily, and she's great with kids. I hope to still be here when Isabela is old enough to learn to ride. Penny would be the perfect horse for her to practice on.

The sun should be setting in just over an hour, but I plan to make this ride as long as possible. Now that Ryder's home, and especially considering what day it is, I have no intention of making it to the main house for dinner. So, instead, I make sure her saddle is on properly before climbing on and leading her out toward my favorite trail, just past the big red barn.

As the day ends, the wind starts to pick up, chilling my skin. The frogs and cicadas can be heard for miles, their high-pitched clicking and rhythmic croaks filling the silence. The sound takes up enough space to keep my anxious thoughts and regrets from tumbling in. It's a welcome reprieve.

"We should probably start to head back," I tell Penny, reluctant to put an end to our ride. The sun is setting on the horizon, casting a stunning display of pink-and-purple cotton candy clouds around us. The wildflowers are in full spring bloom, and the rolling hills surrounding us stretch far and wide, reminding me what an insignificant role I play in the grand scheme of life. It's a thought that should make me feel small and worthless, but it has the opposite impact. Instead, it's reassuring to know my actions are a part of a greater sum, that what I choose to do with my life won't have some huge domino effect that'll leave the world around me in ruins. Leaving my fiancé at the altar only changed the trajectory of my life and his, no one else's. I refuse to feel guilty for leaving Russ; the truth is, I hadn't been happy with him in a long time, and he made sure of that.

As if to say, *"But I know someone who could make you happy,"* the universe laughs at me as I hear hooves hitting the dirt trail. From the sounds of it, whoever it is is in a hurry, and I'm nearly certain I know *exactly* who's chasing after me.

Some things never change. If only he'd chased me when I needed him most.

"Lola!" I hear my name from that deep, familiar baritone, and a shiver travels down my spine. It's been a year and a half since I'd last seen him, and the sound makes my chest ache.

I whip my head around to catch a glimpse of him, and sure enough, Ryder Lockhart is behind me, seated atop Asier, the Friesian we rescued from auction my freshman year of high school. He sidles up beside me, nudging Asier to a slow stroll.

I shake my head at him, steering Penny toward the house, Asier following suit and making a big horseshoe turn as we do.

"Hey there, birthday boy," I tease, swallowing around the lump in my throat. I run the tip of my tongue along the backs of my teeth, steadying my breathing before continuing with a charade of confidence. "Fancy seeing you here."

"Lola Lima. Aren't you just the best birthday present I could ever ask for?" He chuckles, allowing his accent to thicken with his last few words.

Sucking my lower lip between my teeth, I worry the thin flesh before making an easy mistake that threatens to unearth all the pent-up emotions chained beneath the prison of my last relationship. My gaze flits over him, drinking in every inch of his familiar physique, broad shoulders, biceps that ripple beneath the thin fabric of his button-down. I trail back up to his face, cataloging each freckle, the hint of stubble along his strong jaw and square, dimpled chin. I avoid his eyes like my life depends on it, *and it just might*, because those luminous baby blues have always snared me, lighting the darkest, most anxiety-riddled confines of my mind with warmth and light. It's a feeling like no other — toasty, inviting, and undeniably like *home*.

What I couldn't possibly realize would be my downfall is the faint white scar barely hidden beneath the curve of his full lower lip, dragging me into a memory of a day I hadn't thought about in years…

"Ryder! Hurry! We need to run faster, or we'll never make it!" I screeched, my feet pounding against the dusty, sunbaked road as we chased after any horse's worst nightmare.

"Lols, we'll make it!" he hollered back with a false bravado that did nothing to settle the angry swarm of bees in the pit of my gut.

I glanced at him long enough to see the way his thick brows pinch together, eyes set on the trailer ahead. My arms pumped at my sides, my calves burning as I willed myself forward. Don't worry, big guy. We're coming.

The massive Friesian horse was the sleekest shade of midnight black, so dark, it appeared almost blue in the hot summer sun. His mane was a stunning wave that fell below his chest, blowing in the light breeze as he stared out the metal grate, his dark eyes pleading with us to move faster.

"You need to get your freaking driver's license soon, Ry!" I yelled in frustration as my muscles fatigued, sweat dripping down my brows, burning my eyes.

"I promise, I will! We've almost got him, Lols. They've gotta slow down at the turn ahead. There's no way we'll miss him!" he assured me, and I let his confidence swaddle me, giving me the strength to push forward.

"What's the plan?!" My voice was shrill over the crunch of gravel from the truck ahead.

"I'll use my momentum to jump onto the back edge, unlatch the trailer, and then you'll have to grab the reins and hope like hell he has the same will to save himself as we do!"

My tongue raked across my dry lips as I beat back the fear this could all go so terribly wrong. I squeaked out a less-than-assured, "Great, what could go wrong?"

Ryder's playful grin and twinkling eyes met my twisted expression, sending a fluttering of warmth low in my belly.

"I'll count down from five, Lols. Got it?" he asked.

"Sure!"

"Five. Four. Three," Each descending number pressed more firmly on the heavy weight over my chest. "Two. One!"

The white trailer rig tilted slightly to the left, kicking up clouds of dust that concealed us from the truck's side mirrors as it made the wide turn. Ryder sprinted ahead, pushing off the balls of his feet and catapulting himself high enough to grab hold of the door, steadying his lanky body on the metal lip of the trailer.

My pulse roared against my eardrums as I continued sprinting, waiting for a signal. He unlatched the door, yanking it open and grabbing for the reins, tugging firmly to urge the hulking horse to make the jump. He shot me a thumbs-up when the horse cleared the trailer and got to work grappling for the door.

I reached out for the end of the rope, my heart soaring when I grabbed it on my first try, and the Friesian made the leap out of the trailer.

The trailer buckled from the fourteen-hundred-pound loss. The rear right tire hit a rut, jostling the trailer with Ryder still on it. With wide eyes and a still, beatless heart, I led the horse in the direction we came as the metal doors swung back, slamming into Ryder's face before he fell off the back into a heap on the dirt road.

"Ryder!" I screamed, the sound deafening.

"I'm fine, Lola! Just keep going!" he shouted back, rolling over and pushing himself up before following me. My heart rate calmed, and a wide smile stretched my lips as he sprinted to catch up with us.

I turned my attention to our new friend, gesturing for him to slow as I ran my hands over his sleek coat. "Good boy," I cooed. "See? I told you we'd get you in time."

Ryder let out a huff as he sidled up to us, bending forward, his hands on his knees as he panted, catching his breath. Sweat trickled down his temples, his high cheekbones flushed, dark waves curly at the sweat-dampened ends.

God, he's beautiful.

He straightened, meeting me with a heart-stopping smile that left the organ clenching painfully in my chest. "I can't believe we did it," he said with a deep chuckle, his voice no longer cracking as he settled into his post-puberty voice.

I smacked his shoulder, shaking my head and rolling my eyes. "Seriously, Ry? You seemed so confident!"

He shrugs. "I didn't want you to lose hope! See how far it got us?"

We continued walking for a few more minutes, peering behind us several times to make sure they weren't coming back. Ryder took the reins from me, pulling the horse to a stop along the shoulder of the empty clay road.

"What should we name him?" Ryder mused, stroking a hand down the nameless horse's back.

"I'm not sure, but I wish we'd known what his name was before. Imagine living almost three years of your life under one identity, only to be taken to auction all because you can't be used to reproduce," I huffed out, crossing my arms over my chest.

"It's a shame. He's beautiful and well-mannered. Great temperament. It's unfortunate he wouldn't survive in the wild. I think he'd have been happiest grazing, running of his own will."

"We'll give him a good life," I said with conviction, nodding for good measure.

"What about 'Asier'? It means 'new beginnings' in Basque," he suggested.

I shot him a side eye. "And how do you know that? Have you suddenly become worldly or learned a new language outside of English and a tragic attempt at Spanish?"

His shoulders shook with laughter before he pushed himself up and over Asier's back. Once settled on top, his legs straddling the wide birth of the giant horse's sides, he leaned down, extending a hand for me to take. Ryder's face was mere inches from mine, my breath catching in my throat, the world growing fuzzy around us as his musky, sweat-tinged scent enveloped me in a heady warmth. My eyes dilated, landing on his lips before his next words shook me from the fog. "I learned it yesterday in History." A drop of blood pooled at the edge of his lips, my eyes growing wide as he swiped his tongue over it, licking at the fresh wound.

"You're bleeding! Are you okay?" I gripped his cheeks, inspecting the shallow gash.

"I'm fine. Just a little cut," he assured me, and I bristled, his warm breath skating over my lips, sending a tendril of something I shouldn't be feeling zipping up my spine. I rocked on my heels, meeting his gaze. I took his large hand in mine, his fingers wrapping around my palm, eating up any space left between us.

I cleared my throat, averting my gaze before we could make a huge mistake that could cost us our friendship. "I didn't know the football coaches teaching history actually taught anything," I muttered.

"They don't," he said, tugging me up, his free hand slipping around my waist to ease me onto Asier's back behind him. "We had a substitute."

"Oh, right," I answered, dizzy from the press of his skin against mine.

"Hold on tight, Lols," he whispered, looking ahead as he steered Asier onto the main road. I wrapped my arms around his trim waist, pressing my cheek between his shoulder blades, and relaxed against him. I listened to the steady beat of his heart and the gentle sigh of his lungs as we headed back to the ranch, where we had to explain how we'd just stolen a horse worth fifty grand.

"Lola?"

I shift, blinking rapidly at the sound of my name coming from a much older man than the one I'd just experienced in my memories. "Lola, you alright?"

I shake myself out, my eyes locking on Ryder's. They're crinkled at the edges, his brow furrowed as he assesses me. "Where'd you go, darlin'?"

"I was just thinking about when we rescued Asier," I admit, fully returning to the present.

His smile is broad and gleams in the last remnants of the setting sun, my heart taking flight with the small movement. "That's one of my favorite memories from high school," he tells me.

I quirk a brow, knowing I shouldn't ask but unable to help myself. "And what's your favorite?"

He gives me a knowing smirk, and I feel as gone for this man now as I was then. It knocks me off kilter, and as I fight to regain my balance, he finishes me off with a simple sentence that shouldn't mean *so much.*

"The night you convinced Mayte to help us sneak out to the fair," he drawls.

My pulse picks up speed, but I do my best not to seem as affected by his words as I am. Steeling my spine, I tear my gaze from his. "That was a pretty fun night," I allow myself to say.

Tension-filled seconds pass in silence, unable to resist the press of his searing gaze against my overheated flesh. I peer up at him, his eyes searching mine. There's a faint tremor in his voice as he asks, "Are you here for good, Lols?" His gaze lingers, as if my answer could change everything, the quiet hope in his expression trembling like a delicate thread between us.

"At least for the foreseeable future," I say, giving him a non-answer to avoid breaking his heart if I wind up being pulled somewhere else. His eyes widen, and the edges of his lips twitch, but he quickly schools his expression, nodding his cool understanding. He's careful not to show the hope I see brewing in that gorgeous head of his, his lips parting slightly, bright eyes holding mine. I'm thankful for him because if he were to show half as much of the hope I fear he's clutching, I might allow myself to fall face first into it.

We continue down the path to the stables, catching ourselves staring as if we're in high school all over again.

Maybe life would be less complicated if we were.

"Is it alright that I'm here?" I ask him, my voice quieter than I'd intended. "I realize I never asked you, and I hear you've officially taken over as the ranch manager for your dad."

Ryder's bright-blue eyes hold my brown ones. I could swim away in those pools of cerulean. But that's the thing about Ryder Lockhart, isn't it? He made me feel fearless, like I could take on the entire world with him by my side, but in recent years, I've realized we aren't living in a fairytale. Life is hard. Shit happens. And Ry can't change that fact.

"Rosa Ranch will always be your home, darlin'. Of course you're welcome here."

A small smile works across my lips. "Thanks, Ry," I tell him, slipping into our old, comfortable bubble. *Even if I have no right to.*

"Anything for you, darlin'," I hear him say quietly.

After we've put the horses back in the stables for the night, I rush to my childhood home, desperate for a full breath of air after riding beside the man I'd spent more years loving than not, dredging up feelings from the past.

It isn't until hours later that my parents return home from dinner at the main house. It's not a surprise, seeing as Bee and Harlan have always treated my family as their own.

There's a light knock at the door before *Mami* pushes it open and strides inside, taking a seat at the end of the bed.

"We missed you at dinner tonight, *mijita*." She reaches out to nudge my shoulder, silent laughter dancing in her eyes. She wears a relaxed smile that warms my chest, and I'm thankful to be here to see it.

"I'm sorry, *Mami*. I just wasn't feeling up to it yet. I'll be there for family dinner this weekend, I promise."

She nods slowly, averting her gaze to the papers littered around me. She lets out a sigh and sinks further into the mattress. "*Ajá,* so you *did* remember." Her smile shifts to a knowing smirk that has me rolling my eyes. "*¡Lo sabia!*"

"Of course I remembered."

"I bet he would've liked it if you'd been there tonight. *Pero,* judging by the way he ran out as soon as his plate was clean, I imagine you already know that."

My cheeks heat, and I refuse to meet her gaze, studying the paper in my lap as I meticulously fold the edges and roll the papers. "He didn't say as much, but I got the picture," I answer.

"*Tá bien*. I'll leave you to it. Keys are by the front door in case you decide to drive those over to him tonight." She stands, but before she makes it to the door, she bends down and cups my chin, lifting my gaze to hers. "I'm proud of you, Lola. *Tan orgullosa*. I just wanted to remind you in case I haven't said it enough."

"You have, *Mami*. I promise. You say it plenty," I assure her, my voice cracking on the next words, "and thank you."

"*Duerme bien, hija*," she says, kissing my cheek.

"*Buenas noches, Mami*."

Once she's gone, I finish the bouquet of origami flowers, my hands shaking by the time I'm done. My joints hurt, and I'm aching for a bubble bath, some painkillers, and ice for my hands, but I persist, tying a blood-red ribbon around the paper stems to hold them all together.

I hoist myself up, grab the keys from the hook by the door, and sprint through the sprinkling rain to Dad's truck. I make the quick drive to Ryder's cottage, and as my heart pounds faster, I'm starting to think this might have been a bad idea.

When I broke up with Ryder, we had both messed up. He had been grieving the loss of his best friend after a tragic accident and had kept me at a distance in an effort to protect me from his overwhelming grief and worsening depression. Meanwhile, I had been working my ass off to maintain my spot at the dance program I'd had to work twice as hard to get into as a woman of color. I was learning my craft from some of the most talented dancers in the country, and I'd more than earned my place there.

Ryder hadn't wanted to burden me, knowing I'd have given it all up to return to him and be his rock when he needed me, and I think I was too afraid to do just that, so I never pushed for answers because he was right.

By the time he'd gotten the help he needed and we'd matured enough to have that conversation, it'd been too many years too late. He was already engaged to Lemmon, and I was in a committed relationship with Russ.

We let time and space create a divide that never felt natural when he was always the other half of my heart, my partner in crime, sometimes *literally*. So how could it be wrong to show him I still care? With Ryder, it's never been that simple, though maybe he's changed.

He chased you down on horseback today, Lola. Nothing has changed!

I huff out a breath, throw the truck in park, and run to his door, banging on the thick wood before looking for some place to put the flowers where they won't get soaked.

I set them on the small glass table beside the rocking chair and haul ass down the short porch steps, effectively ding-dong-ditching a grown man.

I've been here for only four days, and it's already glaring that my roots run deeper than I remembered.

Ryder

Chapter Five
BIRTHDAY WISHES

WEDNESDAY, APRIL 23

I JERK the door open in time to see José's black pickup truck pulling out of my driveway. My brows draw together.

I swing my gaze around the porch, looking for any reason José would've stopped over in this weather, but the question falls away when my eyes land on a tiny bouquet of origami flowers.

My heart swells, soaring to new heights, reminding me just how dangerous Lola Lima is for my health. She's too sweet. Too beautiful. Too thoughtful. Too *perfect*.

Too mine.

And if she ever leaves again, it'll break my goddamn heart worse than it did the first time.

I pick up the tiny bouquet, heading inside to place it on the mantle next to fifteen others like it.

I'd thought all this time away from her might dull her shine, but I was wrong. With Lola home, I'm done for, and I'll be damned if I let her get away again.

Ryder

Chapter Six

SINS PAID IN KIND

FRIDAY, APRIL 25

IT'S BEEN three days since I got home from my fishing trip to find Lola living on the ranch as if we were in high school all over again.

And just like back then, I can't keep my mind right when she's around. Just knowing she's here, within walking distance, where I could finally wrap my arms around her and kiss the life out of her, has my heart threatening to explode in my chest.

She's still the prettiest sight I've ever laid eyes on; time and distance has never changed that.

I've spent my entire life in what I consider the most beautiful place in the world. I've been surrounded by wildflowers horticultural enthusiasts pay hundreds of dollars to get a glimpse of each year, sunsets that could rival the brightest rainbow in their intensity and complexity, and a sky full of bright, twinkly stars thanks to the low light pollution out this way. And still, Lola Lima is so stunning, each of those dim to nothing more than a grayish hue in her presence.

With her parents both living on the ranch, it isn't like we hadn't spent almost every major holiday together until last year, when her fiancé refused to join us, *again*, and instead, demanded Lola spend the holidays with his family. I have no reason to be *this* blinded by her beauty, but I am. She usually just drops by like a bat out of hell, and just as soon, she's gone again, leaving me yearning for more of her time and attention in any way I can have it. I know I'm partially to blame for her absence, avoiding conversations with her out of respect for Lemmon and likely making her uncomfortable, even if it damn near killed me.

Part of me admits I never loved Lemmon the way I had Lola. I only stayed with her to keep *me* tied down so I wouldn't do the same to Lola, fearing I'd chase after her and ruin everything she'd been working toward. And I realize how terrible a person that makes me. The thought eats me up inside.

Maybe I never deserved Lola either.

When Logan died, it gutted me, but more than that, it made me question everything I'd known about myself. I'd quit playing football for good, something I'd been planning to do anyway, but without the physical outlet it had provided, I'd needed Lola by my side more than ever. She'd just gone off to Dallas, living out her dream, and I was determined to keep her out so she wouldn't come running back to pick up my broken pieces like I knew she would. Whether it was by chance or not, I'm no longer sure, but Lemmon went to the same state college as I had, and having a familiar face to speak about Logan with was a comfort I desperately needed at the time.

It wasn't until Lola returned home for winter break my senior year that she'd gotten to truly see how devastated I'd been, and overhearing me speaking with Lemmon about it was the nail in the coffin I hadn't seen coming. It wasn't until Mayte verbally kicked my ass and *literally* beat me with her flip-flop after we'd eloped that I'd found out Lemmon had bullied Lola in our childhood. I hadn't realized just how bad her torment could be until I'd lived it. I married her after years of an on-again, off-again relationship that was never meant to work out, sticking around through the gaslighting and manipulation that only worsened as my resolve to repair our relationship plummeted. In the end, I finally chose myself for once, and it breaks my heart to know that Lola hadn't been as happy as I'd hoped. She was off to do bigger, better, more interesting things with her life than work on a ranch for the rest of forever. I don't think this is a bad life. Hell, I *love* this life. But I'd be lyin' if I said having Lola here wouldn't make my days a million times better.

I've spent a decade paying for my sins with Lemmon, and I think it might be about time I quit begging myself for forgiveness and work toward earning Lola's trust the way I always should have. I just need to avoid crawling on my knees and begging her to stick around. Surely *that* would have her up and out of here in a flash.

Lola

Chapter Seven
LIKE SOMETHING YOU SEE?

FRIDAY, APRIL 25

"AND YOU'RE ABSOLUTELY certain there's no other option?" I ask for the tenth time today, pleading for a chance that this insurance salesman will have a different answer for me than the last nine.

"I really am very sorry, Miss, but as I said, the open enrollment period is closed until November, and we don't have any plans that meet your needs and fit your budget without an employer package. I wish I had better news for you," the agent says, his tone earnest and sincere.

"Okay," I choke out, tears welling in my eyes before I can blink them away. "Thank you for your time."

I end the call, the phone heavy in my hand, and a wave of restlessness crawls under my skin, defeat gnawing at me from the inside.

I'm grateful I'm here and not the alternative, but being in a small town has its downsides. The thing about Hidden Valley is everyone knows me, and while the urge to get out of the house is suffocating—the need to clear my mind and escape the heavy weight of impending doom caused by my ex-fiancé's radio silence—I can't shake the dread of running into anyone who'll ask too many questions and make a fuss over my return. I want to avoid those encounters, if only for one more day.

All I want to do is move, but everything hurts, so going for a ride or a walk is out of the question right now.

My aching joints act as an unfriendly reminder that, sometimes, doing the right thing comes with a price. Like, you know, leaving your fiancé at the altar because you've finally come to terms with the fact that he's an all-around shit human being. It turns out, all those times he made you feel as though you were only marrying him for decent health insurance were, in fact, true. And then you realize maybe you are *also* a shit human being.

Or maybe you're just in pain, so much pain that you convinced yourself you loved him, that he loved you.

I slump against the kitchen counter, marveling at the field of wildflowers and the cloudless sky through the small bow window above the sink, and sucking in a deep, steadying breath. My lungs fill with the familiar scent of the incense *Mami* burned last night, and it helps to steady me.

It's a beautiful day outside, and I want nothing more than to be out there right now with the horses, the wind in my hair, but the idea of moving anything is just too painful.

"*¿En qué tú piensas?*" Mayte's voice startles me upright as she asks what I'm thinking about. When I realize it's just her, I slump against the counter again.

"Just wish I could be outside, moving," I tell her, shaking my head in frustration. Mayte bumps me out of her way, grabbing a grocery bag from under the kitchen sink before making her way to the small white refrigerator my parents refuse to upgrade.

"Feeling like hell, huh?" she asks, her soft, honey-brown eyes seeing right through the walls I try to put up as she fills her bag with *malta*.

"You stealing from *Mami*?" I ask, and she levels me with a glare.

"No," she answers with a grunt. "She asked me to stop over and grab some drinks before heading to the main house for dinner. She has a craving for *malta con leche condensada*. Now, tell me how you're doing, and cut the bull crap."

I sigh loudly, not wanting to have this conversation. "Today's worse than it has been in the last few weeks," I admit, shrugging. A flush creeps up my neck, the weight of my own stupidity sinking in for not getting a "real" job that pays me consistently and offers health insurance. But I love dancing, and I love teaching. More than that, I know a traditional, structured job wouldn't be good for me, not mentally or physically.

Maybe it would be better than nothing though. Because right now, that's exactly what I've got: nothing.

I could go back. Not to Russ but to the studio. I know Karmella and Yanet would gladly have me, but is that what I want? *No.*

"We'll figure it out. I have no doubt." If anyone can help me get through this, it's her. She's managed to overcome a surprise pregnancy with a one-night stand after *finally* allowing herself to let loose, just once. She's turned out to be the most incredible mother too.

Not that that's a surprise to anyone. She's been mothering me my whole life.

"I'm sure. It's just a matter of figuring out how and when because I feel like I'm falling apart over here," I admit, annoyed it's gotten to this point.

"Don't worry about that now. Just get ready for dinner, and we can put our heads together afterward."

Like I said, always mothering me. Honestly, I've missed it.

I nod, pushing myself off the counter and heading into the bedroom I grew up in.

The lace curtains and little trinkets are the only remaining relics from my childhood after *Mami* decided to turn this room into a crafting space a few years ago. She's not one to let go of anything, so the closet is filled with plastic totes containing the beaded curtain *Papi* hung over my door that I thought was the coolest thing in the world at the time, ceramics I kept my jewelry in, and my many Celia Cruz, La India, Daddy Yankee, and the Salsa queen herself, Yolanda Rivera, posters.

It takes forever to decide on an outfit now that all my belongings are here. I guess it was sort of convenient to have my parents in town for the wedding that never happened. As soon as my girls and I got on the road, Karmella called my parents to tell them I wouldn't be there and to grab my stuff from Russ's place.

Not to anyone's surprise, but my parents were stoked. They couldn't have been happier to break the news to everyone and get out from under the judgmental eyes of Russ's stuffy, uppity family.

I've pretty much torn through my entire closet, and I've got less than twenty minutes before I have to be at the main house for dinner. Anxiety climbs up my throat like bile, but I push it down, unwilling to wrestle with the "why" right now.

I hear a knock at the front door. It couldn't be my parents or Mayte because they'd just let themselves in, so that pretty much leaves one person.

I make it to the door, willing my shaky hands to calm before I open it, finding Ryder mere inches away, his fist raised as if he was about to knock again.

Giving him a smirk, I open the door wider and step to the side for him to come in. "I take too long to answer?" I ask, batting my lashes.

His gaze rakes over my skin, taking every inch of me in. Goosebumps erupt under his scrutiny, and, embarrassingly enough, my nipples pebble just the same.

Ryder finally recovers a moment later. "I'll wait as long as you need me to, sweetheart," he drawls.

Now it's my turn to stare.

I ogle at his lean, muscular frame, working my gaze from

the tips of his ruddy-brown waves over his plump lips and strong, stubble-covered jaw. By the time I make it to those thick biceps straining against the seams of his black button-down, his brows are raised, eyes twinkling with amusement.

His hands are on his hips, and he wears a playful smirk. "Like something you see?"

I love when he's playful like this. It makes it easy to slip back into our easy banter and out of the awkward tension that feels so unnatural between us. I put a finger up to silence him. "One second. I wasn't done," I joke. I wasn't entirely kidding, considering how I avert my gaze to his thick thighs honed by years of hard work and riding. *Horses*, of course. His dark jeans hang over the top of a pair of brown leather cowboy boots I recognize from helping my mom pick them out for him as a gift last Christmas.

When I'm done with my shameless perusal of him, I meet his pretty blue eyes again and can't help but step into his embrace.

His arms widen as if on instinct, enveloping me in his warmth, and I'm surrounded by his signature scent.

God, *I've missed this.*

"It's good to have you home, darlin'," he whispers into my hair.

"It's good to be back." I pull away to end the hug before I lose all sense of reality and allow myself to become a permanent garment for him.

"You almost ready to head to the main house for dinner? I figured I'd drop by and give you a ride since I was passing by this way." My family's cottage is literally on the furthest end of this property. There is zero reason he'd be working over here.

"Uh, yeah. I just have to get dressed," I say, rushing over to my room. I instantly regret that because he doesn't stay put like he should. He's never been good at keeping his distance.

He follows me over to my room, which presently looks like an outlet mall threw up in it.

"I see some things never change," he chuckles beside me. "When will you realize you look incredible in everything? Just pick something off the floor, and let's get going."

I roll my eyes, facing him with my hands planted on my hips. "When will *you* realize I'm unaffected by your charm?" That's a total lie, and I'm sure he knows it too. I am but a puddle at this man's incredibly large feet.

"Mhmm. Whatever you say, darlin'." That smirk of his remains fully intact as he traipses into my room—uninvited, might I add. Maybe I should get some garlic for my door to keep him out, seeing as he's become a vampire to my heart, sucking me dry of my mental fortitude and the strength to keep him at arm's length.

He looks around for a moment, making a decision far more quickly than I could have. Ryder grabs the white linen sundress with tiny floral cutouts off a hanger and tosses it at me. I catch it just before it hits the ground.

"For the record, I'm glad this is the only white dress you've got in that closet." He drops that bomb on me and strides out of my room, the door clicking shut behind him.

I guess *everyone* is glad I didn't marry that *pendejo*.

His opinion shouldn't matter. I'm not ready for another relationship, and I have no idea if staying here will be sustainable.

Ryder Lockhart is *not* the kind of man you do casual with. *He's the one you marry.*

Chapter Eight
MOUNTAIN OUT OF A MOLEHILL

FRIDAY, APRIL 25

LOLA'S PRESENCE beside me on the bench seat pulls a tight knot in my stomach, leaving me unnerved, hyperaware of the minimal space between us. It would be so easy to slide her over to me, but I *can't*.

Lola has always been the first to dive into any situation — unless it involved *me*. She's *always* been a runner where I'm concerned, at least when it mattered most. And if I have any chance in hell of convincing her to give us another shot at a relationship, I need to let *her* come to *me*.

As she gazes out the window, her dark curls hanging like a curtain over her smooth, bronze shoulders, I can't help but recall the very first time we were in this position…

"How did you convince your dad to gift you a truck for your seventeenth birthday, Ry? What happened to 'working hard and earning the things you want most'?" Lola chided, her lips pressed together in a smirk that set my world on fire.

"Obviously, he saw how unbelievably hardworking, talented, and deserving I am and decided now was the perfect time to show me that," I

teased, my chin held high as I turned the corner at the outer edge of the property, passing the red barn at the top of the hill.

"Mhmm, and the real reason?" she asked, a dark brow quirked.

I released a huff of laughter. "Okay, fine. He wanted a new truck, and this one wasn't worth enough to warrant sellin'."

"Ajá, and the truth is out!" she shouted playfully, pointing a finger at me in mock accusation.

I rolled my eyes, grabbing her outstretched finger and twining mine into hers, bringing her hand to my mouth, pressing chaste kisses against each knuckle.

She squirmed in her seat, rubbing her thighs together, but she made no effort to pull away from me. "We really shouldn't, Ry," she whispered, her small voice booming in my ears.

I released her hand, mine quickly growing cold with the loss. "I always want you to feel safe with me, Lola. No matter how our lives pan out, that'll be true. So, if you don't want me to kiss your knuckles or tuck your hair behind your ear"—or any of the other small gestures I'm desperate to do—"we won't."

"The barn. Park at the barn," she rushed to say, her dulcet tone a complete one-eighty from her quiet words moments before.

I did as she said without hesitation, pulling up beside the barn and shifting into park. She stole my hand, clutching it to her chest, and raised her other hand to my cheek, dragging my face to hers. Our noses pressed together; my breath caught in my throat as she stared into my eyes with longing.

"I don't want you to think I don't want those things, Ry," she said, her warm, sweet breath coasting over my lips.

"Then why can't we?" The words that left my mouth nearly brought me to tears. Even then, I'd known I'd loved her for every moment of my life that mattered, and if she'd been too scared to take our friendship any further, I'd live, but it might feel like I was dying.

"Because—" She averted her gaze, biting her lower lip before saying, "I want you too much, and if things get weird between us, I'll never forgive myself for losing you."

"You'll never lose me, Lola," I assured her, swallowing thickly.

"You can't know that," she whispered, her voice wobbly, chin quivering.

"I love you, Lola Lima, and neither time nor distance will ever change that. I swear to you."

She blinked away the tears, a stray one slipping free of her clumped, damp lashes, falling down the curve of her cheek. I swiped at it with the pad of my thumb.

"I love you too," she said, dropping her hands to wind her arms around my neck. My body hummed with approval, pulse pounding in my throat as she climbed into my lap and rested her cheek over my heart. I reveled in the weight of her in my arms, holding her until the sun had set and there were a million stars lighting the sky. I knew without a doubt that I had the brightest one of all right there, in my arms.

My throat burns, heat licking up my neck at the memory as I pull up outside of the main house, parking beside my dad's truck. I nearly toss my body out in an effort to get around to her door before she can haul ass inside.

Her wide smile greets me when I open her door, a shimmer of butterflies swarming in my stomach. She reaches out her hand to take mine without a second thought, and I help her out onto the dirt-covered ground.

"Always the gentleman," she says with a smirk. "I see you're the same Ryder Lockhart I once knew."

"Oh, I don't know about that, darlin'. I'd say plenty's changed with me. I don't think you've gotten a good look at *all* the things that've *improved* in the last few years," I tell her with a wink, and her cheeks turn rosy.

"Your ego certainly hasn't suffered either," she jokes, smacking my bicep and heading inside.

I follow her, being sure to keep my gaze averted to my own feet as we make it up the porch steps. The last thing I need is my mother's prying eyes catching me staring at Lola's wide hips and firm ass.

Once we're both on flat ground again, I peer over at the kitchen window a few feet from the front door, where the white lace curtains rustle as Mom hurries away.

I shake my head in silent laughter, heading into the home I grew up in. *Some things never change.*

Dinner goes exactly as expected. No one brings up the elephant in the room: that Lola was supposed to get married, and now she's here. Alone. Instead, my brother, Zeke, sits in brooding silence beside me, a trait that only became more prevalent after his service in the military, and our parents fawn over Lola, overwhelming her with questions about her plans for work while she's here. Except Lola is Lola, which means she doesn't show her discomfort. No, instead, she's politely engaging in this conversation while her foot taps incessantly beneath the table, giving her away.

"I'm excited to teach again, but"—she flutters her lashes in a uniquely Lola way and smiles at my mom—"I don't know if there's much of a market for Latin dance lessons in Hidden Valley, Oklahoma."

My parents chuckle, hanging on her every word, and for good reason. Lola's the kind of woman who lights up every room she's in. She could be speaking about the most mundane things, and you'd still find yourself absolutely enraptured by her. I know I might be biased, but it's clear as day when you've seen it for yourself time and time again.

"Oh, Lola, when will you learn, precious girl? If you provide it, they will come! I'm sure you'd be surprised to find out just how many of us unsuspecting small-town folks are interested in something new and exciting like your dance class-es!" My mom has always been team Lola, in all things.

"*¡Sí, mija!* They will come," Bexaida, Lola's mom, assures her.

"Thank you, Mrs. Lockhart," Lola says, her cheeks turning that pretty rose color again.

Mom waves a wrinkled hand at Lola. "Oh, you stop with

that! You've been gone a few years, but you didn't hit the reset button. I'll always be Bee to you!" Mom peers at me with a sly grin on her lips before adding, "Or maybe, one day, you can call me Mom."

I nearly choke on my own spit, but Lola takes it in stride, completely unfazed by her antics.

"Sorry, *Bee,*" Lola emphasizes with a wide grin and raised brows. "I appreciate your support. Really, I do." Her dark-brown eyes soften. "I appreciate *all* your support," she says, addressing everyone at the table. "I know we haven't spoken about it, and I'm thankful you've all given me some time to just be here without having to talk it out."

Her leg is shaking a million miles a minute under the table, and I'm certain I'm the only one who notices. I'm sitting directly across from her, just like old times, so I settle my foot overtop of hers, and the shaking stops. Her eyes shoot up, sheepishly meeting mine in a silent "thanks."

When will she finally believe there isn't anything I wouldn't do for her?

We finish dinner without any more wayward glances. Lola volunteers to do the dishes. My chair scrapes across the hardwood floors as I stand, immediately making my way over to her at the sink. "You wash, I'll dry?" I ask her.

She gives me a small smile, nodding her agreement.

My cell vibrates in my back pocket, and when I see who the message is from, it doesn't take any time at all before I'm turning the power off entirely and tucking it away.

Lola and I fall into a rhythm, her meticulously washing each dish before rinsing and handing it to me to dry and stack.

With each dish, her posture becomes more and more rigid, her hands shaking the smallest amount, and a strained look passes across her face.

I lower my head to her ear so only she can hear me. "Darlin', let me finish up these dishes, yeah?"

I get a quick flash of her eyes in my direction, but that's the only acknowledgement I receive to confirm she's heard me.

"I'm not sure what's going on, but you look like you're in pain, and we can't have that. I promise, I don't mind takin' care of these." *Or you.* 'Please, let me!' I want to shout but bite my tongue.

She blows out a breath through pursed lips and mutters, "I'm fine. Just let it go."

I finish drying the glass in my hand, tuck it into the cabinet, and turn to face her. "Lola, please. There's clearly something going on. You don't need to be so strong all the time."

Is she upset about something? Am I misinterpreting a battle of emotions with physical pain?

Her sharp gaze cuts to me, her cute little nostrils flaring with annoyance. I shouldn't be as happy as I am to get this kind of response out of her, but at this point, any attention she'll give me is plenty. It's enough to know she's not in so much pain that she can't speak.

"All these years, and you *still* haven't learned how to leave well enough alone, have you?" she grits out, snatching the dish towel from me to dry her hands.

"When it comes to you? Absolutely not, and I never will. I don't want 'well enough' for you, Lola. I want perfection."

She clenches her eyes shut, drawing in a deep, steadying breath before blowing it out and meeting my eyes with a much softer expression. "Ryder, I appreciate that you care, but I'm tired. I'm going through a lot right now, and I'm sore from moving my things around. *Please* don't make a mountain out of a molehill."

My shoulders sag as I resign, not wanting to push her too far out of fear she'll shove me away instead.

"I'll let it go for now, but you're clearly in pain, Lols, and you don't have to carry the weight of the world alone."

She gives me a solemn nod, leaving me to sulk with the dishes until she and Mayte leave with Isabela. I'm left alone with my thoughts racing, full of worry over Lola and what she could be hiding behind a mask of unbreakable strength.

My night is spent restlessly replaying our conversation until I've picked it to pieces, and I'm certain her pain was, at least mostly, physical. It was clear in the way her posture was slumped over the sink, hands shaking, and a grimace so unfamiliar pinching her expression. I can't just stand by and wait for her to come to me if there's something I can do to help.

Chapter Nine

VIVE UN POCO

SATURDAY, APRIL 26

THE MORNING SUN streams in through the light-blue lace curtains above my bed, but that isn't what woke me.

There's someone pounding at the front door, practically rattling it off its hinges.

"*¿Qué pinga está pasando?*" I grumble, rolling out of bed and padding across the worn-out wooden floors. My parents aren't out here, so they must've already started their day.

When I wrench open the door, the sun is blinding behind Ryder's head. He stares down at me, his jaw hanging as I squint up at him. All my annoyance from our encounter last night has vanished, replaced with hints of desire that shouldn't even be in the same room with us.

A shiver races through me as a light gust of wind travels into the house and past my legs.

My bare legs.

"Oh shit," I say, slamming the door in his face before sprinting to my room to grab shorts or anything to cover my naked lower half, barely covered by panties and an oversized t-shirt.

I hear a light knock on my bedroom door, and of course, it's still Ryder. This time, though, he doesn't wait for me to let him in before he tentatively opens it, the old hinges creaking.

"Darlin', we've gotta talk about this pain you've been havin'," he says, as if he's already decided on this as a fact. If he wasn't coming into my personal space, acting as if my problems are his to bear, I'd find the way he's standing in my room with his hand smacked over his eyes both adorable and hysterical.

One thing he clearly doesn't remember about me is that I don't like being told what to do or having my decisions made for me. That's at the top of the extraordinarily long list of reasons things didn't work out with my ex-fiancé.

"No. No, we do not. I have it handled, and it's none of your business," I tell him, my voice growing louder with each word. It's possible I'm overly sensitive to this kind of thing because of Russ, but the words had already left my mouth before I could stop them. "And the coast is clear. I have shorts on now."

He drops his hand to his side, and his expression quickly shifts to one filled with sadness. "Darlin', I didn't mean to upset you. I'm just worried, is all."

I huff out an annoyed breath, but I work to calm my frustration.

This is Ryder we're talking about. Sweet, loving Ryder, who cares about your health.

"I'm sorry I snapped at you." I apologize, my shoulders sagging.

"It's alright. If you aren't ready to talk about it, the good news is, your pain isn't the only reason I dropped by."

I arch a brow at him. "It isn't?"

"Nope," he says, popping the *p*. "I came to invite you to the county fair with me tonight. I have to judge the annual chili contest." He groans.

Gross. *Sounds gassy.*

"And I thought you might have fun. Call it your first major outing since being home. Plus, Mayte and Isabela could come."
Home.

I guess this *is* my home again. Who am I kidding? Rosa Ranch is the only place I have *ever* truly felt at home.

"Alright." I nod. "I guess that sounds like fun."

Who am I kidding? I *love* the fair.

Ryder knows that, too, judging by the smirk he gives me. "I'll pick you up at four, and I'll drop by Mayte's to invite her before I work on repairing the fence."

"Okay, see you tonight," I say, walking him out. The moment he's gone, my whole body flutters with nerves.

I haven't seen most of these people since I was in undergrad, and now, I'm here after years of just dropping by with no intention of sticking around.

But there's a part of me that's also excited, and when the voice in the recesses of my mind tries to remind me *why* I'm excited, I squash it, busying myself with cleaning.

My sneakers squished through the mud as we slunk along the perimeter of the property, careful not to be seen.

"Loooola, this is a bad idea," Mayte whined for the tenth time in fifteen minutes. "They're grounded, and we'll be next if we do this."

I rolled my eyes, waving her off, crouching to run past the kitchen window at the main house, where Bee and Harlan sat at the table, playing a card game.

"Vive un poco, aseré," I whispered to her as we approached Ezekiel's bedroom window. I tapped against the glass, waiting for any sign of life, but when he didn't magically appear, I knocked more aggressively, praying he heard and no one else.

His dark-blue curtains shimmied, a scowling face greeting me as he unlatched the window and lifted the lip. "Lola, in case you couldn't tell, you came to the wrong window for whatever mess you're about to get yourself into."

"Oh, stop being such a Negative Nelly! You and your brother need to hug it out and make up because I'm tired of you both moping around. And there'll be no mess because we aren't going to get caught," I told him. "Now, get up and get changed while we grab Ryder."

Zeke grumbled something I couldn't hear, slamming the window in my face. I pressed my forehead to the glass, peering inside, and when he met my gaze, I mouthed, "Go change!" flicking my hand to shoo him off.

He stomped away, but when he made a pit stop at his closet to grab clothes, I knew he was too intrigued not to comply.

"Lola, you're gonna have that type-A boy losing his mind when he figures out where we're going," Mayte said with a chuckle, as if she wasn't also losing her mind.

"You two need to loosen up. We're just going to the fair. It's not a big deal," I told her as we made our way to the back of the house, where Ryder's bedroom was located.

I rapped my knuckles against the window, and all too quickly, Ryder was peering out at me, eyes wide, hair a disheveled mess, as he pushed the window open with a screech that had me biting the inside of my cheek.

"Are we doing what I think we are?" he asked with a boyish grin that left me tingling with excitement.

"We absolutely are! Get ready and meet us out here in five," I told him. Mayte was still groaning behind me about our social lives going down the toilet after being grounded until we're forty.

It didn't take long for Ryder to slip out of his window, falling gracefully to his feet before we rounded the house to where Zeke was nervously picking at lint on his burgundy long sleeve.

"Why did you invite him?" Ryder asked with a groan, tipping his head back in frustration.

I rolled my eyes. "Because he's your brother, and you were arguing over something dumb—"

"You don't know what we were arguing about!" Ryder said, cutting me off, but I swatted at him.

"I don't need to know the details to be absolutely certain it was something dumb. Because it is always something stupid with you two. You're hormonal teenagers, you aren't that hard to figure out. Now, quit wasting our precious time—"

"Yeah, because this might be the last moment of freedom we ever have," Mayte offered unhelpfully.

"Jesus Cristo, let's go." I trudged toward the ATVs parked beside the old barn, counting my stars that they wouldn't run out of gas before we got home.

"Wait, what about Logan?" Ryder asked, never one to leave his best friend behind.

"I called the house, and his mom answered, so I hung up. I'm sorry, Ry. I did all I could do," I told him. I liked Logan. He had always been sweet to me, but he didn't live on the ranch with us, so I didn't have any way to clue him in on this plan, save for a carrier pigeon.

"It's alright, Lols. You tried," he said with a resigned shrug.

Ryder climbed on one of the ATVs, Zeke on the other, a silent understanding passing between the four of us when Mayte hopped on Zeke's and I straddled the seat behind Ryder. The thrill of what we were doing buzzed in my veins, though there was also the edge of nervousness.

The cool night air hit my face, my heart racing not just from the ride but from the thrill of sneaking out to the fair. We were supposed to be asleep, tucked away in our beds, but there we were, barreling toward freedom. The thought made my stomach flutter, and a grin tugged at the corners of my mouth. It wasn't more than a half-hour ride before the faint glow of neon lights began to flicker through the trees, signaling the fairground was just ahead.

The sounds of the fair hit us even before we pulled in: the distant whirr of carnival rides, the low hum of voices blending with the screams of people flying through the air, the intoxicating smell of funnel cake and fried Oreos swirling in the night breeze.

"We don't have a lot of time," Mayte called over the roar of our engines, urgency creeping into her voice. "So let's make a plan. How about we each pick a ride and knock those out first in case the lines are long?"

Ryder, Zeke, and I nodded, agreeing with a sense of shared excitement, the kind that you only got from being young, when everything felt a little more dangerous. We decided on the Gravitron, Swing Ride, Scrambler, and Ferris wheel. It was the perfect lineup.

By the time we'd ridden the first three, my stomach was filled with a sticky, sweet mess of fried dough and lemonade, my cheeks aching from the smile stretching my lips.

"Glad we saved the Ferris wheel for last," Ryder said with a laugh, pressing a warm hand to the small of my back as he steered me toward the ride. "The Gravitron would have me puking by now."

"As usual," Mayte joked, rolling her eyes, "I'll skip this one. No need to get the whole town's view while I'm losing my lunch."

"I'll stay with you," Zeke added with a casual shrug, drawing an exaggerated sigh from Mayte.

Ryder and I stood in line for the Ferris wheel, the crowd around us sprawling in every direction. The air was thick with the hum of excitement, the buzz of voices too loud to make out. Clowns weaved in and out of the crowd, handing out cloud-like cotton candy, their painted faces as familiar to me as my own. I watched them, my eyes flicking over to the entertainers who threw glowing toys into the air. The toys flashed in the dimming light, bright against the dark sky as they tried to catch the attention of all the children.

"You want cotton candy?" Ryder asked, his grin playful, though his lips were still stained a pale blue from the slushie he had just finished.

I shook my head, pressing my hand to my belly, already full from the sweet overload. "Nah, I'm stuffed."

"Oh, come on, Lols. You can't break tradition." His voice was teasing, but there was a warmth to it that made it impossible to resist. He knew I'd never say no when he had that look on his face.

"Fine," I groaned, pretending to reluctantly give in. "I wouldn't want to jinx us by not getting cotton candy for the Ferris wheel."

"That's my girl," he joked, and even though I knew that's exactly what it was—a joke—my tummy still tingled with warmth. "Two blue cotton candies, comin' right up."

He left me to hold our place in line, my eyes glued to his every movement as he chatted with the clown, the same guy who handed out cotton candy every year. Without warning, my shoulder was shoved, sending me tumbling forward into the dirt. My knees hit first, sharp and hard, the ground cold and sticky beneath me as I crashed into the mud. My palms burned from the impact, embarrassment spreading like fire as I looked up to find Ryder already running toward me.

The shrill, too-high voice of Lemmon Meringue, my bully for as long as I could remember, filled my ears. "Oh, Lola Lima! I am so sorry! I must not've seen you when I was walkin' by. Here, let me help you up," she said with a thick Southern accent, extending her hand for me to take.

I pushed her hand away, frustration and humiliation twisting inside me. "No, I've got it," I snapped, wiping the dirt off my hands and scowling.

"Lols, you okay?" Ryder asked, his strong hands steadying me as he pulled me to my feet.

"I'm fine," I grumbled, wiping my palms on my denim shorts.

I turned my attention to Lemmon, who greeted me with her version of a bashful smile. "I'm so sorry, Lola. Will you ever forgive me?" she asked, the faux sweetness lacing her voice sickening.

I didn't have a chance to respond before Mayte was at my side, pinning Lemmon with a look that could freeze water. "You did that on purpose. I saw you!" Mayte roared, coming to my defense as usual.

"Oh, sweet Mayte, it's really so noble of you to come to your friend's aid, but I promise, I did no such thing," Lemmon said, fanning her face as if to repress tears.

Mayte opened her mouth, about to say something, but Ryder stepped in. "She said she's sorry. Let's leave it at that and enjoy what's left of our night, yeah?" Ryder asked, diffusing the situation before Mayte could start pulling hair and throwing punches. She might come across as shy at first, but she's a warrior for the people she cares about.

"Fine. Let's just go," I grunted, allowing Ryder to tug me through the moving line, pulling me into a bucket seat and swinging the door closed. He set his eyes on my face, seeing right through the mask of indifference I tried so hard to wear.

"Are you okay, Lols?" he asked, those baby blues never leaving my face as he reached over my lap for the seat belt, clipping me in.

"Yeah, Ry, I am." The words were choked and small. I desperately wanted to tell him Lemmon had been bullying me for years. I wanted to confide in him about this one thing I'd held close to my chest, never telling anyone but Mayte, but I couldn't bring myself to. I didn't want him to think I was weak, and, more than anything, I didn't want him to fight my battles for me. I tried every day to remind myself she was a bully because she'd had a harder life than I did, but those words only came as a comfort for so long.

The motor whirred to life, the metal creaking as we began our ascent. His hand slid up my waist to my bare shoulder before cupping my cheek, smoothing a thumb beneath my eye, where I'd unknowingly allowed a tear to fall.

"I'm sorry that happened, baby," he whispered, unaware of how that word unfurled a cacophony of emotions inside me, stealing the breath from my lungs. "Accidents happen, but it's still shitty."

If the word "baby" made me feel whole and ready to spill my guts to him, finally letting him into the darkest valleys where I hid my secrets, the word "accidents" had the complete opposite effect, pushing me to shut down and protect my heart in the best way I knew how: with silence.

His hand dropped, his arm winding around my shoulders to tug me against his chest, the place I'd always felt safest. I reveled in the moment, unsure at the time how much longer we had left like that—not just on the ride, but before he realized I was too terrified to lose him to truly give in to my feelings.

A knock at the door pulls me from the memory, pushing me into the present, where Lemmon is still a bully but holds so much less control over me and my actions. I release a sigh, heading to the door to spend the night at the fair with two of my favorite people.

Chapter Ten

SAT ON A FROG

SATURDAY, APRIL 26

EVER SINCE WE ARRIVED, I haven't had a single second alone with Lola. She's been pushed and pulled in every direction by the well-meaning people of this town, but I can see how much it breaks her spirit every time she explains she doesn't have a job yet and she isn't sure how long she'll be in town. It's in the small cracks of her smile, the way her shoulders tighten. It's clear this isn't easy for her, no matter how hard she tries to brush it off.

I press my hand to the small of her back, excusing us from Cindy and Sheryl, two of Lola's past teachers. "Sorry, ladies. If you'll excuse us, I believe I have a chili contest to judge."

Sheryl swats at an invisible gnat in front of her face, scrunching her nose as she says, "Phewie! I'm glad my husband won't be judgin' this year. The day after, he always sounds like he sat on a frog!"

Laughter rips through my chest as I shake my head, steering us toward the white-topped tents a few yards away. "What a lovely picture she's painted," Lola teases.

"I'm glad you live alone, Ry. Hopefully, for your own sake, you took some prebiotics or something," Mayte adds, not helping my case. I'm sure this conversation will really have me winning Lola's heart. *Not.*

"Okay, you two. Quit pickin' on me," I say, quickly changing the subject. "Let me take Isabela. She can hang out with me so the both of you can go on a few rides and enjoy some free childcare."

Mayte's face lights up, hitting me with a megawatt smile as she reaches out to pinch my cheek. "*This* is why you've always been my favorite Lockhart brother," she says, dropping her hand to drag Lola off toward the Teacups and the Swing Ride, the only two Mayte has ever ridden.

The chili contest wraps up smoothly, with Andres Baker claiming victory for the sixth year in a row. I don't even need to try his chili to know it's incredible. The man's got the touch, no question.

I weave through the crowd, Isabela strapped into her stroller, her little head slumped back, mouth slightly open. Drool drips down the side of her cheek, but she's out cold, lost in the quiet of a nap. The noise and bustle of the festival fade into the background, and for a moment, I feel like I'm in a different world, tucked away from all the chaos.

Mayte spots me from ahead, her frantic waving cutting through the crowd like a flare.

"Ry!" she yells, her voice sharp and familiar. I make my way over, maneuvering the stroller carefully, just enough to avoid waking Isabela. She stays asleep, oblivious to the world.

"Hey, y'all have fun?" I ask, trying to keep things light.

"As usual." Mayte grins, though there's a bit of exasperation in her voice. "The problem child here has consumed half her weight in cotton candy and funnel cake, so I think it's time you take over. You can handle her while I get back to my actual child."

She crouches down to check on her daughter, wiping her mouth with the edge of a blanket, her expression softening in a way that makes me realize just how much she's been juggling.

"You sure you're okay on your own?" Lola asks her, concern pulling at the edges of her voice, her brow furrowing like she's been carrying a weight of her own.

"Yep," Mayte says, a hint of humor in her voice as she steers the stroller, taking control of the situation without giving anyone a chance to argue. "You two go ride that deathtrap of a Ferris wheel."

"Well, guess I'll have to get you another cotton candy if we're gonna brave that thing," I say, glancing at Lola with a teasing grin.

Her cheeks turn pink, her eyes shifting, not quite meeting mine. The uncertainty is there, faint but lingering, like we've been away from each other long enough that it's hard to remember what this is or what it could be.

Lola waits in line while I grab the cotton candy. I return with two massive blue cones and hand one to her, and she immediately tears off a chunk, shoving it into her mouth. A piece sticks to the tip of her nose, and, without thinking, I reach out, swiping it off with the edge of my thumb. Her eyes flick up to mine, a quick, sharp breath catching in her throat, the air between us suddenly feeling charged. For a moment, everything else fades, and all I can focus on is the air between us. But the attendant's voice, sharp and insistent, breaks the spell. "Next in line!"

I step closer, pressing my hand to the small of her back, guiding her forward. "Come on, Lols. Don't wanna miss our turn," I tease, my voice light, a little breathless from the sudden tension.

She nods, settling into the seat, her movements quick but purposeful as she clips herself in. The cotton candy cone is wedged between her knees, untouched for the moment. It's clear she's not looking for me to buckle her in this time, not like I've done every other time before. There's a shift in her, something subtle, but it's enough to make me hesitate for a beat.

I do my best to settle in, an electric charge pulsing between us as the bucket seats jostle us, beginning their slow ascent to the top.

"Are you having a good time?" I ask, desperate to break the tense silence.

She glances up, holding me in her searching gaze. "Yeah, Ry. I'm having fun. It's just been a lot. I thought I'd have more time to figure things out before reuniting with the whole town."

My brows pinch, frustration with myself settling in. *How could I have been so thoughtless?* "I'm sorry, Lols. I hadn't considered you might want some more time to settle in before a big event like this." I reach out, taking her hand and giving it a tight squeeze.

She leans into the embrace, almost melting into the small point of contact. "It's not your fault at all. I'd have been disappointed if I missed the fair, and I'm glad I came. I'm a little overwhelmed with all the attention and questions is all."

"They're all well-meaning, but that doesn't make it any less suffocating, does it?" I ask, recalling all the times I'd been asked after graduating college if there was any chance I'd still try to go pro with football or take over the ranch. After what happened with Logan, I had even less interest in going pro than I had prior, but that was too painful to admit.

"No, it doesn't," she says softly, shaking her head, her voice carrying a weight of something I can't quite place. She leans into me, her cheek resting on my shoulder as we reach the peak of the ride. Below us, the town sprawls out, small and distant.

It kills me not to pull her closer, to press a kiss to the top of her head, to wrap my arms around her and just hold her. But I don't. I resist. The tension between us is too fragile, and I know better than to push.

"Remember the time you snuck us out to the fair when Zeke and I were grounded?" I ask, the question slipping out as we begin our descent.

Lola's laughter comes light and genuine, and it wraps around me, filling the empty spaces I didn't realize were there. She leans further into me, her body warm and comforting against mine. "God, yes. I was just thinking about that earlier today. We thought we were *so* slick, didn't we? When we got home, we thought we'd pulled it off."

I smile at the memory. "Your mom scared the piss out of me that night. When I tiptoed through the house and found her lying in my bed, wrapped in my comforter, acting like she'd just risen from the dead, I ran straight into Zeke in the hall, screaming."

She laughs again, a sound that settles deep in my chest, like I'm hearing it for the first time. "Oh my god, yes! I still don't know how they came up with that plan, each of them hiding in our beds to scare us. And here we thought we were so clever."

"I think about that day every year," I say, the words spilling out before I can stop them. "Mayte was so sure we'd get caught, that our social lives would be ruined. And, of course, she was right. After that, none of us could leave the house for anything except school, sports, and whatever random crafting club Mayte was in at the time." I shake my head at the memory, that familiar warmth of nostalgia creeping in.

Lola shifts, her hand brushing mine, her fingers lingering just long enough to remind me we're still here, together.

The breeze cools the air around us, and I realize, as the world below keeps spinning, this simple, easy moment with her is *everything*.

Lola

Chapter Eleven
BULL RIDER

SATURDAY, APRIL 26

WE'VE SPENT the whole night on all sorts of extremely questionable rides, making fun of Ryder and that disgusting chili contest, and eating massive amounts of cotton candy.

Not that it's a surprise, but everyone has been so sweet and welcoming.

I've had a couple of people ask if I was planning to offer dance lessons. It gives me the hope I was missing and the courage I need to stick around and figure out a plan for myself. But every time I answer their questions, I'm reminded I have no idea where I'd even teach these classes. It's frustrating, and after a while, it starts to wear me down.

As we make our way over to the lemonade, *I see it.*

That damn mechanical bull.

I have a love-hate relationship with it. I love it because I'd always been good at it and it's so much fun. But in this moment, *I hate it* because I'm sure it's the last thing I should be thinking about doing.

"Ryder, sweetie! Wait up!" I hear a high-pitched, familiar voice from behind me that sounds like nails on a chalkboard, and it immediately sours my mood, acid burning in my gut.

We turn around, finding Lemmon wearing some ridiculous floral dress that looks like it was designed for women during the patriarchy.

She flits her eyes over me with a disgusted look of disdain before centering her gaze on Ryder.

He tips his chin at her, winding an arm around me and resting his hand on my hip. He pulls me close to him and says absolutely nothing to her before turning us to face the other direction.

A pleased smile curves my lips. *Always the protector*, even if he hadn't known the one person I'd actually *needed* protection from was the woman he wound up marrying.

It's selfish, but I'm glad they divorced. It was difficult to see them together, and while Russ's controlling behavior is mostly to blame for my absence, seeing Ryder with Lemmon didn't help.

When we move to walk past the bull riding machine, I hear my name called by Cynthia, a woman we'd already caught up with today.

"Lola! You've gotta take a turn on the bull, for old times' sake!" she tells me, and others join in when they realize I'm here.

A group of surly men wearing black, gray, and red tie-dyed leather jackets, a stack of books embroidered in the bottom right corner of the back panel, turns to face us, smiling widely when they see Ryder.

They're the owners of the only faces in this town I *don't* recognize.

"You must be the one that got away," a man with a red beard and blue eyes says to me, sticking his hand out. I reach to shake it tentatively, my head tilting in confusion.

"Sorry, what was that?" I ask.

"Ryder's told us *all* about you, Miss Lola," the oldest of the men says, and my heart seizes in my chest for a beat before I brush the panicked feeling away.

"Oh, well, I regret to inform you gentlemen that Ryder hasn't done his part for any of you. I think I'd have remembered if he told me Hidden Valley has its very own biker gang now." I smile brightly at them, their hearty laughter wrapping around us.

"We're bikers, but I assure you, we aren't in a gang. The closest we've come to one is our book club," the redhead says.

"And how do you know Ryder?" I ask.

"When they stopped in town, they dropped by Rosa Ranch looking for work. We didn't need any more ranch hands at the time, but I got them set up with a few others around town. They invited me to their book club shortly after I finalized my divorce, and I hadn't been expecting the book of the month to be a second-chance, childhood-best-friends-to-lovers romance," Ryder explains, staring pointedly at the redheaded man.

My shoulders shake, picturing these burly men poring over romance books. They're the true epitome of not judging a book by its cover. "Sounds like a great time. Maybe I'll join you if you've got room for another member," I tell them.

"We'd love to have you, Miss Lola," the older man says. "I'm Levi, and this is Rhett." He points to the man with the red beard. "Teddy is the blond over there." He motions to the group of three standing in line for chicken wings. "Wyatt and Callaway are brothers, the dark-haired guys behind Teddy."

"I won't lie and say I'll remember any of that, but I promise to give it my best shot," I tell him.

"No worries. Now, how's about you get up on that bull? Sounds like you were pretty good in your day," Levi challenges, wiggling his graying brows at me.

Several thoughts war inside me, the loudest being that I shouldn't do it, but the actual voices of real people shouting for me to give it a go are rapidly becoming louder.

"Yeah, Lola. Wouldn't wanna miss out now, would ya?" Lemmon's shrill voice grates at my nerves.

When had she shown up again?

I take a deep breath, stepping out of Ryder's grasp and heading up to the mechanical bull operator. I count my blessings that Ryder doesn't try to stop me, though maybe he *should*.

"Hey there, Lola. Good to see ya," Nate says, opening the gate for me.

"You too, Nate," I tell him with a warm smile, despite the nerves bubbling in my gut.

I tiptoe along the edge of the slippery rubber mat and hoist myself up.

Everything beyond this moment happens too quickly to decipher exactly where I went wrong.

One moment, my thighs are hugging the sides of the bull, my hands clutching the handle. *And then, I'm not.*

As the speed picks up, my legs shake, doing most of the work. My hands slip all over as I struggle to stay put. Every joint in my body is on fire, and my heart is bounding.

I fall backward, hitting the mat with a loud thud. My vision starts to dim at the edges, but not before Ryder rushes to my side. I hear him drop to the mat behind me, his hands warm against my cheeks, fingers brushing softly, grounding me. "Darlin', you've gotta stay awake," he tells me firmly, as if his words alone could make my body's protection mechanisms halt in their tracks.

Turns out *he's right*.

I blink rapidly, regaining my vision, and soon, I'm being thrown over Ryder's shoulder, carried down the stairs and out to the parking lot.

"Ooh, better luck next time, Lola. Seems you're just a tad rusty," Lemmon taunts.

"Back off," Ryder roars at her, stealing the breath from my lungs as he continues carrying me toward his truck.

"I can walk by myself," I whine.

"Do not test me right now, Lola," Ryder grits out. His words have the hair on my neck standing on end. "You just did something so goddamn dangerous. I don't wanna hear it from you."

My nipples have *no business* perking up at the demanding tone in his voice.

Mayte rushes after us, Isabela in her stroller. "Lola! I'm gone for ten minutes to pee, and you can't help but try to get yourself killed!" she shouts at me.

I slam my eyes shut, the tension tightening in my jaw as I brace myself, dreading the sharp sting of the mental ass whooping these two are clearly planning to dish out tonight.

Once we're at Ryder's truck, he gently lowers me down without a word, proving me wrong as he drives us home in silence.

I make it to bed in record time, wanting nothing more than to curl up under the soft quilt. My phone pings with messages from my group chat, a smile returning to my face as I read the string of messages.

> KARMELLA RENAMED THE CHAT "BRIDE SNATCHERS"

> EWELINA RENAMED THE CHAT "KARMELLA IS AN INSENSITIVE ASSHOLE"

> KARMELLA RENAMED THE CHAT "BRIDESMAIDS"

> YANET

> Sigh

> KARMELLA

> You guys are no fun.

> EWELINA

> Ignore her.

> How are you holding in there, Lols?

MY WIFEY FOR LIFEY

She's doing great... Ry is officially in his daddy era. Speaking of which, he's about to drop me off at home, and I'm pretty sure I'm about to get in trouble?

KARMELLA

What??? Why???

MY WIFEY FOR LIFEY

Not totally sure, but there's a vibe. Just parked. I'll update later.

YANET

No, you won't.

MY WIFEY FOR LIFEY

You're right. I won't remember. Sorry! Love you guys!

Sorry, I've just been... Dealing? Not sure how I feel lately, but I know this is for the best. I just wish you guys didn't live so far. I miss you already.

YANET

Getting old sucks.

KARMELLA

You're thirty-six. That isn't old. STFU.

I'm inclined to agree with Mella, but you guys know how much I hate doing that...

Also, Mayte... You BETTER update us! So a girl falls off a mechanical bull. What's the big deal? 😬

KARMELLA

1. It's true. You DO hate to agree with me for some reason 🙄

2. YOU WHAT?!

It's honestly not a big deal. I'm fine.

EWELINA

You wouldn't tell us if you weren't, so I have a hard time believing that. I have to run, but I love you guys. Talk soon!

YANET

Goodnight, guys. I've gotta get the kids showered and to bed. Love you!

KARMELLA

Love you!!! Can't wait to catch up in another two months! 🩶

I love you ladies. Have a good night, and thanks for checking in.

Seven hours later.

JOHANNA

Hi! Sorry, did I miss something? Love you all!

Ryder

Chapter Twelve
PROBLEM SOLVING

SATURDAY, APRIL 26

I'VE WATCHED that woman ride that mechanical bull every year at the county fair when she'd drop into town for a short visit.

If the fair was happening, she was there.

And she loved nothing more than to show off.

Never in a million years would I have thought she'd go flying off that thing. Sure, I could chalk it up to her being out of practice, but after seeing the way her hands struggled to get a good grip and watching her do those dishes last night, I'm not convinced.

The moment we're parked in front of Mayte's cottage, I swivel in my seat to face her.

"We need to talk," I tell her.

She stares up at me with those giant, honey-colored eyes, blinking rapidly before nodding. "We do. Come inside. I've gotta get Isabela to bed first."

I unstrap Isabela, and Mayte unclips her car seat once I get her out of it. We head inside, and I plop down on the couch, waiting for her to get Isabela settled and ready for bed.

When she's finished, she waves a hand at me to follow her to the kitchen.

We take a seat at her small dining table, and she places her forearms on the worn wood, leveling me with her signature stare.

"Alright, sweetness. Let's get into it."

I chuckle at how straightforward she is.

"I noticed Lola was in pain yesterday, and then tonight on the bull…" I trail off, unsure of what else to say.

She smacks her forehead dramatically. "Oh, god! You noticed that too!" she nearly shouts, uncovering her face as her big eyes meet mine. "Gosh, she's worrying the hell out of me. I knew her condition would get worse as time went on without treatment, but I didn't know how fast!"

My stomach drops to my toes as I struggle to put the puzzle together, eventually working it out. I'm unable to clear the shock written clear as day on my face.

Mayte smacks her hand over her mouth when she realizes what she's done. "You didn't know," she breathes out quietly.

I shake my head. "I didn't, but now that I do, I'd appreciate it if you explained."

I lean forward onto my forearms, settling in for what I'm sure is about to be one long explanation.

Twenty minutes later, I'm fully caught up on Lola's rheumatoid arthritis diagnosis, her lack of treatment the last few years thanks to her lack of health insurance, and, of course, the bastard she almost married, who used her diagnosis against her as a manipulation tactic.

"So," she says, slouching in her seat, "what are we gonna do about this?"

I close my eyes, rattling any semblance of an idea around in my mind, and come up short. "I don't know, but I'm gonna figure it out."

She nods slowly, her messy bun bobbing with the motion. "Just let me know how I can help," she tells me.

"Will do. Now, go on and get to bed with that sweet little dumpling. I've taken up too much of your time tonight already."

I stand, heading to the door. Before I step out, she surprises me, wrapping me up in a tight hug and pressing a kiss to either of my cheeks. "Thanks for caring, Ryder. Goodnight."

I tip my chin at her, heading out onto the porch. "Always will. Night."

Lola

Chapter Thirteen

LENGUA SUELTA

SUNDAY, APRIL 27

MY HEAD POUNDS as I sit at the dining table, my elbows sticking to the clear plastic *Mami* keeps over the white lace tablecloth as I ice my swollen knuckles.

As usual, everything hurts, though today is worse than my new baseline.

Struggling with my grip last night had strained my already-sore joints, and falling flat on my back only made matters worse.

There's a knock at the door, and when I answer it, just like yesterday, I find Ryder standing on my porch.

Except this time, he's got a bouquet of white roses.

He thrusts them into my arms and lets himself inside. "Mornin', darlin'," he says, taking a seat at the table. Where the hell are my parents when I need them? "You may not've been ready to talk about it yesterday, but I sure hope you are now."

"I'm not sure what you're talking about," I say, feigning indifference as I take a seat across from him.

His eyes narrow before landing on the bags of ice sitting on the table. "You sure about that?"

"I am," I huff out. "It's none of your business, Ryder. I can take care of myself. I have for a long time now."

His eyes soften as he takes in my annoyed expression. "I'm not telling you what to do, but I want to help," he says, the words coming out like a plea. "I spoke with Mayte…" Those words hang in the air between us, threatening to shatter the stillness. Once sacred, quiet, and peaceful, now nowhere seems free of the thoughts threatening to strangle me at every turn.

He scratches the back of his neck, averting his gaze for a beat.

"And she told you what?" I tread lightly, hoping with every fiber of my being that she hadn't opened her big mouth and spilled the news of my diagnosis to the one person who would do anything in his power to help me.

"Now, don't go doin' that thing you always do," he chides.

I quirk a brow at him. "And what would that be, exactly?"

"Where you close off and pretend like nothing's wrong when it clearly is. You can't be mad at Mayte. I'm nearly certain I tricked her into telling me without intentionally doing so." That wouldn't surprise me in the least. *Lengua suelta.*

"Fine. What's this big discussion you came to have?"

"Marry me, darlin'."

My eyes bug out of my head, threatening to fall to the floor like an overexcited chihuahua. "I'm sorry, what? You're gonna have to repeat that for me because I'm certain I didn't hear you right."

"Marry me, Lola. *Please*," he says earnestly.

"You do realize I *just* got out of a relationship and narrowly *avoided* getting married, right?" Not that I'm mourning the end of my sorry excuse of a relationship with Russ.

"You need health insurance, Lola, and I looked into my policy last night. I can't add anyone on until the next enrollment period in November—*unless* there's a qualifying life-changing circumstance, like *marriage.*"

He researched all this just last night?

"What's in it for you?" I ask, suspicious of his intentions. I haven't seen this man since the Christmas before last, and we've spoken to each other less than a handful of times since then. I know he cares about me, but enough to lock himself into another marriage?

He looks down at his feet, clearly uncomfortable, before his eyes finally lift to meet mine. "I really do want to make sure you get treatment, Lola."

"I'm waiting for the 'but', Ryder," I tell him, folding my arms over my chest.

"*But* I know I messed up when Logan died, and I didn't tell you how badly I was struggling with the loss. I know we've been over this before, but it kills me that I kept you out because of some poorly rationalized belief that you'd have run to my rescue. I should've leaned on you like you wanted me to, and then when Lemmon showed up, ready to listen, there was absolutely zero romantic intent behind it from my end. I only had eyes for you, but after you'd moved on and I was forced to listen to your mom and Mayte's updates about your love life and how things had gotten serious with Russ, I thought marrying Lemmon just made sense." He hangs his head, running a ragged hand through his unruly dark strands before meeting my eyes again. "I hadn't known how badly she bullied you when we were kids. You were so good at keeping that hidden, never wanting to add more fuel to her fire, but I should've known, Lola. I should have asked more questions or done *something* to protect you from her." His voice lowers in a way that tells me he's exhausted by this part of the conversation already. "I hadn't taken care of your heart then, but *please*, darlin', let me take care of your health now."

Now *that* makes sense. Guilt is something I'm familiar with.

I get it now, but when Mayte first told me they'd eloped, it was hard to understand how they ever got married in the first place.

Lemmon comes from a well-off family in town, and nothing

ever seemed to be good enough for her. Even as kids, she was always trying to prove she was better than me, but it wasn't until we were adults that others started to see through the facade. You'd think that sort of thing would get exhausting, even for her.

When I broke things off with Ryder, the son of the largest rescue ranch owner in western Oklahoma, who happened to be a football superstar, I'd given her everything she'd ever wanted: the perfect opening to prey on a young man who was just desperate for someone to listen.

Lemmon was catty, entitled, and downright cruel in the way she spoke to me, but she acted like the perfect Southern belle when she was around Ryder.

Besides, she hadn't even liked him for who he really was. She assumed he'd head to the NFL, make them both famous, and they'd ride off into the sunset together, preferably on a private jet rather than a horse.

If she'd known the first thing about Ryder Lockhart, she'd know he'd wanted to earn a degree in civil engineering with a focus in environmental protection. He had big plans for when he graduated to test out new methods of farming and raising cattle so he could pass the wisdom down to other ranchers and farmers for the betterment of our environment.

I imagine finding out he not only planned to do exactly that but that he accomplished it would have been a low blow to her perfectly curated plans.

But none of that is my problem, and I'm not running away from one marriage into another just for health insurance.

I'll find my own way.

"No." I point to the front door. "I think it's time for you to go."

Ryder

Chapter Fourteen

FUTURE PLANNING

SUNDAY, APRIL 27

SHE MAY HAVE SAID no this time—not that I had made the proposal seem all that enticing— but I'm not giving up that easily.

I want to help Lola more than anything, and if I can earn back some of her trust after marrying Lemmon had broken us, for what I'd thought was for good, it's more than worth the bruised knees and hours of groveling I'm happy to do if it changes her mind.

It's strange having her back. It's only been a few days since her arrival, and it's like she never really left.

I know this life may not have been what she'd been planning, but maybe she could learn to love it. *To love me again.*

She was my first love, the first and *last* person I've ever felt something *real* and lasting with, and I'm determined to work for what I want.

For now, I have responsibilities to keep my racing mind occupied. I continue up the dry dirt path to the greenhouses, determined to make my last project of the day worthwhile.

The only thing that has ever rivaled my love for Lola has been reworking the world around me in an effort to better the way we do things. For our environment. For the children and grandchildren I someday hope to have. For this town that filled me with hope when I wasn't sure there was any left to be had after Logan's death, and then again after Lola left me and didn't plan to return.

They rallied behind me, and I have every intention of doing the same for them. That's why this experiment *has* to work. This fertilizer has the components necessary to be versatile for all plants commonly grown on farms. It's safe for cattle to feed on plants sprayed with it. It doesn't harm the waterways in any capacity or disturb the local wildlife or insects. It also costs next to nothing to make, thanks to recycled materials, and would increase yearly production tenfold, making it so much easier to provide healthy, balanced meals to our schools.

I'm so close to the right formula, I can *feel it.*

If only I were as certain about my standing with Lola as I am about this.

Lola

Chapter Fifteen

HITCHED OR DITCHED?

SUNDAY, April 27

I march down to Mayte's cabin, hearing Isabela's wailing cries from five yards away as I approach.

I let myself in, not bothering to knock when I know not much can be heard over those crocodile tears anyway.

Mayte stands in her small living room, a red-faced Isabela on her hip as she bounces her, soothing my little niece.

She looks up at me, and a guilty smile curves her lips. "Hey, Lols. About what I said to Ryder—"

She doesn't get to finish her sentence before I cut her off. "*He proposed.*"

Her eyes are the size of saucers, but she kicks her feet on the carpet, jostling Isabela as she does. "That infuriating freaking man. He didn't even let me be there for it? I could've taken pictures!" she whines, her face reddening with outrage.

"I didn't say yes, *idiota*!"

Her mouth forms an *o*, and she says, "You didn't?" She sounds genuinely surprised, her voice quiet. Her pink cheeks return to a smooth, warm tan as she pouts, waiting for an explanation.

"No! I'm not marrying him for health insurance."

"Well, why the hell not? You need health insurance, and he has it to offer. Jump on that train, Lols. Choo, choo!" she says, pumping her fist in the air, mimicking a train conductor.

"You cannot be serious right now, Mayte. Didn't we *just* agree I couldn't marry someone for health insurance?"

"No, we agreed you couldn't marry someone *just* for the health insurance. You love Ryder! You always have! And *he* loves you," she tries to reason with me in her own, completely ass-backward way.

"Who's to say he really even loves me anymore? We broke up when I was twenty-one. Newsflash, but I'll be thirty-two this year. As much as I like to joke that nothing ever happens around here, I'm not that dense." I throw my hands up, collapsing into her worn-out, black leather loveseat. "Ryder is a thirty-four-year-old divorcé with an ex-wife who has hated my guts since we were kids. He probably just wants to marry me out of guilt. He practically said as much."

Mayte scoffs at that. "Lemmon's nothing but a two-faced high school bully with no dreams or aspirations of her own. The only reason she hated you so much was because Ryder always loved *you*. She was jealous of your carefree nature and that you had that man's eyes locked on you every second of the day. He *still* loves you, and even if he is doing it out of guilt, who cares? You need health insurance, Lola, one way or another."

I sincerely hate to admit when Mayte's right, mostly because she's a tremendous pain in my ass about it, but she *is* right. About some things anyway.

"Fine. I'll think about it," I tell her.

"*Eres más rollo que película,*" she mutters under her breath.

I roll my eyes at her, standing and reaching my arms out for Isabela. "Hand over my niece."

When she places her in my arms, my hands almost give out under her weight, and I fight to clutch her to my chest.

"Whoa there, Lola," Mayte says, grabbing hold of her daughter. "Take a seat. You can hold her then."

Hot tears fill my eyes, and a watery cry leaves my trembling lips.

This disease has taken so much from me already. *And now this?*

"It's okay. We'll get it figured out," Mayte tries to assure me, her tone hushed. She sits beside me, resting Isabela in my arms, but my heart cracks further and further with every minute her arm remains wrapped around her daughter, ensuring I don't accidentally hurt her.

I might have just reached my breaking point.

It's dark out by the time I make it out to the stables to see Penny, and no matter how much my hands shake with the effort, I'm committed to grooming her the way I should.

I may not be able to ride her at this point, but I need to at least do this. If not for her, then for me.

Living with a chronic illness is a horrendous thing.

It isn't just the physical symptoms or the visible changes in my body that wear me down. No, it's a mental battle too.

The thing I love most in this world, other than my friends and family, is dancing. It was my first true love, and knowing that one day, very soon, if I don't get medical help, I won't be able to dance anymore, crushes me.

A thread of hope I might figure out another way still hangs on, but a much thicker piece of twine is attached to the idea that marrying Ryder might be the kind of luck I need right now.

I tug on the thin rope by the stable door, yanking on it to illuminate the entry in a soft yellow glow. The usually empty first stable now houses an unnaturally small horse. Its cream-colored coat is bristly, black splotches litter its chest, and warm-brown eyes meet mine.

Ryder reserves this stall for the new intakes, the ones he's rescued that require the most attention. He keeps them close to the entrance so they're checked on more frequently than the rest of the more established horses, just like his father had when he was in charge.

I slowly approach the horse, gripping the rough wooden door as I peer into the small enclosure.

"Hi, new friend," I whisper to her, keeping my voice low to avoid spooking her. I see she's got raw skin around her neck, likely from an abusive owner who incorrectly harnessed her, rubbing the skin with the throat strap. "Don't worry, little lady. Ryder is the best. He'll take care of you," I tell her, extending my arm to stroke the soft hairs between her ears. Her wide-eyed expression visibly softens with the gesture, and she pushes into my hand for more attention.

I barely register the soft sound of boots over hay-covered concrete before warm arms wrap around my waist, clutching me tightly to a firm chest. My spine goes rigid, the embrace startling me, but I immediately register that it's *him*. That I'm safe in these arms.

"I've missed you, Lols," he whispers hoarsely against the shell of my ear, a shiver climbing from the base of my spine. I arch into him, greedy for his touch, though I have no right to seek it, to *crave* it.

"I've missed you too," I admit, my voice catching as my chest tightens, like the weight of the words is pressing on me, leaving me stripped bare. I'm not ready to lay myself out for him to see all the broken and messy pieces my ex spent the last few years creating.

He nuzzles the side of my neck, his breath warm and steady against my chilled skin as he drags in a deep breath, a quiet pulse of something unspoken giving me permission to do the same. I'm greedy as I relax into him, allowing the familiar scent of his cologne, a lethal combination of vanilla, whisky, and leather, to wrap around me, invading my senses as his stubble scrapes across my jawline. For a quiet moment, I allow myself to imagine a world where I *do* give in to Ryder, one where I take the advice I'd given to the small horse and allow him to take care of me. Where we get married, he supports me in any way he can, where I have insurance and my pain lessens, and I'm able to hold my niece without fear I'll drop her.

The thought comforts me in a cocoon of hope. I peer down to where Ryder's tan, corded arms are wrapped so firmly around my waist, I *know* he would never let me fall. I find myself letting go of the tension in my shoulders, something inside me softening, becoming more pliable to the idea of letting someone take on some of the weight I carry.

"It feels good to hear you say that," he answers, his deep baritone gruff as he skates a rough palm up my arm, sweeping my hair to one side. His fingers wrap around my jaw, commanding me to shift my gaze to meet his over my shoulder. "You seem exhausted. Mayte mentioned you might want to be alone right now, but I couldn't help myself. You're hurting, and it's breaking my heart to see you suffering."

His eyes are glassy with unshed tears, and I have to swallow around the lump in my throat. This man sees right through me.

"I'm *so* tired, Ry," I whisper, my lip quivering, giving in to my need to be cradled against his chest and cared for. My stone walls have turned to glass, and they're quickly falling around me, resolved to allow Ryder to sweep up every piece. I'm inclined to let him, knowing a few shards of glass piercing his flesh won't break him like it might me.

"Let me make things better. I *need* to make it better for you, Lola." A tear slips down my cheek, and I try to turn away, but he tightens his grip on my jaw, swiping the lone tear away with the rough pad of his thumb. "Come on, darlin'. *Let's get hitched.*"

I take a deep breath, allowing his familiar, comforting scent to envelop me. I hold it, the stillness and comfort he provides slipping into my bones, before I push it out and whisper, "Okay."

Ryder

Chapter Sixteen

RULES ARE MEANT TO BE BROKEN

SUNDAY, APRIL 27

"OKAY?" I ask, just to be sure I'd heard her right, though I know not to look a gift horse in the mouth.

"Let's get married," she confirms.

I spin her around to fully face me, gripping her hips, lifting her up off the ground with ease, and twirling her around in circles. Her arms wind around my neck, and a boyish grin curves my lips when I hear that whimsical, carefree laugh of hers.

Her head is tossed back as laughter fills the void of years without it, without *her.* All the emotions I'd been holding in since she left me seem to flood in, threatening to drag me out to sea, but instead of allowing them to, I hang on to Lola like a buoy.

When I finally put her down, her expression smooths, and she distances herself from me. "This isn't real though, okay?" Ah, setting expectations already. Probably for the best. "This place is our home, Ryder. Even if I haven't lived here in years, it's still home. These people? *They* are my home. So if at any point this becomes too much for either of us, or one of us changes our mind, we have to let it go and figure out another way to work out our problems."

I nod, the thrill of her saying yes far more potent than the disappointment at her rationale.

"Boundaries. Got it," I tell her. "Whatever you need, darlin'."

She steps further into my space, wrapping her arms around my waist and resting her cheek on my chest. "Thank you, Ryder," she whispers, and my heart constricts from her soft-spoken words. I love Lola Lima, and regardless of whether she still feels the same, I'm determined to treat her with every bit of respect and love she never got from the man before me.

It's late, *really late,* as I sit on the sofa in my living room beside Lola.

"I think that's about it," she says. "Anything else to add?"

I stare down at the yellow-lined page of the legal pad in my lap, and I shake my head no.

1. No PDA unless surrounded by town gossips.
2. If one of us is uncomfortable with something, we're open about it, and the other person backs off.
3. If romantic feelings begin to develop, we tell the other person immediately.
3b. If our emotions start to develop and threaten our friendship, we end things.
4. We support each other like a real couple would.
5. After Lola has found a job that offers adequate

health insurance, the marriage will end (unless we both agree to stay married forever and always – Ryder).
6. No sex.

"I don't think so, darlin'. We've been at it for an hour, going over every possible rule rolling through that beautiful head of yours."

A blush creeps up her neck, and she turns away in embarrassment.

"This is a strange arrangement, and I'm sure there isn't some checklist we could find online for this sort of thing, seeing as it's literally *insurance fraud*," she points out, making me feel queasy.

"Which is exactly why our families and Mayte need to be in on it too. Without them understanding and helping us sell this, we'd have people investigating us for sure."

"And that's the last thing either of us needs," she agrees.

Chapter Seventeen

TYING THE KNOT

MONDAY, APRIL 28

MY HANDS SHAKE as we stand on the porch of the main house. Ryder grabs one of them, pulling my knuckles up to his mouth, but before his lips can make contact, he drops them, squeezing gently. "Sorry, boundaries," he explains, as if he just remembered they exist at all.

Ryder and I have never been good with boundaries. We've always jumped headfirst into everything, and I'm terrified this will be no different. I'm basically about to be living out every childhood, middle grade, and high school fantasy I ever had with this man, and it's all *fake.*

Eighteen-year-old Lola would be extremely disappointed at how our life has panned out so far, and she'd be *screaming* at me for putting any kind of distance between me and Ryder.

"Ready?" he asks.

I shake my head, wind tangling my curls around my face. He reaches out on instinct, brushing the errant curls away with a grimace.

"It's going to take some getting used to that I can't—" His words die on his tongue when the door is yanked open.

"There they are!" Harlan says, his rugged, tanned face

greeting us with a wide smile. "Come in, come in." He ushers us inside with a wave of his hand.

We follow behind him, bile churning in my gut. I chew the inside of my cheek, greeting everyone with kisses and hugs before taking a seat on the worn leather loveseat beside Ryder.

I wet my lips as all eyes land on us, tension climbing high in the room, both of our families seated or standing around us.

Ryder takes my hand in his, and even though it breaks one of our rules—no PDA unless surrounded by town gossips—I allow it, letting the gesture calm the war waging in my chest.

"*Suéltalo ya*," *Mami* says, waving her hand through the air.

I work on a swallow, my mouth dry as I recite the words I've been planning to use to break the news to them all night, unable to sleep.

"We're getting married," Ryder says, and with his words, all of mine die on my tongue.

Everyone is silent, wide eyes and gaping mouths greeting us. Even Ezekiel, Ryder's quiet and brooding brother, a man I've never quite figured out, has the good sense to raise his brows and bite his lip.

Ry rests a hand on my knee, giving it a reassuring squeeze, but it does nothing to soothe me.

Another couple of seconds stretch on, thick with tension, each one dragging on like an eternity. Then the air shifts, lighter, almost electric, filling my lungs with something that makes my limbs feel weightless. Our families explode in a flurry of movement, leaping to their feet, clapping and shouting, while our mothers' tears spill over, glistening with joy.

Our fathers are embracing in the biggest man hug you'll ever see. Mayte is clapping Isabela's hands together, and Zeke is wearing a warm smirk.

"Thank God!" Bee shouts.

"*Por fin*," *Mami* says with a wide smile.

"Only took them two decades to get their heads out of their asses," Harlan agrees.

Before they can take their celebrations further, Ryder speaks up, clearing his throat. "There's more, and you better sit down for this," he says.

They all shoot sideways glances around, taking a tentative seat, and quieting down.

I address Ryder's family first. "I'm sure my parents have told you about my diagnosis by now. I have rheumatoid arthritis, and while it presents differently for everyone, I've been ignoring it as best as I can for too long. My joints ache, and it's becoming hard to do the most mundane tasks, let alone keep up with the things I love, like dancing and riding Penny."

"So, while our marriage will look real to everyone else, we need you all to know that it's not. *Yet,*" Ryder adds, nudging my shoulder with a playful smirk. "Lola's health is our first priority, always. We know it might be hard to sell to the townspeople that she up and left her fiancé for me, but if we want to evade insurance fraud claims and prison, we'd appreciate it if the truth of our marriage stays under wraps."

"Of course, Ry, your secret is safe with us," José assures us. "And maybe Lemmon will let up once she knows about you two."

Harlan's lips quirk at the suggestion, and unease stirs in my gut.

"She still buggin' you?" Bee asks, head tilted toward Ryder.

When we discussed our ground rules for this marriage, he told me that Lemmon had been pretty persistent in reaching out to him, but he had no interest in chatting with his former abuser, and I can't say I blame him. I feel the same about Russ, though he's taken our breakup far better than it appears Lemmon had.

"It's gotten better. Just a few calls and texts periodically. I've blocked her number, but I think she's using a burner phone because the syntax is always the same, but the number changes no matter how many times I block them. It's nothing egregious though. I dealt with her manipulation and belittling for years. I can handle a few text messages," Ryder explains, but it doesn't escape me the way Zeke rolls his eyes, crosses his arms over his chest, and huffs. I'm seeing more emotion out of him in the last few minutes than I have in all the years I've known him.

"We decided getting married would be good for the both of us. I'd get access to Ryder's health insurance, and he will hopefully get Lemmon off his back." I decide to leave out the fact that he feels guilty for ever marrying her; I'm sure they know this without me having to rub it in.

Harlan lets a laugh slip out, shaking his head. "I'm in support of absolutely anything that helps you, sweet girl, but if either of you think for a second Lemmon is going to let up because y'all are married, you've got another thing comin'. That girl has been jealous of you since the day you showed up on Rosa Ranch."

"I doubt that's true, Pops," Ryder interjects, but his mom stops him.

"It's true. That woman is vindictive and conniving. I don't think you'll be doing yourself any favors by getting married if you think it's going to make her go away, but I support the decision anyway."

How come I didn't consider that? I *should* have, knowing the way she acted at the fair. She's still the same high school bully I knew and despised.

"Do you agree, Ry?" I ask, my voice a soft whisper as I turn to him.

His eyes hold my gaze, gripping me with their serene pools of blue. "I'm not sure I care one way or the other, Lols. I just want you to have adequate healthcare. I can deal with the rest another way if I need to." My heart seizes in my chest, and my lungs threaten to give out as he leans into me, his warm lips grazing the shell of my ear as he whispers for only me to hear, "Let me do this for you, darlin'. It's all I want."

My fingers throb from how tightly I'm clutching them, a reminder of how badly I need treatment.

My eyes brim with tears as he pulls away, straightening in his seat. "I'm really sorry," I say, my lip wobbling. "I don't want to cause any more problems than I already have, but—"

"Cut that out. You haven't caused any problems, Lola. This is your home just as much as it is any of ours, and if you and Ry want to get married for *any* reason, we'll support it. But if this isn't what you both want, we'll find another way," Bee says, taking her turn to speak as the head of the family.

Power dynamics have never been a thing here, and that's why I always felt comfortable speaking my mind. It wasn't until Russ that I started to lose myself, falling into a pattern of forgetting my voice existed because it was easier not to say anything at all.

The safety and security Ryder and his entire family fill me with is what makes me speak the next words. "I want to marry Ryder Lockhart, and I want to do it just like we had when I was twelve," I tell the room, my cheeks twitching with a smile as Ryder's laughter bubbles over.

He squeezes my hand, and I can tell we're both recalling the time Mayte declared she wanted to be a wedding planner and demanded Ryder and I let her practice with us. The ceremony was small, and our parents pretended to cry, dabbing at the fake tears rolling down their cheeks. The sun set behind us as we said our vows on the top of the hill on the farthest edge of the property. It was small, adorable, and hysterical. My thoughts on my perfect wedding haven't changed, despite Russ's determination to bulldoze *right* over them.

"Consider it done, darlin'. We're tying the knot," he announces to the room.

We spend the rest of the morning making breakfast in the kitchen of the main house, eating with our families, and catching up.

Lola

Chapter Eighteen

QUE SE VAYA PA LA PINGA

FRIDAY, MAY 2

"I STILL CAN'T BELIEVE they were all okay with the idea of Ryder and I getting married," I tell Mayte, shaking my head.

"Stop moving so much. I'm gonna stab you with these pins if you keep acting like a damn bobble head," she threatens as she continues working on pinning my curls on top of my head for our little ceremony tonight. "And what did I tell you? Those people? They are your people, Lola. Your parents and his want you to be okay, and *god*, they hated Lemmon."

I can't help but laugh at that. When we were kids, Lemmon had done a much better job at acting like the sweetheart she so desperately wanted everyone to believe she was, but her grudge against me grew every year, and Ryder's parents weren't shy about telling me how upset they were that he and Lemmon had gotten together. At the time, I'd thought it was solely out of loyalty to me, but Mayte's kept me in the loop on his relationship, and it was clear she was worse to him than she ever was to me.

"Regardless, I think we're all excited to see this happen. We've been rooting for the both of you to wind up together since middle school. You were inevitable, even if the way you've wound up doing this is less than traditional, and you've had some hiccups along the way."

"We aren't really together, Mayte," I remind her.

"Yeah, yeah, yeah. Let me dream."

The thing about that is Mayte doesn't just dream. She dreams big and then does her damndest to bring those goals to fruition—much like this wedding she managed to plan in less than a week. Granted, it's nothing big, exactly how I wanted. Our parents, her and Isabela, and Ezekiel will be there, but she still managed to throw it all together so quickly. That's the benefit of having an event planner for a best friend.

"Dream a little smaller this time," I say, but I know it'll go in one ear and out the other.

"Agree to disagree," she says, and I can see her wide, mauve-lipped smile in the mirror. "We're almost done. Give me a couple minutes and then we'll get you dressed and in the arms of that sweet man."

She continues fussing over me until she's sure I look exactly as she envisioned.

"Okay, now don't be mad," Mayte says, refusing to make eye contact with me.

A knot twists in the pit of my stomach. "What did you do?" I groan out.

Instead of answering, she heads into her closet, pulling out a black garment bag she holds in front of me. "I didn't like the idea of my best friend getting married in a sundress off the clearance rack, even if it is pretend."

"You didn't need to do that," I breathe, but my words get caught in my throat as she unzips it.

Inside is a cream gown with thin straps, with what looks like a long lace train bundled at the bottom. There are delicate lace appliqués over the entire dress. It's *stunning*, everything I could have ever wished for, and perfect for an intimate sunset ceremony.

"It's too much," I croak out. My throat grows impossibly tight at the gesture.

She waves her hand dismissively and then pulls the dress out of the garment bag. "Don't worry, it's not. It's a rental. I'll return it to Ever After on Monday."

Tears prick my eyes, and her expression softens. She places the dress down on the bed, winding her arms tightly around me. "This is going to be good for you — *both* of you. I promise. I can feel it in my bones. And you need to get better so you can dance and live your life the way you want and deserve to," she says into my hair, pulling away and cupping my shoulders. "You look gorgeous, Lola. Ryder's a lucky man."

We spend the next few minutes getting me into this gorgeous gown and simple flats before making the short trip to the field at the furthest end of the property.

My heart is pounding out of my chest when I see Ryder looking as mouthwatering as ever, standing in front of a thin gold arch facing the setting sun. The field is overflowing with vibrant wildflowers in a rainbow of colors, and our parents stand on either side of the arch, Isabela in my father's arms.

Mayte takes my hand in hers, walking the rest of the way with me. She whispers, "You ready?"

And I am. I see Ryder in his navy-blue suit, his eyes raking over me with a look so fiercely confident it settles the anxiety brewing inside me.

My parents smile brightly at me, and *Mami* wraps me in her arms. "I've never seen a more stunning bride, *mija*. I'm so glad things turned out this way. It would have broken my heart to see you marry that other man." Her words cut through me, and the realization I would have never been happy with Russ finally hits home. I knew this; I'd known it for far longer than I'd care to admit, but my own mother confirming those thoughts does wonders for the guilt I've been pushing down.

"Thank you, *Mami*." I give her a kiss on either cheek and

press one to the top of my niece's head, her soft brown curls pulling a smile across my face.

Mami cups my shoulder and whispers into my ear, "*Ay mija, ahora sí vas a respirar tranquila. Y que se vaya pa'l carajo.*" My shoulders shake as I playfully roll my eyes.

My dad and each of Ryder's parents give me a hug as well, and Ezekiel tips his chin at me.

I move to Ryder, taking a deep breath before meeting his eyes.

The sun hits his baby blues just right, so I'm able to see how glossy they are as he takes me in. There's not a chance Russ would've been half this emotional on our wedding day.

He saw me as a prize to be won, a means to an end. Nothing more.

And after years of being told I wasn't worthy of more, I started to believe it.

A deep sadness grips my heart, but Ryder reaches out for me, taking my hands gently in his, drawing me to the present. He pulls me into his strong arms, pressing a warm kiss to my forehead.

Mayte takes her spot between us, preparing to officiate this ceremony.

"You are so gorgeous, Lola," he whispers into my hair. *Lola.* Not darlin', but *Lola.* I love it when he says my name like that, like it holds a million emotions and incredible memories in the four letters of my name alone. "I know this probably isn't how you'd envisioned your wedding day, but if I'm going to fake marry anyone, I wouldn't want it to be anyone else."

My whole body warms at his words, but this is already touching on dangerous territory, so I pull out of his arms and give him a small smile before turning my attention to Mayte.

Because, ultimately, *he's wrong.* This is *exactly* how I always imagined my wedding day.

"You lovebirds ready to do this?" Mayte asks, her eyes glowing brightly.

We both nod, but Ryder's eyes widen, and he says, "Wait!"

My heart sinks as he runs across the small hill to one of the work sheds. Did he get cold feet all of a sudden?

My worries are silenced a moment later as he runs toward us with something hidden behind him. "You needed a bouquet," he explains, producing a tiny bundle of origami paper flowers.

There's a tingling sensation at the nape of my neck, and my face heats as I will the tears not to fall. "They aren't as pretty as the ones you make, but I did my best," he says, thrusting them into my hands.

I clutch them in my left hand, running the pads of my fingers over the delicate edges of the petals. A sob threatens to choke me, but I swallow it down. My eyes flit up to meet his, and the world falls away as I'm met with a look that could end a war or bring world peace. It's in this moment that something becomes incredibly evident to me: Ryder Lockhart will go to the ends of the Earth to make me happy, and I'd be a fool not to let him. He's forgiven me for leaving him when he'd needed me most, and I can forgive him for marrying Lemmon. He hadn't known the full extent of our history, and now that he does, I truly believe he'd never have betrayed me if he were aware.

"They're perfect, Ry," I finally choke out. "Thank you."

"Anything for you, darlin'."

Mayte swipes at a tear, clearing her throat. "Sorry, allergies. Too many damn wildflowers out here."

We go through run-of-the-mill vows Mayte picked out for us, but every word Ryder speaks feels too personal, like he isn't really following a script at all. I can't see what he has written on the paper in front of him through the thick curtain of tears gathered in my eyes. I latch on to his declaration of devotion and protection, allowing them to soothe the sting of a marriage that never was. *Gracias a Dios.*

When he slides the gold band on my finger, I can't help but

stare in astonishment at the marquis-cut diamond flanked by two tiny triangular stones. It's elegant and beyond perfect.

This is another unnecessary stab to the heart, one Ryder would have no way of knowing he'd cause.

The giant, gaudy ring Russ gave me was everything I detest. It was flashy and served only the purpose of showing off how much money he has.

But this ring? It shows Ryder put a whole lot of love and attention into picking out something that reminded him of *me*.

Mayte's voice drags me back. "By the power vested in me by the online officiating course I took last night, I now pronounce you wife and husband." A chuckle escapes my lips, and at the same time, Ryder pulls me into him, clutching my cheeks in his warm hands and planting a firm kiss against my mouth that knocks the wind from my lungs. It's so chaste my lips miss him when it's over.

Or maybe that's just me.

Ryder

Chapter Nineteen

OURS

LAST NIGHT, after the ceremony, we all met at the main house for family dinner. It was casual, everything Lola and I had talked about.

Small and comfortable with our immediate family.

José, Lola's dad, made *choco-flan* as a makeshift wedding cake, and afterward, Lola and I went on a ride with Penny and Asier.

It was perfect, despite having to pull her onto Asier with me when she felt too weak to lead Penny herself.

My feet are heavy as I make my way up the steps of her parents' cottage. *This is really happening.*

My knuckles scrape across the worn wood of their front door, and it bursts open, Lola standing on the other side. Her curls frame her face in a halo of perfectly styled ringlets, those big brown eyes of hers wide, her pouty lips in a surprised *o* as she stares up at me.

"I-I thought you'd be here later. I'm not packed yet," she tells me.

I chuckle, moving past her into the cottage. "I figured, darlin', which is why I came over early. I wanted to help you pack." Despite having about a million things to get done on the ranch today, I'll always make time for Lola. *Always.*

Her throat bobs as she gulps, still wide-eyed in those black spandex shorts and her oversized white sweatshirt. And of course, she still looks just as beautiful as she did yesterday, all done up.

When will the sight of her stop being so potent? Like I'm a caged animal, dying to break free of my restraints so I can wrap myself around her and kiss her every moment of the day. It's clear following our rules will be harder than I'd believed when I first agreed to them, but I'm pleading with a higher power that she'll eventually come to agree that our *rules* are merely suggestions made to be broken.

"Okay," she finally says. Lola blinks rapidly, as if clearing her mind, before heading to her room. I follow behind her. "I guess there's not a whole lot left to do. I hadn't had a chance to fully unpack since I got here, and most of my stuff wouldn't fit in my room anyway."

"So what's left? Put me to work, darlin'."

We work in silence, packing up the photos on her walls and dressers, making sure to take extra special care of each knick-knack. We're almost done. Her clothes are the last thing to be packed, and when I open the top drawer of her dresser, my tongue feels thick in my mouth.

Silk, lace, satin, and everything in between is shoved to one side of the drawer, but her panties are the least exciting part. Lying beside the underwear are vibrators and other sex toys in varying shades of purple and pink, a large black toy with a curved nub that looks like a tongue on top. I gape at them, jaw unhinged, my dick stirring to life in my jeans, balls tightening as I swallow around the lump in my throat.

Lola's hand smacks down on mine. "I'll get that," she rushes out.

I manage to nod, very fucking slowly. "I'll, uh, start taking these things over to our place." *Our place.* The words settle on my tongue like a secret I've been holding for too long, a warm rush spreading through me, as if saying it somehow makes it *more* real. Look at me, already breaking rule number three: *If romantic feelings begin to develop, we tell the other person immediately.* If I tell her how I feel the day after our wedding, she's going to regret ever having agreed to this in the first place, and I'll never have a chance to convince her we could give a relationship, a *real relationship*, another shot.

"Thanks," she says, positioning herself protectively in front of the drawer.

"I'll be back soon, darlin'," I tell her, my voice hoarse.

Lola

Chapter Twenty

CLEANIN' UP

SATURDAY, MAY 3

RYDER SAW my fucking *underwear drawer*.

Not only that, but the other things *in* my underwear drawer.

It's already bad enough that I'm moving in with him today in order to sell this marriage to anyone who might question it. I didn't need him catching a glimpse of my toys too!

Toys I'm absolutely going to become extremely familiar with now that we'll be sharing space.

Thank God we won't be in the same room.

Ryder pulls into the dirt driveway, parking outside his white, cottage-style home, the black slate shingles reflecting brightly, nearly blinding me as I hop out of his truck.

"It looks different than the last time I was here," I tell him, staring at the dark-stained wood pillars holding up the roof of the wraparound porch.

"Lols, you were here a few nights ago, and I distinctly remember being ding-dong-ditched by someone who drove a truck a lot like your dad's," he says, shamelessly calling me out on something I'd thought we held a silent agreement not to mention.

"It was dark the other night, and," I side-eye him, "I don't know what you're talking about."

His deep chuckle rumbles between us like thunder on a hot summer night, and the accompanying lightning must be what zaps straight to my core, heat building at the sound alone. This man is *dangerously* sexy. Dangerous with my heart, that is.

We carry all my boxes into the house, *our* house, and he says, "Alright, darlin', I think that's all of it. You ready to see your new room?"

I nod, following him through the living room, passing the grandfather clock we used to hide notes in as kids, the picture-covered mantle with photos of us throughout our childhood and young adulthood that are so picturesque they look like stock images. The three-seat beige sofa with wide cushions calls to me, practically *begging* for me to take a nap on it as exhaustion settles into my joints.

He opens the white-paneled door to what is now my new bedroom, and here I go again, getting choked up.

I expected the room to be bare bones, with just a bed and nightstand. I had anticipated going into town later this week to get some things to personalize it and make it feel more like me.

But here I am, standing in the doorway to a room that couldn't be more *me* if I'd decorated it myself.

The walls are painted a light cream, there's a rattan bed frame, the mattress is made up beautifully in a white comforter set, and a vibrant-red quilt hangs over the end. There are photos hung on the walls in light wooden frames, and they aren't ones I brought.

I run my fingers over the delicately woven, thin pieces of wood that make up the frames. My eyes flash to Ryder. "Where–Where'd you get these?" I choke out.

"I know living with me isn't ideal, so I wanted your space to feel like yours. Mayte and your mom helped me go through photos they had of you, and I did my best to pick out ones I'd thought you'd be happy to look at each day." He grins, and his eyes twinkle. "And a few of you I couldn't help but have in our home."

The way he says "our home" so naturally has my heart panging in my chest. This sweet, thoughtful man is going to be my undoing all over again.

His eyes flick to one of the larger pictures hanging in the center of the wall. It's a photo of me wearing a silver sequined dress that ends right above my knees. My partner's hand is the only part of his that can be seen in the photo as he twirls me out, both of my arms extended in a *T*, and the brightest smile lights my face. My curls are swirled around my shoulders, and I look more carefree in that photo than I've felt in the last three years.

This man.

He clears his throat. "I'll give you a minute to look around. I'll start bringing in the boxes from the living room."

I take a seat at the end of the bed, running my hand over the soft quilt as I let out a long, calming sigh.

We're really doing this.

Chapter Twenty-One

SAY YES TO THE DRESS

SUNDAY, MAY 4

LAST NIGHT AFTER DINNER, Lola and I sat on the couch together, talking for hours.

It was like when we were kids. Everything about being with her is so familiar, and just like in college, all I want to do is hold her tight to my chest and never let her go.

But that's no longer our reality, no matter how much I wish it were.

She mentioned Karmella and Yanet, her friends from Dallas who run the dance studio she worked at, had checked in on her and made sure she knew she could always go back. I'm thankful for them, for their capacity to love her and provide the friendship I know she needed while away from Rosa Ranch, but it doesn't make the thought of losing her all over again any less painful.

I'm glad she has somewhere she could go to continue living out her dreams, but I'm determined to find a way for her to do that without leaving me again. Though this time, I think I'd follow her if she let me.

Lola heads out of her room with a massive black garment bag draped over her arm, successfully snagging my attention.

"Whatcha got there, darlin'?"

Her gaze flits to mine. "It's the dress I wore the other night," she says, and a pretty pink hue colors her cheeks.

I chuckle deeply at that. "It's okay to say wedding dress," I tease.

"It's weird," she admits. "Anyway, Mayte is picking it up to return it to the boutique. It was a rental." She lays it over the back of one of our dining room chairs, spinning to face me. "Mind if I join you?"

"Not at all," I tell her, patting the seat beside me. "You wanna watch something?"

"Whatever you want. I'm not picky," she says, taking a seat at the opposite end of the couch.

I change the channel to something I think she'd enjoy, but she doesn't react. Her eyes stay glued to the screen, yet there's a distance in her gaze, like her mind's already miles away. The longer the silence stretches, the more the knot in my stomach tightens, my fingers drumming nervously against the armrest.

I scoot over to sit closer to her, and when she doesn't notice, I cover her hand with mine, draping my other arm along the back of the couch. "Darlin', what's going on in that beautiful head of yours?" I ask softly.

"Hmm?" she asks, her far-off gaze making it clear she's still somewhere else. "I'm sorry, what'd you ask?" Her eyes look sad, and she seems tired, her eyes sunken and her lips turned down. It's not the kind of exhaustion a nap could fix.

"You've got something on your mind. Care to let me in?"

She breathes out a long sigh, clamping her eyes shut for a moment, before she scoots around to face me. She adjusts her grip so she's holding my hand now, and it sends tingles up my arm.

"It's the dress."

I stare at her, no less confused than I had been moments ago.

"Do you not like the dress?"

She shakes her head, those gorgeous curls flying all over in the way I love so much.

"No, the problem is that I *love* the dress. I know it's silly because we're only married on paper, but I'd always dreamed of keeping my wedding dress, having it preserved, and saving it for my daughter." Her cheeks heat again, and it travels down her neck onto her chest. If it moves beyond that, I can't see it through the sheer fabric of her cropped white tank top. "And then the realization I may never *have* a daughter kind of…"

"It kind of what, darlin'?" I ask, my voice a strained whisper.

Her cinnamon gaze meets mine now, and she chokes on a sob. "It sort of crushed me, Ry."

I can't help myself, overwhelmed with the need to comfort her. I drag her into my lap, kissing her shoulder, then the top of her head. "You'll have anything you want in this life. I can't promise you a lot, but I can promise you that."

I'd burn down the whole world for this woman.

We sit like this for a while until her body relaxes in my hold. I hear her soft snores, and when I can't hold my eyes open any longer, I carry her to her bed, tucking her in under the covers.

"Goodnight," I whisper, pressing a kiss to her forehead.

The sliver of moonlight shining in through her blinds cuts across her beautiful face, and I feel weak in the knees, like the ground beneath me just got a little too far away.

Anything she wants, she can have. *I'll make sure of it.*

Ryder

Chapter Twenty-Two

HEAVENS TO BETSY!

MONDAY, MAY 5

THE SUN IS RISING on the horizon, and the morning air has a sharp edge to it, crisp and biting, the kind that doesn't linger long after the sun rises. My boots crunch over dew-covered grass as I make my way to the north fence. Dad called early this morning, letting me know the horses had been restless last night, pacing the pasture, their whinnies cutting through the quiet like warning bells. Animals always know first when something is off, and something definitely feels wrong to me.

Dad had been worried, but he didn't get a chance to make it down here to check it out because he couldn't get ahold of Zeke.

I wonder where Ezekiel was since he's never far from the ranch.

The thought is fleeting as the fence comes into view, and my gut clenches. Even from fifty feet away, I can see the problem. The wire sags unnaturally, curling like it had given up on holding itself together. I continue my approach, peering around, as if something, *or someone*, might jump out of nowhere.

The tension wire has been cut clean, *too* clean. This wasn't wear and tear or an accident. Someone had done this deliberately.

I crouch down to get a better look, running a finger over the edge of the wire. Smooth. Fresh. My jaw tightens as a chill creeps up my spine, and it has nothing to do with the cool air.

The ranch stretches out around me, wide open, and what I'd usually consider peaceful under the pale morning light. But it doesn't *feel* peaceful. I feel exposed. Vulnerable.

The horses are clustered closer to the barn than usual, their ears twitching and heads bobbing nervously. They aren't relaxed; they're waiting, waiting for me to tell them everything is okay.

But I'm not so sure it is.

I pull the pliers from my tool belt and start fixing the wire, my movements quick and precise. I've done this a thousand times before, but today, it feels different, like the air itself is holding its breath. I'm hyperaware of every creak and whistle of wind.

I finish up, and a flash of silver near the fencepost catches the light from the rising sun, glinting off it enough to momentarily blind me.

I step closer, kneeling to get a better look.

A knife. Small, practical, the kind you'd pick up at a hardware store without thinking twice. But it isn't mine, and no one who belongs on this ranch would leave something like this behind.

I turn it over in my hand, the handle smooth, the blade clean, save for a streak of dirt. My chest tightens as I scan the horizon, my gaze locking on the tree line at the edge of the property. The shadows are longer now, stretching across the grass like they want to pull me in.

Blades of grass dance in the wind, a faint but unmistakable scent fluttering around me.

A clean, earthy cologne like patchouli.

No one on the ranch wears cologne while working with the animals. Not out here, not when the wind carries scents for miles.

A cold knot forms in my stomach, twisting tighter with each breath. This isn't an accident. It isn't random.

Someone was here.

And they want me to know it.

I gather my tools, heading into the stables to check on the horses, and spend the rest of the day trying to push the thought from my head.

When the sun starts to set, I hurry to my truck and make it to town just before Ever After is due to close for the day.

The bell over the door rings loudly as I enter Ever After Boutique, filled wall-to-wall with dresses for every occasion.

"Ryder Lockhart, is that you?" Betsy, the ancient woman who's owned this place longer than I've been alive, asks.

"It sure is, Betsy. It's good to see you," I tell her with a warm smile.

"Come here and give me some sugar," she drawls, opening her arms wide for me. I give her a tight hug and straighten. "Now, what can I do for you?" She pats my cheek and sits on her stool behind the counter covered in fabric swatches.

"Mayte dropped by with a wedding dress she was returning today." She nods, waiting for me to continue. "Any chance I could purchase it from you?"

Her face contorts, confusion written plainly across her features. "Sure, hun. Might I ask why?"

"Lola and I got hitched, and I know it would mean a lot to her if she could keep it."

Her light brows shoot up her forehead. *"Lola Lima?"*

I nod. "Yes, ma'am, the one and only." My lips don't get the memo that we're playing it cool; just the mere mention of this woman has me grinning ear to ear.

Not only do I get to surprise my girl, but now the rumor

mill will effectively spread the news for us. We won't have to lift a finger.

"Well, my, my, Ryder. I always knew you'd get the girl," she says brightly, hopping off her stool and making her way toward the back, disappearing behind a door that reads "staff".

When she returns, she's carrying a large white box with a blush-pink bow tied around it. "I just finished dry cleaning it. It's all yours, on the house."

I shake my head. "No, ma'am. That's too kind, and I'm happy to pay for it."

"I've known your momma a long time, young man, so I know she taught you manners. Accept the gift, hun. Think of it as a wedding present. Besides, you've done more for me and this shop than you realize. You were always a good boy, and I'd love her to have this. Please, take it." She pushes the box into my arms; I wrap my hands around it, holding it to my chest.

"Thank you, Betsy," I tell her with a small smile I hope conveys just how thankful I really am.

"You're very welcome. Now, get home to that wife of yours." She smiles, shooing me out of the store.

By the time I get home, Lola's in the kitchen, swaying her hips to music playing in her earbuds. Long ringlets fall around her heart-shaped face in a stunning cascade of curls. It's the same rich, dark brown that has always artfully painted her head, sun-kissed streaks of chestnut and iridescent gold drawing out the olive undertones in her smooth complexion. She's wearing one of my t-shirts that hits her mid-thigh as she stirs a pot, and my mouth is *watering*, but not for food.

She spins, hearing the door shut behind me, her eyes wide with surprise. "Hey! You're home early."

I smile, setting the box down on the dining room table behind her. "What's all this?"

"I figured I'd surprise you by making dinner tonight."

"It smells delicious, darlin'. Thank you," I tell her, sincerity lacing my words. A grin pulls at the corners of my mouth as my gaze trails down her body. Her tan legs are bare, and the sight of her in my shirt has me damn near losing my mind. "And what's that you've got on?" I ask with a smirk.

She looks down at herself, suddenly aware of how short my shirt really is on her. She tugs at the hem, but she meets my smirk with one of her own. "It was in with my laundry, and I figured you wouldn't mind."

Goddamn, this woman. "I don't mind at all, darlin'. What's mine is yours," I assure her.

"Thanks," she says sheepishly, that pretty blush swirling on her cheeks. She tucks a rampant strand of hair behind her ear, and my belly warms at the sight of her.

I clear my throat. "Why don't you go take a seat at the table, and I'll serve us up this fine meal you've made?"

She gives me a shy smile, tucking her chin as she pulls her chair out.

She sets her hands on the box I left, and her gaze flicks up to me. "What's this?"

"Go ahead and open it."

Lola

Chapter Twenty-Three

BORN PROTECTOR

MONDAY, MAY 5

MY FINGERS TRAIL over the smooth edges of the box and wrap around the perfectly tied blush-pink ribbon, pulling it loose.

I can hear Ryder a few feet away, plating the *congri, maduros,* and *pollo guisado* I made us for dinner. The least I can do for him is cook, considering I feel like a *mantenida*. It's only been a couple of weeks since I moved back, but not having a job or any prospects is really wearing on me.

Plates clang, but those sounds become faint behind the noise my heartbeat makes, pounding in my ears when I lift the lid of the box to find my wedding dress inside.

My eyes shoot to him. "Ryder," I breathe out.

"Yes, darlin'?"

"What's this?"

"It's your wedding dress," he tells me, as if that answers anything.

"And what's it doing on our kitchen table?"

"You said you wanted to keep it, and I promised you'd have what you want in this life. It seemed important to you, so it's important to me."

A sudden pressure clamps down on my chest, and before I can stop myself, I'm up on my feet, the chair scraping loudly against the floor. My legs move on their own, and in a blur, I'm right there, colliding into Ryder's arms, his warmth grounding me. I stand on my tiptoes, winding my arms around his neck. He reacts immediately, pulling me against his hard chest, which rumbles with laughter.

"Well, hello to you too, darlin'."

My heart bursts into a million beautiful, glittery pieces around me. In just a few days, Ryder has managed to be a better partner to me than Russ ever was, and that should make me sad, but it doesn't. It makes me so unbelievably grateful to be in his arms instead.

"Has anyone ever told you you're perfect?" I tease as I reluctantly pull away from him.

"Not that I can remember," he says, tapping his chin. "But I'd love for you to be the first." He winks, and sparks zip up my spine from that alone. *I'm in so much trouble.*

I ignore my brain's warning. "You"—I point directly at his chest—"are *perfect*, Ryder Lockhart."

"Right back at ya, darlin'," he tells me, warming me from the inside out. He reaches for a plate beside him, piled high with food, and shoves it toward me. "Now, go eat. I'll grab us some drinks and be right there."

He takes a seat across from me a couple of minutes later, and instead of the awkward silence that had always encompassed meals spent with Russ, we jump right into casual conversation.

"Do you remember the time in second grade when Ashley McAllister decided on the first day of class she didn't like you?" he asks.

"How could I forget? That little brat put glue in my shoe!"

"She didn't get much better as we aged either," he says with a light chuckle. "I swear, she enjoyed bullying you more than anything, including arts and crafts."

"She did." A smirk curls my lips. "Until *someone* pushed her into an ant pile, and when she yelled at that someone, claiming he couldn't do that because she was a girl, he told her it would be sexist not to treat her the same way he'd treat any boy." A sharp laugh bursts out of me at the memory.

"She was lucky it hadn't been a fire ant pile," he says. "And I stand by my words. She was a tyrant then, and the fact that she works in politics now makes entirely too much sense. Though I don't believe it was the ant pile that got her to leave you alone," he tells me with a quirked brow.

"No? Do tell."

"Did Mayte ever tell you about my tenth birthday party after you had gone home with a sore throat?"

I shake my head no. "All I remember after that party is you stopping by to bring me a slice of cake after everyone went home," I say with a smile.

He casts his eyes downward before snapping up to meet mine again. "Well, after you left, Ashley made a nasty comment about you, and Mayte nearly flew across the table. She grabbed the first thing she saw, which happened to be a full rack of baby-back ribs covered in barbecue sauce. She slung that thing across that girl's face so hard she fell out of her chair. Mayte screeched about there being more where that came from if she ever bullied you again. Ashley called her mom crying, and after she picked her up, my mom gave everyone an extra bowl of ice cream with dessert." He lets out a loud laugh that matches my own. "And she gave Mayte the biggest scoop." His shoulders quake with laughter as he admits his mom condoned the whole thing. I can't say it surprises me in the least.

"The fact that no one ever told me that is criminal," I wheeze out between laughs.

"Sorry, darlin'," he says, averting his gaze, the smile that had been present just moments ago seems to melt away, and my spine goes rigid, preparing for impact. When his eyes meet mine again, he reaches across the table and takes my hands in his. "I don't think I can properly express how sorry I am for not seeing through Lemmon's fake niceties. I hope you know that if I'd known, I never would have married her." The words hit me right through the heart, and even though he's told me this before, it's never meant as much as it does coming from my husband.

I give his hands a gentle squeeze. "It hurt, Ry, it did. But I *do* know that had you known, things would've been different. I shouldn't have hidden it from you, but I was just so determined not to let her know that her antics bothered me as much as they did that I refused to tell you. I knew you'd try to fight my battles for me, and it's not what I wanted."

"I just keep thinking that I should've paid more attention. It's hard for me to understand how I missed it."

I shake my head. "She very rarely bullied me when there were witnesses, Ry. She was good about keeping her torment to private spaces or making it look like an accident. She'd had the nice girl act down pact for so long, I'd thought there was something wrong with me because everyone else seemed to adore her."

He clenches his teeth, the muscle in his jaw ticking. "Believe me, Lola, I'd thought there was something wrong with me for not realizing everything she'd ever said to me was with the intention of making me feel safe enough to confide in her, only for her to prove to be the most dangerous person I knew." It kills me to know what she'd put him through, and even more at the thought that I probably don't even know the half of it.

"I want to apologize too," I tell him, blowing out a breath.

His brows knit, and he tilts his head. "What for? You've done nothing wrong."

"Please don't do that. You're not the only one to blame for our failed relationship. I should've known you wouldn't just move on after Logan's death. I should have done more to help you, to be that safe space for you to let it all out when you needed me. Maybe if I'd tried harder, you wouldn't have ended up the perfect target for Lemmon." My throat feels thick, eyes burning.

"Lola, listen to me. I wanted you to stay in Dallas and accomplish everything you set out to. I'd have been far worse off if you'd up and left to run to my rescue. That's a guilt I'd never be able to live with." He peers up at the ceiling, blinking away tears. "Do you think this could be our second chance, darlin'? Could we just promise to work toward being better together and agree to get over the guilt we've both been carrying with us for things we'd done when our frontal lobes were barely formed?"

That makes me crack a smile, relief washing over me, but there's still the thread of tension weaving through my heart. Of course I want those things, but I need to be more careful with my heart this time around. It's what pushes me to say my next words. "I think if we can forgive each other, then the next step should be forgiving ourselves."

He gives me a small smile. "Thank you, darlin'. That means more to me than you could ever know." The thing about that is, I do know, just as well as I think he does.

We continue eating with comfortable conversation, and when we're done, Ryder scoots out of his chair. He gathers our plates and takes them to the sink.

"Hey, I'll get those," I tell him, but he waves me off.

"You cooked. I'll clean. I don't want you doin' any dishes 'til you get in to see the specialist once your insurance is active and your medication has had a chance to kick in." His words warm me to my core, and the fact that he's thought about my health beyond getting me on his insurance plan is so sweet. It feels like my heart is *literally* melting in my chest. "How've you been feeling this week? You haven't seemed like you've been in any visible pain, but that might be optimistic of me."

I give him a small smile, remaining seated at the table. "I'm definitely not pain-free, but I'm doing better this week. I have my highs and lows, but I was dancing while cooking earlier, so that's an improvement for sure."

"I'm glad to hear that, darlin'. You have any plans for what you'd like to do as far as teaching again?"

I shrug, unsure what to really say at this point. It's all been such an adjustment from my old life these past few years. "I've started calling around to studios nearby and haven't had any takers yet. My dream has always been to open my own studio, so maybe this was just a push in the right direction." Images of dance classes taught at the old red barn flit through my mind, the same way they have off and on for years. "I'm hoping I can offer classes remotely soon since I'm worried there won't be much of a clientele around here, but that doesn't feel sustainable long-term."

He hums, deep in thought, as he rinses the last dish. When he's finished, he turns around, drying his hand on the dish towel slung over his shoulder, and leans against the kitchen counter. "I'd be happy to put out some feelers in the area and find out if any studios are hiring or would be willing to add on Latin dance lessons," he tells me.

My first instinct is to tell him no, but frankly, I need this to work, and if that's going to happen, I have to be able to do what I love. His help would make things so much easier. "That'd be really great, Ry. I appreciate it."

He finishes the dishes and takes his seat across from me again, reaching out to cradle my hands. His eyes flit from our hands, where our new rings sit as evidence of the massive change we've just committed to, his teeth buried in his plump bottom lip. "I want you to know I support anything and everything you want to do, okay?" he asks, and my gut starts to somersault with tension. *This doesn't sound good.*

"Okay…"

He gives my hands a quick squeeze before his eyes finally find mine again. "You mentioned that if things got really tough, you could go back to Dallas and work with Karmella and Yanet again. Is that what you want though?"

I shake my head, no thought necessary. "No, Ry. I've missed entirely too much of Isabela's life already, and *this* is my home. If I can make things work here, I want to. I just find it comforting to know there's somewhere I can fall back on."

He nods slowly, then runs the tip of his tongue over the slope of his bottom lip. The movement has no right to be as sinfully delicious as it is, but here I am, clenching my thighs together at the sight. His next words take me off guard.

"I won't pretend to fully grasp the weight of what being Latine, especially in Western Oklahoma, means for you, your job prospects, or any of the other ways that you've always had to work harder to earn the respect that's freely given to those who aren't BIPOC. So I don't want you to think I'm dismissing any of your concerns or how they might impact your ability to start your own business outside of this town." My brows pinch, and he continues. "I *know* you're willing to put in the extra work, but what if things could be a little easier for you by having the support of people who watched you grow up?" He squeezes my hands again in a reassuring gesture. "When we were kids, you always told me the red barn would be the perfect place for a dance studio, and I couldn't agree more. What do you think about that now?"

My mouth hangs open. I blink slowly at him in bewilderment. He takes my silence for something it isn't and backtracks. "I don't want you to feel stuck here or anything, but I don't want you to leave or give you another reason to leave me again, and I just thought that maybe—"

I pull my hands from his grasp, lean over the table, and slap a hand over his mouth. "Stop," I whisper. "Just stop talking."

I suck in a breath and will my racing heart to slow. "It's perfect, Ry. It's just what I've always wanted."

He rewards me with a massive smile I can feel beneath my

palm. I drop my hand to get a glimpse of it, and it's every bit as stunning as I'd expected. "But we need to figure out a payment plan because I don't have much in savings."

"You're my wife, Lols. What's yours is yours, and what's mine is also yours," he says with a lopsided grin.

"It's not real, Ryder. I couldn't accept something like that. I'm willing to offer you fifty percent of the income I collect from classes until I've paid off whatever amount we agree upon, and then I'll continue giving you twenty percent each month," I tell him with finality in my tone.

"You really don't have to —"

"I want to, Ry. It's important to me."

He gives me a resigned nod. "Anything for you, darlin'. Now, you wanna watch a movie? Tonight's your pick."

He's made *every night* my pick. And now, he's managed to help me make my dreams come true with a gesture he doesn't fully understand the weight of.

Ryder

Chapter Twenty-Four

IN MY ARMS

WEDNESDAY, MAY 28

REGGAETON MUSIC and familiar savory scents waft through the air, greeting me as I hop out of the truck. Lola's got the kitchen window cracked open, and I can hear her horrendous singing, the sound bad enough that it rivals nails on a chalkboard. It's her one and only fault, and yet, I'm still grinning ear to ear at the sound of her making herself comfortable in our home.

The sharp clang of my ringtone chiming in my pocket makes me groan, my shoulders slumping when I pull my cell out, only to be greeted with the name of a man I'd hoped I'd never hear from again.

"This is Ryder Lockhart," I answer quickly, stopping at the bottom of the porch, hoping to save Lola from any reminder that my ex-wife even exists.

"Mr. Lockhart, this is Chad Calhoun, Lemmon Meringue Lockhart's attorney," he says, his hoarse, cigarette-roughened voice greeting me, grating on my nerves at my last name being attached to Lemmon in any way.

"I know who you are, Chad, and I sincerely hope you'd know your client's name, considering *you* were the one who represented her in court when she tried to convince the judge that half of *my* family's ranch belonged to her."

"Yes, well." He clears his throat, clearly flustered by the memory of Judge Barnes ruling in my favor, seeing as the ranch wasn't in my ownership until after my divorce was finalized, a decision on my parents' part that I don't think was coincidental. "I'm calling on behalf of Miss Meringue, as she has heard of your recent marriage to Lola Lima and wants to discuss the matter of a non-compete clause."

I groan loudly, unafraid to let him know how annoying this song and dance with Lemmon is becoming. Why he continues to work with her, I'll never understand. Most of the town wouldn't work with him if he were the only lawyer left on this Earth after he agreed to represent Lemmon over me. "Chad, I've got to tell you the truth; I'm a little miffed you're wasting both of our time like this. There is no such thing as a non-compete clause when it comes to *marriages*, and even if there were, I'm certain I'd have had to *sign* this agreement for it to be held up in court. So," I huff out, "if you'll just tell Miss Meringue our business is over, and not to contact me in any form or fashion, we can both be on our way."

Chad's coughing fit cuts through the line, and I hold the phone away from my ear, not wanting to lose my hearing because he can't handle the stress of his job. When he's finished, he mutters, "I'll do that then, I suppose." I tell him to have a good night before hanging up and blocking his number.

I jog up the porch steps, excited to see Lola after a day without her.

It's been almost a month since she and I got married, and she was able to get in with the rheumatologist, thanks to a favor his nephew owed me.

She's moving around a lot more, despite the fatigue she's experiencing as she adjusts to the medication, helping around the ranch. She might not realize it, but the way she's been caring for the cattle has lessened a massive strain. She's even helped Betsy and a few of the other shop owners in town when they needed an extra pair of hands, and I know they've been grateful to have her.

Any moment she puts into the ranch or helping the people in this town is time I can better use to tend to her needs, getting home earlier to help around the house and spend time with her. It leaves me feeling more rejuvenated than any nap could.

Watching her dance around the kitchen when she cooks has become one of my absolute favorite parts of my day. The only thing better is those rare occasions when she plays a song slow enough for me to keep up with her and join along.

But she hasn't found any work prospects, and I can tell she's mentally struggling with that. We have plans to start fixing up the barn soon, but we've been waiting for her energy to improve. Though I haven't mentioned it to her, I've been paying a few of the ranch hands extra to help me clear out the barn so it's ready to start renovating whenever she is.

I know these plans help keep her spirits up, but not having work in the interim has become a sore spot for her.

Dance has not only become her career but her source of therapy. It's her creative release, and without that, I see her spark dim the slightest bit each day.

I have a little surprise for Lola to go with something I've planned for her that I hope she'll be excited about, and I think it'll improve her mood.

I carefully navigate the creaky steps, doing my best to remain as quiet as possible, before heading inside with the giant bouquet of red roses.

I set up my phone to play "Turn off the Lights" and pluck a single rose out of the bouquet before heading inside.

Lola smiles over her shoulder at me from the couch, and when she settles those beautiful brown eyes on me, I set the bouquet down, spinning so my back is to her, and turn the music on.

She's giggling from the very moment I turn around, taking off toward her with the rose between my teeth. My strides are long, and my movements are sloppy, but she doesn't seem to mind. I gather her hands in mine, leading us around the living room as La India's low rasp wraps around us. Lola plucks the rose from my mouth and tosses it to the couch, resting her hands on my chest and upper arm.

"Ryder Lockhart, what's all this for?" She continues laughing as I twirl her poorly, practically letting her loose to fly into the coffee table. She saves herself, gripping my bicep tightly and swinging her body back into mine, giggling, her eyes glimmering up at me.

My entire heart is in my throat. *And my whole world is in my arms.*

I dip her, and her hair grazes the floor. She clutches my shoulders, holding on tight, and we swap our pace to an easy sway that allows me to drink in the sight of her, fueling my very being with our proximity. "I know you miss it, darlin'. So I called around a few places, and while I wasn't able to find anyone who's hiring yet, I did find a spot just outside of town that offers classes, and I signed us both up."

Her mouth is agape as she stares up at me. "You'd do that," she says, her words sounding choked, "for me?"

I nearly roll my eyes at the absurdity of that question. "Of course I would, darlin'."

And I have so much more planned, *all to make you happy.*

Lola

Chapter Twenty-Five

NUTTIER THAN A SQUIRREL TURD

THURSDAY, MAY 29

I'VE MADE it a point to call at least five dance studios of any genre within fifty miles of the ranch each morning to kick off my day. They've all led to absolutely nothing, but I'm putting my best foot forward and committing to sticking around while accomplishing my dreams. None of that dulls the ache in my chest at the realization that I've been here for a month and have absolutely *zero* prospects and haven't felt well enough to start the renovations on the barn.

Sure, I've been helping on the ranch as much as possible, mostly feeding the cattle because their big brown eyes make me smile, and I'm not at any real risk of injury, but I fully intend to carry my weight around here once I'm physically able. I refuse to sit around and wait for life to hand me something when I could grab it by the balls and do something meaningful.

Other than the quiet nights in with Ryder and family dinners at the main house, the best part of each day has been spending my afternoons with Mayte and Isabela.

Mayte laughs beside me as we stroll through the quiet

town. The storefronts are all small businesses owned by locals I've known my whole life, large window displays with an awning covering the walkway shielding us from the blinding spring sun.

Caitlyn, the owner of Bake My Day Bakery, pops the door of her shop open, sticking her head out and waving at us. "Hi, ladies! Care for a chocolate chip cookie? They're fresh!" she says in that sing-song voice of hers, her curly strawberry-blonde strands piled on top of her head fluttering in the wind.

"I'll never say no to one of your famous cookies," I tell her, hurrying to the door to grab the two she has wrapped in brown napkins for us. "Thank you so much."

She waves me off. "Consider it a welcome home treat," she says with a wink, letting the glass door close behind her as she makes her way back behind the counter. The sweet smell of brown sugar, vanilla, and dark chocolate chips envelops me, my mouth watering as I take a bite of the warm, gooey cookie after passing one to Mayte, who's outwardly moaning beside me. Her head is thrown back, eyes rolling with her theatrics. I smack her shoulder, unable to contain the laughter bubbling out of me. "Cut it out. You're embarrassing."

"I'm just enjoying the little things, Lols. I'm a single mom. A warm cookie that isn't a hockey puck by the time I get around to eating it is *my* version of an orgasm."

My heart lurches at her words, guilt gnawing at my gut for not being around to help her more. She narrows her gaze on me, brows pinching as she says, "Whatever you're thinking that has you looking all mopey, stop it before I pull my *chancla* off and whack you with it."

I put my hands up in surrender, chuckling as she steals the other half of my cookie, sucking the chocolate off her fingers after finishing it off.

"Now, tell me more about these dance lessons Ryder plans to take you to," Mayte says, her brows bouncing with mischief as she returns to the conversation we were having before making a pit stop for baked goods. *"Dale, suéltalo ya."*

"I honestly don't know much as far as details go. He didn't even tell me what kind of dance lessons these are, but that he realized how much I've missed being in a class setting, even if I'm not teaching, confuses me."

"Confused how?" she asks, a dark brow raised.

"He has always been the sweetest, but I hadn't been expecting him to take dance lessons with me too," I admit. "It's easily in the top five kindest things anyone has ever done for me, and I'm unreasonably excited about it, but it feels like"—I stop to peer around, ensuring no one is within earshot of what I'm about to say before I go incriminating myself—"he's leaning into this marriage more than I'm ready for him to."

"I get that it's scary to let someone else take care of you, Lols, but it's Ryder. That man has only ever had eyes for you," she says, and before I can protest that he was literally *married* before me, she cuts me off, slicing through the tension with her excitement. "I can't wait to hear all about it! I bet it'll be super sexy. God, that man is like a nice, smooth whiskey, aged just right and with so much more flavor each year."

"Haven't you always said he's like a brother to you?" I tease with an arched brow.

"Hey, I have two working eyes, Lola."

"I can't argue with that." We giggle like schoolgirls, and the fact that I'm living so close to my best friend that we can have these talks in person and not over the phone has me bursting at the seams with gratitude. I miss Karmella and Yanet, but our friendship was never the same as mine and Mayte's. If I have to leave her again, it might just kill me.

The sound of chimes is quickly followed by a door swinging out in front of us, nearly knocking into Isabela in her stroller.

"What the hell?" Mayte says, our laughter cut off.

Lemmon barrels out of the store, her arms full of bags from various boutiques. A redheaded woman and a brunette trail behind her, stopping abruptly to turn and face us. Their wide eyes shift to what I believe is supposed to be a glare, but it looks more like they're squinting at us.

If it weren't for Lemmon's cold blue eyes snapping to me, full of hatred, I might laugh at the absurdity. She scowls, and it sends a shiver down my spine that makes me want to crawl out of my skin, but I hold my head high, refusing to back down to someone who doesn't deserve my fear, nor my respect. "You," she seethes between gritted, glittering white teeth smeared in her classic cherry-red lipstick.

I knew she'd be a problem, but I hadn't thought she'd go off the rails like this, confronting me in town looking like a rabid animal. I'd really hoped to avoid any in-person encounters with her since that day at the fair.

"You good-for-nothing little skank! You think you can come into my town and steal *my* man?" The exaggerated accent really does make her sound like she walked off the set of *Hart of Dixie*. She sounds ridiculous.

I roll my eyes, working to calm my breathing and appear unfazed by her behavior. "I didn't steal your man, Lemmon. You and Ryder have been divorced for over a year now. *Let it go.*"

"He and I have history. We're merely taking a break. Unlike you," she says, piercing me with another deadly look. "You didn't bother letting the ink dry on all those refunds for your wedding before you ran back here crying for Ryder to save you, like always."

"Lemmon, give it a rest. You're acting like a villain in a poorly written soap opera," I chide.

"Oh, *I'm* the villain? Seems to me you broke up with some poor man, left him heartbroken at the altar, only to arrive back in town, steal another woman's husband, and why? That's the real question here, Lola. You weren't there for him when he needed you, so why now? There *must* be a reason."

My jaw clenches as I resist the urge to flinch at her words. *Does she know?* How could she possibly be aware we got married for health insurance? *I'm being paranoid.* Yeah, well, insurance fraud will do that to a person.

I refuse to let her know she's riling me up, so I keep my tone even when I answer her. "We're not doing this. Not now, not ever. You aren't worth my time, and what you think of me has absolutely no impact on me."

"Oh, but it will," she seethes. "You think the people of this town are going to take your stupid little dance lessons, if you ever even manage to teach again? Certainly not when the mayor's daughter suggests they'd *better not.*" She sticks out her hip, sizing me up.

Mayte's laugh bursts between us. "You have lost your goddamn mind. You're named after a fucking fruit, for crying out loud. That poor man left you because you made him unhappy, because you, at your core, are an unhappy, evil little slimeball. Your daddy isn't your pawn either; he's a decent man, and it's a real wonder you turned out the way you did. Your mother leaving when you were a kid must've done a number on you." Mayte's words are laced with venom, and for her final blow, she adds, "Move on with your life like Ryder has, Lemmon! And get the fuck out of our way. It's Isabela's lunchtime."

She rams the stroller into Lemmon's leg, careful to draw back immediately to avoid Lemmon landing on Isabela. She hauls ass past her, Lemmon on the sidewalk, clutching her leg to her chest. "You'll pay for this!" she screeches in a voice so shrill it nearly pierces my eardrums.

"Yeah, yeah, whatever, *puta,*" Mayte calls over her shoulder, waving her off as we pass.

We hear her cursing at her "friends" to hurry up and help

her, but I don't bother looking back to see how bad the damage is.

"You good?" she asks me, her voice hushed as we continue to the parking lot.

"Yeah, my heart's in my damn ass, but I'm good," I mutter.

"Good," she says, moving on as if I'm not shaking like a leaf from that encounter. "So, speaking of exes who deserve to be locked up, has Fussy Russy tried contacting you?"

I shake my head. "No, he hasn't..."

"And? There's clearly something you're leaving out." She pressures me to continue.

"I should be happy he isn't trying to reach me, but it's so out of character for him. It makes me feel really unsteady because he's someone who acts on emotions, most of them being volatile and impulsive. The silence makes me worry he's planning something, but then I remember this isn't some movie, and I'm probably being paranoid."

"You were with that man for entirely too many years. You know him well enough to trust your gut. Keep an eye out for anything strange, and *please* tell someone if you notice something. There's no fault in being abundantly cautious, especially with a man like that. Ryder will always protect you, Lola."

"You're probably right."

"I usually am," she says with a smirk. What had I said about her being insufferable when she's right?

I give her an eye roll and head toward the parking lot where we left her truck.

I clip Isabela into her car seat while Mayte gets her stroller and our bags in the back. My pocket vibrates with a text as we peel out of the parking space.

My brows pinch as I read the message, and, of course, Mayte notices. "What's up?"

I shake my head. "Nothing, just got a message from an unknown number. It's probably spam."

UNKNOWN
How's life?

It's such a benign message, and yet, it still manages to make my skin crawl with dread.

You're just being paranoid, Lola.

The motto of the day, and, God, I hope it's true.

Chapter Twenty-Six

DOWN BAD

FRIDAY, MAY 30

"DARLIN'!" I shout excitedly, heading into the house.

She pops her head out from behind her bedroom door, and a smile so bright it stops me in my tracks spreads across her gorgeous face. "Hi! I'm almost ready to go, I swear!" she says, slamming the door behind her.

A deep chuckle leaves my throat as I make my way to my room to change. I got an email this morning suggesting shorts be worn for the class, so I hurry to change. By the time I make it to the living room, Lola's already in the kitchen, filling our tumblers with water.

Her eyes trail down my body and snag on my legs. "Ryder Lockhart, are those *shorts*?" she asks.

"Why, yes, darlin', they sure are." I wink at her, her dazed expression setting my skin on fire. "Like what you see?"

"I-I'm afraid I do," she breathes out. *Whoa there, Lola.* Don't go saying things that are bound to send my heart into a tizzy. Her eyes snap to mine, and as she closes her mouth, a slow grin spreads across her glossy lips.

She grabs the bottles of water and makes her way around the kitchen counter. The moment she does, my whole body is on high alert. I let out a low whistle, shamelessly appraising her smooth, tan legs on full display in those tiny spandex shorts. She's wearing a white shirt that hangs off her shoulders, and it looks like she cut the whole bottom part off herself. That large strip of smooth skin leaves me aching in more places than one. I swear I feel my dick twitch to attention.

"Like what *you* see, Ry?"

A chuckle reverberates through my chest. "Always, darlin'. There's never been a time in our lives when I hadn't loved the view when I'm with you."

Her whole body takes on a deep flush as my words settle in. She shoves one of the tumblers into my hands and keeps her eyes down as she practically sprints to my truck. Lola Lima, so confident and fearless, but the moment I compliment her, she turns into a puddle of goo. *And I love it.*

I lock up and follow her to the truck, opening her door for her and buckling her in before hopping in on my own side. I start the truck and make it off the ranch in record time.

"It's just outside of town, darlin', but feel free to put on whatever music you want," I tell her, nodding to where my phone sits on the dash.

She picks it up, her eyes flashing to mine again. "Mind unlocking it?" she asks, trying to hand me the phone, but my hands never leave the wheel.

"The password is 0502," I say. "And go ahead and add your fingerprint." I want it to be abundantly clear to her this marriage may not entail all the things a regular relationship would, but I'll treat her with the same respect. Lola is her own person, and I have no desire to change that, but *I* most definitely belong to *her.* I know I need to prove that if I'm going to have a shot at unlocking her heart.

I keep my eyes on the road ahead of me so I don't see the rosy tint I'm sure is creeping up her neck as she puts the pieces together. I do, however, hear the intake of breath she takes before saying, "You corny man," with a chuckle. "Our wedding date is your new password?"

"Sure is. I'm a smitten man, Lola. I can't help but be a corny bastard with you."

She laughs, and it's beautiful, a full, genuine sound that fills the tight space of my truck, as well as my ever-growing heart. "And before we got married. What was it then?"

"Your birthday," I answer.

I can practically feel her eyes roll as she says, "Yeah, sure it was."

I don't say anything more. No need to scare her off, especially since it's the truth.

She puts on some Latin hip-hop, and the way she shimmies in her seat as she sings along fills my heart like a balloon, ready to burst at any moment.

Lola's special. She's always been so exceptional, but in these quiet moments, just her and me, when she's totally relaxed, *god*, I've never seen anyone more beautiful.

We pull up to the studio, parking in one of the spaces in front of the strip mall. She stops abruptly and says, "Sorry, have to tie my shoe."

Before she can bend over, I drop to a squat, saving my knees from the hot asphalt as I tie her sneaker with little rabbit ears, double knotting it the way I know she prefers.

Her cheeks are flushed as she squeaks out a quiet, "Thank you," and we head to the studio doors.

Something catches my eye, causing my steps to falter. There's a white vinyl cutout of a dancer on a pole plastered to the outside of the tinted windows.

"Ry… What kind of dance class did you say this was?" she whispers beside me.

I scratch my neck, trying to recall the words of the woman I'd spoken to when I'd called. "I'm, uh— Well, I'm not really sure I asked, darlin'."

Her wide eyes meet mine, and in a burst of laughter, she

bends forward, her whole body shaking. "Oh my god, Ry." Her laughter is still uncontained. "This is amazing," she says, finally able to speak clearly. When she straightens, her eyes meet mine, which are likely full of fear. Her tone softens. "We can just go home. It's okay. You tried, and that's more than anyone else I've ever dated has bothered to do."

"Wait–what? None of your past partners ever danced with you?" She shakes her head no, and uninhibited annoyance curdles my blood. "They were all trash, Lola. You won't be feeling like that with me. Never again, okay? And we aren't going anywhere," I tell her, pulling the door open.

She gives me a small smile, and her little finger grazes the top of my hand as she passes me, heading to the counter to check in. That seemingly insignificant gesture leaves tingles trailing up my arm.

I take my hat off as we enter, and a woman who looks to be in her late thirties, with blonde hair and colorful streaks through it piled high on her head, greets us with a smile.

"Hey, y'all. You must be Lola and Ryder, the new additions to our class today!" she greets us excitedly.

"Yes, thanks for having us," Lola says, returning the woman's grin with a megawatt smile.

"I'm Sarah. I'll be your instructor today. You can follow me, and I'll show you around and get you set up."

Nerves settle in my gut as she leads us into a large room with shiny, light wooden floors and about a dozen silver stripper poles scattered throughout. *Good lord.* What have I gotten myself into?

She shows us to the cubbies, where we leave our shoes and other belongings. "Go ahead and pick whichever poles you'd be most comfortable at. We don't have a full class today, so there should be plenty of room," she tells us.

Small blessings.

"We're also going to dabble in a little chair routine today, so you picked a perfect first day. It'll be loads of fun," she assures us, but I'm not so certain.

Lola takes my hand, tugging me toward one end of the class. "I'll take this one, and you can stay behind me or beside me," she says.

I smirk, nodding my agreement as I stand by the pole directly behind her. There's not a chance I'm giving up an opportunity to watch my girl dance, and definitely not like *this*.

Several people pile into the room, each of them dressed similarly to Lola, except that most of them end up changing into extremely high heels.

The other people in the class smile enthusiastically at us, introducing themselves, and by the time we get started, the tightness in my chest has loosened, and the nausea rolling around in my stomach is mostly gone.

Chapter Twenty-Seven

MAGIC...RYDER?

FRIDAY, MAY 30

I'M ABSOLUTELY giddy as we get started.

No one has ever done something that made them so visibly uncomfortable with no other intention than to make me happy and feel cared for. And, *of course*, Ryder would be the first.

"Alright, class, we're gonna get started with a simple warm-up routine. For those of you who are newer to pole fitness, don't be afraid to ask for help, and have tons of fun!"

Everyone claps, ready to begin, even Ryder, who looks slightly less green than he had moments ago.

"Start with your right hand at the top of the pole. Now, you're going to walk around it, and when you get to the two o'clock position, you're going to use momentum to swing your legs up and around. Use your tummies to grip the pole and follow through with the movement." She performs the movement faster this time to show us how it'll look when it's all put together.

"Give it a try!"

I do as she says, nearly landing on my ass the first time, but by my second try, I get it! My whole body fills with the hum of satisfaction that comes with succeeding at something new, one of my favorite parts of teaching.

"Hell yes, Lola! Just like that!" Sarah shouts encouragingly, and her praise and the thrill of trying something new and getting it right seeps warmly into my bones.

I beam over my shoulder at Ryder, who's staring very frustratedly at the pole in front of him.

He tries, *and fails*, to perform the movement a handful of times before he takes a step away from the pole. His dark brows are pinched together, and he worries his bottom lip in the cutest scowl as he observes the women. Many who clearly know their way around a pole have taken to much more advanced movements. He faces the shiny silver pole, peering over at me, and that annoyed expression of his morphs into a smirk. Ryder grips the collar of his shirt, yanking it over his head and tossing it to the ground beside him.

His tanned, rippling abdominal muscles are smooth all over, aside from a fine trail of hair from his navel that disappears under the waistband of his shorts. He tries the movement again, this time performing it perfectly.

He grins at me, clearly enjoying the way his half-naked body distracts me. "Much better, isn't it, darlin'?" He winks at me, and Sarah's voice, announcing it's time to try something new, saves me from my wandering eyes.

We work our way through several movements, each one increasingly more difficult, and the entire time, I can feel Ryder's gaze searing my skin.

Each time I allow my eyes to wander over to him, he's already staring at me, and it makes my heart beat that much faster.

The movements are difficult, and my joints are really starting to ache. I can tell the knuckle in my right index finger, the one that's thicker than the rest, is going to be screaming in the morning, but I couldn't care less.

This is already such an improvement from last week, and

the fact that I'm able to dance in any capacity, especially with others, is nothing short of incredible.

I think I'm ready to get started on those renovations and work toward building the life I always wanted.

We continue through the class, Ryder's confidence growing each passing minute, and my hope for the future renewing.

"As promised, today includes a little chair work. Not to put you on the spot, but are there any volunteers to help me demonstrate to the class?" Sarah asks.

"We'll do it!" Ryder says, his voice booming in the small studio space.

"Well, alrighty then," Sarah says, smirking at us.

My eyes swing to Ryder's, and he picks up his cowboy hat, placing it on his head, and grabs my hand, bringing me to the front of the class. *Is he being for real right now?* I'm not giving him a lap dance. *Le falta un tornillo!*

Sarah slides a chair out, placing it in front of us, and my stomach drops. The thought of saying no, with everyone watching, makes my skin tighten, like the room's shrinking around me. My pulse quickens, and I can't shake the weight of all those eyes on me.

"Okay, one of y'all take a seat," Sarah says.

Ryder tips his chin at me. "You heard the lady. Take a seat, darlin'."

I stare at him, my blood buzzing to life under his gaze. My mouth is open, and I'm gulping air like a fish out of water, but my legs finally decide to work, and I nearly collapse into the chair.

"This okay, darlin'?" he asks, his voice low enough that only I can hear him. I meet his eyes, nodding my consent.

He gives me a reassuring smile, and suddenly, my whole world is thrown off kilter.

"Ryder, start by standing in front of Lola. Take a moment to tune into the music before you do anything. Pole dancing is about mastering specific moves and stitching them together when they click. Chair work, though, is different. It's all about syncing with the rhythm, letting the music guide you. Trust your instincts, and follow your partner's lead. Go ahead and give it a try. I'll walk you through it."

He stands in front of me, a glint of mischief twinkling in his bright-blue eyes as he looks down at me. When she starts to play "Pony" by Ginuwine, he closes his eyes for a moment, really feeling the music before moving.

God, does he.

Ryder leans forward, resting his hands on my knees, and gently pushes them together. He slides a rough, calloused hand under my jaw and trails two fingers to my chin, pulling my face up to his.

He straddles me with his thick thighs and moves that hand to the nape of my neck. My core clenches, and a whimper almost escapes me as he rolls his chest against mine. His bare skin is overheated with a light sheen of sweat. It's no match for the thin, cropped shirt I'm wearing. His warmth seeps into me, pebbling my nipples, as I suck in a breath, desperately begging my lungs to work more efficiently.

His vanilla-and-whiskey scent wraps around me, making me dizzy, and as if that weren't enough, he takes his hat off and *puts it on my head.*

My head spins as he rolls his hips over me, grabbing hold of my hands and pressing them to his chest, sliding my palms down the expanse of smooth muscle. I nearly pass out, the catcalls from the women around us the only thing reminding me to keep my wits about me.

I swear, I can feel *him* through those thin shorts. Before I can investigate further, he scoots off me, rounding the back of the chair. I faintly hear Sarah's voice and the claps of the women in the class, as well as their amused whistling, but I can't make any of it out through the rush of blood behind my eardrums.

His hands scrape down my arms, leaving goosebumps in

their wake. My breath gets caught in my throat as they travel down my chest, over my stiff nipples. Whether intentional or not, I'm not sure, but the effect it has on me is downright embarrassing.

My body is certainly not getting the memo: *This is not fucking real, Lola!*

He continues dancing, his movements not particularly smooth but sexy as sin all the same. My mouth is watering by the time the music finally stops, and my panties are absolutely soaked.

I suck in a deep breath, clenching my eyes shut for a moment to center myself as I unhinge the death grip I had on the sides of the chair.

Ryder holds his hand out, and I take it, standing on shaky limbs.

"That was excellent! Who'd have known this was y'all's first time?" Sarah asks, and the applause-filled room settles as Ryder leads me back to our side of the studio, looking like the cat that got the cream.

"We took a little longer than I'd planned because I wasn't expecting such an *enthusiastic* first lesson, but all that means is you've all got something to practice at home! I'll see you all next week, I hope," she tells the class, and again, everyone claps.

My heart rate is finally starting to slow, the room clearing out as Ryder bends down for his water bottle. He straightens, gaze roaming slowly over my body. And just like that, my pulse is ratcheting up again.

Why is it so damn hard to follow the rules with this man? Boundaries exist for a reason, but it feels nearly impossible to adhere to them when he's looking at me like he wants to take a bite out of me. *No*, like he wants to devour every goddamn inch of my body and come back for seconds *and* thirds.

"You feeling okay, darlin'?" he asks, clearly trying to fight the humor worming its way into his question as he lifts his water bottle to his lips, taking a slow sip. His Adam's apple bobs, lips glistening with moisture as he screws the lid back on.

My thighs squeeze together of their own volition, and I fight back a whimper, unable to stop myself from tracking the movement as his tongue darts out, licking his full bottom lip, and it's hard not to picture what that tongue would do between my l—

"Darlin'?" he asks, a thick, dark brow raised, and those lickable lips are quirked in a lopsided smirk.

Ay, Dios mio. I am so screwed.

"Huh? Oh, uh, sorry. Did you ask me something?" My voice is breathy as if I'd just run a half marathon and not sat in a chair while my pretend husband engaged me in foreplay in a room full of people.

His smirk only grows. "I asked if you're okay, Lols. You're lookin' a little flushed."

As if on cue, my chest heats, warmth spreading up my neck and over my chest. He reaches forward, tucking a stray curl behind my ear, and steps into my space, invading me with the intoxicating scent of him. It's clean, warm, and entirely *him.*

"Y-yeah, I'm all good." My gaze darts around the now-empty room. I clear my throat, refusing to meet his gaze. "Looks like we should get out of here."

"You're right, we should. You mind if I keep my shirt off? I'm feeling pretty… hot."

I gulp down a lungful of air. *I am not God's strongest soldier.*

"You should probably—"

"Does my good little wife not want anyone else to see what's hers?" he asks, and my eyes dart to his, brows climbing my forehead.

Shit. I played right into that.

I take a gulp of water, stalling. "I just think it's… inappropriate. You know, small towns talk and all that."

This time, a deep chuckle fills his chest, and my blood hums again.

"Noted, darlin'," he says, bringing his mouth impossibly close to my ear without actually touching me. "But I can't make any promises when you look at me like that, eyes all glazed with nipples that could cut glass." He looks down at the offending body parts, and my face flames.

I smack his chest. "None of that," I scold.

"Right. 'Boundaries'," he says with a chuckle, taking a step away from me, hands up in surrender.

We head out to the parking lot with his hand on the base of my spine, his impressive body now covered by the shirt he was wearing earlier. Several women stop to tell me how lucky I am to have a man like Ryder who isn't afraid to make a fool of himself for his woman. Though "fool" is not a word I'd ever use to describe Ryder.

Like the gentleman he is, Ryder runs ahead to grab my door handle, just in time to open it for me. I roll my eyes at him, hoisting myself inside as he makes his way around to his door.

He cues up the music but turns the volume down.

We head home, and he raps his knuckles against the steering wheel, an anxious habit I've seen him do our whole childhood.

I reach out, pressing my hand gently on his to still the motion. His eyes flit to mine before fixing on the road. "What's on your mind?"

He flips our hands, placing them on the seat between us and rubbing soothing circles on my wrist with the pad of his thumb.

"Was that too much, darlin'?" His words sound so small and unsure, and it tugs on the strings of my heart.

"Not at all, Ry. The class was incredible. It was so much fun getting to dance in a class setting, and…" I trail off, not sure if I should actually speak the next words.

"And?"

I let out a huff of air before finishing. "*And* that last part was—" I clear my throat. "It was really fucking hot," I finally say, the words coming out in a rush.

A deep rumble leaves his chest, and his thumb clamps down on my pulse point. "You're not allowed to say things like that," he scolds, shaking his head but keeping his eyes trained ahead.

"I guess it's a good thing we don't share a bed," I joke, trying to lighten the mood.

"You can say that again," he agrees, his voice deadly quiet. It sends another thrill of need racing through me before I can stop it, but thankfully, we're almost halfway home.

"Wanna order in for dinner and watch TV? I'm kind of beat after that class," he tells me when we get inside.

I release a little sigh of appreciation. "That sounds amazing. Pizza good?"

"Hell yes," he says, sounding excited at the prospect of carbs and cheese. Who doesn't love carbs and cheese? "I'll place an order. Go wash your smelly ass," he jokes, setting our water bottles on the kitchen counter.

After I've showered and slipped into a pair of worn-out sweats and another one of Ryder's shirts I'd stolen doing laundry, I curl up on the couch and check my texts.

MY WIFEY FOR LIFEY

How'd dance class go?

You won't believe me when I tell you...

Puta, spit it out and quit toying with me.

He accidentally booked...

Always the fucking suspense with you. Jesus Cristo.

A pole dance class. And it was really fucking hot.

My coochie is SCREAMING!!! Ring, ring, ring! It's your ovaries calling! They're telling you to let that man slide on in.

I'm afraid you're forgetting what this really is... But also... Would it be so bad? If I did give in??? Ugh. So hard to resist, especially after that lap dance.

LAP DANCE? You said POLE dance! When did the lap dance happen?!?!

End of class, Ryder volunteered us to be the example for the class on a little chair routine. Except, it turned into a not so little lap dance, with Ryder making good use of his namesake, GO, RANCH DADDY, GO! Yeehaw, little doggy!

"Ranch daddy?" I hear Ryder call from the kitchen. My head is on a swivel, and my heart plummets. Is he monitoring me like Russ had been? "I got a text from Mayte that says, 'Yeehaw, Ranch Daddy,' followed by a GIF of a muscular bottle of ranch riding a horse. Is there something I'm missing?"

My shoulders shake with laughter, and my heart climbs back into my chest cavity. *Of course*, he doesn't have my phone tapped. "She's a tyrant," I confirm.

He takes a seat beside me on the couch, stretching out his long legs in the gray sweatpants he's now wearing.

Facing me, he quirks a brow and asks, "If I'm Ranch Daddy, does that make you Ranch *Mami?*"

"Definitely not, and don't repeat that to anyone else," I tease.

Ryder smirks, shifting closer to me, his gaze flicking across my face. "Ranch is my favorite dressing."

Because it's creamy and delicious just like...? Nope, definitely don't say that out loud.

The doorbell rings, saving the day.

We decide to watch something on cable that neither of us is really paying much attention to, and when I open the pizza box to pull out a slice, my jaw nearly drops.

A white pizza with ricotta and hot honey. My *favorite*.

"How'd you remember?" I ask, my eyes swinging to his.

"I remember just about everything when it comes to you, Lola."

I swear, if he keeps on like this, I might combust.

To make matters worse, he picks up a slice of his own and dunks it in a cup of *ranch*.

This man has *no right* to make salad dressing erotic. *No fucking right.*

Chapter Twenty-Eight

CAUGHT OFF GUARD

FRIDAY, MAY 30

LOLA'S LYING beside me on the couch, her eyes closed and her breathing relaxed. I cover her with the throw blanket from the back of the couch and flip through channels.

I land on a local news station and sit back, propping my feet up on the coffee table.

They talk about a group of Girl Scouts who outperformed every other troop in the state, then about something going on in the school system, and I've officially lost interest. Instead, I sit beside Lola, watching her sleep, feeling like a total creep, but I can't keep my eyes off her. I wish I could curl up behind her and hold her in my arms.

Minutes that feel like hours pass, and when she rolls over, I've officially decided it's time to head to bed. I grab the remote, ready to turn off the TV, when a new headline pops up.

"Tonight, at Hidden Valley High, a student by the name of Wade Sansbury has been pronounced dead after being rushed to the hospital during tonight's game. As you can see in the footage, the student was hit in a tackle that..." Her words are silenced by the rush of anxiety screaming in my blood.

It sounds like a whistle is being blown directly into my

eardrums as I clench my eyes shut, warring with the sudden panic taking over my body. My lungs are tight, and no air seems to inflate them.

"Ry?" I hear faintly, but I can't focus as I struggle to breathe.

"Ry?"

My hands are balled into fists at my sides as I rock back and forth, pleading with my brain not to take me there.

Please, God, don't make me relive it.

Images of Logan flash in my mind.

That day, that awful fucking day that changed everything. The day that took my best friend from me.

My chest tightens, each breath coming slower, heavier, as if something's pressing down on me. My throat feels thick, like I'm swallowing around a boulder. The weight on my chest is suffocating, and all I can think is that I just want it to end. My jaw throbs from where I'm grinding my teeth, muscles tensed.

Soft warmth envelops me, pulling me out of the suffocating cloud of panic, its steady presence easing the tightness in my chest, calming the tremble that started deep inside.

"Ryder, hey," the soft voice says, and I feel something wrap tightly around me. "Ry, fight whatever demon is raging in your mind, *please*."

My body seems to fall with the heavy weight over me. My eyes burst open as I crash into the cushions.

A steady hand brushes my cheek, and *finally*, I take a deep breath when I see it's Lola. She's curled tightly around me, employing herself as my own personal weighted blanket.

"Hi," she says, smiling softly at me. "You came back to me."

She brushes a tear from the corner of my eye and continues rubbing the scruff along my jaw.

Worry plagues me.

"I'm sorry for scaring you, darlin'," I tell her, my voice thick and my mouth dry.

"You didn't scare me, Ry. You just had me worried for a

minute." She rests her head against my chest, remaining curled around my body as if she were a koala and I'm a piece of eucalyptus.

Several long minutes pass as I work to control my breathing, and when I'm finally able to breathe easily, Lola mumbles into my chest, "I didn't know you had panic attacks."

I run my hand up and down her spine, not wanting to have this conversation, but I'm determined not to hide things from her and desperate for her not to leave yet. "I haven't for a long time, but there was a football player near here who…"

I can't finish the sentence.

"It's okay, Ry. I understand."

"Thank you." My voice breaks on a silent sob.

Exhaustion settles into my bones, and I let sleep drag me under.

Lola

Chapter Twenty-Nine

TAKIN' CARE OF...HIS WIFE

SATURDAY, MAY 31

IT BREAKS my heart to know Ryder carries the weight of Logan's death like this. I know he'd gone to a dark place afterward, almost failing out of college his senior year, but hadn't realized he'd be triggered a decade later. It makes sense. If anything ever happened to Mayte, I'd be grieving that loss for the rest of my life.

These are the thoughts looming in my mind this morning as I fight to fall asleep.

When Ryder knocked out on the couch last night, I stayed with him as long as I could, but the inflammation from the class started to set in, and I couldn't fathom a night of sleep anywhere but my bed.

I wriggle my toes and fingers, slowly trying to awaken my body before finally opening my eyes and giving up on any hopes of rest for the day.

My phone vibrates on the nightstand, and before I can reach for it, another message comes through.

My heart stops beating as I open the text, finding a picture of Ryder and me taken in the parking lot of the pole fitness studio.

UNKNOWN

I see you.

My still, beatless heart plummets to my toes.

I roll out of bed and run into the living room to find Ryder with his thick-framed glasses hanging off his nose as he reads with a book in one hand and a coffee in the other.

He glances up and smiles brightly. "Morning, darlin'."

"Hey, um, I have something I need to show you." Worry colors his face as I take a seat beside him. He takes off his glasses and sets them down beside his book on the rustic wooden coffee table.

I hand him my phone with the messages open. His gaze flits across the screen before meeting mine, his brows pinched in anger.

"Is this from your ex?" he asks, his voice hard.

"I'm not sure who else it could be from, but—" My stomach churns with anxiety. "I haven't heard from him at all, not a single peep since I left for my bachelorette party and never came back. My parents told him we were over, grabbed my things, and got the hell out of there. He hasn't so much as called."

He hums beside me, clearly mulling over my words. "Seems he'd be coming a long way out of the city to take a photo like this. Is there anyone else who would want to scare you?"

An exasperated sigh leaves me when I realize, *yes*, there is someone who would want to scare me. "Yes, God, I'm so stupid for not realizing sooner." I drop my head into my hands, groaning with annoyance at myself. "*Lemmon*."

"Lemmon?" he asks in confusion.

"Yeah, Mayte and I ran into her the other day, and she basically told me to watch out because she wasn't gonna let me steal her man," I tell him, rolling my eyes.

"Why didn't you tell me about this?" he asks, his tone unnervingly clipped.

I shrug, unsure of what to say. "She mentioned something that made me worry she knew we'd gotten married so I could get on your insurance policy, and when I'm anxious about something, I develop avoidant behavior. Basically, I pushed it out of my mind so I wouldn't have to deal with it, and now, here we are, being *forced* to." Lemmon is not someone who deserves a moment of my time, not physically nor mentally, but Ryder and I thrive on open communication, and I should've known he'd want me to tell him.

He scrubs a hand down his face, and I think I'm about to be sick. My jaw is locked as I prepare for the lecture I'm about to receive. *Just like my ex always had.*

When his eyes meet mine, they crinkle at the edges, and he rests his palm in my lap. "If anything ever happened to you, I'd never forgive myself, Lola. I would die an empty man, so *please*, if she ever says anything to you again, let me know. Can you do that for me, baby?"

I blink at him, his words slowly realigning into full sentences as my poor, groggy brain tries to catch up. *No lecture?*

"Can you do that, Lola?" he asks again, and the haze finally clears.

I nod. "Yeah—yes. I can do that."

"Good. Now, quit worrying. The only people besides us who know our motivations are our family." He squeezes my thigh and stands before bending down to kiss my forehead, disappearing into the kitchen. I'm left sitting here, thrown off by his ability to make me feel cared for and respected.

When he returns a minute later, he has a mug in one hand, a bag of ice in the other.

I cock my head at him in confusion as he takes a seat beside me.

"Go ahead and lie back, darlin'. I've got you a cup of coffee, and I'm gonna rub your feet while you ice those hands."

I look down at my aching hands, and sure enough, the joint in my index finger is red and swollen, with a few fat knuckles on the others.

The urge to argue that he doesn't have to take care of me is overwhelming, but the desire to be cared for is so much stronger.

I take the coffee, sipping it. The familiar taste of *café con leche* hits my tongue, and I release a moan.

"Oh my god, Ry, this is so good," I tell him. I don't miss the way he smirks or the bob of his Adam's apple.

"Mhmm, now lay back."

I set the coffee down on the table beside me and rest my hands on my tummy, which he covers with the bag of ice before he pulls my legs across his lap.

He starts with my calves, working his way down each leg, digging his thumb into the arches and balls of my feet.

I groan and make several other unattractive sounds as he works his hands over my muscles and sore joints. By the time he's finished, I'm absolutely blissed out, lids heavy with the desire to nap.

He picks up his book, starting to read again, as he mindlessly rubs circles into my calves, as if this is a daily occurrence for us.

As if we've been married for years.

As if this were real.

Ryder

Chapter Thirty

WORRY WART

SATURDAY, MAY 31

NOT ONLY DOES it piss me off that Lemmon would come after Lola, but it also scares the shit out of me, especially with what happened with the fence the other day. Could that have been connected to this?

Those text messages are creepy at best. At worst, they're an outright threat.

But for Lola's sake, I plan to pretend like it doesn't bother me as much as it does. I don't want my anxiety to add to hers for no reason, and I definitely don't want her to hold back on telling me if something else happens just to avoid ramping up my worry.

The thoughts scrambling my brain make me restless, and I've finally managed to finish the last chapter in my book. It's probably best I get started on the barn anyway.

I tap lightly on Lola's bedroom door, my knuckles rapping firmly against the thick wooden frame. "Hey, I'm heading out for a bit," I call through the door. The usual hum of water from the shower is steady, but no response comes. I wait a moment, my hand lingering on the doorknob. The silence stretches a little too long.

I knock again, firmer this time, and listen closely—still nothing. A knot tightens in my stomach.

I crack the door open and hear the water in the shower stop. "Ryder, is that you?" she calls out.

"Yes. Just wanted to let you know I'm gonna be gone a few hours. Got some work left to finish before the sun goes down."

"Oh! Would you mind dropping me off at the barn? I'd like to get started on it or at least figure out some solid ideas for the design," she calls.

I clear my throat, my brain overwhelmed with the thick scent of her and the knowledge that she's naked behind this door.

"Uh, yeah, Lols. No problem," I tell her, scratching my neck.

"Is something wrong?"

"N-no. I was just heading over there to get some electrical work done on the building. You sure you're ready to start working on it?"

Truthfully, I'd hoped I could work quickly enough to get it all done before she was up for it. I wanted to surprise her, but I'm realizing that might have been a bad idea. This is meant to be her baby, and if there's one thing I know about Lola, it's that she *wants* to work for what she has. I'd been stupid to think this would be any different.

Lola tugs the door open, popping her head out. A blush-pink, waffle-knit towel is wrapped around her, tucked under her arm, another plopped on her head.

She's so beautiful, it hurts to look at her.

"I appreciate you, Ry, but I have to put the effort into this too, okay? You can't protect me from everything," she says, her voice quiet and her eyes crinkled at the corners.

"I understand, Lols. I'm sorry."

She gives me a tight-lipped smile. "Don't be. I know you mean well. I'll toss on some clothes and be ready in five."

I busy myself with locking up the house, double-checking the windows and back door while she gets dressed.

Having this place for Lola to control her lessons, when she teaches, what she teaches and knowing no one can ever take it away from her provides me with a heavy comfort.

It's all hers.

And so am I.

Lola

Chapter Thirty-One

RANCH DADDY

SATURDAY, MAY 31

IN THE LAST FEW DAYS, my fatigue has lessened, and I've been able to accomplish a bit more around the ranch, broadening my daily tasks from feeding the cattle and calling dance studios to helping Ryder in the greenhouse, working on some of the experiments he's been running to see which bioavailable fertilizer produces the best tomatoes, Swiss chard, and bell peppers.

It's nice to see his education being put to work, and it loosens the tight knot in the pit of my stomach now that I'm making myself useful.

It's also been satisfying to see the barn coming to life with every hour we put into it. It's still a long way from perfect, but it shouldn't be long before it's good enough to run a few trial classes. Maybe if I weren't so worried about something going wrong, I'd quit calling around to other places. I don't even want to dance anywhere now that my dream of owning my own studio is at the tips of my fingers, but I can't give up the idea of stability and a fallback plan either.

And as usual, Ryder all but demands I take the afternoons off to spend time with Mayte, Isabela, and *Mami* when she's around. It's that selflessness that I have to thank for my ability to be sitting here on Mayte's sofa, about to witness my niece taking her first steps.

"That's it, Isa. You can do it!"

"Yes, yes! Just one big step for *Mami*!"

"Come on, *mija*, you've got this!"

"*Dale, que tú puedes, muñeca!*" *Mami* shouts at Isabela, clapping her hands.

My niece stands on her chubby little legs, wobbling as she stares straight ahead at Mayte. She hesitantly picks up one foot, balancing on an unsteady leg, and manages to take her first step!

Her first freaking step!

"You did it, *mamá*," Mayte tells her daughter proudly, holding her arms out for her to waddle to where she's crouched a few inches away.

When she makes it into her mother's arms, I lose it.

My heart cracks wide open, and the floodgates cannot be controlled.

"*Mi bebé*, what's wrong?" *Mami* asks, wrapping her arms around me in a tight hug.

I suck in a breath between sobs and manage to stifle the tears. Sniffling, I wipe my nose with the tissue Mayte thrusts into my hand and clear my throat. "I'm just so thankful to be here," I tell them, my voice quivering. "If I'd have married Russ, I wouldn't be here for this. I'd miss all these precious moments."

I've already missed out on so much, and I know I've made the right decision to stay. No matter what Lemmon does, being here and not missing another second of my family's lives far outweighs whatever challenges she plans to throw my way. A few creepy messages and bitchy monologues won't deter me. She won't get rid of me that easily.

"Oh," Mayte says, crushing me in a hug of her own. "I'm so

glad you're here too. Now, let's go eat ice cream and watch *Siempre Bruja.*"

By the time I get home, Ryder is already in bed. He left the porch light on, as well as all the lights in the house, with a note saying he didn't want me to trip. I chuckle as I read it. *This ridiculous man.*

I turn out all the lights, and when I get to the one in the hall that separates our rooms, I realize he's left his door cracked open too. Just in case he can hear me, I pop my head in and whisper, "Goodnight, *Ranch Daddy.*"

I hear his bed creak, and a moment later, "Goodnight, Ranch *Mami.*"

My shoulders shake with the quiet laughter, and it isn't long before I'm dressed for bed and blissfully asleep.

Lola

Chapter Thirty-Two

WEIGHTED BLANKET

SUNDAY, JUNE 1

A SCREAM RIPS through the silence, yanking me from sleep.

I toss the covers off, gaze darting across the room, shadows stretching long in the moonlight, but nothing moves.

A soft whimper floats in from across the hall. It's not sharp like the scream, but just as unnerving.

Releasing a heavy sigh, I sit up on the edge of the bed, bare feet pressed to the cold floor. The whimper rises, fractured and panicked.

Ryder.

I hurry to his room, finding the door still cracked open from when he went to bed, so it's easy to slip inside without waking him.

I'm inches from his bedframe when I realize the *massive* mistake I've made.

Seeing this man in nothing but his briefs is going to make every encounter going forward that much more difficult. Thankfully, it's dark, save for the small stream of moonlight through the blinds, so I can't make out details.

"

He lets out another whimper, tossing in his sleep, his eyes clenched shut. There's nothing peaceful about him right now.

Come on, Lola. *Get a grip.*

I reach for the comforter he's kicked to the end of the bed and toss it on top of him before climbing in. My arms wind tightly around him as his large body shakes beneath me.

"Ryder," I whisper into his hair, not wanting to startle him awake.

He continues trembling, and his breaths come out in short, shallow gasps.

"Ryder," I say, louder this time. "Come on, you've gotta wake up for me. *Please,*" I plead with him as he continues to struggle.

My arms feel weak, unable to keep holding him like this.

Weighted blankets can be good for panic and anxiety attacks, which I only know because I was desperate for anything to help suppress the restless energy I experienced while planning a future I didn't truly want with Russ. Unfortunately, the weighted blanket didn't do shit for me, but, according to Dr. Google, the weight triggers the nervous system to lower your heart rate and slow breathing. That's why I laid on top of him like I had the other night, and *it worked.*

Since he seems to have no plans to wake up anytime soon, I do the same as I had before. Rolling on top of him, I practically straddle his lap before lowering my upper body to cover as much of his massive frame as I'm able.

It kills me to see him like this, struggling with memories — or maybe new fears, I can't be sure. This steadfast and self-assured man has always seemed so solid. It physically hurts to see him crumbling like this.

I start to count down from sixty, planning to try to wake him again if he doesn't on his own. By the time I reach twenty-six seconds, his breathing has evened out, and a moment later, his warm hand is on the back of my head, caressing my curls through my silk bonnet.

"Thank you," he whispers quietly, pressing a kiss to the top of my head. I blow out a contented sigh, relaxing into his embrace.

I fall asleep just like this.

Lola

Chapter Thirty-Three

NEW REALITY

SUNDAY, JUNE 1

WHEN RYDER ENTERS THE KITCHEN, his hair falling in damp waves over his forehead, I'm still standing with the injector pen in my hands.

"Time for your next shot?" he asks, opening the fridge and grabbing a carton of orange juice for himself and, as usual, the chocolate almond milk for me.

"Yeah," I say, a little wary.

He must hear the apprehension in my voice because he sets the cartons down and turns to face me, giving me his full attention.

He's leaning against the counter, his hands gripping the smooth granite, waiting for me to explain what's going on.

"I know I should just be glad I have medication at all. And *I am*," I emphasize. "But it just dawned on me that *this*," I say, swinging the injector pen through the air. "This is my new normal. I'll probably never have the luxury of not jabbing myself with this thing from now until forever, and it just—" I drop my head into my hands. "It sucks," I whisper.

Ryder's warm arms envelop me, squeezing me tightly to his chest. He buries his face in my curls at the crook of my neck, and I swear I feel the feather-light touch of his lips graze over my bounding pulse point.

"I need you to keep being the strong, brave, determined woman I know you are, darlin', because you need this medication to keep doing what you love. Okay?" he asks, and I give him a non-committal nod, my head now tucked under his chin.

He pulls away, his warmth immediately following him, but his hands remain on me as he slides them down my waist to my hips. He hoists me up onto the counter in one smooth movement.

"Now, tell me which thigh we're doin' this in," he says.

His eyes meet my wide ones, and his dark brows climb his ruggedly handsome face. "Come on, Lols. I've got breakfast to make, so you've gotta hurry, darlin'."

I shake myself out of the daze as I roll my denim shorts up on my right thigh. I can't get the hem much higher, as my thighs start to eat the shorts the higher they climb.

Ryder grabs the box I keep my medication in, and he pulls out an alcohol prep pad, setting it on the counter before washing his hands. When he returns, he tears the packet open, working the alcohol in a small circle that widens with each stroke. My skin is littered with goosebumps by the time he's finished.

He takes the pen from the counter beside me and peers up to meet my eyes. I nod, reassuring him it's okay.

He uncaps the pen and says, "Almost done, darlin'," before he plunges it into my skin, pressing down and counting backward from ten to allow all of the medication to disperse.

When he's done, I reach out for him, my fingers biting into his forearm. "Ry," I say, the words barely above a whisper. "Thank you."

Those cerulean eyes peer into mine. He takes my expression in, pressing his forehead against mine. "Thank *you*, Lols."

"For what?"

"For—" he drags in a breath, clenching his eyes shut for a

beat before returning them to me, "For last night. For being there. For… everything, Lols. Allowing me to just be in your orbit. And, more than anything, letting me help you with this," he finishes, pulling back and tossing the used injector pen into the small sharps container on the cabinet beside me.

His words send a warmth like molten honey pooling in my veins, and it takes every ounce of my resolve not to cup his cheeks and press my lips to his. Luckily, he doesn't wait for a response from me, gripping my hips and helping me off the counter. We get everything cleaned up before he takes me over to the couch to rest while he makes breakfast.

It doesn't escape me that in less than one month, he's able to determine my every need and actively wants to make sure they're met. Russ had never done that over the length of our entire pitiful relationship, and I think it might be about time I stop comparing these two incredibly different men. Russ and I were never meant to be, and I think, possibly without knowing it, Ryder is healing all the cracked pieces Russ tried so hard to turn to ash around me.

Chapter Thirty-Four

CHICKEN NUGGIES

FRIDAY, JUNE 6

MY TIRES ARE KICKING up dust on the sunbaked road, and Beyoncé plays over the speakers. The land around me is in full bloom, all that pale-green grass having turned lush, patches of wildflowers dancing in the wind along the edges of the road, mostly blue bonnets. They're Lola's favorite, but I can see a few splashes of orange, red, and yellow too.

I ease the truck around a curve, and the road opens for a minute, giving me a good view of the horizon. There's something about this land that's hard to explain. You'd think it's just dirt and grass, but the more time you spend on it, the more you feel like it's got a pulse of its own. It's just waiting for you to pay attention before allowing you to discover all the hidden gems.

I keep driving, the wind in my hair and the hum of the engine under my seat, feeling the pull of the place I've always known. This land, this road, it's more than just a way from here to there. It's home. That word acts as a reminder that I should check in on the person who makes me feel most at home, no matter where we are.

"Ari, call 'My Wife.'"

The music stops, and I'm met with her robotic answer. "Calling 'My Wife.'"

The line rings a couple of times before she answers. "Hey, Ry. You finished dropping off the feed and fertilizer?" she asks, sounding a bit out of breath.

"Yeah, darlin', I'm just calling to see if you wanted anything before I got home. I'm a few minutes out," I tell her.

There's more heavy breathing across the line, a crash, and then she mumbles something in Spanish I don't quite catch. "Everything okay, Lols?"

"Sorry! Yeah, now that the kid can walk, she's a little menace." She blows out a breath, and her voice sounds closer to the speaker. "What were you asking again?"

I chuckle, a smile tugging at my lips at the mental image she's painting for me. "You're watching my favorite kid *without me*?"

She releases a small laugh, the sound light and airy over the phone. "Mayte works so hard all the time, and it can't be easy being a single parent, so I kidnapped our niece and paid for Mayte to get a massage and pedicure," she explains, and my whole body squeezes like I'm being hugged, pride overflowing inside me.

Isabela isn't technically our niece, but it feels good to hear her call her ours, and even better to know she's making sure Mayte takes care of herself. I'm overwhelmed with how thoughtful she is. Lola will be an amazing mom someday, and I hope she keeps me around to see it. "That's so sweet, darlin'. Next time, I'll watch her and send you *both* out for a spa day so you can spend some extra time together."

"That'd be nice, Ry," she says, and I can picture her smile without seeing it. It blinds me from here.

"Do you want anything before I get home?" I ask again.

"Oh, uh, how about chicken nuggets? I kind of have a craving for them, and Isabela might actually eat those."

"Nuggets, comin' right up. I'll be home soon."

"See you soon, Ry," she says, and the line goes quiet.

I make a U-turn, traveling down the road another minute. A tiny tan blob that looks suspiciously like a chicken nugget sprints along the side of the road; it's so fast, it seems to be keeping up with my truck. I must be hallucinating, or maybe I have an unknown nugget craving myself. I slow to a stop, squinting to get a better look at the tiny thing.

A tannish-orange and white ball of fluff stops alongside the road, panting, its tongue hanging all the way out of its mouth, and it's the cutest little thing I've ever seen.

I check the road for any oncoming traffic, and when I see none, I toss my door open and sprint around to the front of the truck. "Hey there, little buddy. Are you lost?"

He tilts his head, sucking his tongue back in his mouth as his butt wiggles. Yes, his butt, because evidently, corgis don't have much of a tail. "Do you wanna go home with me until we can find your parents?"

He runs past me, and before I can make a sprint for him, I see him jump into the passenger seat through my open door.

I get buckled in, rolling down his window for him, but I decide better of that when I realize he's so small, he might fly right out.

With a tentative hand, I reach out, and when he doesn't back away, I scratch behind his ears and feel around for a collar, finding nothing. "Don't worry, little guy. Tomorrow, I'll take you to meet Dr. Becerra at the vet clinic, and she'll scan for a microchip. We'll get you home soon," I say, patting the top of his head and pulling onto the road, making my way to Lola's favorite fast-food restaurant.

The rest of the drive passes in a blur of waiting in line for Lola's order, fighting the urge to call her back and tell her about our new friend, and feeding the little dog a few fries. He gazes out the passenger window, his tiny nub of a tail wagging, long pink tongue hanging from the side of his mouth as we pull through the gates of Rosa Ranch.

"This is your new home, at least for the night. Do you think you could be happy here?" I ask him, my heart thumping violently in my chest at the two high-pitched yaps he barks out in agreement.

The little fluff ball scoots across the seat, nuzzling his long snout under my arm as I park in my usual spot to the left of our cottage-style home. The lack of another car makes me think I should broach the question of whether Lola wants to learn to drive, and if she does, maybe she'll let me teach her. I know years of living in the city were her excuse for never bothering to get her license, but I can't help but think her ex might have fed into her fears.

I know as well as she does how suffocating it can be to have free will, two working legs, and someone to come home to each night and *still* feel completely, utterly *alone*.

After a quick potty break in the yard, the little guy follows me up the porch. The way he sticks by my side makes me think he has a family looking for him somewhere, and as much as I'd love to welcome him home permanently, I wouldn't keep him from the people who love him.

I crack the front door open and stick my head in. "Hey, darlin'. I've got something for you," I holler inside.

"Oh my gosh, you're a saint!" she says, grabbing the brown paper bag from my hands and clutching it to her chest. She leans forward, pecking me on the cheek and turning toward the kitchen.

"Lols, there's something else," I say, and she twists around, cocking her head to the side.

"Did you get ice cream too?" she asks, her eyes glittering.

I take a step back, making a mental note to run out for ice cream before bed, and open the door wide. The little dog sprints inside, jumping up her legs.

Her eyes light up as she bends forward, picking him up with zero hesitation. "Oh my goodness, hello," she says, kissing his head as he shimmies in her arms.

"I'd like you to meet Nugget," I tell her.

"Nugget? I asked you to get me chicken nuggets, and you came home with a *corgi named Nugget?*" she asks in disbelief.

"To be fair, I *also* brought the chicken nuggets. I don't really know his name, but that's what I'm calling him since he looks like a chicken nugget."

"You don't know his name?" she asks, her dark brows pinching together.

"I found him running along the road. He's got no collar, but I'll take him to scan for his chip in the morning. For now, we'll just make sure Nugget has a good dinner."

Lola smiles and steps forward, cupping my cheek. "You're a good man, Ryder Lockhart."

My cheeks heat, and I'm reminded of the many impure thoughts I've had about Lola since the day she stepped foot on Rosa Ranch. I most certainly do *not* feel like a good man, not by a long shot, but I won't tell her that.

I clear my throat. "Ready for dinner?"

Chapter Thirty-Five

MAMI'S BOY

FRIDAY, JUNE 6

I SLUMP AGAINST THE CUSHIONS, kicking my feet up into Ryder's lap. He already has the TV queued up with what's quickly becoming Ryder's new favorite *telenovela*, *Secrets Signed In Ink*. I love that he doesn't bother acting like he isn't just as enthralled by the plot twists as I am, and the other day, I came home from Mayte's to find *Mami* folding laundry with Ryder while they binged the first season to get him caught up. My chest warms at the thought.

Nugget jumps onto the couch and settles beside me.

"I have no idea how she's managing the life of a single mom while keeping her business open too," I say, almost moaning when Ryder begins his ministrations on my feet, just like he has every night this week.

"Mayte is basically superwoman. All single moms are," he says, agreeing with my unspoken sentiment. "We've all taken turns watching Isabela the last year, but I'll definitely admit the task was much easier when she was sleeping half the time and she couldn't physically go anywhere. Now that she's walking, it's a whole other ballgame," he sighs.

Sadness and guilt settle in my chest. "Thanks for being

there for her, Ry," I tell him, stroking a hand down the length of Nugget's spine.

"That woman is like a sister to me, Lols. I would never expect her to do it all on her own," he says, and a choked cry slips past my lips, startling me as much as it does him. "Darlin', what's wrong?"

I swipe at the unruly tears. "Nothing, sorry." I try to push the emotion down, but the guilt and resentment come on so strongly, I'm not in control of my body.

"Lola, I didn't mean it like that," he assures me, but I already knew he hadn't. He'd never say something to intentionally feed the guilt I'm already living with. "I meant I live right around the corner from her, so of course I'd watch Isa when I can."

I sit up, and Nugget stands, shaking himself out. He slips behind me, making himself comfortable on the stack of throw pillows I'd been leaning against. I guess lying down is officially out of the question now.

Ryder chuckles, reaching for my waist, pulling me into his lap. I melt against him despite knowing this is the last thing I should be letting him do if I really want to maintain that this is *not* a real marriage.

He runs a soothing hand down my back and kisses my temple. "No one expected you to be here, Lola. You were off living your life, and we'd all hoped it was a better and more fulfilling one. I'm so damn sorry it wasn't, but *please*, don't feel bad you weren't here. You haven't missed much, besides a lot of cow crap and Isabela learning to do anything other than drool all over herself."

That makes me crack a smile. "Thanks, Ry," I say, leaning against his chest and turning my attention to the TV.

"Hey, Lols?" he asks before I can fully escape back into the show.

"Yeah?" I twist in his lap to get a better look at his face. His sharp jaw covered in scruff, full, biteable lips, and soul-searching blue eyes have my breath caught in my throat, his handsome features always enough to throw me off kilter when I least expect it.

"Would you like to learn to drive?" he asks, and my brows knit together, unsure where the question came from.

"I, well, I'm… Maybe?" I answer, unsure. "I haven't given it much thought. Why do you ask?"

He smooths a palm down my spine, tugging on the hem of my shirt that's ridden up, smoothing it over my skin. "Earlier, I was thinking about how you don't have a way to leave if you need something, want to go somewhere, or just need to get away for a while. It reminded me of how many people I had in my life when I was married, and yet how incredibly alone I felt. Some days, I would go on long drives to clear my head, not returning until well into the night and I knew she was asleep so I wouldn't have to listen to her yell." His admission is like a gut punch I don't see coming. I grip his cheeks in my palms, anchoring him to this moment with me. "I never want you to feel like you can't get away or your options are limited. So, if you'd like to learn to drive, I can teach you, and we can go down to Dingo's Dealership to pick out a safe vehicle for you."

Hot tears pool in my eyes, my heart tugging in every direction from his thoughtfulness. "There's a lot of newness happening all at once, Ry. I'm not sure I'm ready to add another thing yet, but I'd love that once I've settled in and have a better idea of how the studio is doing and whether or not I'll need to pick up jobs elsewhere for a while," I say, the words sounding watery.

He nods, leaning into my hold as he slides a hand between us to grip my chin and turn my cheek. He presses a soft kiss against the smooth skin, his scruff prickly, lighting up all my nerve endings before he pulls away, leaning into the soft couch cushions and pulling my body into his.

We lie here for hours, the soft rhythm of Ryder's teasing

filling the space between us, and with every laugh and comment, the *telenovela* becomes even more enchanting. His words lift me, deepening my connection to the drama unfolding on the screen, making it feel brighter, richer somehow.

"I'm glad Bexaida came over last week to explain the first episode to me because I was admittedly a little confused."

"Oh?" I ask, my brows raised. "About what?"

"Well, my Spanish isn't exactly fluent, so when the tattoo artist with a chip on her shoulder suddenly seemed to fall head over heels for the women's health physician assistant, I thought I'd missed something."

I wave a hand at him. "No, no. It's a lust-at-first-sight sort of thing, but they eventually—"

"Stop! Don't ruin it for me!" he shouts, cupping a hand over my mouth to silence me.

I chuckle lightly. "Okay, I won't," I say, rolling my eyes.

We continue watching until we're all caught up and the newest episode that's airing now starts to play. My eyes grow heavier by the minute.

"Oh my god! No!" he shouts at the TV, fully immersed. He pats down the couch cushions and grabs his phone from where it slid between the armrest and the corner cushion.

I hear a ringing tone, and my brows climb high on my forehead. "Who are you calling?"

He doesn't get a chance to answer before the person on the other end of the line answers. "Are you seeing this!? I *cannot* believe they would arrest her for something like that!"

I adjust in his lap to snatch the phone out of his hand and bring it to my ear. "*Mami?*"

"*Sí, mija!* That *caballito* arrested her for doing the right thing! I can't believe it. *Ese cara de culo se equivocó si pensó que ella aceptaría 'tu cuerpo, mi elección'!*"

"Darlin', that's very rude. Your mom and I were having a conversation," Ryder tells me, grabbing the phone and rolling his eyes playfully with a lopsided smirk that sends my heart soaring.

I gape at him jokingly, but I'm not offended at all. If anything, these interactions between Ryder and *Mami* are quickly climbing high on my list of reasons I might fall in love with him again, *and that is dangerous territory to be in.*

Lola

Chapter Thirty-Six

GRANNY'S PERFUME DRAWER

SATURDAY, JUNE 7

MY JOINTS FEEL like they're on fire by the time I've finished up at the barn for the day. Ryder's been pleading with me to let him hire contractors to help me, but I don't want him paying for anything else. Plus, it feels good to put in the work for what I want.

What doesn't feel good are the inflamed joints and angry muscles I've been pushing past their limits each day.

It isn't long after I've showered before Ryder enters the house, one hand wrapped around a stack of mail and Nugget tucked under his other arm. "Looks like Nugget is ours unless his owners manage to get ahold of us somehow. He doesn't have a microchip either," Ryder tells me as he sets Nugget down and kicks off his boots, setting his hat on the hook by the door. Nugget sprints to his blue-and-white porcelain bowl, lapping at the water.

"That makes me kind of sad. I love him already, but I can't help but think about the family probably missing him right now," I admit, patting the seat beside me for Ryder to sit down.

He does, stretching out his long limbs with a satisfied groan. He's mindlessly sorting through the mail, listening to me talk about my day, which was uneventful, per usual. His thick, dark brows pull tight, casting a shadow over his eyes.

"What's wrong?"

He shakes his head, tearing into the large white envelope. "It's from the permitting committee," he answers, his eyes roaming over the crisp letterhead. He flips each page, his expression softening with each turn until he's relaxing back into the cushions, shaking his head with a huff of laughter. "These aren't real."

"What are you talking about?" I ask, grabbing the stack of papers he hands me.

He explains further as I read the legal jargon. "My family has been above board since the day my grandfather opened this ranch. If there's an update to the rules, we comply with those updates whether we're grandfathered in or not, and with all the work I've done to the ranch to make our work more environmentally sustainable, none of the problems listed in these documents are remotely possible."

"But what if Lemmon had her father—"

"Lola, her father hasn't been in contact with her in three years. They live in the same town, but that's the only proximity they share. He grew tired of her games, so he set boundaries that she tumbled right over every chance she got. Seeing the way he handled their relationship was one of the things that pushed me to do the same with Lemmon despite years of gaslighting. Fred Meringue isn't going to play any part in Lemmon's games, I assure you. She's threatened to do exactly this to me before. Now, go ahead and give it a sniff."

His words take me from relief to confusion with a snap of his fingers. "I'm sorry, what?"

"Sniff the papers, darlin'."

I bring them to my nose, taking in a good whiff. The smell of magnolias and lemons lingers on the pages, and my brows climb high as shock floods my heart. "Are you serious?"

"Lemmon prides herself on smelling like the inside of her

granny's old perfume drawer. *That* is her rather unfortunate signature scent."

"God, the lengths that woman will go to create tension between us."

"She's got a lot of trauma from her mother leaving her so young, but none of it is an excuse for how poorly she treats everyone. I'm not sure we'll ever work out the real reason, and I don't think I care so long as she stays away from you."

I bristle at his words, not wanting to admit my discomfort at being the target of her abuse again, but he sees right through me.

He widens his stance, spreading his thighs, meeting me with a mischievous glint in his eye. His hands are suddenly on my hips, hoisting me into his lap.

"Ry," I whine, unsure what's going on.

He lifts the hem of my shirt, tickling my soft belly. I squirm and squeal, wriggling out of his grasp to no avail.

"Ry! Stop!" I screech, and his hands lower to my hips with a tight squeeze.

He levels me with a serious look, pouring his intentions right into me and soothing the nausea building in my gut. "If it'll make you feel better, I'll give Todd at the permitting office a call on Monday to make sure everything is sorted."

"It would. Thanks," I admit, toying with a loose thread on his collar.

"And Pops and I will put up fliers across town for Nugget. If his parents see them and give us a call, they can have him back," he says, kissing my forehead, acting as if this touchy-feely business I've been letting him get away with is our new normal. I hate how much I love the thought of that being true, of me and Ryder just *being.* "But for now, we can be his parents," he finishes, completely unaware of my internal monologue running wild. "I'd like to take you somewhere tonight, darlin'. Is that okay?" he asks, tilting his head just enough that a loose wave flops to the other side.

"I'm an unfortunate sucker for surprises, so... I guess so," I agree, a grin tugging at my lips as a flutter of excitement warms my chest. The idea of some Ryder Lockhart-type of fun has my pulse picking up, and I can't help but feel lighter at the thought.

The smile he aims my way could light up the whole world, and it has a similar effect on my aching heart.

He smacks a sloppy kiss to my cheek, gently shoving me off his lap as he swats playfully at my butt. "Go on and get changed, Lols. We'll leave in ten minutes," he says, heading to his room without another word.

"Ry! What should I wear?" I shout through his door.

"Anything or nothing at all, darlin'. It doesn't matter, but I prefer the latter if you're taking requests," he says, pulling the door open to pop his head out, showing off his shit-eating grin. He winks and blows me a kiss, leaving me standing here, momentarily stunned.

Heat creeps up my neck and swirls around my cheeks. He's too damn cute and disarming for my own good.

Lola

Chapter Thirty-Seven

HIDDEN OASIS

SATURDAY, JUNE 7

RYDER DRIVES us down past the horse stables behind Mayte's cottage, pulling onto a back road I don't often travel.

"Where we going, Ry?" I ask when we still haven't made it off the property.

"It's a place I discovered a few years back. I've lived here my whole life but never had a clue what was hiding in this corner. When I took over Rosa Ranch, I decided it was time to check the fence line and make sure there wasn't anything that needed replacing," he says, nodding his chin toward the dense maple trees crowded together at the furthest corner of the property. "I always thought this was just a wooded area, good for the wildlife on the fringes and to keep the ranch somewhat secluded, but—" He trails off as he parks his truck to the side. "God, Lols, I was so wrong."

He turns the engine off, pocketing the keys and making his way around to my side of the truck. He holds my door open for me and hoists me out of the seat.

I take his hand and revel in the feel of his fingers slipping between mine. We walk in comfortable silence between the thick trunks of the maple trees. After a while, the trees start to open up, eastern redbuds in full bloom, surrounding the center of a secluded space with their bright-pinkish hue.

"Ry, what is this?" I ask in awe. Never would I have expected *this* to be here. The further we walk, the more I realize there's truly more than meets the eye in Hidden Valley because what's hiding in these woods is enough to stun me into silence.

A pool of glimmering water fills the space; the sound of the running water trickles over smooth stones.

"It turns out my dad knew about it all along. He kept it a secret for him and Mom. It was their little oasis until now. Will you share it with me, darlin'?" he asks, and my eyes swing to his, tears pricking at the corners of my vision.

I don't say a word, letting my actions speak louder. I finally give in to the moment rather than overthinking about what I *should* be doing.

My fingers find the hem of my top, tugging it over my head, leaving me in a white lace bra with sheer cups. Ryder sucks in a breath, his head falling back on a groan. "This might've been a really bad idea."

I chuckle softly, unbuttoning my shorts and sliding them down my thighs. I tilt my head to the side, a teasing smirk on my lips. "What is it, Ry? Does the sight of your *wife* have you riled up?"

He scrubs a hand down his face, rubbing at his dark scruff. "When I open my eyes again, are you going to be naked? I need to know so I can thank God for everything she's done for me so far and let her know I'm ready to be called home. I know I'll die a happy man if that's the case," he says dramatically.

"I don't know, Ry. Why don't you open your eyes and find out?"

His eyes snap open, and the loud groan he releases sets all my nerve endings alight. "Jesus, darlin'. You're a fucking stunner," he says, his voice husky. The sound scrapes along my overly sensitive skin.

"It's your turn," I tell him, and it takes some work to keep an easy smile on my face when all I want is to fall to my knees for this man. *Being fake married is already harder than I thought.*

He gets this playful glint in his eyes that always reminds me that with Ryder Lockhart, I'm never truly in charge of my own heart. He grabs the collar of his shirt, tugs it off, and tosses it to the side, leaving me gawking at his impossibly wide shoulders, corded muscles, and firm pecs. I could lick every square inch of this man and never get tired.

"It's okay, darlin'. You're allowed to ogle your husband. And maybe later, if you're a good girl, I'll let you put that drool to good use."

His words take a moment to catch up, and when they do, I'm left to do what every adult in my situation would. I unclasp my bra, toss it at his face, and run toward the crystal-clear water.

I hear him coming before I see him, suddenly blinded by the splash of water from his cannonball.

I swipe at my eyes with the heels of my palms. "Ryder Lockhart, did you just spray your wife with water?" I ask in mock annoyance.

"Sure did, sugar. Now, show me what you're gonna do about it," he says, leaning back and kicking off the edge, water lapping over the smooth, wet stones.

I swim after him, and the cool water chills my overheated skin. When I'm a foot from him, he winds his arms around my back, pulling my front to his chest. Ryder doesn't dare look down at my breasts, locking his eyes on mine like a lifeline.

I wrap my legs around his waist and wind my arms around his neck, bringing us impossibly close.

His lids fall shut as he presses the tips of our noses together. His fingers spread wide over the expanse of my back as he clutches me to him. My heart starts to stutter against my rib cage, and my breaths tangle in my chest with each passing beat.

"Darlin'," he breathes out.

"Mhmm?" I ask, molten lava pooling in my core. God, I haven't been touched in so long.

"Can I touch you?" he begs, and the words leave me reeling, digging through the trenches of my mind to uncover their hidden meaning. With Ry, nothing is ever hidden, not his meaning or his intentions. He wants me because I'm *me*, not just to have a piece of arm candy or to joke about sharing me with his friends. Not to use and abuse, mind, body, and soul. No, this is Ryder Lockhart, the man I've known all my life. He was my first kiss, my first crush, my first *everything*, and I've been aching for him.

So when I've gotten enough air in my lungs, I whisper, "*Please, Ry*," shock flickering through me momentarily.

All these goddamn boundaries, and now *I'm begging?*

He sucks a breath through his nose, his hungry eyes searching mine as his hands wander over me, leaving sparks of heat in their wake.

The sun is setting, leaving the sky looking like cotton candy clouds on a vibrant-red-and-purple watercolor background. The sun's rays glint off his wet strands, and I brush them out of his face, suddenly aware my nipples are stiff peaks, Ryder's thick length growing between my legs.

Fuck, I want this. I want *him*. Preferably, inside of me, but I'll accept his tongue or fingers too. Anything to dull the ache between my thighs.

He holds me tight, surprise stealing my breath as he dunks us under the water. My eyes snap open, adjusting to the almost effervescent, fresh water surrounding us. My hair floats around my head, tangling in his hands. He pushes it away, sliding those rough palms down my shoulders.

We're encapsulated in a moment of silent, sheer bliss. He pulls me up, and I gasp, filling my lungs with the air I've been deprived of as he sets my ass on the edge of a smooth rock.

He ducks his head, brushing his lips against the shell of my ear. "Can I taste you, Lola?" he asks, his voice barely above a whisper.

The muscles in my abdomen coil tightly, heat practically dripping from my pussy.

Snap.

The sharp sound of a branch breaking startles us back to reality. My head swings around, searching for the intruder, but with the setting sun and our heavily wooded surroundings, I can't make anything out.

"It was probably a deer. They sometimes jump the fence line," he says, but something about his darting gaze and rigid spine makes me think he's not so sure of that. "Come on, darlin'. Let's get you somewhere dry," he whispers, climbing out of the water and pulling me to my feet.

He keeps his eyes turned down, careful not to look at all my bare skin. My pebbled nipples haven't gotten the memo that our little moment was shattered. *This was a mistake.* A moment of weakness, a sign I need to make up with my vibrators. I'm horny and touch-deprived, and my *fake* husband shouldn't be the one to give me what I want right now.

Even if he wants it too, not until we've had a chance to talk about our feelings and the aftermath if we were to go any further. We're quickly tearing our predetermined rules to shreds, and the thought is exhilarating.

Ryder

Chapter Thirty-Eight

HORNY DREAMS

SATURDAY, JUNE 7

LOLA IN A WHITE LACE THONG, an expanse of bronze skin over long legs and wide hips, her small, perky breasts uncovered and begging to be sucked. _That_ is what dreams are made of.

Horny teenage dreams and some of my wildest fantasies as an adult, but dreams, nonetheless.

I hadn't brought her out here to get her naked. I wanted to spend time with her, show her a place I've come to love. A place she can escape to with or without me. A place where no one else will find her if she doesn't want to be found.

But I should've known better, because with Lola Lima, I could never get my fill.

She taps me on the shoulder when she's dressed and ready to go back to the truck. I spin, my heart fluttering and my pulse bounding in a way I'm nearly certain it shouldn't. Her long, curly strands hang in wet sheets down her back. The tiny baby hairs near her temple sprouts out, drying much faster than the rest.

I clear my throat, working my saliva around the dry lump

in my throat. "Ready to get out of here, darlin'?" I ask, swallowing thickly.

She nods, reaching out to grab my hand. The atmosphere is charged, and I can't shake the feeling we're being watched. The hair on the back of my neck stands straight, but I ignore it, focusing on Lola's movements instead.

We make it through the heavy brush, and I lift her over a stump on instinct, pulling my hands away abruptly when she peers over her shoulder at me.

I drive us to the barn at the top of the hill, parking the front of the truck under a weeping willow. "What are we doing, Ry?" she asks, her voice small and hesitant.

I flick my gaze out the window, giving her a small smile. "Follow me and find out." She grips the handle, pushing the door open. I meet her on her side, offering my hand, which she takes, twining her fingers in mine, warming me with the small touch.

We approach the freshly-stained, smooth barn doors, sliding them open with ease thanks to the new metal brackets we installed the other day.

I flick on the light, illuminating the room in the warmth offered by the chandelier and strings of cafe lights. The floors are nowhere near finished, but the concrete has been cleaned, and all the dust, dirt, and cobwebs are gone.

Lola stands beside me, unmoving as the corners of her lips quirk in a contented smile, her eyes crinkling as they roam over the room. "I know it doesn't look like much," she whispers, "but it's mine."

I squeeze her fingers, bringing her knuckles to my mouth to press a kiss to the back of her hand. "It's all yours, Lols. No one's going to take this from you."

She bats away a tear, releasing a small laugh that gets caught on a silent sob. "There's still so much to get done, and I know the medication is working, because if I'd tried to accomplish something like these renovations without it, I'd have been on bed rest for a week after a single day. It's just so frustrating to know I'm this close," she says, holding up her thumbs and pointer finger a millimeter apart, "but it might not work out in the long run because of a million factors I can't control."

I shift our bodies so we're facing each other, lifting my hands to cup her face. It's an awkward position because I refuse to release her hand, but I manage. "Lola, if it's not complete by the time we do the trial run, the town will understand. If there are days you need to cancel a class or you realize you need more help, *we will hire someone to help.* If the scheduling and marketing make it hard for you to enjoy yourself, we'll find someone to take over that part. But what I need you to do is let go of all those fears for just a few minutes right now and bask in the fact that you're *two weeks* from making your dreams a reality."

She nods slowly, clenching her eyes shut for a beat before meeting my gaze with her glossy cinnamon one. "I can do that."

"Good, Lols," I say, reluctantly dropping her hand to get my phone connected to the speakers. I open my *For Lola, With Love* playlist, and 'Levii's Jeans' by Beyoncé filters through the speakers.

Her eyes light up as I set my phone down, reaching out for her. She wraps her arms around my neck, swaying to the music with me, rolling her hips over mine. I go dizzy as all the blood from my brain rushes to my dick.

When the song ends, it transitions to one of her absolute favorites. *"La Vida Es Un Carnival"* is an upbeat song that has Lola cracking a smile so wide it rivals the moon outside.

She slides her hands down my arms, loosely taking my hands in hers. Her hips shimmy, feet moving as she takes control, reminding me of all the years we spent dancing together as kids.

I spin her out, pulling her back into my body with a little too much force. Her back knocks against my chest, and she lets out a little "oof" but quickly recovers. She grinds her ass against me as she slowly sinks down my body, nearly killing me, my eyes rolling back from the friction. She pops back up to shoot a smile over her shoulder at me.

"Little minx," I tease and allow my hands to roam freely over her body.

We continue dancing until we're both out of breath and Lola's lightly flushed cheeks are quivering from smiling so much. My heart feels beyond full as we close up, exiting to head to my truck bed in blissful silence. I open the tailgate, revealing the blankets and pillows I've laid out for us. "I've got no ulterior motive here, Lols. I figured a night under the stars would be nice," I tell her, carefully choosing my words so she doesn't think this night was all a setup to get in her pants.

She steps into my arms, wrapping hers around my neck and pressing up onto her tiptoes. "It's perfect. Thank you, Ry," she whispers into my neck. The sound is so sweet it makes my teeth ache.

I help her up into the truck bed, closing the tailgate behind me, and lie out on the blankets, resting my head on my arms.

We spend hours staring up at the sky, recounting all the stories our moms used to tell us when we were kids, making up the most random fairy tales about the stars and the people living within them. For the night, we get to be a part of that, too, a world of our own making, free of Lola's health problems, my panic attacks, Logan's passing, and the exes who haunt us.

Crickets chirp in unison, and fireflies zoom by, flickering in and out as they pass. Lola has her head tucked under my arm as she peers up at me. "Thanks for being the best fake husband I could ask for."

"Thanks for being the best fake wife I could ever want." What I don't say is how much better it'd be if she were my *real* wife, but I think we've toed that line a bit too much tonight. I know that's a tightrope I have to walk really slowly.

We pack the blankets and pillows up and drive over to

Mayte's, walking hand-in-hand to her cottage, picking up Nugget. Lola carries him to the truck, Mayte pulling me aside. "I'm rooting for you," she says with a wink, all but shoving me off her doorstep.

The added vote of confidence from Mayte, the person Lola has always trusted most, has me walking to my truck with an extra pep in my step. A lightness fills me as I drive us home.

Lola stretches her arms over her head, yawning in a high-pitched way that tickles my ears. Her shirt lifts, exposing her soft tummy, and butterflies take flight in my chest.

I settle my hand on her lower back, guiding her to the porch after Nugget had a chance to pee. He runs up the steps, sniffing around with vigor, and as we approach the door, his hackles raise and his spine stiffens. My brows knit together, and dread churns in my gut, dousing out the earlier butterflies.

"Ry, is something wrong?" Lola asks, eyes searching my face for reassurance.

"I'm not sure, darlin'. Stay behind me, would ya?" I approach the door with caution, reaching for the knob, but then I notice the door is *already* cracked open.

"Ry," she whines, her hands trembling at her sides when I look at her.

"It's okay, baby. I'll never let anything happen to you," I assure her, kicking the door open in one swift motion. It ricochets off the walls, but I hear nothing, and no one stirs inside. I reach in, flicking the lights on. Again, nothing happens. "I'm gonna go check it out. Stay right here," I say, but she grabs my forearm, tugging me to her.

"Have you never watched a scary movie, Ryder? They *want* you to leave me out here so they can attack while you're inside!" she whisper-shrieks.

"Darlin', you *know* I'm afraid of scary movies! Of course I haven't, but fine. Come on, stay close," I say, tucking her to my side. She reaches down, grabbing Nugget and holding him to her like a football under her arm.

We walk quietly inside, and I grab the baseball bat mounted to the wall from a game I went to with my dad as a kid. We walk into each room, flicking on the lights and checking for anything out of the ordinary, making sure to check every closet, every window, and close each one when we're done. Nothing appears to be misplaced, and my racing heart slows down, the raised hair on my arms settling.

"Well, it looks like the coast is clear, but someone was definitely here," I grumble. To say I'm frustrated is an understatement. I want Lola to be safe. I promised her that when we got married. It doesn't matter why we got married; those vows meant something. They meant *everything*, and I refuse to let her down.

"Why would someone break in and not take anything?" she asks, rubbing a hand up her goosebump-covered arm.

"I'm not sure, but we'll figure it out," I tell her. She nods, setting Nugget down. He bolts away from her, sprinting into the kitchen. He stops at his food bowl, about to take a big bite out of whatever's in there, but I shout at him to stop, scooping him up before he has the chance. He looks up at me with a grumpy expression, but I don't care—we didn't leave any food in his bowl.

Lola grabs the ceramic dish, looking inside, and when she meets my eyes, hers are tear-filled, and they crack my heart right open. "Ry," she says on a watery cry. "What kind of monster would try to hurt a dog?"

I look into the bowl she's holding out in front of me, and my stomach plummets straight to my toes. Nugget has been with us for barely over twenty-four hours, and whoever knows we have him just tried to kill him with razor blades shoved inside a hot dog.

I take the bowl from her, setting it down in the sink before I place Nugget on the floor. I grip her wobbling chin, dragging her sad eyes to mine. "I don't know what's going on here, what they want, or how they know we have Nugget, but I'm going to get to the bottom of it. I'm going to keep you *both* safe. Do you understand me?"

She nods slowly, her shoulders shaking with a fear I've never seen from her. "Lola, baby." I wrap her in my arms, pulling her to my chest and carrying her to her room, setting her on her bed. "We'll get to the bottom of this," I tell her again. She sniffles, blinking the tears away.

She puts on a brave, uniquely Lola Lima expression and says, "When we catch them, *se lo voy a meter por el culo.*"

I choke out a laugh, covering my mouth with my fist as I sputter. She pats me on the back and leans in close, invading my space with her warm vanilla scent. "Can I sleep with you tonight? I don't want to be alone in case anything goes bump in the night."

"Of course, darlin'. We can have a slumber party," I tease. Nugget jumps up on her bed, panting and shaking his whole ass. "All *three* of us," I clarify, and Nugget releases a loud, happy bark at the notion.

Chapter Thirty-Nine

"TAKE WHAT YOU NEED, SWEETHEART."

SUNDAY, JUNE 8

THE WAY we fell asleep last night is certainly not the way we're waking up.

A bird chirps loudly outside the window, and the heat already radiating from the window over my head tells me we've slept in. *A lot.*

Lola's lying on her side, now mostly hidden under the covers, nothing but a few dark curls hanging out from the top, her bonnet somewhere beneath the covers with all the tossing and turning she does in her sleep. As to how she's breathing, I'm not sure.

None of that is the problem though.

It's what's between my legs, and now *hers*, that's going to be an issue.

Somehow, she went from lying on top of me, *over* my comforter, to having herself plastered to my front, lying on our sides.

My dick is hard as a rock. I'm taking short, shallow breaths, allowing the absolute bare minimum oxygen into my lungs out of fear of waking her. With every breath she takes, that sweet spot between her legs rubs against my shaft a little more.

When she starts to wriggle awake, my cock pulses, and a loud groan escapes me.

I feel her body stiffen immediately, but instead of staying put, she does the opposite.

Lola shifts again, this time arching into me, and I swear to God, this must be punishment for every wrongdoing I've ever committed.

I need to stop this, but she feels so fucking good.

Bracing my hand on her hip, I try to slide away from her, but she looks over her shoulder at me. The fact that she's awake and not just following some completely physiologic response as she sleeps is baffling.

"Ry," she whispers. "Is this okay?"

"God, yes," I moan, holding her against me now. Her shoulder blades are flush with my chest, my cock burrowed so deeply between her thick thighs, I swear it feels like I'm already inside her.

I hear a scraping sound by the door and peer over her shoulder, finding Nugget glaring at us before excusing himself.

Good riddance, Nuggs.

This is every fantasy I've ever had finally coming true, and I'd rather not share the moment with any innocent eyes.

She rocks her hips against me, keeping a steady rhythm as I do abso-fucking-lutely nothing. I can't move or I'll lose my mind.

I haven't slept with anyone in so long, and nothing has ever felt as good as *this*.

As *her*.

"Ryder," she moans, her dark eyes still locked on mine. "I need more," she rasps, and if I thought I was hard before, I'm a fucking steel pipe now.

Another groan leaves me, and I have to clench my eyes shut to tamp down my breathing. With Lola here, watching me with lust-filled eyes, there's not enough oxygen in the world that could satisfy my lungs.

When I finally uncover my eyes, she's wearing this needy expression that undoes me. I pull myself out from behind her, and her brows pinch on a gasp as I roll over onto my back.

This needs to be her decision, not mine. "Take what you need, sweetheart," I tell her, nodding to my lap.

Chapter Forty
STRADDLE THAT SADDLE

SUNDAY, JUNE 8

"TAKE WHAT YOU NEED, SWEETHEART."

Goddamnit! Why is this man so attractive? It should be illegal. Clearly, it's messing with my head.

When I woke up this morning with his absolutely massive dick wedged between my thighs, I was in shock, but that only lasted for a split second before the desire to come all over him took over.

And now, as he tells me to take my pleasure from him, it requires even less time before I do exactly that.

I roll over to face him and swing my leg over his waist, straddling his hips.

Just gotta get back in the saddle.

I brace my hands on his chest, sucking my lower lip between my teeth as I glide over his rigid length. His quick intake of breath and the way his eyes roll back tell me everything I need to know about whether he's okay with this.

And right now? Ryder is *more* than okay.

"Touch me," I whisper on a moan as I increase the speed of my movements and roll my body over his.

"I can't," he grits out, clenching his eyes closed once again.

"If I touch you, I'm liable to do other things, and I can't think about that right now, Lola."

Understanding sends a thrill of satisfaction up my spine.

I love how unhinged I make him.

Grabbing his hands, I place them on my hips before leaning forward. My face is mere inches from his, and when those full lips open on a puff of air, it all becomes too real.

I want nothing more than to kiss him right now, but I can't. If I'm going to ride this man fully clothed until I get myself off, I can't break this boundary too. We need to have a conversation about what we both want. The sooner we do, the sooner we can get these clothes off. But right now is not that time, not when he's likely to tell me anything I want to hear.

I focus my attention on the utter magic happening between my thighs as my clit meets the head of Ryder's length with each roll of my hips.

"Oh, god," I cry, and, *finally*, he starts meeting my movements with thrusts of his own.

"Climb up here and ride my face, Lola," he pleads.

"I thought," another sweep of heat dips in my belly, "you said," another moan, "you couldn't handle *more*, right now." *I can't handle more right now.*

He releases a strangled groan, bucking up into me with renewed vigor. The thin, silky pajama bottoms I'm wearing and his boxer briefs do nothing to dull the pleasure searing through me as I come undone over top of him.

His blue eyes, framed in dark lashes, pierce me as my body ripples with pleasure.

"Fuck," he grunts. *"Lola,"* he moans, and it's the sexiest sound I've ever heard, doubly so as his hot cum coats my seam through our layers of clothing.

I should regret this, but I don't. I don't regret a single thing about Ryder Lockhart, except for ever leaving him.

"Darlin'," he says, his voice cautious as his calloused fingers dig into my hips.

I give him a reassuring smile and bend forward to plant a chaste kiss on his sharp jawline. His stubble leaves my lips raw, and I climb off his lap.

He jolts from the bed, rushing to the bathroom.

"Ry, what are you doing?"

"Getting something to clean you up," he says, the words coming out in a rush.

I chuckle. Ryder, always the gentleman. "Ry, I'm going to take a shower," I tell him, hoping to ease his mind, but instead, his eyes go wide, and he stammers on his words.

"Oh, yeah, okay. I'll go grab you a towel."

I shake my head, a grin plastered on my lips. "I meant in my *own* shower," I clarify.

He runs a hand through his disheveled, sleep-ridden brown waves and clutches the short hairs on the back of his neck, chewing on his lip. "Yeah, okay," he says, suddenly so damn shy I have to suck my cheeks in to stop myself from laughing at his expense. "That, uh, makes more sense," he says, unable to maintain eye contact any longer.

I get out of the bed and stop to squeeze his bicep. "Hey, quit freaking out. We're *married*," I tell him, trying to lighten the mood, but it has the opposite effect.

His eyes flash with need before he's able to cover the expression up with a more serene one that feels more like him. "Want anything for breakfast?" he asks, but his cheeks turn pink almost immediately, and it feels damn good to have him flustered for a change. He clears his throat. "After I shower too."

"Sure. Breakfast would be good," I say, heading to take that much-needed shower in my own room. Because truthfully, I can't stand to watch him flounder for a second more.

Chapter Forty-One

SECURITY

SUNDAY, JUNE 8

IT'S SUNDAY, which means I have slightly less work today than usual, but with everything that happened last night, I figured it would be a good idea to up security around here. Dad and I spent the morning installing a few cameras around the property, focusing them on Mayte's cabin, the main house, Lola's parents' place, and ours. I also installed new door locks, in case Lemmon had somehow gotten ahold of the old key or made herself a copy.

Hopefully, whoever broke in last night will be deterred by the new equipment, and we can put this all behind us. Though this gnawing feeling in my gut tells me even I don't believe that.

"Thanks for helping me out with this, Dad. I know we'd said you were retiring, but it's nice to have your help," I tell him, housing the last bucket of red paint for the barn into the truck bed.

"To tell you the truth, son, I've been bored out of my goddamn mind," he chuffs. "This retirement thing was fun for a month, but I'm ready to work wherever you need me. I don't necessarily want to take on the same amount of work, but I'd really like to have something to do."

Worry pings in my chest, toying with the edges of my frayed heart. "Dad," I say softly, "Rosa Ranch is still *yours* too. Nothing will ever change that, so whatever you want to take on around here, feel free. You don't need my permission, but let me know so I don't worry, all things considered."

He pats me on the back, giving my shoulder a squeeze. "We'll figure out who's behind this, Ry. You know we will," he assures me. I believe that, I really do, but what happens if we find out *too late?*

"I see the wheels churning up there," he says, shaking his head. "Stop your spiralin' and tell me where to set these boxes."

Hours pass, and with my dad's help, we've made remarkable time, though I've had a great motivator this past week. Winning a Lola Lima smile is enough to make me do just about anything to be on the receiving end of one.

The electric work has all been updated, and I managed to install a chandelier from the center rafter, stringing strands of lights outward from that, covering the whole ceiling.

Lola pushed herself too hard, finishing the last coat of paint by herself. I know she wants to do as much of the renovations herself as she can, but it shattered my entire soul seeing her legs shaking on that ladder with the energy it took to hold herself up. The last straw for me was the stream of tears she couldn't help but let fall.

Mayte picked her up under the guise of needing something in town. I hate lying to her, but I texted Mayte to come get her, knowing she wouldn't leave on her own.

Lola's too independent sometimes, and I refuse to allow that stubbornness to harm her in the long run.

After the paint dried on the far wall, Dad hung another strand of lights at the top; as soon as the paintings I had commissioned arrive next week, we'll work on getting those up too. All we'll have to do afterward is hang fliers to advertise Lola's new dance lessons.

I just hope we aren't inviting more trouble with these classes. Who knows how Lemmon will react when she realizes Lola's here to stay?

"This is gonna be good for her, Ry," Dad says, standing beside me with his hands on his hips as he takes in our handiwork.

"I think so too."

"Now"—he wipes his hands on his jean-clad thighs— "Ezekiel invited me over for hot dogs, and he said he made his own sourdough buns. Wanna join us?"

"Hot dogs?" I ask, my brows pinched in confusion. "Since when does Zeke eat hot dogs?"

Dad gives me a "no idea" look but says, "Knowing him, they're probably some vegetable concoction he put together."

"Thanks, Dad, but not tonight. I wanna get home to Lola."

"Good man," Dad says, tipping his hat at me with a suggestive wink. "Happy wife, happy life, son."

"Happy spouse, happy house, Pops."

He nods, scratching his jaw. "You know, I like that better. I'm using that from now on."

I chuckle, locking up the barn and following after him to the truck before dropping him off at Zeke's and heading home to Lola.

Lola

Chapter Forty-Two

NO SEAS COMEMIERDA

WEDNESDAY, JUNE 11

I'VE SPENT every morning sobbing at that godforsaken barn.

I *know* it'll be worth it when it's finished, to have a place that's all my own, something no one can take from me. As much as I miss Karmella and Yanet, I have no desire to go back to Texas, to leave Mayte, Isabela, Ryder, or my parents. The circumstances suck, but I think everything I've ever needed is finally falling into place.

I stretch out on Mayte's couch, my body humming with an undercurrent of pain that gets worse with each day that I overexert myself to get that barn ready for classes.

I've started to spread the word about my first class, knowing there's not a chance the studio will be completely ready by then, but having a grand opening with a few people from town might raise the rest of the money I need to perfect it.

"Are you sure it's all Lemmon? Any chance Russ might be behind some of this stuff?" Mayte asks, closing her eyes and breathing in the hot steam from her coffee mug.

I glance around *Grind*, our favorite coffee shop in town,

ensuring there aren't any prying eyes or ears in the vicinity. "The permitting situation was *all* Lemmon. Ryder spoke with Todd on Monday, who confirmed she'd tried to blackmail him into fining Ryder. When he refused and said he'd call her father for even suggesting such a thing, she clearly decided to take matters into her own hands."

"And everything else? The texts, the razor blades, and feeling like you're being watched?"

I shake my head, shrugging my shoulders. "I'm not sure." I sigh. "The text messages seem childish enough to be Russ, but I can't imagine him playing the long game. If he were in town, hours away from home, he wouldn't have just left. He'd have stayed behind and waited until we got home to make his move, whatever that may be. That, and for all that man's faults, he *loved* dogs. I can't imagine him ever hurting one."

"Lemmon probably wouldn't think twice about hurting a dog. It's totally her," Mayte grumbles, humming into her mug.

"What about her friends? You think they might be involved?"

She scoffs and dismisses the suggestion with a hand flick. "You mean Dumb and Dumber? Definitely not. They're both sweet but misguided. She probably pays them to stick around."

That *almost* makes me feel bad for her, but not quite.

Movement to our right steals my attention. Sebastian dances around the counter, lifting the glass dome off the tray of pastries and plucking a couple, placing them onto a plate. My eyes follow his movements as he sways his hips to the music from the speakers; he twirls until he's standing beside our small rainbow-painted table. He places the plate down, winking at us, and says, "On the house for my favorite ladies."

"Quit flirting with me, Sebby!" Mayte says, fanning herself with one hand as she snatches one of the flaky pastries and brings it to her lips. She takes a bite, moaning loudly. Her eyes roll back, and Sebastian swats at her arm.

"You quit that moaning, Mayte. I don't want the single

ladies in this town to get the wrong impression! I don't need that kind of pressure," he jokes, bending to press a quick kiss to her cheek before sauntering off behind the counter.

"You're the best, Seb," Mayte says, blowing him a kiss that he grabs from the air, twisting his body to press his palm to his ass, as if placing her kiss there.

We both chuckle, loving the way his lighthearted antics momentarily rid us of the tense topic we'd been discussing.

"Okay, where were we?" Mayte asks.

I glance around for good measure, knowing no one has entered the small shop in several minutes. "Maybe if we lie low, it'll all blow over, and whoever it is will go away."

Mayte rolls her eyes, taking another massive bite of her pastry. She mumbles around the flaky dough, *"No seas comemierda."*

"I'm not," I groan. "I'm being optimistic."

"All I'm saying is that you need to keep a good head on your shoulders."

The weight of her words, and the insinuations that follow them, settles like a loaf of stale bread in my gut. Like Ryder, I never loved horror movies, but I'm afraid I might be *living* one.

Chapter Forty-Three

DINNER & A SHOW

THURSDAY, JUNE 12

IT'S dark out by the time I make it home, and knowing Lola, she's probably already in bed. She's been going to sleep early after spending hours each morning poring over her work at the barn. She's been exhausted but refuses to quit, and as much as it pains me to see her struggle to get it done, I'm damn proud of her for it.

I'd dropped by the barn earlier to check on her and let her know a local cattle driver had a herd run off his property. The whole town has spent the last several hours searching for them, and now that they're all home, I can't wait to shower and crawl into bed.

The lights in the house are off, save for the one illuminating the kitchen from beneath the microwave. Lola refuses to turn it off, and I've grown to like it. It's like a comforting night light leading me straight to the pantry.

"Oh!" Lola shouts from her room, my heart racing as I take off toward her room. As I get to her door, I'm met with a sound so sexy my cock swells in my Wranglers.

"Yes, that's perfect," she moans, voice ragged. "Ry, oh god! Yes!"

I'm panting as I edge closer to the door, delighted to find it's cracked open wide enough that I catch a glimpse of Lola. She's sprawled out in bed, her head thrown back in ecstasy, one of *my* shirts pooling around her waist as she plunges a hot-pink toy inside her plump, shining cunt.

I shouldn't be out here right now, but she keeps shouting my name, and my mind is fuzzy, my dick aching for release.

I'd rather she know I'm here and send me away than not give her the choice at all, so I nudge the door open, unintentionally silencing her cries of pleasure.

"Ry?" she whispers hoarsely.

"Yes, darlin'. I'm home, and I was wondering if you needed some instruction on how to deal with this little problem you seem to be havin'." My tongue feels thick in my mouth as I watch her expression shift from fear to surprise to *lust.*

"You can look, but you can't touch, Ry," she agrees, her voice rough and sultry. "Tell me how you want me to make myself come," she whimpers, nibbling on her lower lip.

I'm hit with a wave of elation that she wants me here, that she feels comfortable being vulnerable with me. My heart swells as much as my dick does at the notion. "You're so damn beautiful, Lola," I praise, drinking in every inch of her soft, fuckable, *gorgeous* body glowing from the moonlight. "How's that toy feel?"

"Not as good as you would," she pants between gasps of pleasure, cresting closer to her peak from my presence alone.

"You're absolutely right, but we aren't going there now. Your rules, not mine. I want you to pretend it's me fucking you right now," I tell her, unbuckling my belt, the sharp sound of metal clanging through the small room.

She plunges the toy deep inside until it disappears, save for the rounded handle.

"That's right, Lols. If I were inside you, I wouldn't be able to help myself. I'd have to be *all the way inside you.*"

"Mhmm, I— Oh god, I want that," she cries out, the hand

pumping the toy in and out of her moving quicker and more erratically.

"Slow it down, baby. I'd take my time with you, burying myself in your perfect pussy like it was my one and only opportunity to make up for lost time." She slows her ministrations, pulling her lip between her teeth as she watches me unfasten my jeans, my cock springing free.

"So big," she mutters, her back arching into her hand.

"Remember how I'd stretch you out so well, darlin'? You'd milk every last drop of cum from me, wouldn't you?"

I wrap a hand around my base, tugging gently, making sure I don't finish before she does. It's a damn hard task.

"Yes! I want you in my mouth, *please*," she whines, and I almost give in, but I'm determined to keep my distance until she can tell me she wants me when she doesn't have an eight-inch silicone rod in her wet cunt.

"Uh, uh, you said no touchin'. These are your rules. Now, lift your shirt and let me see those pretty nipples."

She does as I say, and I just about die right here. I'd die a happy man, though, so I'm not complaining. *R-I-P to me.*

"Show me how you like them touched," I demand, my tone harsher than I meant it, but it's difficult to keep my voice even with how goddamn hard my cock is. I run the pad of my thumb over the head, lubricating my tip with precum.

Her desperate moans fill the room as she plucks at her nipples, twisting and tugging on them the way I plan to with my mouth as soon as she realizes *she's mine*, in every sense of the word.

"What about your clit? Do you need to touch it to get off?" I ask, delirious with need. I want her orgasm as badly as she does, and I'm three seconds from sucking on her clit myself to see to it.

"Usually, but right now, I think a warm breeze could finish me off," she groans, and I chuckle in response.

"Unless you've got a window cracked, I think I'm gonna

need to see my wife pull that vibrator out and coat her fingers in her wetness."

She does as I command, removing the vibrator with a soft *pop*, only to be separated by her delicate fingers. She removes them, now coated in her arousal, quick to replace them, plunging the vibrator deep, releasing a loud moan that tightens my balls and makes me feel like the luckiest man on the planet to be in the presence of such a magnificent woman. I wish I could suck her fingers clean and have her coming on my cock, but I can't. Not yet. *Not tonight.*

"Now, spread those pussy lips for me, Lola. I wanna see your needy clit before you come around my cock," I tell her.

She slides her fingers through her slickness once more, spreading her middle and ring fingers to splay herself open for me. "So stunning, Lola. There isn't a single part of you that isn't perfect."

"If I'm so perfect,"—she pauses only to moan, swirling her fingers around her clit as if to enunciate each word—"why won't you let me choke on your dick?"

"You know why. Now don't be a brat. I want to see what a mess you can make, darlin'."

She throws her head back, soft curls spread out around her. Her tits heave, both hands working as she plunges the vibrator deeper, her movements frantic. My hand matches her pace, the edges of my periphery blurring.

I'm struggling to take a full breath as she calls out my name, her eyes locked on me as she comes, her moans loud. It isn't long before I'm following quickly behind her.

I imagine her contracting around my hard length, my cock pulsing. Never once do my eyes leave her beautiful, writhing body. Heat rises in my throat, my neck arching as a guttural groan leaves my lips, and my dick spurts into my calloused palm.

I steady myself against her dresser, tucking my slowly deflating cock back into my jeans before heading to her bathroom for a couple of washcloths. I dampen one with warm water and take a seat beside her on her bed, feeling a lot less awkward than I had the other morning when she was writhing against me.

Lola's lying with her forearms crossed over her face, her breaths shallow, dropping her arms to her chest when she feels the dip of the mattress from my weight.

She greets me with a sated smile and rosy cheeks, and my lips twitch with the knowledge that *I'm* the one responsible for the look of contentment warming her face.

"Mind if I clean you up?" I ask, and her gaze drops to the cloths in my hand.

"Not at all." She reaches between her legs, her fingers wrapping around the silicone cock she's apparently decided to *kill* me with. My soul leaves my body at the sight of her like this, and when she pulls it from her warm, soaked pussy, I nearly melt.

"Christ, Lols. You can't do things like that without warning me," I groan.

She peers up at me, all doe-eyed and innocent. "I'm sorry. Like what, Ry?" she asks and then proceeds to bring the toy to her mouth. She swipes her tongue over her bottom lip, opens wide, and wraps them around the toy, sucking herself off it with a loud moan that has me seeing stars.

She removes it from her mouth with a *pop* and says, "You want a taste?"

Because I am a weak, *weak* man when it comes to Lola Lima, I say, "I've never wanted anything more in my life, darlin'. *Please.*"

I'm rewarded with a lopsided smirk as she dips two fingers into her dripping cunt and holds them to my mouth. "Suck."

I wrap my lips around those two digits, reaching out to hold her wrist in both my hands as I savor every last drop of her slightly sweet flavor. A burst of something so uniquely *her* hits my tastebuds, driving me absolutely mad as I lick her fingers clean, smacking a wet kiss to her palm when finished.

"Dinner was *delicious*, darlin'. Thank you for that home-cooked meal," I say, shooting her a cocky wink as I pick up the wet cloth, swiping it between her thighs and patting her dry with the other.

"Dinner and a show, Ry. What more could you want from your domestic little wife?" she teases.

I roll my eyes, pressing a kiss to her forehead before I exit her room, feeling like the first man to land on the moon, except I'm not just surrounded by stars. No, Lola is the whole damn *sun*. She lights up every dark corner of my life, and I feel so honored to spend any part of this existence with her.

Chapter Forty-Four

GAMES & STOKING FLAMES

FRIDAY, JUNE 13

OTHER THAN WHAT conspired between Ryder and me last night, things have settled down a bit. No break-ins, creepy texts, or anything amiss. I guess the new cameras have deterred whoever was behind it.

Nugget is snoring in my lap by the time Ryder gets home from finishing his fertilizer experiment for the night. I was forced to take the day to rest after waking up with a red, swollen knee that was hard to bend for the first few hours of the day.

I hear the familiar rap of his fingers on the door. We've developed a new system for entering the house after I tried to hit him over the head with a frying pan the other night when the door stuck and he needed to muscle his way inside.

Three fast, followed by three slow knocks, and then the jingle of his keys as he unlocks the door, setting my overly jumpy heart at ease. Of course, Ryder gave me an earful about how unsafe it is to stand outside that long, knocking on a door before unlocking it, when we had an intruder less than a week ago. It's good to know it's okay when *he* does it, but not okay for *me*.

A crack of lightning vibrates the walls of the cottage, startling Nugget awake as Ry lets himself in. His grin is wide. "Hey, darlin'." He tips his hat at the oversized chicken nugget in my lap. "Nugget." He hangs the hat on a hook, shaking the fat rain droplets off and kicking his boots beside the door.

"I *was* wondering if you'd want to go to the new outdoor rollerblading rink in High Crest, but now"—he points out the window to emphasize his point—"I'm not so sure that's a good idea."

I hadn't told him about my knee this morning, not wanting to worry him or be forced to go to the rheumatologist. The rain makes my joints ache, but there's not a chance I could rollerblade today.

I let out a puff of laughter, his sheer presence throwing me off tonight. Must be my period coming up. Having him home right now is making honey flow through my veins, and I'd be lying if I said I didn't love the feeling. It's warm and intoxicating, just like him.

"I guess we'll have to figure something out here," I say.

"Have anything in mind?" he asks, standing beside me and scratching behind Nugget's ears.

I beam up at him. "How about a horror film?" I joke.

He rolls his eyes, bending down and planting a loud kiss on my cheek. "Not a chance, darlin'. I'm gonna go get cleaned up; we can think of something in the meantime."

"Alright, darlin'," he says, exiting his bedroom wearing a pair of dark-gray sweatpants that hug his thick thighs and a black t-shirt that stretches over his wide shoulders. His hair hangs in loose, wet waves. He looks like a male model exiting the ocean in a cologne campaign for something like Dolce & Gabbana

Light Blue, and it's making my mouth water. "How's about we head to the main house?"

"That sounds perfect, Ry." I beam up at him, carefully maneuvering off the couch to change into a lightweight floral dress and rain galoshes. Friday night parties at the main house when it rains are a well-kept tradition at Rosa Ranch. The ranch hands join everyone for dancing, drinks, and games, knowing the next morning will require extra work thanks to the soggy landscape.

A thrill of excitement lights me up at the prospect of getting to see everyone and regaining some semblance of normalcy. Besides, it's probably best I'm not left alone with Ryder any more than necessary; I've found myself falling harder and faster for him than I ever thought possible. I love him. I never fell *out* of love with him, and that scares me most of all.

But I can't be everything Ryder deserves until I've worked through my own worries, so instead of putting that on him, I'm going to face the problem head-on and use my fancy new insurance to get scheduled with a therapist.

I meet him in the entryway, and he slides my raincoat over my arms, spinning me to face him so he can zip me up before tugging his boots and jacket on. "I already called Mayte to let her know we're heading over," he says, opening the door wide for me before he scoops Nugget into his arms and locks the door behind us.

We sprint through the rain to his truck, and despite the torrential downpour, he still runs ahead of me, tugging my door open and helping me inside.

He turns the heat on, angling the vents toward the mushy pile of fluff in my lap. Nugget peers up at me with an unbothered smile, his tongue hanging out as he pants.

Ryder takes his time, driving carefully down the dirt path to the main house, both hands remaining on the wheel the whole way. My fingertips itch to reach out and squeeze his thigh, but I hold back, knowing I shouldn't poke the beast.

When we get to the main house, it's all lit up. We park along the back, where all the ranch hands are gathered with our family, dancing and playing games under the warmly lit, glass-domed back patio.

"Ready to make a run for it?" Ryder asks me, his smile wide with a boyish charm I love to see, especially in light of all the creepy shit going on lately.

"As I'll ever be," I tell him. He reaches across my lap, his fingers lingering on my waist a beat too long after he unbuckles me. His lips and warm breath hover just above my bounding pulse point, but when he leans forward, further invading my space, it's to grab Nugget, tucking him safely beneath his jacket before righting himself and jumping out of the truck.

I push the door open and sprint out before he can get absolutely drenched being a gentleman. Meanwhile, I'm *already* drenched for him, no door holding necessary.

We run inside, shaking ourselves out like wet dogs. Ryder sets Nugget on the ground, and he goes straight to the white plastic banquet table set up at the far end of the space, the biker gang seated in their tie-dye leather jackets around a plate of pastries. *Mami* is seated with Papi next to the oldest in the group, Uno cards clutched tightly in her grip as she leans in, explaining the rules.

Nugget catapults himself into the redheaded man's lap like he's done it a hundred times before, and the man doesn't even flinch. He just picks him up, nuzzling against his head and placing a kiss between his eyes.

"Looks like your mom has found a new group of people to fool into playing Uno with her," Ryder says with a light laugh. He hangs our jackets up, wrapping a warm arm around my waist and steering us toward Mayte. She's bouncing Isabela in her arms, her head thrown back in laughter as she talks to Troy and Ben, two of the ranch hands who work most closely with the horses.

Her eyes land on me with a wide smile. *"¿Aseré, que bola?"* she asks.

"Not a whole lot has changed since I saw you at lunch," I tell her, chuckling. I pluck Isabela from her arms, holding her to my chest as I kiss Mayte's cheeks. With a smile, I turn to greet Troy and Ben, who slip away after saying hello to find their wives in the small crowd dancing in the center of the room.

"I'm glad you decided to come after all," she says.

Ryder slips past me, and my eyes follow him. "I'll just be a second, darlin'," he assures me.

"You up for games, or are you too busy eye fucking your husband?" she asks with a sly smirk.

I roll my eyes.

"Games sound good," I grumble, following her. She parks us in front of the massive wall of bookshelves leaning against the house, most containing games we've been playing since we were kids.

I take a seat, Isa nestled against my chest, staring out at the room full of people dancing. I wish I could be with them right now. This is what I get for pushing myself too far, and it terrifies me to think I might have to cancel classes at the whims of my body, even after the barn is open for business.

Ryder strides over to us, some metal-and-plastic contraption in his arms. He plunks it down on the floor, pushing it open until each leg snaps in place. He reaches for Isabela, settling her into the pink pack n' play covered in white bunnies between me and Mayte.

"All set," he announces.

"You and Lola having a kid I don't know about? Why do your parents have a pack n' play?"

"I figured if Isabela was going to come over more often, we better have a good place for her to nap and hang out with us, so I got one for each of our houses. I don't want her dunking

Nugget's toys in his water bowl for entertainment anymore," Ryder explains.

Mayte's eyes snap to his, and she tilts her head. "You let my kid play in your dog's water bowl?" she asks, her voice indignant, but she breaks into a laugh that settles Ryder's tense shoulders. "That kid, I swear. She's on something. I'm gonna need to get her an *azabache* bracelet to ward off the bad energy. Haven't been able to find one."

"That's no surprise considering we're in *Oklahoma*. Not exactly a lot of Latine-owned businesses around." Just another reason I'm worried my classes won't fill up. "We should see if Joanna can ship us some *agua de Florida* though."

"For sure. I've got some you can use in the meantime; you could use a good cleansing," she agrees, pursing her lips. She reaches beside her to grab the wooden box of Dominoes from the shelf, setting it on the table and cracking her knuckles before sliding the panel off the top.

"You remember how to play *Domino*, right?" she asks Ry, and he sighs heavily.

"Yes, and I also remember that you two are ruthless and have kicked my ass since we were kids. After this, we're playing something else. *My* pick," he says, but the words sound almost pleading.

I pat his shoulder. "Okay, Ry. Whatever you need, but we're playing to one hundred," I tease, and he slumps into the chair beside me. His bouncing thigh rubs against mine, and I place a steadying hand on his. His eyes flicker to me, and the anxious movement stops.

The game leads to tons of trash talk from Mayte, and, for once, Ryder is kicking her ass.

Ryder's proud grin sends fireworks shooting off in my chest. He's adorable when he finally wins at something. "Oh, was that your last play? Too bad."

I swoon dramatically, grabbing his forearm and leaning my

weight against him. "Ry, I never thought I'd say this, but you're my hero."

Mayte throws a chip at me. "Traitor."

Ryder leans back in his seat, crossing his arms over his chest. "Alright, enough whining. It's Lola's turn. Let's see what my wife can do with the mess I made."

I straighten in my seat, looking down at the last of my tiles as I chew on my lip. I've got nothing good, that's for sure. I place a tile, one I know won't help me win a damn thing.

Mayte's eyes glitter under the warm kitchen lighting. She slow claps. "Truly an inspiration."

She sets her next tile down.

"Yeah, an inspiration for *me*. Both of you are, really," Ryder says, winking at me and effectively soothing some of the sting from my impending loss. He slaps down his final tile and whisper-shouts, "*Domino*, baby!" He tosses his hands up and smacks his lips together, shooting a kiss across the table at Mayte, who's fuming.

"What?!" she asks, infuriated.

"That's right, ladies. I'm the new champion," Ry says, slinging an arm over my shoulder and leaning in to whisper in my ear. "What's my prize, darlin'?"

I swat at his chest, rolling my eyes. "Your pick, Ry. What are we playing next?"

He grabs a small black box from the top of the bookshelf, setting it on the table as Mayte finishes putting the game away.

"The voting game. I'm not sure there's actually a winner with this because I've never played it, but I picked it up a while back and figure we can all learn together."

He unwraps the clear plastic from the box and tosses it in the trash by the back door, lingering by Ezekiel where he's leaning over the small bar, thick-framed glasses sliding down the straight bridge of his nose, a book in hand.

"Hey, Zeke. You wanna join?" Ryder asks. He peers up

from the book, glancing over to us, but he quickly returns his gaze to Ryder, shaking his head before refocusing on the book.

"Okay, so it sounds like we have a stack of cards with questions that sit in the middle. We each have numbered cards. Lola is number one, Mayte is two, and I'll be three. We pick a card from the center, read it aloud, and everyone turns in a card with the corresponding person's number. We're voting for who is most likely to do whatever's on the card. Does that make sense?"

Mayte's shoulders shake with a chuckle. "Leave it to Ryder to pick a get-to-know-you game where no one wins."

I can't argue with that. It certainly is a very Ryder thing to do.

"Also true," he says. "How about we also assign card numbers to people who aren't playing so we can include them in the vote?"

"Hmm, sounds interesting, but why don't we just invite other people to play?" Mayte asks, pushing out of her seat, not waiting for a reply. She saunters over to the table where *Mami*, Bee, and the biker guys are all seated, returning with them in tow a moment later.

"I don't know anything about those guys. How am I supposed to guess?" I whisper to Ryder.

"Levi is the oldest of the group. He's the leader and stand-in father, and Teddy's the youngest, really easy going. Just go with your gut," he tells me.

"Nice to see you again, Miss Lola," Levi says, smiling warmly at me as he takes the seat across from me.

Everyone drags chairs over, and Ryder starts scribbling names on a sheet with the corresponding numbers so we don't get lost.

1. Lola

2. Mayte

3. Ryder
4. Ezekiel
5. Bee
6. Bexaida
7. Levi
8. Teddy

"Why'd you include Zeke?" I ask.

Ryder chuckles. "He never joins us for anything, so I figure this is the only way we might get the chance to change that."

I roll my eyes at him, and Mayte explains the rules to everyone based on what she's read on the back of the box. She picks up the first card and reads it for us. "Who gives the most awkward hugs?"

My shoulders shake as I put down a four. We flip them over, revealing seven fours. "It's not his fault," Mayte whines. "He's an awkward man. Very cute, but *so* awkward and grumpy."

Bee snorts at this assessment but makes no move to come to her youngest son's aid.

"As his brother, I agree. The man is adorable, like an angry grizzly bear squeezing a cute plushy version of himself. His attitude only got worse when he returned from his last deployment."

"I wish he'd join us for once. It always feels like we unintentionally leave him out of things," I say, my shoulders deflating.

"I invite him to everything, Lols. He keeps to himself, is all. Maybe another time. I keep trying because he's my little brother, but it's hard when it feels like he doesn't put any effort in himself."

"I'm sorry, Ry. It's just hard to believe things are still so tense between you two."

He shrugs. "They're not. He's been like this since high school. I think he never grew out of the brooding teenager phase," he says with a chuckle, attempting to lighten the mood.

Levi and Teddy keep their gazes cast downward, not wanting to get in the middle of this conversation.

"Orrr maybe it's because you married his childhood crush?" Mayte interjects, making our heads snap to her.

"Excuse me, what?" I ask in shock.

Mami and Bee ask the same, our voices melting together.

"When Ezekiel was a freshman in high school, there were more than a few times I caught him and Lemmon getting frisky on the ranch, but as soon as she got her sights set on Ryder, she dropped that boy like a hot potato." She says it like it isn't news to anyone, nonchalant and totally relaxed as she leans back in her chair.

"How on Earth have you never thought to share that with anyone?" Ryder asks, dumbfounded. His jaw is practically hanging on the floor.

"It wasn't my business to share." She shrugs.

Mami smacks Mayte over the back of the head, shouting, "*¡No mames!*"

Mayte rubs her hand over the spot while she pouts. "That wasn't very nice, *Tia*," she grumbles.

"I don't know if you've *met* you, but you didn't get the nickname '*lengua suelta*' for no reason," I chide.

She rolls her eyes dramatically. "When I drop the good *chisme*, it's usually by accident. How am I supposed to know what everyone already knows and doesn't around here?"

"Well, that would certainly explain why he's so closed off," Ryder groans beside me.

Mayte waves a hand around. "No. Your brother is the broody type. He wouldn't have been happy with Lemmon anyway. It was probably just the thrill of an older woman. Anyway, *moving on.*"

How can she be serious right now? She dropped a massive bomb on us and acts like it's nothing, but for Ryder's sake, I let it go and read the next card.

Who's most likely to marry someone who isn't born yet?

I scrunch my brows, unsure of what to do with this one since Isabela isn't an option. I decide to put Mayte down, and when we flip them over, there are several for Mayte.

"You voted for yourself on this one, didn't you?" Bee asks with a knowing smirk.

"Hey now, it never specified which marriage this would be. I could get a divorce from the husband I don't currently have and then wind up a cougar and marry someone thirty-four years younger than me. I'm already a MILF; what's stopping me from being a GILF too?"

"What the hell is a GILF?" Ryder asks, scrubbing a hand over his jaw.

"Grandma I'd like to fuck, obviously. *Dios mío*, how old *are* you?" *Mami* asks.

"You know what? I like the confidence," he says, nodding his approval as he picks up the next card.

Who has the most awkward middle school yearbook picture?

My eyes widen. I push out of the chair and run to the bookshelves, standing on my tiptoes to reach for the highest shelf housing our old yearbooks.

I find the year I'm looking for and pluck it down, taking a seat and searching through the list of *L*s. Ryder's picture is right next to mine, just like it was every year until he gradu-ated. The school system here is small, so we didn't have a ton of students. Everyone knew everyone, and the yearbook was in alphabetical order, not split between grades.

I pick up a card and set it in the middle of the table with theirs. "I've brought proof in case anyone tries to disagree with me."

Mayte rolls her eyes, flipping the cards over. Four for me and only one for Ryder.

"I feel like I'm at a severe disadvantage here," Teddy says, running a hand over the back of his neck.

"Then it's a good thing Ryder picked a game where no one wins," Mayte says, crossing her arms over her chest.

"Yeah, yeah, yeah. It's time for me to defend my honor," I announce. "I knew neither of you would remember this picture; you've spent entirely too much time ragging on me for my sixth-grade photo, but *this* is truly the stuff of nightmares." I lay the book down in the center of the table, and Mayte leans over it, studying the pictures.

"Oh, Ry," she clucks, shaking her head slowly. She takes one of the ones off the table and replaces it with a three. "It's a good thing you've grown out of this," she whispers to him, sitting up.

"Jesus, Ry. You had a bowl cut?" Levi asks in feigned horror.

I absolutely lose it, a cackle ripping through my chest. "It was so bad, Ry," I whine, tears pooling in my eyes.

"Oh, god, it was," he says. "I'm sorry for every time I made fun of you the year it rained before photos and your hair was three times bigger than your head."

"Apology accepted," I say, and he kisses my cheek, sparks tickling my skin.

His eyes roam the page and land on Lemmon. His shoulders start to shake, and he bites that full bottom lip. "The devil horns and red eyes were a good touch, Lols," he chuckles, squeezing me to his side.

The first several questions are easy enough. They're funny and lighthearted, but the further we get into the stack, the more I think Ryder is starting to realize what a bad idea this game might have been.

Chapter Forty-Five

IS IT HOT IN HERE?

FRIDAY, JUNE 13

I HAVE NEVER LOVED Isabela more.

If not for her crying, our moms would still be seated here, and I'd have just about died. Levi and Teddy left shortly after with their usual crew when the rain let up, leaving Lola, Mayte, and me to dive into the hard stuff.

Who regularly dreams about someone else in the room?

Well, shit.

I pick a number three, lying it face down on the table. Lola flips all three cards over, and her eyes lock on mine, stealing the breath from my lungs. When she releases her gaze, I gulp at the air.

It's wild what one look from Lola Lima can do to a man. To *me*.

"So, Ry, what have you been dreaming about? Is it me?" Mayte asks, batting her lashes to stifle some of the tension building in the room.

The night winds down, only a few stragglers remaining. My dad's friends all sit around the table, playing poker and smoking cigars with him and José.

The room feels smaller without the cacophony of voices

and laughter. While love in this family can be loud at times, the quiet makes every unspoken word louder.

"I can't say it's you I've been dreaming about. Sorry to disappoint." I run my foot up Lola's shin, and she squirms in her seat.

Which player would make the best adult video with the players on either side of them?

I fan myself, blowing out a choked breath, suddenly overheated.

"Well, looks like we can't answer this one," I say, raising my brows and preparing to move to the next card.

Lola sets her hand on mine, stopping me. "Come on, Ry, don't be a cheater. Let's pick two or three numbers each," she says.

I don't miss the warning look Mayte shoots across the table at Lola. I gulp, picking the only answer that'll ever make sense to me and setting the one and three down on the table.

Lola sets her two down, and of course, Mayte, the troublemaker, sets her *three* down.

"Alright, what've we got here?" I ask, flipping the sets over.

Warmth spreads in my gut, and I feel my balls tighten. Lola has a three and a one. *Me and her.*

When I look at Mayte's cards, they're not at all what I'm expecting. She shrugs. "What? I'm a year postpartum. No one wants to see this body on camera."

Lola kicks her under the table, scowling at her. "*Deja la bobería, que tú eres una dura.* Don't talk about yourself like that. That body you're so mean to safely carried my niece for thirty-two grueling weeks and brought her into this world, despite all odds. So don't you dare talk down about it again." This is so contrary to the brave face she puts on, joking about being a MILF and all.

It breaks my heart that Mayte thinks so poorly of the way she looks. The woman is beautiful, always has been. There aren't two women in the world who could shine a candle to Lola and Mayte. My wife and sister, for all intents and purposes, are stunning, and everyone knows it.

Mayte waves Lola off, but I see the tears pricking the edges of her eyes. "Whatever. You with Ryder and Zeke would still be way hotter," she says, her words sounding watery and choked up.

I gag. "Absolutely not. That's disgusting," I say, pretending to vomit into my fist.

Lola pats me on the back, picking up another card.

Who has a secret crush on someone in the room?

"I'm not sure it's a secret. You might be *fake* married, but you're *real* turned on by each other," Mayte deadpans, and heat creeps up my neck, threatening to strangle me.

I cough. "Next question."

Who would be most willing to kiss the person to their right?

We look around the table, and I smack down a three.

When I turn the cards over, they're straight threes.

I wink at Lola, seated on my right, and a rosy blush flashes on her cheeks. She leans across the table, grabbing another card.

Who has seen the most players in this room naked?

My eyes go wide, and I toss down a six. We turn them over, revealing a mix of two sixes and a five.

"*Tia* and Mama Bee did get an eyeful when we were kids," Mayte says with a chuckle, placing another card in the center.

Who isn't wearing underwear right now? Prove it.

My eyes grow wide, and I scratch the back of my neck.

We each glance at one another. Lola nibbles her bottom lip, and I have the urge to pluck it out and suck on it for her.

Woah, calm down, big guy.

I set my card down, selfishly hoping I'm right. Mayte turns the cards over, and a wide grin curves her lips. She nods her chin at Lola and says, "Go on, hot stuff. Show us what you're workin' with."

Lola rolls her eyes, standing. My lungs squeeze in my chest as her chair scrapes across the floor. Nugget jumps from his place on the floor, barking incessantly at the sudden break in silence. *Saved by the bell, or the puppy, rather.*

"I think that's my cue to get out of here. I should probably get Isabela to bed anyway," Mayte says.

I drop Lola and Nugget off at the house first, passing it on the way to Mayte's, walking Lola in, despite knowing she can take care of herself. "I'll be right back, Lola. Don't answer the door, okay? I've got my keys. I'll knock and let myself in," I tell her with a pointed stare.

I'd never be able to live with myself if something bad ever happened to her.

"I'll be fine, Ry. See you soon," she says.

I nod, stepping out onto the porch, but I poke my head in one last time.

Lola holds my eyes, unspoken words traveling between us. Her lips tilt, and as she turns, she lifts the skirt of her dress over her *bare* ass. "See you soon, Ry," she says, shooting a wink over her shoulder and dropping the dress in place, sauntering out of the living room. My tongue sticks to the roof of my mouth as I gape at her, unable to move yet.

"Everything okay?" Mayte calls out to me from the open truck door. I turn, shutting the door behind me, and jog over to her.

"Yeah, yeah, everything's fine."

Lola

Chapter Forty-Six
PHOTO ATTACHED

FRIDAY, JUNE 13

TONIGHT HAS BEEN SO *GOOD.*

It was the perfect reminder of why I loved growing up here so much, the community we've built, and the amazing people and all their wonderful personalities that make Hidden Valley *home.*

By the time Ryder makes it back from dropping off Mayte, I'm riding on a high despite my earlier worries about my knee.

Ryder knocks three times fast, followed by three times slow, turning the key in the door and letting himself in. He's scowling when he enters the room, locking the door behind him.

"Did you unlock the door for me?" he asks, and I shake my head.

"No. Maybe you left it unlocked?" I ask, a cold chill making its way over my skin at the insinuation that if he hadn't, we have bigger problems.

I rub my hands up my arms on instinct, and he takes a seat beside me, cupping my face in his hands. "Lola," he says, his words so small they shatter my heart. "I'm so sorry, baby. I was distracted, and that's not an excuse, but—"

I grip his cheeks, stopping his word vomit. "Ry, it's okay," I say, emphasizing the last word. His hands start to tremble, and his breaths come in short, fast bursts. "Nothing happened. No one is in here. I'm fine. *I'm safe.*"

I hope.

He clenches his eyes shut, blowing out a long, sweet breath that tickles my lips. Pressing his forehead to mine, he winds his arms around me and holds me close to his chest.

"I don't want to live in a world without you in it, darlin'. And if I were responsible–"

"Stop. Nothing has happened, and nothing *will* happen," I tell him, keeping my voice as low as possible, despite the very real fear gripping me by the throat. But that fear isn't for myself. It's for Ryder's sanity and his shaking body in my arms.

We hold each other like this until his breaths have leveled out and he's no longer trembling against me.

He runs a hand over my hair, smoothing it out of my face. "Mayte was right, Lols," he whispers. "I do love you."

I close my eyes, taking a steady breath. My heart continues to hammer against my ribs, but I somehow manage to speak. "I know, Ry. And I love you too."

He pulls back, peering into my eyes, and those blue orbs of his glitter with so much hope. It kills me to crush those dreams, not only because they reflect my own, but because hurting Ryder is the last thing I'll ever want. "*That* I'm sure of. What I'm not certain of is if I'm ready to offer you everything you deserve."

His shoulders slump, and the brightness in his eyes dims. "You are all I've ever wanted, and having you home has made me happier than I can describe. But I also know you just left a man who never treated you how you deserved, and I don't want you to feel like you're running into the arms of another person. So, I'll wait for your brain to catch up with your heart, okay?"

I swallow, willing the tears stinging my eyes to dry up. Ryder Lockhart has been the man of my dreams my entire life, and I'm officially deciding not to let fear get in the way of that. "Be gentle with me, Ry. I'm yours," I whisper. "I always have been, but I need to take things slow. There's just so much uncertainty, and our lives have changed so quickly, I'm just a little overwhelmed."

He tucks a loose curl behind my ear, rubbing the tip of his nose up the length of mine. "I love you, Lola Lima. We can take things at whatever pace you need."

I feel my shoulders pull as my upper body slackens, releasing the tension that had gathered there. My nasal passages feel like they're tingling from the deep, contented pulls of my breath, and it's this moment I realize everything really *will* be okay—because there's no other way.

Time passes slowly, but somehow, over the last hour we've been watching this snooze-worthy rom-com, I've slid down Ryder's lap, landing like a puddle between his legs.

"We should head to bed," I say, stretching my arms over my head as I yawn.

Nugget's yawn matches mine from the chair he's lying on beside the fireplace, the TV mounted above it.

Ryder sits up, setting his hands on my hips, his eyes a silent plea. My brows pinch, unsure of what— "Oh."

His thick length presses against me, and if I rock against him, he'll— "Lola," he whines, moaning loudly, desperately.

Heat worms its way through my body, and I sit up, unintentionally straddling his lap. I plant my hands on his shoulders, hovering my lips above his ear, ignoring the ache in my knee.

I know we'd said we'd take it slow, but my body is so familiar with this man, I'm not sure *how* slow I really want it.

And after what we'd done last night, a little taste won't hurt, right?

The fire building in my core is responsible for the next

words I breathe. "Your wife still doesn't have any panties on… in case you're hungry."

A growl rips from his chest, and suddenly, I'm on my back, Ryder between my legs. He grips my ankle, bringing it up to his mouth, planting a kiss on the inside. "I'm fucking *starving*."

"I thought so," I say with a smirk.

He continues traveling up my calf, planting kisses every couple of inches, and when he's traveled so high that he can see between my legs, his pupils visibly dilate, blowing out the baby blue of his irises. He releases a strangled groan that vibrates straight through me.

"Enjoying the view, Ry?" I ask, panting as I run my hands up his chiseled abdomen.

"You know I am, darlin'." He lowers himself further, pushing my thighs apart to accommodate his wide shoulders, but before he can settle between them, the thick silence in the room is shattered.

His phone rings and rings as he scrambles to grab it, and his brows climb his forehead. "Blocked number," he says, answering the call and putting it on speaker. "Hello?"

Creepy clown music fills the small room, and Nugget jumps from his seat, sprinting to the window by the door, barking at whatever—*or whoever*—is lurking behind it.

My vision turns blurry as I suck in ragged breaths, trying to remain calm when I feel anything but.

Ryder hurries to end the call, and as he does, my phone goes off with a text.

1 ATTACHMENT LOADING

A photo of us, moments ago, his face between my legs, stares back at us on the screen.

"Oh my god," I whisper, clutching a hand to my chest.

"This ends *now*," Ryder declares, standing and grabbing the baseball bat.

"Ry, wait!" He spins to face me, and his pale expression

gives me pause. "Whoever it is probably *wants* you to go outside. Please, sit down. We need to call our families to warn them and check the cameras."

He sucks in a breath, setting the bat down between us, and starts sifting through the footage on his phone.

I work on making the calls, warning everyone on the property.

MY WIFEY FOR LIFEY

The cops better get her before I do. I'm tired of this shit.

Please stay safe.

1 ATTACHMENT LOADING

A few seconds pass before the photo loads, shocking me into near silence as I stare down at a photo of Mayte holding a gun.

When the hell did you get a GUN?! You were in the fucking Peace Corps for two years after I went away for college!

I have a kid now, Lols. I have a safe for it, and Isabela will never get her hands on it...but this creepy shit is ramping up, and I'm not taking my chances. I refuse to wind up in the headlines or on the cover of a true crime podcast. I listen to them, but I don't want to live it!

My heart sinks in my chest. It's my fault we're in this mess in the first place. If I'd never come back, these people I *love* would all be safe.

Ryder finally stops his pacing and slumps into the seat beside me, the couch sagging under his weight.

"The cameras are no help. Whoever's responsible for this must've hacked into the cameras through the Wi-Fi because the footage stops just before we received the text messages and restarts shortly after." He rubs at the spot between his brows and meets my eyes. "I'm sorry, Lols. I don't know what to do at this point, but we'll come up with something."

"Let's head to bed, I guess. Whoever it is, they're probably gone now. No use staying up all night worrying about it."

He stands, taking my hand to pull me up with him. "Stay with me tonight?"

I reach up on my tiptoes, pressing a kiss to his cheek. "I'll stay with you forever, Ry." I can't take back the words or make myself regret them once they're out, but I can add this to the list of things my therapist and I should work on: not jumping into things just to soothe him.

He rubs his thumb over the top of my cheekbone, drawing my face to his. "Where you belong, darlin'," he says, dipping his head and planting a need-filled, bruising kiss to my lips that leaves me panting when he finally pulls away.

This night has certainly taken a turn.

Chapter Forty-Seven

RESTING IN FOREVER

FRIDAY, JUNE 13

"LOLA, what are you doing right now, darlin'?" I ask, humor lacing my words for the first time in the last hour.

She doesn't answer me as she gets on her knees, crawling on the floor, and reaches under the wooden frame to the center of the bed with the bowl of water.

I take my glasses off, set them on the nightstand, and close my book, sitting up to get a better look at her. She's got her ass in the air, now covered with her tiny, silky night shorts, as she shoves the bowl further under the bed. She presses the tip of her tongue to her teeth, groaning, and when she's satisfied, she sits back on her shins, slapping her hands on her thighs. "All better," she says, reaching a hand out for me to pull her up. I tug her into my lap, swinging her legs over the side of the bed so she's resting on my thighs.

"What's better? Do we have a cat hiding under the bed who needs a bowl of water or something?"

"No," she says, indignant, as if *I'm* the one who's being ridiculous. "The water is to ward off negative energy. Don't worry, I'll take care of changing it each day."

Okay, turns out I *was* being ridiculous. I should've known

better. I've been surrounded by Cuban culture my entire life, and I'm thankful for that. It's given me a unique perspective into the lives of people so different from where I've grown up, and I couldn't be more grateful for it. I might not always understand why Mayte or Bexaida do the things they do, but I'm glad they do them.

It's that insight that tells me I should nod my head and accept her answer for what it is. So that's exactly what I do.

"Ready to go to sleep?" I ask, pressing a kiss to her temple.

"I'm not sure I'll ever sleep again after what happened tonight," she groans. "But I'll try."

I roll her off me, setting her on her preferred side of what I'd like to start calling *our* bed. I keep all the lights on in the house, lock our bedroom door, and double-check the closet, bathroom, shower, and windows. Nugget gets into his bed in the closet, where he apparently prefers to stay, and I flip off the lights before climbing into bed beside Lola.

She rolls on top of me, weighing me down with comfortable ease, as if this is how we sleep every night. And I hope it is, for the rest of *forever*.

"Goodnight, darlin'."

"Goodnight, Ry," she whispers, pressing a warm kiss to the side of my neck that makes my insides turn to goo.

Chapter Forty-Eight

ENERGÍA PESADA

SATURDAY, JUNE 14

SWEAT DRIPS FROM MY BROW, stinging my eyes as I swipe it away, but the discomfort is just a blip on my radar compared to the all-consuming, excruciating pain radiating through my joints.

I have six days to get this place ready.

Six days to prove to myself and this town I still belong here, that I can do this. That I can make my dreams here a reality.

When we picked the date for the soft opening, it felt like I had forever to get everything done, but now that it's rapidly approaching, that is so far from the case.

My paint-covered hands hang loosely at my sides, my muscles quaking with fatigue as I stare up at the outside of the barn, red drips drying in an unruly disarray down the side.

I squint up at the massive structure, the sun's rays burning my retinas.

It looks better. The inside is nearly complete, and Ryder and Harlan are planning to hang the mirrors tomorrow, but am *I* ready? Can I truly teach like this, with my body threatening to fall apart around me? Is it worth it?

My shoulders sag, chest heaving as I drag in a pained breath, sliding to the grass beneath me, roots thick and painful against my sensitive skin.

I've never wanted anything more than to dance, to teach others about what makes each style so uniquely beautiful and magical, but maybe Russ and his family were right. Maybe I need to accept this dream was just a childish endeavor, never meant to be a career.

My phone vibrates in my back pocket, startling me enough to distract me from my downward spiral, even if just momentarily.

I answer it, bringing the speaker to my ear. "Where are you? Bee and *Titi* are gonna watch Isabela for a couple of hours while we go into town."

"Hello to you too, dearest," I snark back. "I'm at the barn, same as I have been every afternoon at this time."

"I don't know what crawled up your ass and died, but you better get it out before I get there. You've got approximately seven minutes," Mayte says before hanging up without enough time for me to apologize.

I don't wait for her to get here, opting to call her back immediately. "When someone hangs up on you, it usually means they're annoyed with you and need a minute," she grunts.

"I know, and I'm sorry. I shouldn't have snapped at you. I'm exhausted and in pain. It's not an excuse, but it's all I've got," I tell her.

"I'm here. You can apologize properly by buying me a pastry on our way into town," she says at the same time I hear the roar of her Jeep as she pulls up the side of the wildflower-covered hill. "Get in, loser!" she shouts through her rolled-down window, a wide grin plastered across her face that makes me feel about a million times better.

We spend the rest of the afternoon eating baked goods and gathering supplies for the cleansing rituals *Mami* and *Tía* Maria taught us as teens. It's no small feat, seeing as Latine-owned businesses are few and far between out here, but we make do with raiding *Mami's* cabinets.

If there's anything my little pity party taught me this afternoon, it's that something can only tear me down if I let it. I refuse to let the shadow of my ex make me feel bad about myself. I'm determined to cleanse my body, mind, soul, and home of all this *energía pesada*.

Mayte parks her lime-green Jeep beside the large chicken coop. "How many eggs do we need?"

"The egg *limpia* just requires one egg per person we're cleansing, but we should try to get a few extra in case we break any before we're supposed to."

"Got it," I say, unlatching the tiny metal lock on the coop. "Hello, ladies," I say, speaking directly to the hens.

They squawk and flap their wings, feathers flying all around us as they leave their perches. I tiptoe around their water and food, careful not to step in too much poop and find myself at the end of the row. Mayte and I look in each nesting box, coming up almost empty.

My shoulders sag as I grab just one from the second-to-last box. "Only one," I say, pouting.

Mayte leans over the last box, squinting to see inside. It's dark since it's a corner box, so I turn on my phone flashlight and shine in it. She screams, jumping a foot in the air, and runs straight out of the coop. "What the hell, Mayte!" I yell at her, turning my attention to the box.

A brown-and-tan rat snake lies inside, coiled around the eggs. Its little tongue flickers at me, and I'm out of there before you can say *pinga*.

I suck in a breath, holding the single egg, and close the latch on the hutch. "I don't know that snake's name, but whoever the hell she is, she can keep them. Those are her eggs now."

"Sure are," Mayte agrees. "You keep that one though. You

need it more than anyone," she tells me as we walk to her Jeep. I'm careful not to squash the egg as she drives me home, dropping me off in front of the cottage.

Ryder meets me on the steps, pressing a kiss to my forehead. He holds the door open for me as I pass through. "You find everything?"

"Yeah, but there's a snake in the chicken coop. It's just a rat snake, but it's holding my eggs hostage," I tell him.

"I'm sorry, darlin'. That's the ecosystem at work. If I wasn't sure she'd come right back, I'd remove her for you, but I think grabbing some eggs from the store tomorrow might be a better idea."

"That's okay," I say, waving him off. "How's the fertilizer coming along?" I ask. He's been working overtime on his experiments the last several nights, and the last I heard, he just needed confirmation from a few more farmers that they'd utilize his fertilizer exclusively on some crops so he could confirm the efficacy.

He beams at me, uncontrolled excitement bursting through him in a way that revitalizes some of my energy. "It's going amazing, Lols. I've had nothing but success with this batch, and the labs I've sent samples to have finished their tests. They've confirmed that the ingredients aren't harmful to plants, animals, or waterways in the current concentrations, so I'm all set to drop them off to the farmers in this area."

God, I love it when he gets all nerdy. "Oh my gosh, Ry! That's incredible!" I shout, slamming my body into his, unable to contain the excitement and pride flowing through me. My arms wind around his neck, and he tugs on my thighs, wrapping my legs around his waist, nuzzling his face into my neck.

"Everything Lemmon told me I couldn't do, couldn't have, all the dreams she tried to crush, they're right here at the tips of my fingers, Lols. I can feel it," he whispers, and my heart aches for a past version of him who believed her cruel words.

"You're amazing," I tell him. "You will have everything you

want in this life and more," I say, returning the words he'd given me not long ago.

He squeezes me tightly, dropping his forehead to my shoulder. "I hate to leave you, but I already promised I'd drop the fertilizer off. I shouldn't be more than a couple of hours."

I release him as his hands guide me gently to the ground. "Go! It's okay. I've got to cleanse this house and get rid of all the bad energy that's been following me. When you get home, we can do something to celebrate."

"Can we go for a ride?" he asks, and even though I know my body aches and I've overdone it today, I can't say no to that face.

"Absolutely, Ry. Drive safe, and I'll see you soon."

Ryder scratches Nugget behind the ears before gripping my chin to turn my face to him. He presses a kiss to my cheek and heads off toward his truck. "Lock the door, Lols!" he shouts.

I roll my eyes at him. *Of course* I'm going to lock the door after what happened last night. I don't care if it's only three in the afternoon and the sun's still up. Whoever's behind this, and I'm almost certain it's Lemmon, probably doesn't care what time of day it is.

By the time I've finished changing the water under our bed and mopping the floors with *agua de Florida*, it's nearly time for Ryder to return, and I still have the egg *limpia* to do. My hands cramp as I wrangle the mop bucket to the front porch, dumping the contents out into the grass.

I use the hose by the door, rinsing the bucket and turning it upside down to dry before going inside.

"One last thing, and then I can take a much-needed shower." I head to the kitchen and get a cup of water together, setting it beside the egg. I take a deep breath, winding the egg around me like wrapping lights on a Christmas tree, careful to start from my head and not my feet. My knuckles ache as I hold the egg, passing it from one hand to the next.

I feel like I've missed some steps, but I can't remember everything Mayte told me to do as I wind it around my back. My hands tremble, and tears stream down my cheeks, blocking my vision. This shouldn't be so *hard*.

The egg slips, crashing to the floor with my spirits. I grab the cup, falling to my knees, the hard crack of the tiled kitchen floor against my kneecaps only making the tears come faster. I scoop the slimy contents up, trying to salvage it as I get it into the cup of water.

My hands are sticky, my knees are on fire, and hair clings to my sweaty forehead. Hanging my head, I deflate. *This is all wrong.*

I barely hear the knocks at the door between my angry cries. Ryder runs into the kitchen, dropping to the ground beside me. "Lola, baby, what's wrong?" he asks, cupping my cheeks in his calloused hands.

"I dropped the egg," I cry, hearing how unbelievably stupid that must sound to him. He looks around us, taking in the full scene for the first time since running in here.

"It's okay, darlin'. I'll get some rags and clean it up. It's not a big deal, baby," he says, his voice calm and soothing. He brushes my hair off my face, and my sanity seems to burn to dust with those periwinkle eyes.

"It's not about the mess, Ry." I shake my head, not having the energy to explain why I'm so upset, but I try. For him, I do my best to explain. "The egg is supposed to act like a vessel for the bad energy. When the body has been cleansed, it should tell me what's been lurking around us, but I broke it before I could finish, and I'm not sure if I even did it right. It's been so many years since I've practiced any kind of cleansing ritual."

"I'm sorry, baby. Just tell me how to fix this, and I will."

I shake my head, pushing off the ground and wincing as I stand. "It's alright. I'll just tell Mayte what happened later. It's better that she help me do it anyway."

"Wash your hands off, and I'll go run you a bath. I'll be right back," he says, turning to leave the kitchen.

"No, I-I don't want to be in this house right now. I think… Can we go for that ride after I get this cleaned up?" Today was supposed to be a good day, but every time something great happens, it's followed by something awful. I refuse to let this keep us from celebrating his accomplishments.

He gives me a small smile with pain hidden behind it, buried deep in the endless expanse of those ocean eyes. "Whatever you want, darlin'."

I wash my hands and press a cool towel to my puffy eyes, glad I have my first therapy appointment Monday to deal with some of these emotions. Ryder cleans up the mess I made and gives me a few minutes to get changed while he drops Nugget off with Bee and Harlan. When he returns, he drops to his knees in front of me, grabbing my left boot and helping me get it on before doing the same with the right.

My joints ache, and as simple a task as putting my shoes on might seem, it's a daunting one when my RA flares like this. Struggling to get a shoe on would have absolutely pushed me over the edge, back into crying territory, and I'm endlessly appreciative of him.

We drive to the stables and get the horses ready. When they're saddled up, Ryder positions his hands on my hips, hoisting me up, not leaving my side until I'm stable on Penny's back.

Penny and Asier walk leisurely beside each other, keeping a steady pace so I don't have to work too hard to hold her reins. A cool breeze blows against my skin, my curls flying around my shoulders as it passes. Crickets and frogs chirp and ribbit as the sun sets and the moon finishes her ascent.

"It's beautiful, isn't it?" I whisper, my voice thin.

"Absolutely," Ryder agrees, his hushed, gravelly tone scraping along my arms like sharp edges of rock, littering my skin in goosebumps.

I twist to find him staring at me, not the giant, glowing moon in the purple-hued sky.

My chest heats, cheeks flushing as we continue down the path to the hill we were married on.

We continue in a comfortable silence, and when he breaks it, his words grate on my nerves.

"I'm thinking about hiring security for the ranch," Ryder says, breaking the easy silence.

"For the whole ranch or just for us? Because I don't want any special treatment, Ry," I tell him.

"Lola, whether it's Russ or Lemmon, they want to scare or maybe even hurt *you*, not anyone else from the looks of it, so yes, I want security for *you*."

I huff in frustration, giving myself whiplash with my sudden mood swings today. "Fine. Where exactly are you planning to find this security guard, huh? Someone off Craigslist who could be working for Lemmon and we'd never know it?"

He sighs loudly, hanging his head as he steers Asier back toward the stables. "I haven't gotten that far, darlin'. I wanted to run it by you first. If you're against it, we can nix the idea for now, but if things keep happening, we're going to have to explore our options."

"If they keep happening, we can pick someone out *together*," I agree, still mildly annoyed.

He reaches for my hand, holding it gently in his and pressing a kiss to my knuckles.

His lips stretch, and the smile he's wearing could rival a thousand suns in its brightness.

"Why the sudden change in attitude?" I ask, smirking at his newfound excitement.

"I've got a surprise for you next week, and I just thought of something that'll make it even more special."

"Is it a personal stalker—" I clap my hand over my mouth, pretending to be sheepish. "Sorry, I meant bodyguard. A personal *bodyguard*."

He rolls his eyes, leans over, and grips my hips, pulling me off Penny's back and settling me between his legs. "Ry!" I giggle as he lifts the hem of my shirt, tickling the sensitive skin there.

"I love it when you scream your husband's name," he taunts, his scruff scraping against my cheek, and I wish it was between my thighs. He continues to tickle me, and I swat at his hands. He slows his movements, only to drag his fingertips over my belly.

"Maybe if you're a good boy, I'll scream it in the bedroom sometime soon." My breath gets caught in my throat as he slides his hand between my thighs, trailing heat with it.

"I look forward to being a *very* good boy for you, darlin'," he whispers against my neck, nipping gently at the skin below my ear. A groan slips past my lips, and I melt into him.

My nipples are peaked, and the chill in the air does nothing to fix it as he continues whispering in my ear the entire ride to the stables.

Chapter Forty-Nine

AND THAT'S ON COMMUNICATION

THURSDAY, JUNE 19

I CHEW on my lower lip, waiting anxiously in the living room for Ryder to finish his shower before we have our video call.

My therapy session with Talia went really well on Monday. While I don't expect it to have completely cured me of my apprehension, it provided clarity.

Which is why Talia suggested we try a couples session with her today. She gave me some homework to do over the last few days, which involved sharing with Ryder one fear, one dream, and one thing keeping me from reaching that dream and overcoming that fear. Not that it's a surprise, but he was so grateful I opened up to him that not only was he totally on board, but he booked himself a solo appointment with someone else from the clinic. He even took the homework assignment we'd been doing for me and did it *with* me.

I feel more loved and understood every day I'm with him, and it's given me a newfound sense of hope for the future. But I have no idea what to expect of couples counseling, and that newness has me feeling a little sweaty and my chest tight.

He's spent the entire week hanging fliers for my first dance class happening tomorrow, picking me up off the floor when I fell apart, sure the studio wouldn't be finished in time. We hadn't even gotten the floors done until yesterday, but our parents came to help, and the guys from the biker book club rented a freaking truck to help us out.

They convinced us all to join them for next month's book club, and I'm looking forward to it.

Ryder strides into the living room clad in a pair of Wranglers and a button-down short sleeve tucked into the waistband, and my anxiety flees the premises. "Ry, what are you wearing?" I ask, trying to contain my laughter. He sets me at ease without trying.

He looks down at himself, swiping a hand over the tortoise shell buttons running the length of his chest and abs. "What? This old thing?" His smirk has my shoulders relaxing from the built-up tension I've felt working its way into my muscles all day. "Darlin', my momma would kill me if she thought I'd shown up to any appointment dressed in less than this."

"We're *at home*. It's supposed to be a comfortable environment," I explain, knowing it's futile.

"And I *am* comfortable." He sits down beside me and pulls my legs across his lap, balancing my laptop over my thighs. "See? Now, I'm extra comfy." His wide grin reflects just how true that is.

"If you say so." I'm not sure if it's because I've got thick thighs or what, but jeans are the furthest thing from what I'd consider cozy.

I log into the website and wait for it to tell me the host will let us in before uncovering the camera.

Talia's bright smile fills the screen, and she greets us with a warmth that has me settling further into the couch cushions.

"Good evening, you two. It's nice to meet you, Ryder," she says.

"It's very nice to meet you too, ma'am," Ryder tells her, laying it on thick with the "ma'am." It's a word I never found swoon-worthy, but I'm ready to drop my panties at the sound of it slipping past this man's lips.

We get started by setting some expectations for the meeting. "We have about an hour, though if we're in a really good place, you're my last session of the day, so I don't mind continuing a little past that. No pressure. We'll see where this takes us, okay?"

"Sounds good," I agree, and Ryder nods enthusiastically.

"Great. So, from my understanding of the questionnaire I had you each fill out, it sounds like you've known each other for a very long time, both of you have expressed feeling very comfortable with the other person, which is wonderful, but you've also expressed some concerns." She pauses in a silent display of understanding, giving us a chance to interject if anything sounds incorrect. "The main concern sounds like you were both in long-term relationships prior to your marriage, and neither of you ever felt loved in the way you deserved by those people. You're very newly married, and Lola," she turns her attention to me, "you mentioned that while you don't feel like your ex ever deserved you and you don't have any positive feelings left toward him, you feel like you should. Could you explain that further if you feel comfortable?"

I nod, pausing for a moment to gather my thoughts. I've gone to therapy before and found it very helpful, but when I turned twenty-five and no longer had insurance under my parents' policy, I quit going and felt pretty well equipped to stop. After years of Russ beating me down, though, this is definitely a necessary step. When I feel like I'm ready, I look to Ryder, who gives me a reassuring smile and squeezes my knee.

"When I first started dating Russ, I was in a really weird mental space. I had been away from my friends and family for a long time, and I was still trying to find my footing. He sort of swooped in at a vulnerable time and encouraged me to pursue my passion for dance. It was something I'd known I wanted to do, but I was also terrified would be a mistake." I take a breath, tugging on the sleeve of my shirt to cover my arms as a chill races through me, recalling those first few months with my ex.

"I think deep down, I knew my family wasn't bluffing when they said they'd support me in anything I wanted to do." My brows pinch together, and I suck my bottom lip between my teeth before continuing. "I was born in Cuba, and I was really young when we moved here. I'd seen my parents struggle financially, and when we moved here, that changed, but it wasn't without a lot of hard work." I hadn't realized how tough our lives in Cuba were until I was old enough to reflect on it. My parents had always done such an incredible job of maintaining joy in our home despite the lack of access to even the most basic medications, the constant power outages, and extreme poverty. Memories of the days and nights after moving here resurface; they'd spent many years learning how to care for the horses and other animals, working late hours, and celebrating a long week with a massive family dinner on Fridays. "Rosa Ranch has grown a ton since we first arrived. It used to be Ryder's parents, mine, and Mayte's, plus three other ranch hands and their families. Now, the ranch has five times that many employees and is making better money than they had at the start."

Talia nods her understanding. "My parents eventually found their rhythm here, and so did I, but I worried that by not having a corporate job, I wouldn't have the financial stability my parents always wanted for me. Then, when I was diagnosed with rheumatoid arthritis shortly after getting engaged to Russ, it felt like all my biggest fears were coming true. I didn't have access to adequate healthcare, and this man who had made me believe he was my biggest cheerleader turned out to be a fraud."

Ryder remains silent, listening to a part of the story I'd never told him before. I'm realizing now that might have been out of embarrassment, but the methodical circles he rubs along the pulse point in my wrist ease my discomfort.

Talia nods. "Now, you mentioned your ex turned out to be a fraud. Could you expand on that?"

I blow out a breath, forcing my rigid posture to relax. "At the beginning of our relationship, he showed up to all my dance lessons and came to a few recitals. But as his startup grew, things changed for the worse. He had never been good about communication in the first place, but it was like that very first day we met was the most open he was ever willing to be with me. As it became harder for me to find a job with a stable income, he shut down further. He changed his tune completely as soon as he proposed, and I foolishly agreed. Instead of supporting me, I never saw him, and on the rare occasions I did, he would make me feel so small." A tear slips down my cheek that Ryder swipes away with the pad of his thumb, his warmth giving me the courage to continue digging into something I hadn't realized was bothering me so much.

"I tried to look for the good in him, but eventually, I came up so short, I stopped looking at all. When I'd had enough and tried to leave him, he brought up my health. He used my diagnosis against me and continually reminded me I needed his health insurance to do the things I loved so much, the things he now despised."

I hear a low sound rumble from Ryder, his jaw locked as I glance over at him. I finish by adding, "I'd never been in love with Russ. I don't think I ever *loved* Russ, but I was so afraid of having to start over again and not having the chance to feel whole again, I quit trying to leave him. It wasn't until my friends took me away for my bachelorette weekend, ready to blindside me with an intervention, that I realized how much of myself had died with Russ."

"That's very good, Lola. I'm so proud of the incredible progress you're making already."

"Yeah," I admit, wiping my tears away. I choke out a

watery laugh and take a deep breath, my lungs expanding fully for the first time tonight.

"I'm proud of you too, Lols. Thank you for sharing that with us," Ryder tells me quietly, gathering my hands in his.

"And Ryder, how did hearing all of that make you feel?" Talia asks.

He releases a short laugh that holds absolutely no humor. "Honestly? I'm not sure you really want to hear what I'm thinking."

I already have an idea of what's going through his mind right now, and it's nothing but a murderous rampage.

Talia smiles, tamping down the laugh I know is trying to come to the forefront, but she has a good poker face and plays it off as a cough. "Tell me what's on your mind, no matter how colorful the language you'd like to use."

Ryder shakes his head. "No, ma'am. I try not to cuss much, but what I will say is that Russ never deserved Lola. I can't say if it was money, or maybe his family, or if he was always a horrific person, but unlike him, I plan to put in ten times the effort I had the day before, every day, for the rest of our lives to make sure Lola is happy, cared for, and feels safe to pursue her passions the way she should have always felt comfortable to."

His words wrap around me like a heated blanket, soothing the sting of the memory of my ex and his unkind words.

"I truly believe that, Ryder. I think you being here at all is a testament to how dedicated you *both* are to making this marriage a success. Couples counseling gets a bad reputation. A lot of people seem to believe it's only for relationships that aren't doing well, but that isn't the case. Sure, that's what a lot of the couples I work with are here for, but I think it can be used as a way to fill your toolbox."

Ryder and I give her a puzzled look, unsure of what she's going on about now. She's lost me with this particular metaphor.

"Essentially, my thought is that you, as a couple, have a toolbox when you enter a relationship, and it starts out empty. Therapy is just another tool, and working through therapy provides you with more of them. You could end today with a more solid foundation for communication, but next week, maybe you add a coping mechanism for when one of you has had a hard day and doesn't want to talk about it. These are all tools you add to your toolbox for when you need them."

Ryder looks at me and then returns his gaze to Talia. "Like having a hammer? I only use it if I have something to hang or nail together, but I have it when I need it."

He's adorable for trying, and Talia lights up at his explanation. "Exactly like that! Great, so you get the concept, but Ryder, could you dig deeper into your relationship with your ex-wife? It sounded like you and Lola both have quite a bit of animosity toward her, which I found very interesting. I think it could be cathartic to get some of it out, but if you don't agree, we can circle back to this another time."

"I'd actually really like to discuss Lemmon if Ry is okay with it too," I answer openly. It's actually laughable to think of a scenario where the roles are reversed and Russ is the one sitting beside me right now. He thought it was a weakness to discuss our relationship problems with other people and would have laughed in my face at the prospect. And *that* is precisely how I know I'm in the right place, with the right person.

"Of course, Lols. I'm okay with it too. Do you mind if I go first?" he asks.

I shake my head. "Not at all."

He starts by talking about the early years of our childhood, how Lemmon was always really sweet to him. Because I was too embarrassed to tell him how she treated me, he didn't know until I was already gone and he was married to the monster. "Things weren't natural with Lemmon the way they had been with Lola, but I hadn't dated anyone other than her and Lola, so I wasn't sure what it *should* feel like. And then, when my best friend died shortly before my college graduation, I'd been desperate to keep Lola unscathed from the depression trying to eat me up. I didn't want to derail her plans by needing her too much, and Lemmon was a familiar face from our same small town." He continues explaining all the things we've already discussed, things I've finally gotten clarity on and had the time to forgive us both for the way we'd handled things in our past. "I carry a lot of guilt over the fact that I think, deep down, I'd stayed with Lemmon to keep from chasing after Lola. The thought makes me worry I'm not the man I'd thought I was."

"Is it okay if I ask him a question? Is that appropriate in couples therapy?" I ask, mind reeling.

"Yes, Lola, of course. Ryder can choose not to answer them, but you are free to ask."

"Okay, well…" I chew on my bottom lip. "Do you think I'm terrible for staying with Russ even after I tried to leave?"

Ryder's brows climb high on his forehead, and he looks like I've just struck him. "What? Of course not. Why would you think that?"

"Because you just explained your guilt surrounding Lemmon. It's the same thing, Ry. I want you to give yourself the same grace you give me."

"Lola, I appreciate that, but I stayed in that relationship with the knowledge I was using her to keep me grounded." His words are rough, and it's hard to listen to him speak so poorly about himself.

"Did you really though? Was it a conscious decision, or have you come to realize that those were your subconscious thoughts all these years later?"

He scratches the nape of his neck, drawing his dark brows together as he sits in silence, mulling over my words. "It was a subconscious decision I've come to realize in the last two or three years as I finally learned how to effectively grieve Logan's death."

"So what I'm hearing is, you were dealing with the death of your childhood best friend, a *sudden* death you weren't equipped to handle, and after years of being in an unfulfilling relationship with someone who didn't make you happy but you didn't outright hate, you learned how to grieve Logan's death. With that, you came to recognize the true reasons you stayed with Lemmon, and then *you ended the relationship.* Is that accurate?"

He stares at me for so long I worry I've said too much or picked things apart in a way that isn't accurate and managed to offend him, but he breaks the silence with a quivering lip and a single tear. I don't think I've ever loved anyone more than I do in this moment. This level of vulnerability feels like he's stripping himself bare for me, trusting I won't do anything to hurt him. It's such an incredible honor.

"That sounds right," he finally manages to say, choking out the words. "I didn't go to therapy, but I started reading a bunch of self-help books, namely ones revolving around grief and childhood trauma. I didn't think I *had* childhood trauma because my parents have always been supportive of me and given me everything I've ever needed to thrive, but the more I read those 'grieving loss at an early age' books, the more I realized trauma comes in so many forms. It was unfair to myself not to recognize it for what it truly was: a traumatic experience in my young adulthood. I might not have been a child, but I was too young to deal with it alone."

"On your questionnaire," Talia speaks up, reminding me she's here, "you had mentioned that Lemmon was not supportive of these books and often weaponized Lola. What does that mean?"

Shock ricochets through me at her words, causing me to recoil in my seat.

"Lemmon often belittled me for reading them, suggesting I wasn't a 'real man' because if I was, I'd have gotten over his death more quickly."

I scoff. "As if grief has anything to do with how manly you are." I'd love to give that uppity bitch a piece of my mind.

"I know she was wrong, Lols, but her words wore me down. Eventually, when she saw how withdrawn I was, she started to use you as a weapon. She'd tell me if I wanted someone to treat me like a child instead of a grown man, I should have continued to follow you around like a puppy dog. She'd say I'm not a man at all, that I'm definitely not man enough for her. She made sure to tear me down at every turn and would yell at me about how she should've been smart like you and left when she had the chance. When *I* tried to leave her time and time again, though, she'd change her tune and make me feel like the villain in my own story."

My heart sinks. "Ry, I never *wanted* to leave you. I just wanted you to feel comfortable confiding in me, and I understand why you hadn't then, but it didn't make it hurt any less that you'd chosen to share with her, of all people. I don't blame you for any of it. We were so young," I tell him, holding his hands a little tighter and pressing a kiss to each of his knuckles.

He smiles, and it cracks my heart in two in the best way, exploding with the love and admiration I can see and feel pouring off him.

"And Lola, do you want to share why you resent Lemmon?"

I let out a huff, not sure I should speak about her at all with how badly she made Ryder feel. I don't want him to struggle any more than he already does, but I know we're sharing, and I think he'd rather I get this out than hold it in.

"Lemmon always acted like the sweet Southern belle when in the public eye, and she was kind to Ryder from what I could see growing up. When they got married, it seemed like an odd relationship, but I tried not to worry myself too much with it because he wasn't mine anymore—"

"I've *always* been yours, Lola," Ryder interjects, and I can't help but roll my eyes at him.

"Okay, Ry, not the point," I say with a laugh, moving on. "I pretended it didn't bother me as much as it did, but Lemmon was always downright cruel from the very first day I met her. She'd kick dirt at me, push me into puddles of water, or trip me in mud. She'd call me names but say it in that sickeningly sweet way of hers that made me feel like she thought I was stupid and wouldn't notice. And as we got older and she became more and more jealous of my relationship with Ryder, she'd make threats about having her daddy get me kicked out of school. It was one thing after another with her, and I was exhausted, so when I found him confiding in her in the way I'd been desperate for him to after Logan's death, it felt like she'd finally won."

"And you resent her for her actions during your formative years?"

"I don't resent her for that, no. I feel pity for her because her father was kind but not around enough, and it's no secret her mother left when she was five. I think she had her sights set on Ryder, and I was in the way of that, so she bullied me, hoping she wouldn't feel so small anymore. What I resent her for is hurting him when she finally got him." I look up to find Ryder already staring at me with tear-filled eyes, and it's like a punch to the gut. I love him, painfully so, and I hate Lemmon more with each passing moment. "Every time I came home to visit, she made a point of running into me for that reason alone, and my visits home became fewer and farther between as a result. I resent her for conditioning me to believe this place was no longer my home, for making the most incredible man I know feel like he's less than amazing."

"It sounds like you've both experienced some very difficult things in your formative years, and while you might have some regrets about how you went about things, I get the sense you're both well on your way to working through those struggles and doing that *together*."

"I appreciate you suggesting this today, Talia. I think we would have gotten here on our own eventually, but having your guidance has been really helpful. If Lola is okay with it, and if you have time in your schedule for us, I'd really like to have these sessions periodically," Ryder tells us.

"I think so too. I've always felt safe with you, and I know I can tell you anything, but therapy has been great at pulling things out of me that I hadn't noticed I was bottling up at all." I aim my words at Ryder so he can feel my sincerity and heal from that too. I never want him to think I don't trust him implicitly.

"I'd love to have you both work with me. I appreciate the time you took to really dig into your pasts. Do Thursday evenings work for you both? Eventually, I'm sure you'll get to a place where you'll want to see me less frequently, but I still suggest checking in every few months once you're in a good spot so you can refresh the tools," she says.

"That sounds good to me."

We end the call after a few more minutes of working out logistics, and Ryder puts my computer away, pulling me into his lap to nuzzle against my neck.

"Do you ever feel guilty for leaving Lemmon?"

He kisses the side of my neck and pulls away to meet my gaze. "I don't. I feel guilty for other reasons though."

"Like what?"

"For not leaving sooner when I realized we were doomed. For not chasing after you. For missing out on years of loving you the way you deserve. For *not* feeling guilty about leaving Lemmon."

I cup his cheeks, his stubble scraping my smooth palms. "You can't change the past, Ry. She was manipulating you, and if you tried to chase me, I would probably have kept on running. We were so young, we can't say what we would have done because we don't know. Who's to say we would have been capable of loving each other the way we deserve? Neither of us knew any better, and I think it took years of being unhappy in other relationships for either of us to truly grapple with an understanding of what we wanted. You don't know what you don't know."

He places his hands over mine, warming my chilled skin. *This* feels right. Everything about this moment feels so uniquely *us*. Opening up, sharing our fears, not hiding from our pasts.

"Besides, the only thing keeping me from diving headfirst into this *fake* marriage is the guilt I've felt for leaving Russ, running straight into your arms, and not looking back. I haven't missed him for a single second, and I feel guilty about that too."

"Let's make a promise then, darlin'."

I quirk a brow. "What kind of promise?"

"I promise to not allow guilt to keep me from the things I love and want most if you won't." His voice rings with such finality I find myself nodding along with him.

"Okay. Pinky promise," I say, dropping my palms from his face as he does the same. I hold out my pinky, and he grabs onto it with his.

"I, Ryder Maddox Lockhart, promise to never let the guilt of the past keep me from the beauty of the future," he says.

"And I, Lola Lima, promise to remind myself there's nothing to feel guilty for in the first place, and to instead allow myself the joy and love of those willing to offer it." His smile matches mine, and it sends a beam of light straight through to my soul.

"Good. Then you shouldn't have any problems letting your husband be big spoon tonight, right?" he asks, standing from the couch with me in his grasp, pulling me against his body. He carries us to bed, tickling me as he does. Nugget follows behind us, barking at my laughter.

Allowing myself to be loved feels so much better than I could have imagined.

Lola

Chapter Fifty

JITTER BUG

FRIDAY, JUNE 20

I FEEL NAUSEOUS, just moments from hyperventilating, as I stand here, gripping the edge of the sink.

My body aches, and anti-inflammatory drugs haven't helped, but it's the least of my worries now that the day has come. It's finally here.

The day that tells me whether this town is ready for me or not. The day that helps me decide whether *I* am ready for *it*.

I hear a light knock on the bathroom door and manage to extricate myself from the spot I'm rooted to.

I open the door to find Ryder smiling brightly at me, his arms behind his back. His smile drops as he takes in my sullen expression.

"Lola, what's wrong, baby?"

"I'm going to fuck this up, Ry," I whisper. "Nothing about this has been easy, and it has me wondering if that's a sign it isn't meant for me."

He shakes his head adamantly. "Cut that out. You know just as well as I do that the best things in life are worth fighting for. Now, tell the nasty voice in your head to shove it where the sun don't shine."

"But Ry—"

He cuts me off, gripping my chin between his thumb and forefinger. My lips part on an exhale with the unexpected movement. "Stop worrying about it, darlin'. Now, go take a seat on the bed so I can give you your gift," he tells me, producing a box from behind his back.

I sit down, holding the box with shaky hands. I take my time untying the black ribbon and slowly lift the top off. Lying between layers of black tissue paper is an eggplant-purple two-piece dance set with a shimmering chiffon overlay.

"This is stunning, Ry," I say, gawking at the fabric bunched in my grasp.

"Put it on, and we can get out of here," he whispers, pecking me on the cheek.

The outfit fits like a glove. It's possibly one of the nicest things I've ever owned, and I think I might want to be buried in it.

The top is a deep purple, an almost eggplant color that shifts in the light. The back is strappy, with gold rhinestone-ed strings that wrap around my neck in a halter. The front is comprised of two pieces of fabric: one that's thicker, sitting tightly across my chest to hold my breasts in, the other a sparkly chiffon piece that gives the illusion of being draped from my shoulders to right below my breasts, tapering in the middle, with a cowl neck in front that shows off the right amount of cleavage to be tasteful.

The skirt is a bikini-style bottom that hugs my waist securely, lots of matching glittery chiffon layers hanging down the sides and back.

It goes perfectly with my black, classic series ballroom shoes.

We lock up the house, and Ryder carries me to the truck, insisting I'll lose my heels in the soft dirt. When we've parked in front of the barn, a calm washes over me at the sight of the trucks, cars, and motorcycles surrounding the back of the building.

They came.

Maybe this really is my second chance.

"You've got this, Lols," Ryder whispers, leaning across the seat to plant a kiss on my cheek.

He exits the truck, rounding the front to open my door, unbuckling me and lifting me onto the ground before closing the door and locking it. The sun has set, and the sky is bright with stars, the crescent moon hanging overhead.

He slides the door to the barn open and leads us inside to the studio of my dreams that has just become my reality. It feels so damn *sweet.*

My eyes widen as I stand here, gaping at the fifty or so people standing in their nicest dresses, slacks, and boots. More people showed up than I could have ever imagined; my heart feels so full.

Ryder squeezes my hand reassuringly. Tears threaten to spill, but I coax them in, wringing my hands out as I take everything in. When my gaze lands on the floor-to-ceiling paintings hanging along the back wall, my eyes go wide. These were not here last night when we left to get cleaned up for our counseling session. Each one of them stands at least twenty feet high, and they're all of *me.* These are photos from dance competitions I've competed in, wearing some of my favorite outfits with the widest smiles on my face.

The front of the space has a wall of mirrors, and the floors are a sleek, light-colored pine. There's a central chandelier hanging between the rafters, strands of lights coming off it in ribbons, illuminating the space in a calming but bright, warm light. It turned out *perfect.*

I spin to face Ryder, cupping his cheeks. Emotion takes over, driving my actions. I press my lips to his, reveling in the feel of his arms effortlessly wrapping around me, the taste of his tongue as it swipes over the seam of my lips, delving into my mouth and tangling with mine.

My senses are overwhelmed with him, with the vanilla and bourbon taste of his mouth, even though he hasn't had a single sip of alcohol since we were eighteen. My lungs fill with him, every cell in my body vibrating with need, and when he dips me low, my hair grazing the floor, the room erupts in a roar of catcalls and cheers, breaking me out of the spell.

He lifts me up, severing our physical connection but never the metaphysical.

I suck a deep breath in through my nose, filling my lungs with much-needed, Ryder-free oxygen, and allow thoughts and words to find me. Turning toward the crowd and clapping my hands together once, I project my voice in an enthusiastic tone and ask, "I think I owe you all some dance lessons, don't I?"

My heart beats wildly at the overwhelming amount of support I'm receiving from people who've barely seen me in years. So much has changed in that time, and yet, Hidden Valley's commitment to supporting the people of this town never wavers.

They cheer, and I don't miss the table in the back where Mayte and my dad sit with Isabela, each of them shooting me an exaggerated wink.

Chapter Fifty-One

SWEATIN' LIKE A WHORE IN CHURCH

FRIDAY, JUNE 20

I'M STANDING at the front of the expansive dance studio, the mirrored walls reflecting a sea of curious faces. Fifty pairs of eyes watch me, some eager, others looking a tad nervous, their gazes shifting between me and the neighbors they've lived by most of their lives. I catch the glimmer of Pepto Bismol pink, and the sheepish smiles of Lemmon's cronies greet me, knocking me back with surprise. They greet me with small waves, and I don't feel any bad energy from them. *Maybe they pulled their heads out of their asses.*

The air buzzes with anticipation, and the faint scent of lavender wafts in from the field in bloom at the top of the hill. "Alright, everyone! *Bienvenidos*! Welcome to Cuban Night. As most of you know, my family and I are from Cuba, and while I teach all styles of Latin dance, I feel tonight is a very special one. As such, I'd like to focus on where I came from"—I look across the room, meeting Ryder's eyes—"and where we're going."

The familiar faces all smile back at me, clapping. "Tonight, we're learning *Casino*, or *Rueda de casino*. Many consider this the heart of Cuban social dancing, and it is often referred to as

Salsa Cubana. That isn't necessarily a correct term for it, though, because while Salsa did originate in Cuba and Puerto Rico and was further developed in New York City, Salsa is the genre of dance, while *Casino* is a dance style that falls under that umbrella. But what you all need to know about *Casino* is that it's all about connection, rhythm, and a whole lot of fun. Are you ready?"

"What if we don't have rhythm?" Betsy, the owner of Ever After Boutique, calls out, and several people chuckle.

I wave a hand through the air, meeting her glittering eyes with a smile. "That's what the lessons are for, Betsy! I'll teach you. Don't worry."

A mix of cheers and hesitant nods answers me, and I can't help but smile. Leading large classes always gives me such a rush, like I'm an orchestra conductor commanding a symphony of movement.

As the music begins a vibrant, pulsing *son Cubano* rhythm, I raise my arms and step to the side, my hips swaying naturally to the beat. "Step together, step together, back… and forward! Yes, just like that. The basic step is simple, but it's how you *feel* it that makes it magic."

I move through the crowd, correcting postures and encouraging shy smiles. In the corner, a young couple giggles as they stumble over their feet. My parents are in the back, showing off with exaggerated spins.

Ryder stands by the door, leaning against the frame. His flannel button-down stretches over his broad shoulders, and the overhead lights catch on his dark waves. His arms are crossed over his chest, and he watches me with a feral look in his eye. His attention sends a jolt of awareness down my spine, and it feels impossible to tear my gaze away from him.

"Good, everyone! That's wonderful! For those of you who haven't already, go ahead and pair up," I say, forcing myself to break eye contact with Ryder. "This dance is about partnership. We're going to work on leading and following."

I make my way to the front and watch as Ryder cuts through the crowd with a natural grace, meeting me in front of the mirrors. "Looks like you're without a partner, darlin'," he muses, his deep voice carrying over the music. "Need a volunteer?"

His smile holds a challenge I can't resist. "Do you remember how to dance *Casino*?" I ask, raising an eyebrow.

"Well enough," he says, his lips quirking into a grin.

A ripple of excitement surges through my veins as he tugs me into his chest. "If memory serves, you have no issue moving your hips."

He runs the tips of his nose up my neck, whispering against the overheated flesh in a rumble of approval, "I'd be glad to reacquaint you with my hips tonight."

Sucking in a deep breath, I recenter myself and try to remember we're in public. I place his hands where they need to be, one on my back and the other in my hand, leading him through the basic steps. His movements are surprisingly smooth, and his touch is firm but respectful, rhythm precise. "Well, well, well, Ryder Lockhart. It looks like someone's been paying attention after all."

"It's hard not to pay attention to you, darlin'."

I roll my eyes, peering over his shoulder to see how the crowd is doing. I project my voice over the music. "You're all doing excellent! Now, loosen up and really feel the music. Watch how Ry and I do it."

With every step, the room seems to blur. The other dancers fade into the periphery. The two of us are caught in a rhythm both electric and intimate. Ryder's eyes hold mine, and I can feel the heat spreading throughout my limbs.

He holds me close, our chests brushing, and desire settles deep in my core, where I wish he were right now. I suck a breath in at the thought, pulling away from him to get a good look at the crowd. I feel the snap of the tether drawing us together, but instead of breaking, it acts like a rubber band, bouncing me back into him. With the prying eyes of a small town, I know I need to remain professional, no matter how difficult that might prove to be. These people are here to support me, but I also need to make a name for myself if I want to continue earning their business after the novelty has worn off.

I leave Ryder for a few moments, making corrections as needed, and when I return, it's like one touch from him could light my entire body on fire.

I swallow thickly, ungluing my tongue from the roof of my mouth. "*Casino* is a conversation, not a monologue. Make sure you're giving your partner enough space to reply," I tell the crowd, keeping my voice even despite the mixture of excitement, nerves, and joy I'm feeling.

Ryder presses his warm hand to the base of my spine, pulling me back into him. I twirl, pressing my backside to his front. He mimics my steps, keeping up nicely before putting a hand up for me to take and spinning me, first in place and then around his body. He turns into me, tugging me tightly to his chest. One of my hands roams over the thick muscles of his bicep, the other bent with his hand in mine, leading us through the moves.

My heart rate climbs, my eyes plastered to his chest, reluctant to meet his gaze for fear that I might see something I like a little *too* much. He can tell what I'm doing, using our clasped hands pressed beneath my chin to lift my face to his. Our mouths are so close, I can feel the tickle of his cool, minty breath coast along my lips.

"Eyes on me, darlin'," he murmurs, just loud enough for me to hear over "*Rosa La Peligrosa*". Those beautiful baby blues are hooded, and I have to count on muscle memory to carry me through the rest of the dance. My brain feels like *un tremendo arroz con mango*, a big, confused mess.

The song comes to an end, and the room bursts into applause. I reluctantly step away from Ryder, suddenly aware of the heat rising to my cheeks. I pray it's not obvious that I'm practically panting after only a handful of minutes in my husband's arms. "You've got potential," I joke.

He ducks his head, his lips brushing the shell of my ear as he whispers, "Maybe my wife will give me private lessons."

My breath gets lodged in my throat, and I avert my gaze, sucking in a deep, steadying lungful of air. The music quiets down, and the loud chatter stills. When I lift my head to see what's going on, Ryder's body goes rigid beside mine, his hand on my back sliding to my hip as he pulls me into his side, as if shielding me from something — or *someone.*

I don't have a chance to ask what's going on before I'm seeing red.

Or should I say: *yellow.*

Lemmon traipses through the middle of the crowd, a pale-yellow lace dress hanging around her slim waist, falling to mid-calf. *Tu De Que Vas* starts to play through the speakers, and it's impeccably timed, given the meaning of the song: *"What's your problem? What were you thinking? Are you joking with me right now?"* None of these are literal translations, but they all make entirely too much sense as Lemmon approaches me, the massive barn suddenly stifling.

She doesn't cross the invisible line between where Ryder and I stand and where the rest of the crowd is gathered.

A tense hush falls around us. It's an eerie silence that makes me feel like there are bugs crawling on my skin, and bile churns in my gut.

Ryder's fingers flex, digging into my hip as Lemmon and I enter a stare-off. "Lola, maybe we sh—" His words are cut off by *Mami's* screams.

"Fire!"

The smell of smoke billows through the room, singeing the inside of my nostrils. I cover my mouth, coughing as panic threatens to seize my lungs.

My gaze swings around the room, the crowd breaking into

hysterics, shouting as they push through the room, but when my gaze catches on Lemmon, it lingers there. Stuck on her shocked expression, wide eyes, mouth open in surprise, and not the theatrical kind, but a genuine sense of fear written plainly across her face.

Ryder tugs on my arm, pulling me back into the present as thick plumes of smoke climb the wall in the far corner, coating the newly painted red in black soot.

He drags me through the room, ushering everyone out. "Stay calm! Just get outside quickly, everyone!"

My heart is hammering in my chest, sweat collecting on my brow as we make it outside, and when I look back, it's the paintings Ryder commissioned, burning to ashes right in front of my eyes, that have my heart sinking. Everything I'd worked for, just *gone*.

I turn away, tears pricking the backs of my eyes. The cool, moist air coats my skin in a sticky contrast to the dry, astringent air inside the barn. There's a stampede of people yelling, and Isabela's cries roar over the rush of blood in my ears, but I'm thankful for the sound, as it pulls my attention right to my family rushing *safely* over to me.

"What's going on?" I plead, trying to gain my bearings and find the source of the fire. I stare at the building in horror as the weeks of pain and anxiety go up in flames with my dreams. If this isn't a bad omen, I don't know what is.

"Don't worry, Miss Lola. We'll get it sorted!" Chuck hollers at me, pulling on the large hose tucked outside of the barn. Ryder is already on the phone with emergency services. Isaiah and Cynthia join Chuck, splitting up to contain the fire.

"Did everyone get out alright?" I pant out.

"They're volunteer firefighters. They know what they're doing, darlin', everyone will be okay. Don't worry. We'll get the damage fixed and your studio reopened in no time."

I cup his cheeks, pressing a firm kiss to his lips as I melt into his chest. "I'm not worried about the barn, Ry. I want to know how this happened." My voice cracks as I try to hold myself together and not shatter in his arms. This night, Ryder's surprise, my love of dance—it's all been so magical, and my chest aches to think of all the hard work that went into it being burned to a crisp, literally. I can't stand the thought of the beauty of this experience being sullied by something so heart-breaking.

Ryder smooths a hand over my head, flattening my curls down my back. "Unfortunately, Lols, I think we know the who and the why," he says. Straightening my spine, I peer over his shoulder, making eye contact with Lemmon. She immediately looks away, scurrying off toward the police car parked down the hill.

I turn in Ryder's arms, grabbing his hand, and drag him behind me as I make a hasty descent, following Lemmon. I do my best not to trip in my heels, stopping momentarily to pull them off. Ryder takes them from my grasp, nodding his chin toward Lemmon to urge me forward, and boy, *do I ever*.

"Sheriff Wilson!" I call with a renewed sense of determination. This isn't a bad *omen*; it's a bad *lemon* spoiling the bunch.

He gives me a smile, but it falls as fast as it appeared. Lemmon has her hand over her heart, tears pooling in her eyes. "Why, Sheriff Wilson, I just don't know how this could happen in our quiet little town. It hurts ma' heart to think someone could be actin' so malicious so close to our home." She swipes a finger under her eye, sniffling.

"Cut the crap, Lemmon. We know you're responsible for this." Even as I say it, the words feel wrong, like they're somehow tinged in soot. It's as if my gut and my heart are volleying with my brain and the facts of our situation. If it's not Lemmon, who else could be responsible?

Her head snaps to me, her tears drying as she narrows her glare on my face. "Now, Lola Lima, why on God's green Earth would *I* be behind such a thing?" She doesn't let me interject with a rebuttal before she's deflecting, and very poorly at that.

"Speaking of suspicious activity, why would someone marry Ryder Lockhart and not take his last name?"

I roll my eyes, crossing my arms over my chest.

"Because, Lemmon, it's the twenty-first century, and I *like* my last name," I huff out.

"You know, something tells me that just ain't the truth. You and Ryder got married awfully quick, didn't you? You sure there's not a more nefarious reason for that? Any chance your marriage is all a sham, and you didn't take his last name because there'd be no point in all that paperwork?" Her words slam into me, knocking me off kilter as the weight of fraud hangs over my head like an anvil.

Ryder wraps his arm around my waist, tugging me tight against his side. "Lemmon, my marriage to Lola is more real than *ours* ever was. You can quit digging for problems that don't exist. Lola and I love each other, and there's nothing you can do that's going to split us up or make the fine people of Hidden Valley turn on her."

Damn right! I fist pump the sky internally, proud of Ryder for standing up for not only himself, but for *us*, even in the face of his abuser. "That's right. Now, if you're done deflecting, why don't you tell Sheriff Wilson where you were for most of my class before the barn went up in flames, making your grand entrance moments before?"

She turns her attention to the sheriff, reaching out to grip his bicep, but he shakes her off. "Sheriff, I can understand why that *would* sound mighty suspicious, but I promise you, there is an excellent explanation."

"Well, let's hear it then," I urge, extremely interested to find out what utter crap she cooked up.

"I—" she glances down at her scuffed ballet flats, kicking at the dirt. *At least she has the good sense to look bashful.* "I'll admit that I was here to kick up a fuss," she murmurs, my eyes growing wide, and Ryder must be sharing my thoughts, tightening his hold on me. "But I wasn't late because I was starting a fire, I swear it. You see, I ran across a baby turtle sitting right in the middle of the road. I just felt so bad, I had to help the little fella across the street."

"You hate turtles, Lemmon, always complainin' they carry salmonella," Ryder says, tucking me under his arm, as if shielding me from her without realizing it.

"You must be misremembering, Ryder, sweetie. I mean—" She tosses her blonde waves over her shoulder. "It's not like you paid much attention to me all those years we were together anyhow. You must be thinkin' of Lola, perhaps." She waves a hand through the air, her glare darting to me, but it softens when she peers over her shoulder at the damage the fire caused. "Never mind that. The sweet turtle needed my help, and I was happy to lend a hand. I came straight here, and well, you know the rest."

"I'm sure, Miss Lemmon, but–"

She cuts the sheriff off. "And why in the world would y'all think I'd be responsible for burning down a building I'm inside of?"

"Making the victims your alibi," I deadpan, but somehow, the words don't feel right on my tongue.

"Well now, that's just ridiculous. I'd never do such a thing, and in either case, *there's no proof.*"

"And I'm sure you made certain of that," Ryder mutters under his breath.

"I'm sorry, Lola. We'll do everything we can in the investigation, but right now, we have no leads because I'm standing here talking to the three of you. If you'll excuse me, I'll be getting to work on this," Sheriff Wilson says. He tips his hat at us and trudges up the hill, leaving Lemmon gawking at his retreating form, dumbfounded and sweating like a whore in church.

Lemmon shakes herself out and spins on her heel, sauntering over to her baby-blue Volkswagen Beetle convertible without another word.

"That bitch has lost her goddamn mind," Mayte grumbles from behind me. I turn to see her standing with her hands on her hips, a look aimed at Lemmon that could rival Medusa herself.

"That'd require Lemmon to have ever been right in the head," Ryder comments.

"Let's focus on making sure everyone is okay, and we can figure out what to do about this mess later," I tell them, heading off to the crowd still standing in front of the partially burnt structure.

Thanks to the volunteers on site, the fire is out, and based on a quick glance, the structure is still salvageable. The paintings are no more, the oil paints only acting as fuel to the fire, the floor-to-ceiling mirrors all cracked from the heat, and the chair where Mayte sat with Isabela now little more than dust.

Chapter Fifty-Two

"DISTRACT ME, RY."

FRIDAY, JUNE 20

TO SAY I'm exhausted would be the understatement of the century. My joints ache, and my eyes still sting from the tears I've been holding in.

Ryder takes my hand, leading me to the truck, driving us home in silence.

There's nothing more to be said right now, nothing more we can do.

Bee offered to keep Nugget for the night so we can settle down and have a breather, which is unbelievably appreciated.

"Stay here for a minute, please. I want to check the house before we go in." I'm too tired to argue, so I give him a defeated nod, letting him lock me in the truck.

I'm not sure anything would surprise me at this point.

My chest feels tight while I wait for him. I watch as each light flicks on inside, Ryder passing the windows and casting shadows that fill me with momentary fear. When he finally emerges on the porch, my shoulders relax for the first time since Lemmon showed her face.

Ryder opens my door and lifts me against his muscular body. My arms wind around his neck, and I breathe him in, allowing his strong arms to cage me like he's physically grounding me to this Earth.

"I'm gonna take care of you, darlin'," he assures me, bringing me inside, walking us through the living room and into our bathroom.

"I know, Ry. You've always taken care of me," I whisper, staring at my reflection in the mirror, black streaks of mascara dried down my cheeks. My hair frizzy, eyes puffy and red.

Ryder's rough palms scrape down my bare shoulders. He squeezes my biceps and trails his fingers back up, brushing my hair to one side, pressing a gentle kiss to my shoulder. A chill races through me as my nipples peak, and my breasts feel heavy.

I watch him as he takes in every detail of my body through the mirror. When his eyes meet mine, I say, "Distract me, Ry."

"Are you sure?" he whispers, knowing exactly what I'm asking for.

"*Please*," I plead, my eyes welling with tears.

That's all it takes for him to take the lead and give me everything I want.

His hands slide down the slope of my spine, and I hear the zipper as he undoes my skirt, his intake of breath when he slides the chiffon over my ass and down my thighs. My skin feels electric everywhere he touches, and as he travels up my body, allowing the skirt to pool at my feet, his warm breath leaves a trail of goosebumps over my leg.

He unzips the side of my top and unclips the halter neck, gathering my hair in his fist and tugging lightly.

I melt into his touch, my head landing on his chest as he takes my top off, revealing my bare breasts.

His eyes look drunk on my very existence. "Look at you, darlin'. All that glowing skin, your stunning face, this perfect hair. Don't get me started on these breasts..." he trails off, cupping my small chest in his large hands.

He pinches my nipples, twisting and kneading. My knees

wobble, and he slides a hand down my abdomen, holding me up while he continues toying with me the way I'd shown him last week.

The tips of his fingers travel lower, tickling just above where I want them most. "You're everything I've ever needed," he whispers against my skin, lighting my nerves and heart on fire. My chest heaves, and the needy whine that leaves my lips sounds foreign to my own ears.

My thighs are coated in my arousal by the time he slides his middle finger through my wetness and circles it over my clit. The most delicious feeling licks up my spine, and heat coils in my belly.

"I can't believe you're finally mine, Lola," he whispers against the shell of my ear, working me to an orgasm with every swirl of his finger. "I've dreamed about you for as long as I can remember. Wished you were in bed beside me when I woke up each morning. Regretted not going after you when you left," he admits for the second time in twenty-four hours. My heart feels like it's being strangled.

"And now that I have you, darlin', I plan to remind you just how *mine* you really are." His hands shift, fingers digging into my wide hips as he spins me to face him and hoists me onto the counter.

"I want that more than you know." Fire blazes behind his eyes at my response.

The cool countertop bites at my flesh, but my awareness of it is erased as Ryder sinks to his knees. He lifts my foot, pressing tender kisses from my ankle up to the inside of my knee, widening my legs to accommodate his broad shoulders.

His head falls back, and he sucks in a steadying breath, turning his attention to what's waiting for him.

"God, darlin'. You're just as pretty between these legs as you are everywhere else. I'll never get over how stunning you are." His eyes flit up to mine. "Can I have a taste?"

My fingers twine into his muddy-brown hair, dragging his

head so his mouth hovers above my needy core. "Take anything you want from me," I plead.

He grips my thighs, laying them over his shoulders, and drags my ass closer to the edge. His tongue darts out, parting me as he groans.

"You taste so good," he praises, and my vision starts to blur. "Tell me what you like, darlin'," he instructs, flicking his tongue over my clit.

"Fingers—oh, yes!" I'm panting, squeezing his head between my thighs as he presses a finger inside me. He draws my clit into his mouth, sucking on the tender flesh and inserting another finger into my pussy.

Every touch and taste consumes me, calling me to the brink of bliss, and when his crystal-blue eyes lock on mine, holding me in a trance, he says, "If you want my cock buried inside you, you've gotta prove you can still take all of me, darlin'." He inserts a third finger, and my mouth drops open, my lip trembling as need ricochets through me. "That's right, Lola. Just like that. *Come for your husband.*"

It doesn't take long. The punishing thrusts of his fingers contrast with the featherlight kisses he presses into my skin, and soon, I'm seeing stars in my periphery.

He slides up my lax body, pulling me against him and supporting my weight as he carries me to bed.

Ryder

Chapter Fifty-Three

IMMACULATE VIEWS

FRIDAY, JUNE 20

LOLA COMING undone around my fingers and tongue is easily the sexiest thing I've ever taken part in, and I want *more*. I'm unnerved, obsessed with the thought alone.

Her chest heaves as I unbuckle my belt, but she bolts upright, her curls flying around her face. She reaches for my hands, halting my movements.

"Can I?" she asks, and I just about come in my jeans.

"Anything you want, darlin'." I mean that literally. She can do anything she wants with me, and I'll beg for seconds.

Lola drags that full bottom lip between her teeth, her eyes dilating. My hands fall to my sides, and her eyes smolder with need as she rubs her hand over my length. "I remember you were big, but damn," she breathes out, and a thrill of satisfaction tangles in my chest.

Her fingers are unsteady, but she takes her time unbuckling my belt, pulling the leather from each loop. She works on the button, dragging the zipper down and dipping her fingers into the waistband.

She tugs, first gently, then with more force, her earlier hesitations gone.

I wish I had this moment on tape. The soft *pop* as her lip is freed from her teeth and the words she says next will be played over and over in my mind until the end of time.

"Your dick is so pretty, Ry. I can't wait for you to fuck me with it."

"Oh, fucking hell, Lola." I release a strangled groan, and her soft fingers wrap around my base. She bats her lashes at me twice, and my knees almost give out. "Will you be a sweet girl for me, darlin'? Will you let your husband fuck your throat like the angel I know you are?"

The small, shy smile she aims at me is enough to break me, but if I thought that was too much to bear, it's nothing compared to the feeling of her soft lips as she wraps them around my length.

She hollows her cheeks, creating a vacuum-tight seal around me, twisting her hand at the base. My ass cheeks clench, and my balls tighten. Fire rips through my limbs. "You're so good at that, Lols," I praise through gritted teeth.

She bobs her head, as if nodding her agreement, and I feel her smile around my length. My fingers settle in her hair, digging into her scalp, tugging on her roots. She whines, increasing her pace, my cock thickening in her throat with each pull. She drops a hand between her legs, the other remaining on my hip to stabilize herself.

"Does that turn you on, sweetheart? Are you aching for my cock to be buried deep inside your perfect cunt?"

She moans around my dick, the sound vibrating straight through me.

I pull her off me, and she peers up, her pretty brown eyes wide as she wipes the saliva from her lips with the back of her hand. "I'm sorry, Ry. Was I not doing it right?" she asks, her lips quirking in a repressed smirk.

"You're the most perfect person I've ever known, Lols, and this is no different. I'm just more than ready to be inside you. I need to ruin you for any other man."

She shifts her weight, crawling up to the head of the bed, lying against the mountain of pillows she insists we need to sleep with. "I'm already ruined for anyone else. Nothing has ever felt as good, as right, as guiltlessly *perfect* as *us*." It's intoxicating to hear her speak those words, to release the guilt we've both been fighting.

My mouth goes dry as she extends her legs straight in front of her, lifting them up and letting them fall to either side in a middle split that gives me the most immaculate view of her plump, wet pussy. Her hips crack with the movement, but she doesn't show any sign of pain, so I'll accept the present I'm given and not look a gift horse in the mouth.

"God, you're incredible." I undress, stripping my clothes off as quickly as I can before crawling up the center of the bed and straight between her legs.

Chapter Fifty-Four

SADDLE UP AND RYDE

FRIDAY, JUNE 20

RYDER PROWLS up the bed with the grace of a panther, but I can't focus on anything other than what might be the sexiest thing I've ever seen in my life—*and it isn't his dick.* Though that's gorgeous too.

His thick thighs flex with his movements, but I press a palm to his chest that stops him in his tracks, my eyes locked on his right thigh.

"Lola, somethin' wrong?" he asks, concern bleeding into his words. "I promise it'll fit, if that's what you're worried about." He chuckles.

That snaps me out of my trance long enough to roll my eyes. "Oh, I *know* it'll fit, Ry. You're a big boy, but I'm not afraid of a challenge."

"Well then, saddle up and *ride,*" he taunts, his brow quirked as a lopsided grin lights his face.

A high-pitched combination of a laugh and cough threatens to take my life as I choke on my own saliva. "Jesus, Ry, that was bad."

"Yeah, but you're worrying me. What's going on, gorgeous?"

I redirect my attention to his thigh again. The crisp, dark lines swirling over his lightly sun-tanned skin reveal a perfect replica of one of the origami bouquets I gifted him over a decade ago. It was some of my best work, with extra intricacy in the defined petals of the blooming roses. I'd been avoiding studying for an exam the night I made them, instead spending hours working on the gift. And here they are, outlined on his skin for eternity.

He looks down between us, following my gaze.

"It's beautiful," I breathe out, barely managing to get the words out as love and lust threaten to strangle me. I've loved this man all my life, and maybe if I stopped running from one thing to the next long enough to realize it, I could've saved us a whole world of heartbreak. I make the effort to stop that thought in its tracks, knowing Talia would redirect me. I can't change the past, and it wasn't our time. *Until now.*

"*You* are beautiful. This," he says, motioning to the tattoo, "is just a little something to carry me through the dark days. Now that you're here, those are few and far between."

Tears prick the corners of my eyes as I peer up at him. "Are you sure about that? Because it sure feels like I've been bringing a whole lot of darkness to your life," I tell him, anger, resentment, heartache, and regret twisting inside me as I mentally recount the recent events that landed us here tonight.

He gathers my hands in his, kissing my knuckles. "Lola Lima, you are *the* most precious gift I've ever received, and every day spent with you has been brighter than the last. Some days have their challenges, but there is no one I'd rather have by my side for as long as the moon dances in the sky than *you.*"

My heart bursts wide at the seams, overflowing into my chest, making it hard to breathe. Relief floods me, as does fear. "But…" He wipes an errant tear from my cheek, dragging me against his body and pressing a kiss to the top of my head.

"But what, darlin'?"

"This marriage wasn't supposed to be real, Ry."

He chuckles deeply, the sound vibrating into my stomach, releasing a horde of butterfly wings. He tips my chin up, forcing me to meet his eyes. "Lola, I've never loved anyone more than I love you. I might have tried to convince myself I was marrying you for any reason besides that, but the truth is it's always been you, always will be. I don't want there to be an end date to our marriage, and I'd hoped couples counseling had shown you that, but since you need the reassurance, understandably so, I'm here to give it to you as long and as often as you need."

He presses a kiss to the tip of my nose and settles his forehead against mine. "I don't *want* you to leave me, not *ever*. This is real for me, darlin', and I want to show you that every single day." He bends further, caressing my lips with a gentle kiss that has those butterfly wings brushing the sides of my tummy. His words calm the restlessness that's been swirling inside me these last couple of months, and I know there isn't anyone I'd rather do life with than him.

"I love you, Ryder Maddox Lockhart. We have a lot to talk about, things we need to work out, obstacles to overcome, but every day from here on out, I'm choosing *you*."

"Now *that* is the dirty talk of my dreams. God, baby, words of affirmation just do it for me," he says, light laughter bubbling between us. "And I love you too, more than you know. I'm about to try and show you," he says, smirking as he tosses me on my back and ducks his head, nipping the skin at the base of my throat. All the tension is suddenly replaced with a newfound wave of lust and desire.

He grips the base of his dick, pressing the tip against my clit. I grind against him, groaning from the sparks zipping up my spine. "Do we need a condom?" he asks.

"I tested negative after the girls rescued me," I tell him. "And I have an implant, so I'm okay to go without if you are."

"I'm also STI-free and haven't been with anyone in years, even since before the divorce."

My eyes widen, unable to stop them as I stare at him in disbelief. "Excuse me, *what?*"

"Don't act so shocked, Lola. The woman was emotionally abusing me. It's difficult to get in the mood when you're constantly under fire like that. I have no regrets about the way things have turned out. In every lifetime, it was always you, Lols."

"Ry, you were *married* to her. Jesus, no wonder she hates me!" I tell him, but I'm only half joking. Mostly, I'm thrilled he's saved so much of himself for me, even if that wasn't necessarily the intent. I wish I'd done the same; instead, it feels like I sold pieces of my soul to the devil in the hopes he'd prove me wrong and show me he wasn't exactly what I'd thought he was: a monster.

I push the unwanted thoughts from my mind as Ryder clasps my jaw in his warm grip, dragging my eyes up to his. "No one else matters here, darlin'. It's you and me. Okay?" I nod, and he gives me a lopsided grin as reward for my stellar behavior. "Good. Now, eyes on me, darlin', because I'm about to fill you until there's no question about who you belong to. Be a doll and grab onto the headboard."

"Yes, sir," I agree, reaching behind me to grip the wooden slats, laughter spilling past my lips. It dies in my throat as Ryder dips his head, pressing a searing kiss to my mouth, now swollen from his kisses. His tongue tangles with mine, and I release a rough moan. He notches himself into me, sliding his engorged tip through my slickness, my thighs clenching around his hips from how damn good it feels.

"I have never seen or known anyone more beautiful, inside and out, than you, Lola," he tells me, his tone reverent. When he says things like this, they dig themselves deeply into the very depths of my soul. With Ryder, *I believe him.* I believe him like I've never trusted another man in my entire life, and instead of terrifying me, *it thrills me.*

"How about you slide on inside and find out *just* how true that is," I say, the joke falling flat as he does exactly as I say.

We both groan loudly, my head falling against the pillows as he stretches me, a delicious touch of pain mingling with pleasure. Heat coils in my center as he edges back out, only to drive his hips further, deepening the stretch.

His mouth finds the sensitive bud of my nipples, sucking and tugging on them. When he slips a calloused hand between us, pressing down firmly on my clit, I almost combust. There are so many sensations swirling inside me, I'm overwhelmed with pleasure, and it's an intoxicating feeling.

"I want all of you, Ry. Give me every inch," I beg, aching for release.

His resolve snaps, a hungry growl ripping from his chest as he ravishes my body, pounding into me. The headboard bangs violently against the wall, matching the rhythm of my rampant heartbeat.

"You can have anything you want, darlin'. I'll. Give. You. Everything." He punctuates each word with arduous thrusts that have me barreling toward my release. He praises me, pushing me over the edge.

My walls clench around his thick length, heat licks up my spine, and my limbs tingle as I lose myself in the feeling of Ryder Lockhart fucking me into our marital bed.

I release the headboard, twining my fingers in his hair and dragging his mouth to mine as he finishes inside me with a loud moan I'm locking away in my spank bank. *Thank God for cowboys.*

"So good, so perfect," he whispers over and over, resting his sweaty forehead against mine as we relax into the bed together.

"It was about time we consummated our marriage, huh?"

He boops my nose with the tip of his forefinger, crawling backward out of the bed, only to grab a candle and lighter from the dresser behind him. "Spread your pussy open, darlin'. I have to see what we look like together," he tells me, and I obey, using both hands to spread my lips for him to see his cum dripping out of me.

"That's so good, baby. Your cunt deserves to look like that every day. Don't you agree?" he asks, climbing over me, straddling my thighs as he lights the candle.

I'd thought I couldn't take a single second more tonight, but it turns out, with the right incentive, the incentive being Ryder Lockhart's massive dick pulsing against my needy pussy again, I can be persuaded.

"I saw this candle the other day when I was in town and thought you deserved a good massage," he says in a husky tone. He sets the lighter down beside my head, leaning over me, scraping his stubbled jawline from the base of my throat to the soft skin under my breast. He kisses that spot gently, lifting to peer down at me with hungry eyes. "Is this okay?" he asks, tilting the candle just shy of the wax spilling over the lip.

"As long as that turns into massage oil and not a waxy mess, yes, absolutely," I pant, which he meets with deep laughter.

"Tell me if it's too hot," he whispers, dripping the hot, silky wax between my breasts. It stings, burning for only a moment before cooling to the perfect temperature. He sets the candle on the nightstand, focusing every ounce of his attention on me. His rough hands slide through the oil, kneading my breasts, flicking his thumbs over my nipples. My back arches, desperate to deepen the way his strong fingers press into my skin. "This feel good?" he asks.

"Y-yes," I whisper, the word getting caught in my throat as my muscles relax beneath him.

"Good. Now flip over," he instructs, standing to allow me the room I need to lie face down, resting my cheek on my forearms.

"I promise I meant this as a nice cool down before I wash your hair and treat you how you deserve after sharing something so perfect with me," he whispers, his tone soft, measured, and filled with respect for me.

"And now?" I ask breathlessly.

"And now"—he taps my ass and pussy with the length of his quickly hardening dick—"I have a little detour planned," he answers, laughing deeply, the sound full-bodied and comforting. "I want your knees bent, thighs spread wide, and ass up. I *need* to see that beautiful pussy while I take care of you."

Without hesitation, I shift forward, bending my legs so my knees are tucked close to my elbows. His sharp inhale is all the satisfaction I need to maintain this position, but what he does next is enough to convince me to do *anything* he asks.

His hand glides down the slope of my spine, hot oil trickling from the top of my ass down the strip to my pussy, where he runs two fingers through the mixture of our cum and the warm oil, slipping them inside me, teasing me with a slow, steady pace.

"It's safe for intercourse," he says, my mind a hazy, blissedout mess.

"Huh?" I ask, rocking against his hand, seeking out the pleasure his fingers provide.

"The oil, darlin'. It's safe for sex. I didn't want you to worry," he answers, and while I know this sort of thing should be the bare minimum, my heart flutters all the same. I'm not sure I know *anyone* who would think about something like that in the heat of the moment, truly taking care of every aspect of my needs.

As if reflecting my own thoughts, he says, "I have to make sure I take care of every single inch of my wife, especially her gorgeous cunt."

"Mmm," I moan. "And how can I take care of my husband's pretty dick?" I ask, heat licking up my spine, tingles burning at the base as a contented ecstasy gathers in my core.

He releases a groan I feel inside me, my walls clenching around his fingers in approval. He doesn't answer, but his fingers leave me, more oil coating my ass before his fingers knead my skin, spreading the oil around. When he's satisfied with a job well done, he swats me on the ass and presses a firm hand on the small of my back, lowering me into the mattress.

The tip of his fully engorged length notches at my entrance, swiping through my folds before he presses in slowly, inch by blissful inch. My neck arches, the backs of my thighs meeting the fronts of his as he fills me to the hilt.

"I'm honored to be here with you, Lola," he tells me, filling the quiet silence of the room with heavy words spoken so low they shouldn't rock my whole world. "To have you all to myself, then to see the way your eyes light up, a permanent smile plastered on your face, when you're with your family. My heart aches with gratitude for the small moments and the monumental ones, knowing you've let me in and given me pieces of yourself."

His words have tears pricking the edges of my vision, my tongue too big in my mouth, unable to speak.

"And I intend to take care of absolutely any pieces you'll let me. Not because I think you need to be cared for. No, you can do that all on your own. I *want* to give you everything you deserve and more," he finishes, his movements slow and deliberate, rocking us gently toward release.

"You *do* make me feel cared for, Ry. More than anyone ever has," I manage to say, fire burning me from the inside changing from pure lust to love. I guess *this* is what those sappy romance books meant when they called it "making love."

He bends forward, pressing a soft kiss to my spine, whispering against my skin, "And I intend to keep it that way."

He straightens, pouring more of the hot oil along my back, massaging the sore, stiff muscles. He digs his thumbs and knuckles into the tight knots in my shoulders where I carry all my stress, maintaining a smooth rhythm with his thrusts.

My body is pliant in his capable hands, and I'm unable to tell where I begin and Ryder ends as we come apart together.

This time, there's no rush as we ride the wave of euphoria, enjoying the gentle tingle of pleasure low in my core as I pulse around him.

He leans down and gathers my lax body in his arms, clutching me against his oil-slick chest, carrying me into the bathroom.

"Well, Mrs. Lima, I think we oughta get washed up so we can do it all over again."

"I could go another round, *Mr. Lima*," I tease.

"Don't play with me, Lola. I'll go down to the courthouse tomorrow and ask for a name change if that'll make you happy." His tone is serious as he settles me on my feet and reaches into the shower to turn the water on. Steam billows around us a few moments later, cloaking us in a shroud of safety I haven't felt in weeks. Not since Lemmon Meringue decided to weasel her way into our lives, but she messed with the wrong woman. I protect what's mine, and Ryder Lockhart certainly is *mine*.

But after seeing the look of what I fear was genuine surprise on her face tonight, I'm worried I've gotten it all wrong.

"Hey, Ry," I whisper, water dripping down my body, his callused fingers gliding over my hips as he lathers his eucalyptus body wash into my skin.

"Yes, darlin'?" He peers down at me, dark clumps of his hair plastered to his forehead, water dripping into his eyes.

"What if we're wrong and it hasn't been Lemmon all along?"

His brows pinch, ocean eyes search my gaze. "What makes you think that, darlin'?"

I shake my head. "It's just—" I glance down to where his hands are on me, gathering mine in his, our wedding bands glimmering beneath the bathroom lights.

He tugs one hand out of my grasp gently, pinching my chin

between his forefinger and thumb to tilt my head back, and I find myself snared in his gaze.

"It's just what?"

"She looked so shocked, Ry. And unless she's been taking professional acting classes, I'm not sure it was all a ruse."

He nods. "I trust your instincts, Lola. No matter what the truth is, we'll figure it out." The fierceness with which he says those words settles some of the unease swirling in my gut, and rather than focus on all the ways my *gut* could have steered me wrong, I focus on Ryder, the man my *heart* has always led me back to.

After a long, well-deserved shower, we crawl into bed together, our bodies sated and clean.

Ryder twists my wet curls, setting them above my head on my pillow, and I just know I'll regret sleeping with wet hair when I'm forced to tame it in the morning, but after the night's events, I just can't be bothered to diffuse. Although he did his best, detangling, raking leave-in conditioner from the mids to ends and even applying my gel afterward, like he's seen me do so many times before, it won't matter in the morning.

He leans in close and wraps an arm around my waist. "Will you please consider a security guard? For me?" he asks, his voice small, but it sounds so loud in the calm silence of our dark room.

The last thing I want is to feel like some mob princess with a price over my head, but I have a feeling Ryder's mental health could really use this, so I agree. "Sure, Ry. We can look into a security guard."

He lets out a relieved breath, his body sagging against me. "Thank you, darlin'."

"Whatever you need, Ry," I say, repeating a version of his earlier words to him.

He falls asleep quickly, but he doesn't stay asleep.

A half hour passes as I stare at the ceiling, my lids growing heavy while I wait for the inevitable to happen. When I hear his whimpers and feel his body go rigid against me, I'm ready for it this time.

I roll over top of him, straddling his waist and hugging my body tightly against him, the same as I have every time panic threatens to strangle him in his sleep.

"It's okay, Ry. It's alright. I've got you. I'm here, and we're safe," I whisper the mantra over and over until his body stills, and I'm able to sleep.

That happens three more times before the sun rises.

Chapter Fifty-Five

COWBOY CROSSING

SATURDAY, JUNE 21

I KNOW she's not thrilled about having a security detail, and, if I'm honest, I have no idea how we'll afford it or where we'd go to look for something like that, but I'll figure it out.

I woke up to the first of what I'm sure will be many threatening text messages. This one was overtly so as opposed to the veiled warnings of some of Lola's earlier messages.

It read:

> Watch your back, cowboy. We know what you're hiding.

The message was so cliché, I actually had to laugh, but the "we" has me worrying this problem might be bigger than either of us realized.

That was followed by another with nothing more than a photo, not of Lola and me together like the ones before, but of the barn bursting into flames. The image was taken from somewhere on the fringes of the property. My hair's been standing on end ever since, skin crawling with unease, and my head has been pounding all day from a lack of sleep and my constant panic from last night.

Lola's tucked into the corner of the couch, a book three inches from her face, when I get inside, an involuntary smile stretching my lips at just the sight of her.

"Maybe you should use that health insurance for an ophthalmology appointment," I joke.

She dog-ears the book and sets it on the end table.

"In case you weren't aware, Ryder Lockhart, this is America. Health insurance doesn't include your eyeballs or your teeth," she says with a light chuckle.

"I know, Lols. I've been in this country thirty-four years. I got you vision and dental too," I say, ruffling her hair and stealing a handful of popcorn from the bowl beside her.

"Well, aren't you just the most thoughtful little peach?" she says, clearly imitating Lemmon's accent.

"You know, I've wondered my whole life if that voice of hers was a choice because I've met her daddy, and he doesn't sound a lick like that," I muse.

"Doesn't matter if it's intentional or not. It's annoying."

"That's a fact I can't deny. Now," I say, moving the popcorn bowl and dragging her into my lap, "how about we move your things into our room and go on a drive later?"

Lola

Chapter Fifty-Six

DRUNK AS A SKUNK

SATURDAY, JUNE 21

"YOU CAN HAVE any drawers and closet space you want. Take your pick, darlin'."

Ryder tugs open the top drawer of the dresser and starts emptying his clothing before I can say otherwise. "Ry, I basically live in leggings and *your* t-shirts. I don't need much room."

"I want this to feel as much your space as it does mine. Please, Lols. Split half of everything with me, yeah?" he asks, his eyes crinkled at the corners with an earnest expression, silently pleading with me to give in.

And of course, I do. "Sure, Ry, whatever you want," I say with a chuckle, sidling up to him and bumping him out of my way with my hip. My fingers curl around the intricate brass handles of the antique wooden chest of drawers, yanking the second drawer from the top open.

My heart stops in my chest for a beat before galloping wildly at the contents of the drawer. I can't pull my eyes away to meet his eyes. "Ry," I breathe out, shock rippling through me as I reach inside to pick one up.

"I used to keep them on the mantle, but when I knew you

were moving in, I thought it'd be best if I hid them until you'd gotten used to the idea of how in love I've always been with you." I finally drag my eyes away from the delicate paper petals littering the drawer to peer up at my husband's chiseled face, his bright eyes swirling with adoration.

"After all these years, you kept them? *All* of them?" I ask, my voice strained as I hold back the tears threatening to fall. The origami flowers I'd made him for his birthday each year, and most recently, this April, are all here, each one in near-pristine condition.

He's been holding on to hope for a future together for longer than even *he* might've realized.

"Mind if I put these on the mantle where they belong, now that I've spilled the beans?" he asks with a lighthearted chuckle.

"Of course, Ry. Let's get these in some water," I joke, plucking them gently from the drawer and carrying them to the mantle, Ryder's hands full of the ones I couldn't carry.

It doesn't take long before we've got our room filled with my things, and then we're in his truck for a drive.

The music is so loud I wouldn't be able to hear my own thoughts if I wanted to. And right now, *I don't.* My mind keeps dredging up reminders of all the hard work I'd put into that barn, my studio, just to see it burning down around me last night.

The damage wasn't completely damning, but it'll still take time to fix. Luckily, Ryder had the building insured, but the claims adjuster isn't working until Monday, so there's no use dwelling on it until then.

After Ryder helped me shuffle our things around, we each got a text that had me crawling out of my skin. Text messages are one thing, but *photos* of us together *inside* our home? That's something I've grown tired of already, and instead of lighting a fire under my ass to put a stop to it, I want to run away for the night. We can figure the rest out tomorrow.

Ryder has the windows rolled down enough that the wind blows through the truck, but not enough that my hair is a complete mess.

He's got Callum Scott playing, and he's been singing the entire car ride down this long highway. We have no plans for where we're going; we're driving until we find somewhere to stop or turn around.

The sun is starting to set, the sky itself a baby blue, but the thick clouds overhead are a bright-bubblegum pink, and if not for the low hum of anxiety simmering in my chest and the way my gut feels a little twisty, I'd be completely at peace right now.

Every minute we drive out of Hidden Valley, my nerves settle a little more.

Fields of crops flank us, barbed wire fences holding livestock every few acres flying by as we drive.

The rumble of motorcycles grows louder until they're passing in front of us, waving as they go. It's hard not to recognize the guys, with their tie-dye leather jackets.

Ryder rolls up the windows and turns the music down.

We continue, neither of us saying anything as we settle into the safety of our own little bubble.

Another ten minutes pass, and we're still behind the guys from the biker book club. They turn their signals on, slowing to pull up a driveway into the only standing structure for miles.

"Can we go there?" I ask, nodding toward the small, rundown bar with a lit-up sign that reads "The Rusty Spur", except the *y* isn't lit.

"Anywhere you want, darlin'."

He follows behind the guys, parking in an available spot on the side of the bar beside a dumpster before turning off the engine and coming around my side to unbuckle me. He takes my hand, steering me toward the doors.

Peanut shells litter the ground, and the smell of stale beer permeates the air as we make our way to the bar.

"I've always wondered how people with a peanut allergy navigate something like this. Obviously, they don't go to places with peanuts all over the floor, but is there a good way to know about this sort of thing?" Ryder muses, his boots crunching on the shells.

"That's a good question, and unfortunately, one I don't know the answer to," I tell him, chuckling lightly.

The bikers are all seated at the far end of the bar, chatting with the bartender. Her hair is all jagged, sharp lines of various shades of blonde, and she's wearing a tight, cropped tank with denim shorts that show off her tattooed abdomen. It makes me think about the tattoo I've newly discovered on Ryder and how unnervingly sexy it is.

It's reassuring to know that, as wild as the last few months have been, Ryder will remain a steady constant in my life. I'll get to be up close and personal with the ink on his thigh *as often as I want*.

I drag Ryder up to the bar, taking a seat beside Wyatt on a wooden stool, leaning over the bar to wave at them. "Hey, guys," I say with a small wave.

"Evenin', Miss Lola," Levi says from the opposite end, his long gray beard hanging to what I'd imagine is where his nipples might've sat in the early two-thousands. Each of the men greet us, and the bartender returns to take our order a moment later.

"Howdy. I'm Raylin." The bartender introduces herself, tipping her hat at me with a wink. "What can I get y'all to drink?"

"A rum and Coke for me, please."

I look over to Ryder, and he smiles at her. I bask in the difference between the polite smiles he gives everyone else and the ones I receive. Each one contains multitudes, with a different level of hidden emotions, ranging from lust and desire to admiration, contentment, and my favorite, *endless devotion.*

"Just a water for me, ma'am," he tells her, unintentionally yanking me from my thoughts as I give him a look. "Don't think you've gotta hold back on my account, darlin'. I'll keep you safe," he assures me when Raylin sets the drinks in front of us. I let the cool, sweet liquid burn as it runs down my throat, warmth settling in my chest.

I turn in my seat, looking around the small room to get my bearings. There's a three-person band seated in the corner closest to the front doors, playing all the quintessential country songs I expect from a place like this.

Tall wooden tables are scattered around the room, but the center is clear of anything besides people and scuffed-up wood floorboards, presumably from years of line dancing. A few couples are dancing, and there's a table near us with a bunch of rowdy guys talking shop.

The twangy opening notes of "Boot Scootin' Boogie" fill the air, the crowd whooping as boots hit the center of the room, people flooding the dancefloor. Strings of fairy lights hang low across the rafters, casting a warm glow over the room.

I reach up, grabbing Ryder's hat from his head and settling it on mine, grinning up at him. "Come on, cowboy. Impress me."

I toss back the rest of my drink, taking his hand and dragging him out to dance.

Couples and groups are already in formation, their boots tapping in time with the music. Ryder slides a hand to the small of my back, guiding me into position as if we hadn't spent the entirety of our adolescent years line dancing together.

The music picks up, the crowd moving as one, shuffling left then right, boots stomping in unison. I throw myself into the rhythm despite the way my joints scream at me to stop. I refuse to have another thing taken from me at the hands of something out of my control.

My hips sway, and laughter bubbles out of me with every step and spin.

Ryder matches me move for move, his pretty blue eyes twinkling under the lights and his grin widening each time our gazes meet.

"Unlike this bar, I see that *you*, Ryder Lockhart, are not as rusty as I'd thought," I call over the music, my breathless excitement giving me away.

He chuckles, spinning me and catching my hand as I swing around. "And you thought I was all for show, didn't ya, darlin'?"

"You're certainly nice to look at," I admit, moving up on my tiptoes to press a chaste kiss to the corner of his mouth.

The song comes to an end, and I'm flushed. I'm sure my cheeks are glowing beneath the shadow of Ryder's hat.

We weave through the crowd, and the bartender makes eye contact with me, giving me a small smile and pouring me another drink. I gulp it down.

"Slow down there. You're gonna be drunk as a skunk any minute, darlin'."

"Maybe that's the point, Ry," I say, tossing him a wink and turning to head out. He snatches my hand, dragging me into his warm body.

Ryder cups my cheeks, kissing my forehead and lowering his voice. "Just promise you won't puke on me because you know that makes me squeamish."

The alcohol is already hitting me, tingling through my limbs as I gaze up at him. "No promises, Ry."

He shakes his head, laughing as he twirls me, the contents of my stomach already swirling with the alcohol. I move past it, determined to have a good time tonight.

We dance for several more songs, taking short breaks in between. When the music swaps to something much slower, couples pairing up to embrace each other, Ryder holds me close to his chest.

My breath catches as I peer up at him, my mind a little hazy. The way he's looking at me, like I'm the only thing worth watching, makes my heart do a little two-step of its own.

At some point, I plopped down beside Wyatt again, the outside of my thigh now pressing against his black leather pants, but I don't have the energy or strength to move.

I vaguely hear Ryder ordering chicken wings and cheese fries as I turn to face the group. "Hi." I wave, a wide smile on my face. At least, I *think* it's wide?

The five men lean over the slippery wooden bar top, their lips stretching into grins of their own as their eyes land on me.

"How's it goin', Lols?" Levi asks, the corners of his eyes crinkling with mirth.

"You doing okay after everything that went down last night?" Teddy, the blond, asks, his voice low and warm. I feel guilty I've met them so many times and don't remember all their names, but I'm sure that'll come with time. Lemmon isn't running me out of town this time, that's for sure.

"I'm doing about as good as I can be. The insurance should cover most of the damage, but it's going to take time to make sure the electrical is salvageable and safe and the roof is stable."

"If there's anything y'all need, just holler. We're happy to help," Wyatt, the one beside me with the short-cropped, dark beard and glittering green eyes, says. He's also got a warm thigh, which wins an extra brownie point, seeing as my skin is littered with goosebumps from the chill in the room.

"Yeah, Lola. We like to stay busy. Keeps our minds from wandering. We're happy to help," the man beside Wyatt says. They share several of the same features, and I recall they're brothers, but his name escapes me.

As if reading my mind, Wyatt pats his brother on the shoulder and says, "That we do, Cal." *Cal.* Callaway!

"We appreciate the offer," Ryder tells them. "And we might have to take you up on that. Lola's worked too hard for things to go this poorly so quickly, but it might be smart to wait to fix things up until after we've figured out the Lemmon issue."

The bartender interrupts briefly, delivering our food. "Y'all need anything else to drink?"

I look over to Ryder, who's got a glass of ice water. He shakes his head no, but I know what this man really wants.

"Yes, please! Ryder would like a Shirley Temple with extra cherries." I beam at her.

"Comin' right up," she says, a smirk curving her magenta-painted lips.

Ryder's strong arms wind around me, holding me up. He presses a kiss to the pulse along the side of my neck, and my skin feels like it's on fire in the best way possible.

Raylin passes Ryder a tall, slim glass loaded with cherries, and his smile at seeing the sweet, bubbly drink is contagious. I watch him suck on the straw, his throat bobbing as he swallows.

"Would y'all mind tellin' us a little about this Lemmon issue? We've heard a lot of talk, but we hadn't realized she might be capable of something as serious as arson," Levi asks, his salt-and-pepper brows pinched with worry.

I breathe a heavy sigh, dragging a long swig of my drink before answering. "I hope you gentlemen have got time on your hands, because it's a *long* and convoluted story, and truthfully, I'm not sure she's capable of arson either."

"We've got nothin' but time, Miss Lola," the redheaded one, whose name I believe is Rhett, says with a soft smile.

And that's how I find myself blabbering about Lemmon for so long I lose track of time. I tell them I've had to give up on romantic thrillers and suspense lately because I've been so jumpy from everything going on. The rum and Cokes keep coming, and my lips grow looser by the minute.

They listen to me with rapt attention, hanging on to every word. Ryder just sits back, rubbing soothing circles over my skin as we chat. It feels good to have gotten it all out, spilling my guts to these gentlemen.

This leads into a discussion about the romance books they read, their favorite authors and genres, and a few romantic suspense novels they've picked up that reminded them of my current situation.

By the time my lids are drooping and I'm sagging into my seat, I've relived our entire history with Lemmon and Russ, and the guys have offered to take turns as my security detail in exchange for dance lessons once the studio is back open.

My mind feels warm and fuzzy, back slumped against Ryder's chest as he holds my weight up. "We should get goin', Miss Lola, but it was wonderful gettin' to know you better," Levi says, wrapping Ryder and me up in a hug. He smells like cloves and leather, and as we wave our goodbyes, my gaze gets caught on their jackets and leather pants.

Ryder would look damn good in leather chaps. "Baby, we should get a motorcycle," I slur.

He chuckles, the sound tickling the skin of my neck. "Come on, darlin'. Let's get you home." Ryder's words are the last thing I hear before I'm home, on my knees, clutching the porcelain throne and emptying the contents of my stomach.

Ryder

Chapter Fifty-Seven

DRUNKEN WORDS, SOBER THOUGHTS

SUNDAY, JUNE 22

"IT'S ALRIGHT, BABY," I coo, piling Lola's hair on top of her head as she empties her stomach. I grab a silk scrunchie from the counter, tying her hair up so I can grab a washcloth.

"I'm sorry, Ry," she cries. "This is so gross."

I chuckle lightly, wetting the cloth with cool water before I get down on my knees behind her, the tile biting into my skin. I wipe her mouth each time she pukes and let her get it all out. "It's not that gross, and it's nothing I haven't seen before." I rub circles along her back, and when she's stopped retching, I stand, lifting her up and balancing her against the sink.

"Can you hold yourself up long enough for me to get you out of these clothes, darlin'?"

"Ry, I'm s-sorry," she slurs. "I'm not in the mood right now."

I chuckle, but the sound is humorless. What the hell had Russ done to her? "I don't want to fuck you right now, baby. I want to help you shower, get you into some pajamas, and tuck you into bed. Is that okay?"

"Mmm," she hums. "That sounds nice. Th-thank you, Ry.

Y-you've always—" She hiccups, slapping her hand over her mouth, eyes wide.

"Okay, baby. Go ahead and lean on the counter, and I'll get you undressed and in the shower." She plants her hands on the counter, making a point of popping her ass out as she peers over her shoulder at me.

"Like this?" she asks, her voice filled with a playful lilt.

"Yes, darlin'. Just like that," I tease, unbuttoning her shorts and sliding them down her legs. She's not wearing panties, but thankfully, my dick gets the message. We're on a mission here, and he stays nice and flaccid. Well, mostly. "No panties? Such a dirty girl." What? I'm a gentleman, not a saint.

"Only for my husband," she says, shimmying her ass. "Is it time for my top?"

My chest expands with laughter, and I feel weightless. "Yes, baby." I help her drag her shirt over her head, her perky little tits popping out from beneath the soft fabric. "And no bra? Well, wifey, were you hoping your husband would fuck you in the bathroom of a dingy bar?"

"I d-didn't know where we w-were going, but I w-wanted you to fuck m-me anywhere," she says, still hiccupping every few words. Heat simmers in my blood at her admission.

"Maybe after you've gotten a good night's sleep and can properly consent, we can revisit this conversation, yeah?"

"Mhmm," she hums, her eyes closing.

"Let's get you in the shower, darlin'," I say, carrying her across the bathroom and setting her on the shower bench, running the water to warm. I step out, stripping down to my briefs before I climb in. "Keep your head up for me," I instruct her gently, taking the shower head and running the warm water over her body.

She sits with a contented smile as I lather her body in shower gel, taking her hair down and wetting it. I wash and condition her hair, detangling it with a wide-tooth comb and then a wet brush like I've watched her do a dozen times.

I help her dry off when I've finished, brushing her teeth as she stands with a grin like the Cheshire cat, one that bares all her teeth to me. I do my best, and she rinses and spits into the sink. I pat her mouth dry and carry her to bed. She's wrapped up in a towel, now fast asleep, so I take my time changing into a fresh pair of briefs. I grab one of my t-shirts, sliding it over her head.

She rolls over, her hair splayed over her satin pillowcase, reaching out to grab my face as her eyes crack open. "Thank you, Ry," she says, planting a kiss on my mouth—or trying to. Her teeth and lips smack at my chin, and she bounces off me almost comically, flopping onto the mound of pillows behind her.

"You're welcome, darlin'." I flip off the lights and climb in beside her, tugging the covers up under her chin. The last words she speaks before passing out nearly steal my breath from my lungs.

"I'm *in* love with you, Ry," she whispers dreamily, falling asleep as quickly as the words leave her mouth, a soft snore rattling through the room.

"I'm in love with you too, darlin'." Maybe when she wakes up, she'll want to tell me while sober.

Lola

Chapter Fifty-Eight

MAMI KNOWS BEST

SUNDAY, JUNE 22

"YOU NEED A GOOD VACUUM, *mija*. You have a dog, and when you and Ryder decide to give me grandbabies, I don't want them covered in hair."

I roll my eyes, continuing to sweep the kitchen floor. "I'll add it to the list, *Mami*. And in case you'd forgotten, we just got married and even more recently decided to make it real."

She waves a hand in front of her face, dismissing me. "Of course it's real. It always has been. You belong together."

I steer her away from the topic of grandbabies and onto something that'll make her smile instead. "I moved my things into the main room with him yesterday."

"Don't think I don't know exactly what you're on about," she says with a pout.

"*Mami*, he kept the flowers I made him," I tell her, my eyes pooling with hot tears, this time joyful ones. Ryder's the only man who has ever made me cry happy tears.

Mami physically swoons, wringing her hands together and tucking them under her chin. "That is so sweet, *mijita*. You'll have to teach your children how to make those flowers someday."

I groan, sighing as I finish sweeping the dirt into a dustpan before dumping it into the trash. "Can we talk about something else? *Please.*"

"Fine. Come here. You need to catch up on *Secrets Signed In Ink* before Ryder gets home."

My brows pinch as I take a seat beside her. Nugget hops up, making little donuts before plopping down between us. "And why is that?" I run my fingers through Nugget's thick fur, relaxing into the tan cushions.

I meet my mom's guilty gaze before her eyes dart away. "What did you do?"

"Nothing, nothing." She waves a hand in the space between us. "It's really your husband's fault, though, if you want to get down to it."

"*Mami, seriously.*"

"Okay, *fine.* Ryder came over earlier and watched the episode from last week with me, so now you're behind."

"Already picking my husband over me, I see," I say, snatching the remote and turning on the TV. There isn't a single ounce of me that's actually upset about it. The fact that Ryder watches *telenovelas* with my mom is the most adorable thing and an absolute panty melter, if I'm totally honest with myself.

We spend the next hour catching up on the episode I missed, and when Ryder gets home from his trip to the feed store, *Mami* insists on cooking dinner. *Papi,* Mayte, Isabela, and Ryder's parents wound up coming over, and despite all the madness taking place on the ranch lately, there's some semblance of normalcy at having all the most important people in my life around for something as simple as a good meal.

Chapter Fifty-Nine

NOT AS IT SEEMS?

WEDNESDAY, JUNE 25

JUST LIKE EVERY OTHER MORNING, Lola's asleep when I leave for work, her body curled around a pillow and the covers tucked beneath her chin.

I press a kiss to her forehead. "I love you, darlin'."

"I luhf woo," she whispers, her breathing still steady and slow, with no signs of her being awake. Every morning, I tell her I love her, and every morning, her unconscious mind registers it, telling me she loves me back.

Warmth spreads through my chest, and a satisfied smile tugs at the corners of my lips.

Nugget blinks up at me, and I lift him onto the bed to snuggle with Lola. He wags his little nub-tail and rubs his head against her back, twirling in place before he plops down.

"I love you too, Nugget," I tell him, kissing the top of his head before gently closing the door behind me. I grab the two breakfast burritos I warmed from the counter and leave Lola a note so she knows there's one in the fridge for her.

After I've made sure the windows are all locked, I head out, locking the door and double-checking the cameras.

Rhett waves at me from his seat in the small garden. "Mornin', Ryder!" he hollers.

"Morning, Rhett," I say, tossing the burrito at our new biker friend. I'd thought what they'd offered to do for us was nothing more than an empty, drunken promise, but Sunday morning, we woke up to a call from Ezekiel. Zeke was absolutely miffed about not knowing about Lola's new security detail, demanding to run background checks on men he's known for two years now.

"I'll keep an eye on things 'round here," he assures me, unwrapping the burrito and taking a bite, returning to reading the book of the month.

"Thanks, Rhett. What y'all have been doin' for us means more than I could express. Truly, let me know if you need anything," I tell him, tipping my hat and climbing inside my truck.

I do my best to keep my mind clear, finishing the backend admin duties as quickly as possible before spending a few hours at the greenhouse.

If this takes off, I'll need to start creating much larger batches, but I already have a plan for that. My hope was always to be able to sustain my community single-handedly if needed, which has come with a lot of preparation on my part. That doesn't make it any less overwhelming though.

In between getting things done, I spend a hell of a lot of time answering calls from people in the community reporting suspicious activity from Lemmon. Most of it seems to be false alarms, with everyone being abundantly cautious on our behalf. Still, more than a few people mentioned seeing her driving out of town in a vehicle they didn't recognize, driven by a man wearing a black hoodie over his face. Then, Betsy mentioned his side profile reminded her of Zeke, and my mind ran wild.

Chapter Sixty
TURNING THE PAGE

WEDNESDAY, JUNE 25

RYDER'S BEEN GONE the better part of the morning, and with Mayte working on an event, I figure I can keep Rhett some company.

I slip a pair of flip-flops on and crack the door open, peering outside and spotting Rhett seated on the wrought iron bench in the small garden. It's overflowing with vibrant wildflowers in various shades of purples, pinks, and blues. There's a blue jay perched on the fencepost nearest to the garden, chirping, clucking, and whirring its liquid notes in a whisper-song that fills the crisp air.

Rhett peers up over his book as I step out onto the wraparound porch, dressed in another one of Ryder's t-shirts, this one a worn-out band tee that feels thin and soft against my freshly waxed skin. My leggings protect me from the bite in the air from the unseasonably cool weather in early June in Oklahoma. I find myself wrapping my arms around my upper body.

"Hey, Rhett. Mind if I join you for a bit?"

"Not at all, Miss Lola. Come on over and grab a seat," he tells me, patting the space beside him as he leans back, ankles crossed. His feet rest on a small ceramic table Ryder, Mayte, Ezekiel, and I helped Harlan glue colorful pieces of glass to as an anniversary gift for Bee. Gifts we helped make litter the entire property, much of it *Mami's* fault, given her affinity for arts and crafts.

I plop down beside him, stretching my sore limbs after another night spent worrying someone is trying to kill me by any means necessary. If you'd have asked me a month ago, I'd have said Lemmon was behind it all. She's like a small dog: all bark and no bite. But now? I'm not fully convinced of anything other than the fact that whoever's behind it is out for blood, and the thought sends a tendril of fear skirting down my back.

"Now, I know you said you weren't sure if you'd be able to commit to our monthly book club or not, but I'm prepared to convince you," he says with a wide grin that crinkles the sun-tanned, freckled skin at the edges of his eyes.

Rhett is a sweet man in his late thirties who opened up to me about his friendship with the other guys. On Monday, when he took his first shift here, he'd kept me company while I worried about what the insurance appraiser would find at the barn. The electric needs to be stripped, a new roof has to be installed, and everything is covered in soot and soggy from the water used to contain the fire, but it could be worse.

Rhett made sure I had my mind on anything but that fire, telling me all about his friendship with the guys in the Ryde or Dye book club.

Levi lost his wife to cancer a couple of years ago. Teddy had been struggling with addiction, which ended his marriage and took his right to see his children. Wyatt has been healing from a long history of depression, and his brother, Callaway, quit his job to support his brother on his self-growth journey. And Rhett, well… He's never been able to move on after "the one who got away" left a few years ago. All the men are open about their experiences, and he assured me they wouldn't mind me knowing what led them all to Hidden Valley. Rhett said

Ryder and I have brought him and his friends a lot of hope for the future, and that makes me more gleeful than it has any right to.

To think, our complicated, messy, and sometimes downright terrifying love story could give way to so much hope. It's like a little miracle.

"Well, I am ready to be convinced," I say, placing my hands in my lap and turning my full attention to the gentle giant before me. His blue eyes twinkle, and he spends the next hour relaying the highlights of his favorite books from book club before giving me a synopsis of the current book of the month.

"So the FMC has ADHD, but she won't medicate because she's nursing?"

"Yeah, basically. I mean, it's a lot more complex than that, but I don't want to ruin it for you. She also does this thing I find hysterical, where she avoids having deep conversations with the MMC…"

"And the MMC used to work on the ranch but left after a one-night stand with the FMC where she wound up pregnant with his baby?"

"Yes! Can you imagine?" Rhett asks, tugging on the ends of his red beard.

Actually, I can imagine, considering that's precisely what happened with Mayte. Maybe she should skip this month's book club.

"Uh, sounds wild," I say instead, because unlike Rhett and his friends, we haven't spoken about whether or not it's okay to air my best friend's dirty laundry to these men, even if Rhett seems totally harmless and is doing me and Ryder a huge favor by being here.

Speaking of the handsome devil, Ryder pulls up in his truck, the exhaust burning my nose as he cuts the engine. "Hey, y'all. Reading anything good?" He chuckles, but the sound doesn't curl around me with warmth it usually would, and the feeling has me worried.

"I'm trying to convince Lola to join our book club," Rhett tells him, shifting to sit straight.

"Well, consider me thoroughly convinced," I tell him with a light laugh. I could use a good distraction from the real world.

"I'll join too. What better way to find out what Lola's ideal husband is than a book club that talks all about it?" he says, shooting me a wink as he produces a small bouquet of wildflowers from behind his back.

"Awww," Rhett swoons. "That's so sweet! You lovebirds get inside. I'm gonna give y'all some privacy. Cal will be here to swap with me soon." His round cheeks pinken with his wide smile, and it makes me sad to think about these guys not being around as often after we get things sorted. Bittersweet, for sure.

"Thanks, Rhett. You guys are the best. Honestly, I don't know how we'll ever repay you."

"Oh, Miss Lola. Dance lessons when your studio is up and running again will be more than an even trade. We're really liking it in Hidden Valley, and the guys and I are thinking it might be time for us to officially call this place our home," he says, and hope unfurls inside me, a grin tugging at my lips.

"We'd love that, Rhett. If there's anything I've learned, it's that Hidden Valley is the perfect place to start over, even when you think your life is unrepairable."

"It sure seems like it," he says, shooing us inside.

Ryder leans over, wrapping his thick, muscular arms around me and hoisting me up as a squeal flies past my lips, replacing any of my earlier apprehension with excitement. "Come on, little lady. You heard the man: We should get inside," he says, playfully swatting my butt once we pass over the threshold into the house.

He sets me on my feet long enough to adjust his position so his arms wind around me, tugging me against his chest. My hands flatten over his firm pecs, the muscles rippling under the bunched-up black fabric of his V-neck.

"Ryder Lockhart, who'd have thought something as simple as a plain t-shirt could look *so* good?" I purr, flirting shamelessly with my husband now that we've both agreed to remove the word "fake" from the title. Our marriage had never been anything close to a sham, and despite the terrifying events since my arrival, I'm so glad we're on the same page with that revelation.

"I could ask the same of you, darlin'. But I won't because I already know the answer," he says, dipping his chin to catch my lips in a hot kiss that melts any remnants of the icy block that settled in the pit of my stomach. "Whether you're wearing my clothes, your own, *or nothing at all*, you're the most magnificent person I've ever laid eyes on."

I push up onto my tiptoes, winding my arms around his neck. I do my best to meet him in the middle, closing the distance between the extra foot of space between our mouths.

The muscles along my neck ache as I crane my head back, meeting his pillowy-soft lips again. His tongue swipes along the seam of my mouth, pleading for entry. His large hand drops to my ass, squeezing tightly as I gasp. It's just the distraction he needed to slip his tongue into my mouth, licking and tasting as my knees wobble beneath me. I moan into his touch, desperate for more of him.

He pulls away just long enough to drag in a ragged breath and whisper, "I still can't believe you're mine."

My heart bursts at the seams before he sews them back together with the firm press of his lips against mine.

Nugget's loud barks from the couch startle me, and I work to suck a few steadying breaths into my lungs before bending to greet him. "Hi there, Nuggs. Have a good nap?" I ask the tiny tan ball at my feet.

He jumps straight up, licking my cheek in response.

Ryder's hearty chuckle fills the room, adding more warmth to the already-warm space with curtains in deep shades of red, tan-colored walls, and framed photographs on every wall.

"It seems I'm not the only one who missed you," he says, reaching down to pick up Nugget, holding him against his wide chest. He presses a kiss to the top of his head, ruffling his big, pointed ears before setting him back down.

The air in the room shifts when he releases a strained sigh. "Can we go sit and talk?" he asks, waiting for my response before hanging his hat on the horseshoe-shaped hook by the door and slipping out of his dark-brown leather boots.

We take a seat on the couch, first sitting on opposite ends as anxiety hammers through me, churning the contents of my stomach. Barely a handful of seconds pass before Ryder gathers me in his arms and places me in his lap.

"I know there was a lot going on the day of the fire, and it's taken us all some time to calm down from it, but I think it's time we come up with a plan now that we've had a few days of reprieve." His soft blue eyes are locked on my brown ones, snaring me in his worried gaze.

"It was nice to pretend everything was okay for a little while though," I admit with a humorless laugh—not that our several-hour-long discussion about saving the barn was easy. "But you're right. It's time we stop avoiding the inevitable and waiting for the other shoe to drop, *again*." There's a war waging inside me between the parts of my past that want to pretend nothing is wrong and the pieces of my future desperately begging me to resolve this.

Ry gathers my hands in his, a subconscious habit at this point, drawing methodical circles along the pulse at my wrist. "I've been thinking about what Mayte said about my brother and Lemmon," he admits, this conversation taking a completely different turn than I'd expected.

"You think Ezekiel might have something to do with this?" I ask, my brows pinched, weariness filling me. Sure, Zeke has never been a very forthcoming person, but surely he wouldn't harm his own family, right?

"No—" He shakes his head before dropping his chin to his

chest, squeezing his eyes shut as he gets his bearings. "God, I don't know. I don't *want* to believe he could be involved in any of this, but he's always been so withdrawn. With what Mayte mentioned the other day, she planted a seed I've been ignoring until this afternoon."

"What happened this afternoon?" I ask without hesitation, my limbs feeling tingly as nausea builds inside me.

"When I went to check in on Dad this morning, he mentioned he couldn't get ahold of Zeke last night. For a man who's rarely anywhere besides his home and the ranch, it makes me anxious to consider what he could've been doing. And then—" He scratches the back of his neck, looking visibly uncomfortable.

"And then what, Ry?" I ask tentatively.

"And then, Betsy called to say she'd seen Lemmon driving out of town with a man she thought looked a lot like Zeke."

Shock hits me square in the chest, and my heart breaks for Ryder. "I can't imagine how difficult it must be for you to consider him being involved," I whisper, pulling him against me for a long hug, prioritizing his comfort over my surprise.

"I truly don't believe he's behind this, but I feel like I need to speak with him, clear the air, and fully convince myself he has no part in any of it," he says, his voice cracking. "And afterward, we need to have a family meeting to solidify a plan."

"Okay, Ry. When do you want to talk to Zeke?"

He releases a sigh and rests his forehead against my shoulder. "First thing tomorrow morning. I want one more night of normalcy to pretend there isn't a possible murderer on the loose."

"Sounds like we're going to have a lot to talk about in therapy tomorrow night," I tell him, joking to break up the tension.

"I look forward to it, darlin'. Any time I can get a glimpse into what's running through your thoughts, I'm a happy man."

Chapter Sixty-One

BOOTY MUNCH

WEDNESDAY, JUNE 25

AS PROMISED, Ryder and I've spent the majority of the evening pretending absolutely nothing is wrong in our world.

We danced around the kitchen before he caught the time and realized the pole fitness studio had a class we could make. He wouldn't give me a straight answer about it, but judging by the much more fluid movements of his hips and the seductive way he pinned me to the chair with both his body and eyes, I'd say he's been practicing. The idea of him rehearsing a lap dance for me with one of the wooden chairs from the kitchen has me equal parts amused and turned on.

Warm water runs down my back, my core tensing as images of Ryder and me the other night flit through my mind, replacing the near equally erotic image of him grinding against me at our class tonight.

Heat pools low in my belly as I open the glass door, sticking my head out. "Ry!" I shout, hoping he'll hear me in the living room.

"Yes, darlin'? Everything okay?" he calls. "Did you forget a towel again?"

"Yeah, Ry, sorry. Could you bring me one?" I ask, a moan

traipsing past my lips as he grows closer, my nipples pebbling with the knowledge that my husband is seconds from falling to his knees for me *and he doesn't even know it.*

I hear the doors of the linen closet creak, sliding open and closed, then his footfalls against the tile floors.

"You have a towel, right—" His words cut off when he sees me wearing nothing but a playful grin.

"Ry, could you help me out here? I can't reach my back, and I'm feeling *extra* dirty right now."

"Oh hell, darlin'," he moans. "I'll be right there." He frantically strips down, joining me in the shower. His hands smooth over my warm, wet skin, and he nips at the sensitive skin along the column of my neck.

I close my eyes, allowing sensations to wash over me with the hot spray of the shower. He plucks one of my nipples, tingles of pleasure zapping through me like an electric current. I moan, the sound verging on a cry.

"Your body is a thing to be worshipped, and I plan on making myself an altar at your feet," he proclaims, his voice gravelly as he moves to kneel on the floor, praising me and ravishing every inch of my body with his lips and tongue.

He makes it to his knees, his large hand gripping the back of my thigh and the other cupping my ass. I twine my fingers in his hair, tugging on the roots as I commit every detail of this moment to memory.

His full, swollen lips from the many kisses we've shared tonight. The wet, shaggy waves plastered to his forehead. Pleading, earnest eyes anchoring me to him. He appears to be as enraptured by me as I am by him, like two sirens calling to one another.

I pull his head into my center, urging him forward. He dips his chin without hesitation, sliding the tip of his nose through my wetness, lapping at the sensitive skin between my thighs, my legs trembling with need. I cry out, desperately wanting more, but he stops, his expression taking on a more feral look of need. His mouth and face are coated in my slick heat, and his tongue darts out to lick his lips clean as a heady groan rumbles through his chest.

"I want to prove my devotion to this delicious pussy, Lola. Do I get to do that?" he asks.

I bite my lip, his words sending heat licking up my spine as I nod my enthusiasm.

"Use your words," he commands, an ache of desire settling into my bones at his demanding tone. Who'd have thought a coarse and formidable Ryder would be as needlessly attractive as a desperate and needy one?

Okay, I guess I *have* spent a lot of time considering that would be a possibility. Either way, my husband is the sexiest man on the planet, and I fully intend to use my words with him.

"I want you to make me come all over your face, Ry," I pant, and he wastes no time hoisting my leg up, balancing it on one of his shoulders to give him better access.

He drags my clit into his mouth, the swollen bundle of nerves vibrating with the sensation of him tugging it between his teeth, eliciting a loud cry from me.

"I need more," I breathe out, aching to be filled. He answers my pleas with an eager mouth, lapping at my entrance and spreading me wide.

"What do you want, darlin'? My fingers? My tongue? My *cock*?"

I groan, sagging against the cold ceramic tile walls partially supporting my weight. Ryder isn't as enthused by my non-answer as I'd been, so he spreads my cheeks wide, swirling the tip of his finger over my tight hole. I gasp, eyes widening with surprise as I clench around nothing, my pussy spasming with need as the leg supporting me trembles.

"Does my dirty girl like that? Can I lick"—he swipes a finger through my pussy before slipping it between my cheeks and using the moisture to rub the puckered hole—"right here?"

I nod, words evading me again, my lips pursed as my knees buckle beneath me. I can barely hold myself up anymore; there's not a chance I'll last if he does that.

"Lola," he grits out, "do you want your husband to eat your ass or not?"

"I do!" I finally shout when he refuses to touch me beyond holding my weight up, a rumble of approval vibrating through his chest.

Chapter Sixty-Two

FLAVOR SAVER

WEDNESDAY, JUNE 25

ONE THING HAS BECOME ABUNDANTLY clear: My wife is a menace to a party of one. *Me.*

I'd crawl on my hands and knees for a chance to praise and worship her body the way I've always dreamt of.

The other night was merely a warm-up for what I have planned for her, and it feels damn good to know we've got the rest of our lives to live out every fantasy.

"Grab the shower head, darlin'."

She takes it with shaky hands, tilting her head, silently questioning me.

"Now, turn around, face the wall, and spread your legs real wide for me."

I lower her leg from my shoulder, and she bites her lip, doing as I say before a squeak leaves her. "Wh-what should I do with the shower head?"

"Beautiful and *so* smart, Lola. I'm sure you'll figure it out," I praise, sitting back on my shins, taking in the glorious sight of her round, tan ass just begging to be spanked. "Hand on the wall darlin'." She nods shakily, putting her left hand up for balance and sliding the other between her legs, blasting her pussy with hot water.

"Oh!" she moans, slumping further against the wall, and the sound has my dick painfully engorged.

I smack her ass, another moan leaving her lips as I groan, watching it bounce with the fresh pink print of my hand. I spread her cheeks, sliding the tip of my tongue over her tight hole, swirling around it before pushing two fingers inside her pussy. She bucks against my face, my nose sliding over her most intimate spots as her arousal coats my hand.

"Ryder, fuck," she cries out, slamming her hips into my hand, my fingers burying deeper with her movements. Her tight cunt clamps around me, my balls tightening, as if my cock were inside her.

"Yes, baby, you're doing so good."

"Spank me again," she begs, panting.

I pull away from her just long enough to fulfill her request before diving back in, lapping at the tight ring, her soft, beautiful body yielding to my control. The expanding tingle at the base of my spine is obscenely good, her rapture becoming my own. Before I can stop myself, my vision is met with the blurry edges of pleasure as I drive her to her release.

She unleashes a strangled moan, need vibrating through us as she falls apart for me. My poor dick forgets the mission, spurting all over the tile wall between her legs.

"Oh, fuck," I groan out, my breaths heavy as I come down to Earth, tracing soft, aftershock-inducing circles over her swollen clit.

Lola's ragged breaths calm as she looks over her shoulder at me. She smiles brightly, spinning to spray my face with the shower head. I swat her away, swiping a hand over my scruff. "Aw, come on, darlin'. That's my flavor saver you just rinsed!" I feign annoyance.

Her deep chuckle fills me with pride—I'm the one who made her laugh. "Ry, that's disgusting," she says, shaking her head. "And you've gotta either trim that thing back or let it grow out till it's softer, because the current situation gave me rug burn."

"I'm sorry, 'flavor saver' was 'disgusting', but *rug burn* is acceptable?" I chide, standing on shaky limbs with sore red knees.

"I stand by that."

"I'm sure you do," I tease, rolling my eyes, grabbing the towels from the counter. I wrap her up in the white fluffy material and carry her to bed.

I deposit her into the center of the mattress and open the top drawer of the dresser, sorting through it until I find what I'm looking for. I flick the light off and climb in bed behind her.

She shifts, tossing a leg over my hip and wriggling against me. "Whatcha got there?" she asks, her pretty, soulful brown eyes glittering beneath the stream of moonlight through the bedroom window.

"Oh, you know—" My words are replaced by the vibrating, sucking sound of the pink silicone toy as I turn it on, slipping my hand between her thighs.

"Mmm, I knew you had more in you," she teases, gripping my swollen dick, swiping the cum beading at the tip over my seam. She grips the base and notches the head against her slick pussy lips.

I groan, trying to slide further inside her, but she holds me still, shaking her head. Wet curls smack my chest with the motion.

"No? Don't you want your husband to fill you up?" I ask, lust strangling the last shreds of my sanity.

"You have to earn it, Ry. You've gotta prove you're a good boy who can listen to rules," she says, planting her hands on my shoulders as leverage to slide over me before resuming her achingly shallow thrusts. My face twists with desire as I try to contain my whimpers.

"Darlin', I don't know if you're aware, but you're toying with your poor husband," I plead with anguish. I've never wanted anyone or anything as bad as I want Lola Lima.

I still can't believe I get to be here at all, so I'll take whatever she's willing to give me. It doesn't mean I won't throw a fit about it in the meantime.

"I love how desperate you are to please me, Ry. I want you crying for your release, and maybe then, I'll let you pump me full."

I swipe at an invisible tear, batting my lashes at her. "I'm ready to cry *now*, Lols. Please," I whine, and she rewards me, arching her back and sinking down half an inch further.

My cock throbs painfully, my balls tightening with need when I realize that I have a real problem on my hands. Every day with Lola Lima makes me want her more, and if that remains true, I'll never get my dick to settle down. It might explode before I have the opportunity to make her come again.

No use wasting time.

I turn the sucker on, pressing it to her clit, and settle for swiping my fingers through her slit, since, apparently, the rest of me isn't allowed to do the same.

"That's *cheating*," she complains. "But you can proceed." Her wide grin is like a beacon to my orgasm, and I chase the high, swapping speeds and rhythms on the sucker, rotating it between her clit and nipples until she's fully seated on my cock.

Her nose presses to mine, her warm breath tickling my lips as arousal builds heavy in my groin. "You feel so right," she whispers.

"You feel so goddamn perfect, baby," I answer. "Thank you for letting me be here."

"Thank you?" she repeats.

"Mhmm. I can die a happy man knowing what it's like to have my dick stretching your pussy, dripping and needy for *me* and no one else. It's the best feeling in the world. Other than, well—"

"Other than what?" she asks, her voice barely above a whisper, her tone reverent.

"Nothing could top the way my heart warms like the sun's rays when it rises high in the sky after a cold winter's night, lighting up the darkest corners of my soul when you tell me you love me, that you're *in* love with me."

She swipes the pad of her thumb over my bottom lip, pressing a searing kiss to my mouth, pulling away enough to whisper, "I love you, Ryder Maddox Lockhart. I am *so* madly *in* love with you."

I bury my face in her neck, repeating those same words, punctuating them each with a thrust of my hips. "I. Love. You. God, I'm so in. Love. With. You."

The words become a jumbled chant, moans and my quiet whimpers filling the room as we fall off the edge together, nothing but our physical connection acting as a parachute for our return.

Every vertebra in my spine roars with ecstasy as my balls tighten, my cock filling her with pulsing gusts of my cum. I mold my lips to hers, drinking in her moans and gasps as we come down from our release, our bodies still twitching with pleasure.

I tuck her against my side, clutching the back of her head in my palm and pressing a chaste kiss to her forehead. She tucks her head under my chin and settles against me, resting her cheek over my heart.

Right where she belongs.

Chapter Sixty-Three

RUNNING FASTER THAN A CREEK AFTER RAIN

THURSDAY, JUNE 26

"I LOVE YOU, DARLIN'," I whisper, kissing the crown of her head where her curls are piled beneath her bonnet.

"I lufh you," she whispers back groggily, rolling over and hugging her body pillow tighter.

It's a quick drive to my brother's cottage, but the elephant sitting on my chest is an unwelcome burden of my anxiety that makes it feel ten times longer.

Zeke is waiting on the porch for me when I arrive, having agreed to meet me this early despite not being a morning person. "Cup of coffee?" he asks, not bothering with pleasantries.

I wave him off. "No, thanks. I'm wired as is."

His dark brows creep high on his forehead, and I'm met with a concerned scowl. "Wired? Ry, what's going on?"

I shake my head, exhaustion weaving into every muscle as I drag myself up the porch steps to his black paneled, cottage-style home. The dark wood beams in front are the only hint of warmth surrounding my brother's unnervingly tidy house.

"Inside, Zeke. We can't talk about this out here."

He has the good sense to listen to me for once, never

having taken my role as his big brother seriously throughout our entire childhood.

His spine is ramrod straight as he leads me inside, his chubby calico cat, Cowgirl, making an appearance. She winds her body through my legs, purring when I scratch between her ears.

I do my best not to trip over her, taking a seat on the gray sectional sofa beside my brother.

"Do you have feelings for my ex-wife?" I ask, too worn-out to ease into this conversation.

His head rears back, light-blue eyes dimming to an eerie gray as he levels me with a glare. "Are you fucking kidding, Ry?"

"*Please* answer the question," I plead, dropping my face into my hands, releasing a low groan.

"No, I don't have feelings for Lemmon," he says, his voice chastising. "Actually—" My head snaps up to meet his glare, but my shoulders sag with his next words. "That was a lie. I *do* have feelings for her: disdain, resentment, annoyance, and, on my off days, pity."

I can't help but chuckle at that very "Ezekiel Lockhart" response. "Isn't disdain your default emotion?"

He rolls his eyes, crosses his arms over his chest, and slumps against the couch cushions. "Ha, ha, ha, *very funny*. But also, yes."

That gets a snort out of me, and the dark cloud looming over my head ever since I'd decided confronting my brother was the only way I'd be able to know he isn't involved dissipates.

"Where is this coming from exactly?"

"A little birdy sort of mentioned you and Lemmon had a thing in high school, and I was afraid you thought I stole her from you or something."

"Ah," he says, shaking his head, his lips pulled up in a grin. "And would this 'little birdy' be a drop-dead gorgeous, five-foot-six woman with dark wavy hair and a beauty mark above her lip?" He quirks a dark brow at me and rolls his eyes again when I don't answer. "You know, that woman's mouth runs faster than a creek after rain."

"Hey, she did pretty good. Over a decade, as I recall." He rewards me with a deep chuckle that nearly shakes me out of my boots.

"Yeah, for her, it certainly is. I never resented you for what Lemmon did, but I was pissed about it for a long time," he admits, and my heart twists.

"What exactly did she do?" I ask, hesitant.

"She and I had been fooling around in high school. I thought we had something special; she treated me like a real person, something she didn't seem to do with most everyone else. Hell, she even let that phony accent drop."

My eyes bug out of my head, jaw scraping the ground as I stare at my brother in utter disbelief. After the last few months, *this* is the thing that shocks me most.

"And you never told me!? Zeke, I was *married* to the devious little thing for a *decade*, and she didn't slip up once!"

He shrugs. "I figured if she kept on talkin' like that long enough, it'd eventually become real. Anyway, she told me about her dreams for the future, how much she wished she could find her mother someday. Then, when she woke up one day and pretended I never existed, it became clear as day that she was using me to get to you, learning every detail about our family during the years we spent together. I'll admit, it grossed me out that she'd move on from kissing me to smacking lips with my brother, but I was too pissed off to talk to you about it. After years of seeing how miserable she made you, I thought I could save you the added disgust of knowing how she'd used me. Until recently, I hadn't thought much about her, but clearly, she's back to wreaking havoc."

After talking to Zeke about Lemmon, clearing the air, and discussing some thoughts he's had about this whole mess, we have a more solid plan for how to tackle this situation. I can thank Lemmon for something positive for once: acting as the catalyst that helped my brother and me start healing our fractured relationship, even if she may have been the one to break us in the first place.

Chapter Sixty-Four

LET'S TRY THIS AGAIN

THURSDAY, JUNE 26

MY THIGHS STICK to the leather seats, sweat coating my skin as anxiety fills the well inside my chest.

The air in the living room at the main house is filled with every negative emotion imaginable as we gather together for a family meeting. The only saving grace is the two-story great room, which adds the extra ceiling height needed to prevent the roof from bursting off from all the pent-up unease in here. This much negativity should *not* be all in one place.

"Have you tried cleansing your home and yourselves, *mija*? Maybe Russ's bad energy has been walking around with you." *Mami* is emphatic, clearly holding on to hope that we can sweep this whole ordeal under the rug.

"I already mopped with *agua de Florida, Mami*," I tell her, my shoulders sagging.

"And *limpieza con huevo*," Mayte adds from her seat beside me on the sectional sofa.

"I didn't get to finish that, actually," I admit, my stomach churning. I'd been so upset that day, I'd completely forgotten to mention it to her.

"What? What happened?" she asks, her honey-brown eyes wide with concern.

I swallow around the lump in my throat, my shoulders growing heavy as I blow out a breath. *I broke it.*

The room goes eerily silent, and I bristle under the boring gazes of my parents and Mayte. Even Harlan has the good sense to tug at his salt-and-pepper roots.

"Please stop staring at me like that," I whisper, discomfort soaring through my body, trying to break free of my skin. They still don't answer, and I catch *Mami* clutching her necklace, rubbing her thumb over the pendant of *La Virgen de Guadalupe,* a powerful protector and guide. "I was having a bad RA flare that day. My whole body ached, and after cleaning the floors, I was barely standing upright. I was so scared, I just wanted to get it over with," I admit, tears pooling in my eyes, my lip quivering.

Ryder slides closer to me, hoisting me into his lap, pressing reassuring kisses to my shoulder. "I'm so sorry, baby. I hadn't realized what you were doing was so important when I found you that day." Bless this sweet man. These rituals are an important part of my community, something I'm honored to get to share with my parents and my best friend, but it means the world to me that he's so understanding of its significance.

"It's okay, Ry. I'd forgotten about it after you helped me clean up. I should've told Mayte or *Mami* and had one of them help me."

"It's okay, *mija*," *Mami* says, sounding much more understanding now than her earlier reaction would have suggested. "Bee, do you have any room temperature eggs we can use?" she asks, standing from the couch and beckoning me to follow her to the kitchen, not bothering to wait for Bee's reply.

I follow her with Mayte in tow, but I shake my head when Ryder tries to follow me. I'm not sure what this egg is going to reveal, and I don't need him to worry more than he already is. Plus, as much as he respects my family's spirituality, I don't know if he actually *believes* any of it, and I can't have him bringing any additional negativity into that space.

"Any chance Bee has *agua de Florida* lying around?" Mayte asks *Mami*, who rolls her eyes.

"Use water with salt to cleanse the egg. Make sure it's cold water."

Turns out, I was right. I had missed *a lot* of steps when I'd done this last time. I suppose that's what happens when you let a man keep you from your friends and family: you forget a lot of the things that make you who you are.

Mami lights a white candle by the kitchen window while Mayte does as instructed, returning the egg to *Mami*, who has me stand in the center of the kitchen after cleansing my hands. "Now, hold it to your heart and give gratitude for its assistance."

I do as she says, praying over the egg, thanking it for helping me rid the *mal de ojo* and for protection against more evil. When I'm finished, she starts from my head, winding the egg around me much more thoroughly and skillfully than I had. I'd also forgotten to cleanse the egg and pray over it the first time, which had done me no favors.

She and Mayte each recite prayers for my well-being as she makes her way to my feet, repeating the process several times, ensuring they start at the crown of my head each time.

A physical weight starts to lift from my shoulders as they continue the process, sending good intentions and hope into my very being. When complete, *Mami* breaks the egg into a glass of water. If I thought the silence was deafening before, it's nothing compared to *Mami's* sickly pale complexion as we stare into the clear glass, now tainted with a bubbly, stringy, cloudy egg.

Nausea rips through me, threatening to bubble over. As I watch the yolk sink to the bottom of the glass, my stomach rages against me, *Mami* and Mayte rushing to my side with panicked prayers falling past their lips.

Chapter Sixty-Five

NEW REVELATIONS

THURSDAY, JUNE 26

"LOLA!" I shout, unable to stay silent any longer as I tear through the living room in search of my wife. They've been gone for entirely too long, and after hearing Mayte's anxious pleas for Lola not to throw up, because *she* will return the favor, I can't sit still for a second longer.

I enter the kitchen to find Lola doubled over, clutching her stomach, green-tinged cheeks filled with air. Sweat shimmers on her forehead, pain evident in her posture.

"Lola, what's wrong?" I ask, frantic as my feet drag me to her. I help hold her up, rubbing her back.

"She needs a goddamn exorcism at this point." Mayte mutters under her breath before clarifying, as if just how screwed we are wasn't clear enough. "Her *limpia* result is not good, Ry," Mayte tells me, and I find myself staring at the clear glass on the counter, as if I have any idea what this rotten-looking egg could be telling us. "Go have a seat in the living room. We'll join you when we've disposed of the egg appropriately."

"Would it be alright if I took Lola to dispose of it off the property real quick, or would that be disrespectful?" I ask, desperate to support Lola in any way I can.

"That's fine, Ryder. We were probably just going to flush it, but—"

Bexaida cuts Mayte off, "No, we were *not!* We aren't keeping this energy in Bee's home!"

Lola's shoulders slump. "I'm so sorry," she whines, her voice small and pained. It breaks my heart. "I didn't mean for all of this to happen. I would never intentionally bring you all into harm's way." She sags against me.

"You are not responsible for the actions of others, Lola. The good news is, while your *limpia* revealed gossip, someone keeping a close eye on you, karmic cords you need to cut, a physical ailment, which you already knew about, the tiny bubbles are a sign the *limpia* cleansed you of those things. The big concern now is the, well—" Mayte's eyes dart away, discomfort twisting her face as she scratches her arm.

"The figure," Lola finishes, and I swear, everyone who wasn't in that kitchen with them has their head on a swivel.

"There was a human figure in the egg yolk when Lola started to feel sick. And shortly after, there were *two*," Bexaida informs us.

Goosebumps litter my skin, bile climbing up my throat. I become acutely aware of why Lola would have a weak stomach after her experience.

"How do we get rid of them? What's the next step?" my mom asks, leaning into the conversation with her elbows planted on her knees, wild blue eyes frantic for an answer.

"A lot of the bad energy was disposed of with the egg, but if there are two people coming after Lola, we have to get to the bottom of it. We need to confront the problem, break ties, and make sure they're not able to spiritually bully her anymore," José answers.

"What if we hire a private investigator? We have messages

from these people. Maybe there's someone who can confirm it's Lemmon behind all this?" Dad suggests.

"I'm not totally convinced it even is Lemmon, at least, not *just* her," Lola admits, rubbing her temples.

"Whoever it is, we'll figure it out, darlin'," I assure her, squeezing her thigh.

"That's actually what I was looking into the other day. I have a buddy of mine from the Marines who can track anyone. He flies back to the States on Sunday and said he can get on it then," Zeke explains.

"Any ideas for what we should do in the meantime?"

"Have you swept your home for cameras or recording devices of any kind?" Zeke asks, and trepidation mingles with the ever-growing list of uncomfortable emotions I'm living with.

"No. As stupid as it is, I hadn't thought about it." *Very* fucking stupid of me, given the circumstances.

"I need to grab a few things from my place, but I can head over after and check things out to be safe," he says, and we spend the next hour going through possibilities for who the second person might be, coming up mostly empty.

"What about those dumb girls always hanging around Lemmon?" Mom muses.

Mayte shakes her head. "Unlikely. Judging by the way they avoided being seen with her at the barn fire the other day, it seems they've cut ties."

"And they'd probably get her caught if they were involved," Dad tells her.

Zeke butts in, stunning us into silence. "Neither of those women is dumb, nor are they girls. Wendy is a pre-school teacher with a sick mom and a special needs child she's fighting to gain full custody of from her abusive ex, but since she doesn't have the budget to afford a home care nurse for her mother, it's not going well. Dana Sue runs a non-profit and can barely afford to feed the stray cats she cares for, let alone fund her little brother's rehab." His gaze sweeps over each of us. "They're *good* people living with unfortunate circumstances. You can't blame them for accepting Lemmon's money."

"So she *does* pay them to be her friends?" Lola asks.

Zeke shakes his head. "No, she just helps fund Wendy's mom's home health aide and Dana Sue's non-profit, I guess so she doesn't have to be totally alone. It started after her dad cut ties with her."

I can't utter a word before Mayte flashes Zeke a smirk. "Well, excuse me, little Lockhart. When did *you* become the town crier?"

"I'm not crying about anything, you brat," he says with a chuckle that warms me to my bones in the same second it acts as a shock to my system. "I *do* have a life outside of this ranch. It may not be extravagant, but it's wholesome. I met both of them while volunteering at Dana Sue's non-profit a couple years back."

Zeke's on a roll, stunning me into silence yet again.

"Are you living a double life or something? Should we call you Hannah Montana?" Lola asks, standing and reaching across the coffee table, pressing the back of her hand to his forehead. "You're not feverish, so there's no good reason for you to be hallucinating."

He gently swats her hand away, rolling his eyes and leaning into his corner of the couch, his arms crossed over his chest. "The point is, it's not them. Moving on, y'all."

"*There* he is," Mom mutters, the corners of her lips twitching.

"What about the bikers?" José asks, receiving a pointed glare from Bexaida. "They've been showing up an awful lot more recently. It could be related."

Bexaida shakes her head almost violently, black-and-silver hair falling loose from the low bun at the nape of her neck. "No, never. *My* Levi would *never*."

"You know, I think *Papi* might have something to say about this," Lola teases, earning a scowl from her mom.

"Those men are good-hearted people who've lived very tough lives. They have vibrant, protective energy around them. They are *not* involved," she insists.

We've officially run out of suspects, aside from Russ, who's acting out of character, according to Lola. Besides that, there's nothing really tying him to any of this.

We move on to discussing strategies for keeping everyone safe: lying low, cleansing our homes and auras, and when we finally leave, I feel a little lighter than I did at the start of the day. Not much has improved; if anything, it's gotten twice as bad, based on the second figure Bexaida saw in the yolk, but knowing we have such a strong support system provides me some much-needed hope for our future.

After driving Lola off the property to dispose of the egg and taking care of a few last things on the ranch, we finish up the last few minutes of our counseling session with a home-work assignment for the week and a plan to meet next Thursday, same time.

"Is there anything else you'd like to discuss before we end our call?" Talia asks.

"Yeah, I was wondering if you have contact information for any therapists trained in animal-assisted therapy. I've been looking into non-invasive treatments for rheumatoid arthritis and came across several articles that outlined the benefits of equine therapy." I scratch my neck, averting my eyes, but I can't escape the way Lola's gaze feels so heavy on my skin. "I figure since we rescue lots of horses to live out their lives here, why not work with someone who can help them rescue others in their own way?"

I finally glance at Lola. She peers up at me with glossy eyes and swipes at a tear that's fallen down her cheek.

Talia smiles brightly at the camera and bends her head, jotting something down in our file before glancing back up at us. "I have a couple of people in mind I'll reach out to and have them get in contact if interested. And for what it's worth, I think that's a wonderful idea."

"Thank you, Talia. I appreciate your help with everything, not just this," I say, a newfound tether of hope attaching itself to my heart, and we end the call after some basic pleasantries.

As expected, we had a lot to discuss, but we each ended the night feeling more equipped to handle the bad days, like today, than we had last week or the one before that.

The only thing left to do for the night is the part I find most daunting.

Zeke agreed to come over after we finished therapy, and I hope whatever he finds doesn't leave me wishing we hadn't waited.

Chapter Sixty-Six

SPY ZADDY

THURSDAY, JUNE 26

"SO, should I ask why you have this type of equipment lying around your house?" I ask Ezekiel, staring unabashedly as he unpacks his equipment from the small black-and-gray fabric case.

He peers up at me, his eyes void of humor, but his response makes me laugh anyway. "Probably not."

"Oh-kay then."

Zeke walks around the house, scanning every inch, but paying special attention to items like paintings, picture frames, light fixtures, smoke alarms, and the carbon monoxide detector.

Everything seems to be going smoothly until the room fills with a shrill beeping. It stops quickly, *as does my heart.*

Zeke's heavy brows pull taut, spine rigid as he removes the pale-blue lampshade from the wall sconce, unscrews the light-bulb, and checks each piece for a positive signal. He comes up empty-handed at first, but the same loud tone blares over a screw at the base.

"Ry, could you turn the power off to this side of the house, please? I've gotta take this apart."

Ryder works quickly, as does Zeke, and a few minutes later, we're staring at a tiny black camera the size of my pinky nail that had been peering at us through the center of the hollowed-out screw.

A chill wracks through me, and I shake like a leaf. All the private moments we shared have been anything but this *whole* time.

Invasion of our privacy doesn't *begin* to describe what's wrong with this situation, and as Zeke combs through the rest of the house, he finds four voice recording devices and another camera that was hidden in my room.

"The night the door was open," I cry. "When they tried to *kill* Nugget. They came here to bug our home, Ry!"

He pulls me into his lap, wrapping his arms around my waist, and rests his chin on my shoulder. "I'm so sorry, baby," he whispers, his voice hoarse.

Zeke clears his throat, quietly dragging our attention back to him. "That's—" He scratches at the nape of his neck, much like Ryder does when nervous or anxious. "Well, Lola, that's not possible. This software is far older than anything you'd get on the market now."

"So, what does that mean?" Ryder asks, swiping hot tears from my cheek.

"It means that while Lemmon has likely been surveilling you for *years*, even while you were married, there is some good news."

Has my gut really been wrong this whole time? Hearing Zeke confirm it was Lemmon leaves me questioning every interaction I've had with her since returning.

"Please enlighten us as to how my ex-wife bugging my fucking house could possibly come with any good news."

Zeke chuckles humorlessly. "She doesn't have a live view. These devices stayed on because she hard-wired them directly into the electric, but she'd have to be physically present to extract anything from them." He shrugs. "My best guess is that she came here for exactly that reason and left the hot dog in Nugget's bowl as a distraction. When she didn't find anything useful, her responses continued to escalate."

Zeke's conclusion and overall believability of the series of events leave me wondering what exactly his job was as a Marine. He never gave us much insight, and I wasn't really around to be privy to those details anyway.

"Is there any way to prove all of that?" Ryder asks.

"I'm going to take these home and see what I can get off them. I don't feel comfortable listening to the audio recordings unless absolutely necessary, and I don't believe the camera hidden in Lola's old room would be of any help, so I'm not going to invade your privacy any further. I'm thinking the camera in the wall sconce should have everything I need to pin her with at least one crime, if not *several*. The angle it was positioned at includes the living room and a partial view of the kitchen and entryway."

"Thank you, Zeke. I'm starting to think I've barely scratched the surface of what you did in the military, but I appreciate you using some of that expertise to help us out," Ryder tells him, reflecting my thoughts.

"It's not a problem, Ry. I sincerely hope that you never have to find out the answer to that question," he says, standing and squeezing Ryder's shoulder before traipsing out of the house without another word.

"Ry," I whisper.

"Yeah, darlin'?" he asks, dazed.

"I think your brother might've been some elite spy," I answer, unsure whether I'm joking or not.

"I think so too," he wheezes out on a laugh, the sound breaking the tension between us.

The rest of the night, it's like we're two ghosts, unable to speak or feel, merely passing through the house in silence as we get ready for bed. Ryder tucks Nugget into his room in the closet, and I pray we don't wake up with our house on fire or whatever Lemmon has planned for us next.

Ryder

Chapter Sixty-Seven

MR. LICKERTON

FRIDAY, JUNE 27

MY POCKET VIBRATES WITH A CALL. Excusing myself from Dr. Becerra, I leave her to check on Daisy, who's due in September, before answering.

"Hello, this is Ryder Lockhart."

I'm met with an unfamiliar male voice, it's smooth and low, with a hint of an accent I can't pinpoint. "Hey, man. A friend of mine sent a picture of one of the fliers you put up in town. It looks like you found my little guy, Mr. Lickerton."

I almost choke on my spit, pounding on my chest to speed up my recovery.

"You good?" he asks.

"Ye–Yeah, I'm good. Must've breathed in some dust," I explain. Now that the coughing fit has worn off, his words fall into place, and I'm hit with a wave of sadness. Nugget's dad wants him back and, presumably, he's been looking for him all this time. I'm conflicted by the loss, happy he'll be reunited with his original family and that Lola and I had the opportunity to give him a good life while he was away from them, but unbelievably sorrowful he isn't ours to keep. "So the little guy is yours?" I ask.

"Yeah, I've been looking all over for him, and when my friend sent the flier, I thought 'no way it could be him.' I'd lost all hope, but sure enough, the photo was an exact match."

"Hey, I'm really glad—" I'm getting choked up, hot tears springing to my eyes that have no business being there. "Glad we could reunite you. Would you mind sending me a picture of you and"—my teeth grind as I scrape the atrocious name past my lips—"Mr. Lickerton? I believe you, but you know how it is. I have to check for his safety and can't just trust anybody." I chuckle to diffuse any potential tension, but he takes it in stride.

"No worries, I get it. I'm sending a pic right now." I wait a few moments for the photo to populate: a handsome guy with dark, short-cropped hair on the sides and a mop of near-black curls piled on the top of his head, Nugget tucked against his chest, staring into the camera with glittering brown eyes and a white, disarmingly wide smile. Nugget's mouth is open, his pink tongue hanging out; he seems completely at ease, no evidence of abuse.

"Got it. Thanks for confirming. Looks like you'll both be happy to be reunited. When would you want to meet?" I ask, pacing the hay-covered cement corridor between the stalls.

"I live a few hours away, but I need to drop into Washita for work. If you're available, I could meet you somewhere around there tonight."

"Washita is about an hour and a half from me." I don't want him to have to drive too far, but I hate the idea of leaving Lola at home or making her sit in a car that long with the weather we've got rolling in. Heavy rain always makes her joints ache. "Would you mind meeting me in Snapdragon?" It's still about an hour out for me, but a two-hour drive seems more manageable than a three-hour round-trip.

"Uh, sure, man. Not a problem. I'll send the address for a place I can stop for a coffee or something before heading home with the little guy. And thanks again for doing this," he says, ending the call and shooting me an address with his ETA a few minutes later.

By the time I make it home to Lola, the sky has opened up, heavy gray clouds blocking what's left of the sun's rays, pouring sheets of rain that show no signs of letting up.

"Hey, Teddy. Sorry you're out here like this. You sure you don't want to come inside?" I ask the blond biker seated on my porch, his feet kicked up, reading a book.

"That's alright. I'm enjoying the rain. If it starts thundering, I'll take you up on that though. I'd rather not wind up with a new tattoo courtesy of a lightning bolt."

"Good deal," I say with a chuckle, kicking my boots off at the door and shaking myself out like a wet dog before knocking to alert Lola I'm home.

She's napping on the couch with her legs elevated, ice packs resting on her knees and a heating pad over her tummy. Nugget is curled up beside her, his snores vibrating through the living room like a motorcycle gang passing through, a sound I've become very familiar with. The little guy needs a CPAP.

"Hey, darlin'," I whisper, crouching down beside her, my knees digging into the thick carpet, my jeans stretching uncomfortably over my thighs.

Her dark lashes flutter open as I gather her hands in mine, kissing her knuckles, then her smooth, rhythmic pulse against the inside of her wrist.

My pulse matches hers, speeding up as she wakes, those cinnamon eyes looking at me like I hung the moon and all the stars in the sky. A small smile curves her lips, and it feels like I'm glowing from within. I earned that look, and I intend to work for it each and every day.

"Hi," she says in a dulcet tone. "How was work?"

"It was good. Daisy's doing well, and Dr. Becerra says she's not seeing signs of the same issues she had last time. We aren't in the clear yet, but we're on the right track."

"That's great news, Ry." She shifts, brushing her lips against mine, and honey oozes in my blood.

"It is, but—" My voice is hoarse as I prepare to deliver a blow she had no way to anticipate. "I got a call about Nugget, Lols. His dad finally got word of him being here, and he wants me to meet him tonight."

Rain pounds on the slate roof, rumbling through the house as she whips her head around to peer out the window by the front door. "Tonight, Ry? The weather is horrible, and we're barely getting to say goodbye," she says, her voice cracking more with each word.

I wrap my arms around her, cradling her to my chest. "I know, darlin', but if he were ours and we'd lost him, imagine how happy we'd be to have him back. His dad sent me a picture of them together; they both looked real happy," I tell her, reaching into my back pocket to retrieve my phone. She rests her hand on my arm to stop me, shaking her head.

"No, that's—" She sighs, slumping into the cushions. "I'm glad Nugget has a good home to go back to, but I don't want to see the picture. Not now anyway. I don't think I can be happy for his dad while being so sad for us."

"That's quite alright, darlin'. Just tell me if anything changes."

She nods in agreement, shuffling to sit up. "When are you meeting him? And what's his name?"

"Six o'clock, and Mr. Lickerton," I tell her, unable to contain my laughter.

"I meant his *dad*, Ry, not Nugget. But that is a terrible name."

My heart sinks a bit. "Oh, I hadn't thought to ask him. I'm sorry, Lols. That was shortsighted of me."

"It's fine, Ry. I'm sure you had a million things on your mind when you got that call."

This is the sort of thing Lemmon would've lost it on me over, and it only acts as another reminder of how right Lola and I are for each other. "How about you stay here till I get back so you don't have to sit in the truck that long? When I get home, we can go over to the main house and have a family night or something."

"Sure, Ry. That sounds good," she says as I stand. She gets up to stretch, Nugget jumping up when he wakes, realizing I'm here. He shimmies over to me, tiny tail shaking with unbridled excitement as he releases a couple of good, yelp-like barks.

"Hi, handsome," I say, picking him up and pressing a kiss to the top of his head. "I've got some good news and some bad news," I tell him, talking him through this evening's plans.

Lola

Chapter Sixty-Eight

APPLES & OTHER FRUITS

FRIDAY, JUNE 27

MY FACE IS PUFFY, and my eyes burn from crying the last hour. Ryder called to say he got to the gas station he's meeting Nugget's owner at. The service was bad, and he sounded choppy, but I appreciate the open communication. I don't need another thing to worry about tonight.

I grab a pair of sweats and one of Ryder's oversized hoodies, carrying them into the bathroom with me. Turning on the shower, I allow the room to fill with a comforting layer of warm steam.

I strip out of my clothes, still unsettled at the idea of showering when it's storming out. I *know* I won't get struck by lightning, and the power isn't going to suddenly go out because I stepped foot in the shower, but old habits die hard. My mother would throw her *chancleta* at me if she saw me right now.

A loud *crack* startles me, causing me to lose my footing. I slip, slamming my hip on the cold tile floor. A sharp, burning pain sears through me, and I bite my lip to keep the scream climbing up my throat from bellowing out into the house. The last thing I need right now is Teddy worried and running inside to see my naked ass crumpled on the floor.

I roll over, reaching for the lip of the counter, and pull myself up. Pain shoots down my leg, and I yelp, but the sound gets caught in my throat as banging and yelling fill the living room.

Adrenaline floods my limbs, and the pain I'd felt dries up. I rush to shut the water off, slipping my hand into the bedroom to turn off the light and avoid alerting anyone to my presence. I hurry to change, my foot getting caught in the pant leg. I want to scream, tears welling in my eyes with frustration.

"Where are they?" A shrill, but familiar voice echoes through the house, and my limbs grow cold, my heart stopping in my chest with Teddy's weak, raspy reply.

"Th-they went to Snapdragon to return N-nugget to his owner. I'm s-sorry, that's all I know," he tells them. I'll be forever grateful for this sweet young man and his bravery. I plan to tell him as much if we make it out of this alive.

I turn the bathroom light off, grabbing my phone and shim-mying into the linen closet, making sure to silence my cell. If there's anything I've learned from TV, it's that people *always* call you during the worst of times. I'm not about to let my Daddy Yankee ringtone be what gets me kidnapped or killed.

I type out a frantic message to the family group chat, my pulse thundering against my ribs, hands shaking with the effort it takes to remain upright. I've never been so scared in my whole damn life.

The bedroom door swings open, smacking the drywall behind it with a loud thud, the spring of the useless doorstop *boinging* with the effort. "All clear. They aren't here."

Scratch that—*now* I've never been so scared.

I haven't heard that voice in months, and I most certainly never intended to again. The combination of the two has my temples pounding, chin quivering.

I have *everything* I've ever wanted, only for Russ and Amy, his spiteful mother, to take it all away. *How fucking poetic.*

If Amy has been behind everything this whole time, we're

fucked. She's too unpredictable, and it's impossible to foresee someone's movement if you had no idea they were ever a player on the board at all.

"What are we looking for exactly?" Russ asks.

The egg *limpia* was right. *Two* figures.

"Evidence. We need proof this whole marriage is a sham if we're going to get her on insurance fraud and ruin her life the way she has ours. That Apple girl said the devices should be in here, and then we'll have everything we need to prove your ex is the trailer trash I'd always suspected she was," Amy says, her tone smug. *Lemmon's been helping her?* Out of everything, that's the only part that makes sense. I hear the whir of a drill and rest my head back on the wire shelves, my legs tingling from the lack of blood flow while standing in this cramped closet.

"If Lemmon knew there was evidence, why isn't she here with us?" Russ asks, and it's a damn good question.

The drill shuts off, followed by Amy's frustrated huff. "*Because*, honey, much like Lola, when things got tough, Lemmon walked away. Something about me 'taking things too far'," she finishes, mocking Lemmon's explanation.

"What the hell do you mean by that, Mom? She was the one who suggested the marriage was insurance fraud in the first place. She's why we're here right now. Why would she have changed her mind?"

Does he not know about the barn fire? *Was Amy behind it all along?* I'd never thought of her as a mother figure to me, but could she really be so cruel as to burn down a building with over fifty people in it?

And for *what?* Money?

"Quit asking questions you don't want the answers to, Russ. You aren't innocent in all of this," she grits out, her tone practically begging him to say otherwise, always looking for a punching bag.

He doesn't say anything else, and the whir of the drill starts back up again. I glance down at my phone, and to my absolute horror, *the text never sent.*

I clench my teeth, holding back a frustrated scream, and try again, smashing my thumb on the red "Message not sent. Tap to retry" button. I jam my finger onto the screen over and over until, *finally*, it goes through.

"They're not here! How could they not be here?" Amy shrieks, her heavy footfalls smacking on the hardwood floors as she paces the living room. "If that girl lied to me, I'll wring her damn neck."

"Maybe this is a sign we should cut our losses. I'd love to get back at Lola for how she humiliated me, but I don't have any interest in getting arrested in the process," Russ tells her throatily.

Russ has managed a relationship where he's the more reasonable one, and that's enough to tell me just how unstable his mother has become.

"I did *NOT* come all this way and work with the likes of a girl named after a goddamn fruit to come up empty-handed."

"Mom, seriously? I just want to go home, *please*. I have *nothing* left. Nothing!" he shouts at her. "I've got no money, no friends, no business, and now, no fucking dog. I'm so damn *lonely*. When you brought me to the shelter, I thought the dog was going to be *mine.* But now all this?"

"Russ," Amy coos, a more motherly tone overtaking her voice, and I'm waiting on bated breath to find out what she could possibly say to justify this situation when the person who was, arguably most impacted is literally begging her to just let it go. "That dog was a pawn. He's played his part. Now it's time for you to play yours. Keep your eyes on the prize, honey. If we have proof of what your ex has done, your investors might consider returning, and we can get our lives back. I've worked too damn hard to make you into the man you were before Lola Lima came along and ruined everything."

My heart cracks, a small fissure of hurt forming on Russ's

behalf. He wasn't a good man by any stretch of the imagination, but no one deserves to have a mother like his.

"Ma, please," he murmurs, and I have to strain my ears to hear. "I just want the dog back. I could've met her husband at the gas station and—"

Ryder. He's either losing his mind with worry or about to walk into a complete shit show.

"We'll get that stupid dog back just as soon as we have our proof. You lost your damn company because of what your ex did to you. She deserves more than the loss of a *dog*." A moment passes in tense silence. "Now, come on—I know exactly the person who can tell us where those recordings are, and if she can't, we'll use her as collateral. Either way, Lola Lima will be locked up for insurance fraud by the end of the night. *Mark my words*."

My heart hammers in my chest, my stomach bottoming out as fear grips me.

I hold my breath, typing out one last message to warn Mayte, waiting for Amy's crusade to be over and the door to slam shut before I jump into action. "Jump" is generous, really. My joints are stiff, I'm shaking violently, and the pain in my hip is back with a vengeance. I push it all to the side, finding my way to the living room on trembling limbs.

"Teddy! Teddy!" I call out, my eyes growing wide when I find him tied to a chair, his mouth duct taped shut. "I'm so sorry, Teddy," I whisper, grabbing the corner of the silver-gray tape and yanking. It tears off his mouth with a shredding sound that makes me nauseous.

"L-lola, I n-need you to listen to me and pay attention. C-can you do that for me?" he asks, stuttering, but he works to keep his tone firm.

I feel lightheaded as the scent of iron fills my nostrils. Teddy's blood sliding down his temple distracts me, but I find my way back to him, focusing on his eyes. "I can," I tell him, my shaky voice not lending much confidence.

"I need you to leave me here." My eyes widen, a refusal on the tip of my tongue, but he finishes before I get there. "I probably have a concussion, I'll be no good to you, and it'll take too long to untie me. Grab my gun before you go. It's tucked into a holster under my jeans. Left ankle."

The seriousness of the situation crashes into me, but I remain strong, focusing on his instructions. With trembling hands, I crouch, unholster the gun, and check the safety isn't on before leaving him shouting behind me to be safe.

Someone coming after *me* is one thing, but my family? That's an entirely different situation, and Amy better hope someone in the chat called the cops before I get to her. I'll prove to be the more dangerous of her opponents if I catch her first.

Ryder

Chapter Sixty-Nine

WEATHER WONDER

FRIDAY, JUNE 27

"WELL, Nuggs, it's been a half hour, and he hasn't answered any of my calls or texts, so I guess we got stood up. I hope you don't think it's too much of a loss," I tell him, scratching between his ears.

I try calling Lola to tell her the good news. I know she's torn up about it, but the call won't go through. "Must be the weather. Hopefully, I'll get better cell service the closer we get to town."

I turn the engine over, pull out of the gas station, and head home for game night with my family.

The closer we get to home, the more my thoughts start to spiral. I'm doing the best I can to focus on keeping my truck from sliding all over the road in this weather, but it's nothing short of treacherous out here, and my mind is at home with Lola.

I pull off to the side of the road and unclip my phone from where it sits on my dash, map up. The offline map is working, but still, I have no bars.

Nugget whines beside me, shimmying to get closer to me. "I know, Nuggs, but you've gotta sit still. We'll be home soon,"

I tell him, guilty that he hasn't been able to pee yet. Granted, he refuses to go out in the rain.

I try calling Lola anyway, but it doesn't even ring, dropping the call over and over, along with my stomach, now nestled somewhere below my feet.

We get back on the highway with not another car in sight, likely because no one else would be stupid enough to drive in this. I keep having this feeling that my nervousness isn't merely a result of missing my wife and some inclement weather. There's something wrong.

I know it in my gut.

Chapter Seventy

TOO LATE

FRIDAY, JUNE 27

MUD SQUISHES through my toes as I climb up the hill, running as fast as I can toward Mayte's home. That's where they would've gone. *I'm sure of it.*

The thought of my best friend, practically my *sister*, in harm's way because of me has the contents of my stomach threatening to make an untimely appearance. I choke the bile down, angry tears streaming down my face. *Isabela.* God, what if they hurt her? I'll never be able to live with myself.

My gut wrenches, joints screaming for me to quit running, but *I can't.* I refuse. I have to make it there in time.

I *have* to.

Lightning cracks overhead, and I jolt in panic, my heart racing, the sound pounding violently behind my eardrums.

The soft, wet earth is unforgiving, and I slide through the grass, falling to my knees multiple times as I make my ascent to her house. I see the small blue cottage on the top of the hill, Russ's black Ford Expedition pulling into the driveway giving me a renewed sense of hope that I might make it in time, and I'm cursing myself for not taking Ryder up on his offer to teach me how to drive.

I drag myself up the hill, my lungs protesting with each wheeze. Rain pelts my skin, everything burning, aching, the pain made up of every excruciating sensation I can think of all mixing into one horrendous potion of my own destruction.

Teddy's gun weighs heavily in my hand, the metal cold and biting, as I sob.

"I'm almost there, Mayte. Just hold on one more minute."

Fear races through me as my feet pound against the hard clay at the end of her driveway. My eyes are trained ahead, thunder clapping around me.

I'm fifteen yards away when my whole world *stops*.

Two gunshots bang through the air, the sound muffled by Isabela's screams, muzzle flash lighting up her nursery window.

I fall to my knees, suffocated, like the walls of despair are closing in around me, crushing me beneath their weight. The lump in my throat feels too thick, too heavy to swallow around.

Isabela needs me.

It's the only thought that has me picking myself up from the water-logged ground, dragging my limp body into the house, where I'm certain the image will haunt my nightmares until the day I die.

I'm glad Ryder isn't here to witness this.

Ryder

Chapter Seventy-One

PANIC CALLING

FRIDAY, JUNE 27

I'M VIBRATING with nervous energy as I approach the gate, my heart sinking to my toes when I see the electric gate hanging off its hinges.

Nugget shuffles around his seat, unable to sit still the entire ride back, his tongue hanging from his mouth as he pants, fogging up the window.

I drive through the gate, cataloging my surroundings as I go, looking for anything else that might be out of place. My phone pings with messages and missed calls, one after the other, the sound grating on my nerves.

Nothing prepares me for the sight before me as I make it further down the dirt path onto the ranch. The little blue house I once went to for morning coffee and game night is now surrounded by an ambulance, a fire truck, and no fewer than six police cars.

Flashing red-and-blue lights surround Mayte's home, and my lungs cease to work.

My heart hammers in my chest, my breaths coming shallow as darkness clouds my vision. I throw my truck into park, unclip my seatbelt with unsteady hands, and toss myself out the door, my legs wobbling beneath me.

Fear. Unbridled fear fills every crevice of my soul as I fight through a panic attack that won't wait much longer before it pulls me into its current, whether I'm *ready or not.*

Chapter Seventy-Two

ANXIETY SHITS

FRIDAY, JUNE 27

LOLA WITH THE PHAT 🍑

Russ and his mom are here, searching for the cameras Lemmon hid. I'm hiding and safe for now.

My stomach rebukes her message, bile, and a three-day-old chicken biscuit courtesy of the "hashtag mom life" stirring in my gut.

I hurry to check the door; it's locked the way I rationally knew it would be, but I couldn't help but make sure anyway.

It feels like I'm vibrating, watching as I move through my motions, as if I'm having an out-of-body experience. *How is this happening?* Is *this* body doubling?

Isabela is asleep in her nursery, blissfully unaware of the utter hell surrounding her. I move on unsteady legs, carrying myself through the house, plugging in the code to the safe and pulling out the Glock I had Cynthia, the town's sometimes-friendly arms dealer and volunteer firefighter, help me acquire.

I'd gotten it for this exact reason, but I'd never truly believed I'd be sitting here, waiting to use it.

My phone pings with another message.

LOLA WITH THE PHAT 🍑
They're coming for you!

I now know exactly what the term "bone-chilling" feels like, and I can say with absolute certainty I hope to never experience it again—and *not* because I'm going to die tonight.

I have too much to live for to let some dumb bitch and her even dumber minion kill me in my own goddamn home.

It's not ideal for my hands to be shaking the way they are while holding a gun, but I'm scared shitless, and thank God for that, because usually, I'd be on the toilet with anxiety shits by now.

When I get to Isabela's room, it's dark, a quiet lullaby playing from the projector of swirling constellations on her ceiling. I open her closet door, setting the gun down on her dresser before pulling her into my arms.

I kiss her forehead, hot tears streaming down my cheeks, my lips trembling as I lower her into the bassinet I have stored in her closet.

She stirs in my arms, but she continues sleeping once I have her down. I count my blessings for that.

"I really should've looked into gun silencers or something," I whine, grabbing blankets and pillows to use as a buffer around the sides of the mesh bassinet, praying no one from the AAP throws a lightning bolt to smite me for the risk of SIDS. I think we have more pressing matters.

I gently place a pair of tiny earmuffs over her head that one of my cousins had sent for my baby shower, not taking into consideration that I live in *Oklahoma*.

Rosalia, you useless pendeja, *thank you.*

I hear something slam against the front door, pounding on the wood, followed by the shattering of my window.

Those windows are *stained glass*. They have gone *too* far!

I rush to shut the closet and angle myself facing the door, my back pressed against the wall.

The Glock I'm affectionately naming "Betty White" is trembling in my hands. Okay, fine. That's me, but I digress. I can do this. I *have* to do this.

They'll come in here, I'll stare them straight in the eyes, and I'll shoot the shit out of whatever body part I can manage. *No, no,* like you practiced, Mayte. You know where to shoot. "Come on, Mayte. Pull your big girl panties on and get your act together," I whisper under my breath.

I hear Amy and Russ as they get closer to the room, the lullaby still playing, obscuring their conversation, but Amy's grating voice is hard to miss. "Don't you mess this up. You got it? We get her to tell us where the recordings are, and if she doesn't know, we use her as collateral." *Goddamn the state of Oklahoma and their one-party consent laws.* "Lola will be forced to admit to insurance fraud, and we can use that to get your investors back. They'll take pity on you once they realize how awful your ex was."

I square my shoulders and prepare for what's next as their footsteps grow nearer.

Door. Open. Shoot.

Door. Open. Shoot.

Door. Open. Shoot. Door. Open. Shoot. Door. Open. Shoot. Door. Open. Shoot.

I chant this new mantra over and over until the door is cracking open, all the chaos in my mind going blank. My eyes zoom in on Russ's shiny kneecaps, and I blow those motherfuckers right off his scrawny body.

It all happens so quickly. Two shots, and Russ hits the ground, shaking the room with the impact, his shouts blood-curdling. Amy shrieks, flipping the light on, her eyes wide, body trembling. Isabela's wailing slices through the room, as if she and Russ are competing for loudest scream, and it jars me out of my stupor.

I keep the barrel of my gun trained on Amy, avoiding looking at what I'm sure is a bloodstained pink fuzzy rug in the center of my daughter's once serene nursery. Blood freaks me out. It's sticky and hot, the smell of iron permeating the air. Because I love myself, I refuse to assess the damage. I've done my part. I've stopped the bad guys. Now, it's everyone else's turn to jump in.

Except, there *is* no one else. Not a single soul is in sight, and if I have to shoot Amy, I might faint. I hate this bitch, but shooting a woman seems so much more impossible than shooting Russ had been. I can't imagine actually pulling the trigger again.

"Russ! Russ, my sweet boy," Amy sobs, falling to her knees beside him, reaching out to tamp his bleeding wounds. I back myself over to the closet, opening the door, keeping Betty White secured in my quivering hand. "Shhh, shhh, *mija*. It's okay, you're alright," I coo, trying to find a twisted balance between *Mami* and my new apparent job title: assassin.

Amy reaches for the gun Russ had dropped when she thinks I'm not paying attention, but I shake my head. "Uh uh. You saw what I did to your son, and I'm sure you don't want that gaudy pleather nonsense you call an outfit covered in blood. If you know what's good for you, you'll keep your ass seated and call the cops so he doesn't bleed to death and traumatize my child further."

She gapes at me, her mouth opening and closing like a fish. My pulse is racing in my neck, and my stomach chooses now to announce I have gas, rumbling loudly through the room. The anxiety shits really need to wait. Just another hour, *please.* I like this house. I don't want to have to burn it down if I shit all over and have this *hijo de puta's* blood splattered all over.

She finally nods, slowly reaching into her back pocket and retrieving her phone.

"I need"—more groaning—"help," Russ says hoarsely between screams.

"Should've thought about that before you entered someone's home looking to kidnap them. Newsflash, Russ: Women aren't your grandpa's victims anymore. *We're armed now.*"

Ringing from Amy's phone drags my attention to her—her brown eyes glisten with tears, pale face red and puffy, gray hair a mess.

"Nine-one-one, what's your emergency?"

"Put it on speaker," I instruct.

"Hello? Did you mean to contact emergency services?" the cool-toned woman answers again.

"Hi, yes. My name is Mayte Avila. I live at sixty-eight Silvercrest Drive in Hidden Valley, Oklahoma. There has been a break-in." I repeat the words Cynthia told me to make sure I say if I ever have to use the gun she sold me. "I felt threatened and shot the first intruder in the knees. I was protecting myself and my daughter. It was an act of self-defense."

"Okay, hold tight, Mayte. I'm Lisa. I'm dispatching to you now. Is there anyone else with you? You mentioned a first intruder. Does that mean there's a second?"

"Thank you, Lisa. Yes, the second intruder is unharmed—" I cut Amy a no bullshit stare and mouth the words, *"For now. Don't try me, bitch,"* before continuing to relay the events to Lisa, impatiently waiting for the red-and-blue lights that'll rescue me.

No, this is not one of those stories where I feel safe and protected by my local law enforcement. What they're rescuing me from, however, is my second worst fear. And since I've overcome the first, my toilet is going to help me prevent the second as soon as I can get my child in the arms of someone I can trust.

Lola

Chapter Seventy-Three

PARTNERS IN CRIME

FRIDAY, JUNE 27

I RUSH through the front door, and when I get inside, I'm stunned and elated to hear Mayte on the phone with a dispatcher.

I run to Isabela's room, and my stomach roils at the sight of Russ curled up on his side, clutching his knees in a puddle of his own blood. Amy is sitting on the ground in one of her signature over-the-top outfits, hands clamped down on her son's knees, her whole body trembling.

Mayte's standing with her body half concealed by the closet door. Her eyes meet mine, lighting up, a wide smile stretching across her lips. It's entirely misplaced given the circumstances, but my blood sings with relief.

I step around the crime scene, rushing to Mayte's side as the dispatcher says, "Okay, Mayte. Help is on the way. Sit tight and stay on the line."

"Thank you so much, Lisa!" she tells her. "My best friend showed up, so she's here too. Her name is Lola Lima. She has dark-brown, curly hair, and she's wearing a red Adidas sweat suit that's at least two sizes too big and makes her look like she belongs in a nineties boy band."

"Can you get to the point?" I ask her, groaning.

"Oh yeah, sorry. She's here, so please tell everyone not to shoot her—" My eyes grow wide, jaw dropping. She mouths, *"You never know!"* before continuing. "I have to step away to use the bathroom, and I'm leaving her with my gun and my daughter."

She looks down to see I have a gun of my own and shoves hers into my hand. "Just in case!" she says before sprinting through the room, her thighs pressed together, ass cheeks dimpled in her brightly colored leggings as she hurries away to do what she does best in high anxiety situations. I'm left here with a million thoughts, but the most powerful is that I'm just glad there's a reason *to* laugh at a time like this.

Which reminds me—there's now a more pressing matter to tend to.

"Hey, Lisa?" I ask, drawing a glare out of Amy at the sound of my voice.

"Yes?"

"Could you send someone to my home too? A friend of mine, Teddy, is over there, and he was assaulted by the same people who broke into Mayte's home." I take a few minutes to recount all the necessary information to Lisa before I hear sirens traveling up the driveway.

When the officers make their way inside, escorting me out, I glance over at Russ. Out of everything, it's the flicker of something inscrutable that crosses his face as he meets my gaze that confuses me most. But whether it's momentary regret, frustration, or something else entirely, I don't care to find out.

Chapter Seventy-Four

TRUTH UNFOLDING

FRIDAY, JUNE 27

LOLA CATCHES SIGHT of me as I fall to my knees in a combination of relief and panic, my vision narrowing as she shouts my name, running to me.

I heave, sucking in oxygen and fighting to keep my eyes open.

"Ryder! Ry!" she shouts, but her voice is barely louder than a hum with the whooshing of blood and adrenaline in my ears.

I give in to the panic when she folds herself around me. My body crumples in on itself as I gasp for air. "Ryder, it's okay. I'm okay. Everyone is alright. Come back to me, baby," she whispers in my ear. The weight of her body over mine acts as an anchor, calling me home to her when the worst of it is over. My extremities quake, chin quivering as I peel my lids open to see Lola's mud-soaked curls and deep, cinnamon eyes.

My heart rate slows, galloping along at the realization that she's here, in my arms, *safe*.

"Wh-what happened?" I ask hoarsely.

She doesn't have a chance to answer before Sheriff Wilson approaches. "Mr. Lockhart, I'd like to get you and Lola out of the rain so we can discuss what happened with her ex-fiancé. If you wouldn't mind followin' me," he says, nodding toward Mayte's porch.

Lola helps pull me up, and I follow her to the steps where Mayte cradles Isabela against her chest.

"Russ was involved?" I ask, whispering to Lola in a daze.

"In a roundabout way," she mutters.

A whole lot becomes clearer once I'm standing in the middle of the chaos, no longer hidden behind one of the many cars and emergency vehicles parked along Mayte's property.

A woman I've never seen before is handcuffed, arguing with two police officers as she's pushed against the hood of one of their Dodge Chargers. She's fighting against them as they shout at her to get in the back seat before they have to resort to other methods of restraint.

I swing around to the sound of a man crying, only to find the guy who looks suspiciously like Nugget's apparent owner being wheeled into the ambulance bed on a stretcher. He's attached to it with handcuffs, and I suppose that would be Russ.

"Ryder! Lola! Oh, my God!"

We all whip around to the sound of that voice, my eyes growing wide as saucers as Lemmon barrels toward us. Her mustard-yellow dress stuck to her, hair drenched and plastered to her head.

"Lemmon, what the—"

She trips, slipping through the mud, body flailing as she lands at Lola's feet. Lemmon clambers onto her knees, chest heaving as she looks up at Lola, tears mixing with rain running down her puffy cheeks.

"Lola, I'm so sorry, I tried to warn y'all, but you have my number blocked, and then my car broke down, and I'm just so sorry," she sobs, choking on a cough. "I never meant for this to happen," she wails. "I just—God, I was just so jealous. You came here with nothing and managed to make friends, living out all of your dreams, and when you left Ryder, I thought—" she sniffles, "I thought I'd *finally* won some of that good luck you seemed to have in truckloads."

"You sure like to talk a lot, don't you?" Russ drawls, and if the circumstances were different, I'd be inclined to laugh. As it stands, I'm in the middle of a goddamn crime scene, and I almost lost my entire world tonight. My stomach churns at the thought.

"It wasn't *luck*, Lemmon. I'm kind to people—*that* is how I make friends. And I've worked my ass off for every single thing I've got, including my relationships. Your jealousy doesn't excuse whatever part you played in this," Lola tells her, and damn am I proud to call her mine.

Lemmon's shoulders shake, and she smacks a palm over her mouth as another sob tears through her. "Y-you're right. Th-that wasn't much of an apology," Lemmon admits, and I'm momentarily stunned.

This *could* all be an act, but I'm inclined to believe that, just maybe, there's some good left in my ex-wife after all. And maybe there's hope for her yet; it just won't be here with me or anyone I love.

"What exactly *was* your part in this?" Mayte asks her, getting right into it.

Lemmon glances up at the sheriff, her gaze quickly darting away. "I wanted to prove they'd gotten married for Lola's health insurance."

"And how did you plan on proving *that* little theory?" Mayte asks, cocking a dark brow as she not-so-subtly tries to get a confession out of Lemmon, but before she can further incriminate herself, one of the paramedics shouts over to us.

"Hey, Sheriff, we've gotta get this guy out of here. He's bleeding bad!"

"Ah, shit. Alright, give me a minute," he tells us. I nod in a daze, my eyes glued to the scene before me.

"I need your phone for evidence," Sheriff Wilson tells Russ.

"Baldy over there already took it," he whines, tipping his chin at Raul, the heavy-set officer.

"Sure did, and you're gonna love what I've found already! We've got everything we need to press charges and make sure they stick," Raul says, waving the phone around with a hearty chuckle. "And it turns out this one named Lemmon's contact with her *actual* name, even wrote out their entire plan in a notes app. Included some information about a break-in, tampering with security cameras, and facts he'd researched about recorded evidence and what the Oklahoma law entails about non-consensual audio recordings."

"Russ! You stupid bastard!" Lemmon shrieks, picking herself up off the ground and stomping off toward the ambulance. Ah, there's the ex-wife I know and detest.

One of the officers reaches out and grabs her by the elbow, tugging her against his chest before she can make an even bigger scene and go after Russ.

"Oh, shut it, Lemmon! You're the idiot who concocted this damn plan that got me *shot*! Now, can someone take me to the fucking emergency room!?" Russ yells back at her.

Lola folds her arm around mine. "It turns out Russ threw a hissy fit at the wedding when I didn't show up. Seems his investors weren't as excited to give him their money when they realized how volatile he can be, so he lost everything. His mom, Amy," she says, pointing to the woman pinned to the cop car with her chin, "did some digging and reached out to Lemmon, who was all too happy to lend a hand in getting their payback," she says, rolling her eyes. She's far more relaxed than I am, clearly having had more time to process everything, but I know the crash will come later, when the adrenaline wears off. *And I'll be there to help her through every second.*

I wrap an arm around her waist, tugging her against me and kissing the side of her head now that I'm more stable on my feet.

Lemmon is escorted into one of the cop cars, climbing into the backseat without much fuss.

Amy, on the other hand, is throwing an elbow into one of the officers' sides, twisting around and narrowly evading them.

I pull away to run after her, but Lola's steady hand stops me. "Just wait."

Nugget whips out from under the porch, lurching forward and gaining speed, yipping as he chases her, putting those tiny paws to good use.

Amy peers over her shoulder, yelling as she runs, scrambling in the mud, looking unbelievably out of place in her red-and-black leather pants and feather-lined coat.

José's black pickup pulls down the path ahead of her, illuminating Amy through the dark and rain. He stops abruptly, the passenger door swinging open.

Bexaida tosses herself out the door, bends over to pull off her shoe, and sends it sailing through the air, nailing Amy right in the head. There's a chorus of "oofs" that meets the *thwack* sound. She goes down like a domino, and Nugget skids over to her, jumping on her back for good measure.

"That woman is *deadly* with a *chancleta,*" Mayte praises beside us.

The officers rush over to her, pulling her up as Russ yells, "Good boy, Mr. Lickerton!" before the ambulance doors are pulled closed and he's driven away with sirens blaring.

Amy is shoved into the back of a police car, still yelling obscenities as the officer slams the door in her face.

When most of the officers and the fire truck have cleared out, my entire family sits down to speak with the sheriff and the few officers left behind. We recount every creepy message, break-in, phone call, and everything else that's happened here the last few months, gaining clarity on Lemmon's part in all this with the help of Russ's phone.

It turns out that Lemmon was suspicious of our marriage from the beginning, leaning on the belief that Lola and I had to have gotten together so soon after she left Russ because we'd been cheating on Russ and Lemmon with each other. After breaking into my home and confirming that wasn't the case, thanks to the cameras *she* had planted, she'd still been hoping to get Lola to leave town out of spite and jealousy. But then Amy hired someone to sneak onto the property and start the barn fire, and everything became too real for Lemmon. She tried to cut her losses and separate herself from the whole situation, but when Russ reached out to Lemmon, worried his mom was going off the rails, Lemmon ran over here, trying to warn us and make amends for her role in everything.

Jealousy is a potent toxin, worming its way into your every action, and while I may never fully understand how deep that poison runs within Lemmon, it certainly makes me feel better knowing my ex-wife wasn't a complete psychopath. And when the night is over, I take my wife and our furry child home to bed, just like I plan to for the rest of forever.

I couldn't be more content knowing that through it all, she chose *me*. And I got to marry my best friend.

Lola

Chapter Seventy-Five

AFTERMATH

SATURDAY, JUNE 28

I WATCH Ryder and Nugget rest beside me, relieved to realize Ryder's night terrors didn't make an appearance for the first time in weeks. He looks so peaceful, his pillow-soft lips slightly parted, face turned toward me.

The bright afternoon sun streams in through the blinds, and I can't help but reach out, stroking my thumb over his cheek. Resting on my elbow, I lean closer to him, desperate to commit every detail to memory.

With the way our first few months of marriage have gone, I know I can't take anything for granted, especially not these serene moments when Ryder is safe and loved beside me. I'm only able to ensure one of those things will remain true forever.

His dark lashes flutter with the next stroke of my thumb, and I almost regret the motion until I'm met with the most beautiful cerulean eyes. A slow, easy smile fills my heart to the brim with gratitude.

"How'd I get so lucky to wake up to my gorgeous best friend?" he asks, his tone gravelly and sleep-laden as he reaches to cup my jaw.

"I wonder the same thing every day," I whisper, content to remain in the quiet space surrounding us and avoid the prying questions from the amazing people in this town who no doubt love us but are, sometimes, a little much.

"Mmm," he hums, wrapping an arm around my waist and tugging me to lie over his chest. He ducks his chin and presses kisses along my jawline and over my thrumming pulse, my body warming.

We spend the next who knows how long whispering our shared gratitude for another day together, a second chance. We explore our bodies, pressing gentle kisses, tentative licks, and nips on every inch. Our touches are slow and worshipping, neither of us rushing to remove our clothes or take things any further. We just soak in the beauty of this moment, free of fear for our safety, the stress of rebuilding our lives, or the anxiety of what lies beyond this.

That is, until the chirping from our phones can no longer be ignored.

I'm straddling Ryder's lap, his arms wrapped around my waist as he sits up, his legs straight beneath me. His scruff-covered chin sits on top of my shoulder until he kisses below my ear and nips at the tender flesh at the base of my neck with a groan. "How long do you think it'll be before they're busting down our door?"

"Probably not long," I ruefully admit.

He lets out a rough exhale, pulling away from me to grab our phones from the nightstand.

The door creaks open, and Nugget waddles in, his entire butt shaking as he attempts to jump onto the bed, hanging onto the edge as I lean over to help drag him up. His tongue hangs as he dances, letting out a couple excited yelps and covering us in affection.

"Okay, good boy, Nugget. That's enough," I say, giggling as I pick him up, sliding out of the bed to take him out.

"Hey, Lols!" Ryder shouts, but I've already made the mistake of opening the door.

What looks like the *entire* town is in our front yard! They all glance up to see me standing barefoot, hair a mess, my pants forgotten somewhere between crawling in the house and waking up this morning. Their brows raise, but they release a collective sigh at the sight of us, alive and safe.

As overwhelming as it is at first, Ryder and I take it in stride, allowing the town that raised us to be here in our most vulnerable moments, giving us over fifty shoulders to lean on when we need them, no questions asked.

After spending the last several years isolated from those I could trust, I'm ready to untangle those feelings and lean into something true: *unconditional love.*

Ryder

Chapter Seventy-Six

LOLA'S

WEDNESDAY, AUGUST 6

MY HEART IS SOARING high today after several long weeks of rebuilding this place, the entire town volleying for us, putting in the extra time and manpower necessary to get the studio back in working order for Lola.

These people, with such massive hearts, stood by us every step of the way. From the court hearing, which was sped up substantially thanks to Lemmon's own father pushing to get it over with, to the nail-biting days of waiting for a decision where Russ was released with a year of community service because ultimately, he'd only gone along with his mother's plans so he could retrieve the dog he'd adopted after Lola left. Not that we returned Nugget to him.

It was Russ's cousin who did all of Amy's dirty work, sneaking onto the ranch to take photos of us and burn the barn down. We learned he lived less than an hour away and was actually the guy in the image I received with Nugget. He had a warrant out for his arrest already as a result of several other crimes he'd committed, and thanks to Teddy, he's behind bars. Turns out Teddy was a bounty hunter in his past life and put those skills to good use, getting back at the family that left him on my living room floor with a concussion.

Lemmon is in a facility, receiving the psychiatric care she needs to help heal from her past traumas. And Amy is locked up in a cell somewhere in Texas, never to bother us again, working through her own divorce after everything came to light and her husband desperately wanted out of their relationship.

The emotional strain, coupled with Lola struggling through some medication changes that had her more fatigued than ever, was painful to watch, and it makes this moment of pure bliss that much more incredible. Her symptoms have improved significantly, and it shows in every step she takes, each sway of those grabbable hips and the distinct lack of a wince when she rocks onto the balls of her feet.

The last several weeks have felt more like months with how much was packed into them. We made time for ourselves, too, acting like recluses, hiding away from everyone for a while to process our emotions, with the help of Talia and my grief counselor, Samuel. I made sure that, above all else, I took care of my wife, giving her the space and time she needed to focus on healing, both emotionally and physically.

Nothing about her wide smile and bright, glittering eyes gives away how much she'd shattered after the adrenaline had worn off and the realization that things could have ended so much differently sank in. The entire experience broke my goddamn heart.

Through it all, we felt an outpouring of love and support holding us up, pushing us from one day to the next.

My gaze flits around the room, landing on the overjoyed faces of the people who'd made all this possible, getting us through the utter hell we'd been served.

Sebastian is swiveling his hips to *"Bailando Bachata"* by Chayanne, dancing circles around his husband, Jeremiah. Their heads are thrown back, joyous laughter pouring out of them as Jeremiah does his best to shimmy and sway. Each day, we were woken up with lattes from Grind that had Lola purring into her mug as I rubbed her feet and calves. It became the perfect morning ritual, especially paired with the baked goods from Bake My Day that Caitlyn would drop off.

The Ryde or Dye book club has taken it upon themselves to pair up with the singles who came to class today, and they've shocked, I think, everyone with how good they are. For a bunch of bikers in leather, they're pretty smooth. I, for one, am extremely grateful they didn't have anything to do with the strange occurrences around town. It would've killed me. Thankfully, Bexaida's instinct to trust them was right, as usual, and they worked every day to make sure our home was always stocked with romance reads, the barn cleaned up quickly and ready for repairs as soon as we were.

Even the lovely ladies at Wigs & Waffles, the newly opened drag brunch spot, brought us meals to get us through each week. They had never met us, and they still jumped in to help, as if they'd lived in this town their entire lives. That's the beauty of Hidden Valley: once you're here, *you're family.*

So it comes as no surprise that the studio is at max capacity. We even had to turn our parents away. There was barely room to breathe, let alone dance. They're set up outside the open barn doors in folding chairs, happily watching Lola take on her first class in the finished studio, no threats of arson hanging over our heads.

And god, my wife is *beautiful.*

I've never seen a more magnificent sight than Lola Lima in her element, dark-red lips stretched across her cheeks, curls cascading down her shoulders, and skin shimmering in her fire-engine-red outfit.

Music plays loudly overhead from the upgraded speakers Zeke helped me install, and Lola's hips sway, re-explaining the basic steps of *Bachata* to the class. She's gone over it a few times, explaining it in different ways and using me as her partner for her demonstration, making sure to change how she teaches to fit different learning styles.

It helps that Karmella and Yanet, her close friends and the co-owners of *Fuego Fusion*, came to cheer her on. They're assisting her, moving through the room to correct form and offer tips.

I move through the crowd when Lola holds out her hand for me, my pulse speeding with the knowledge I'll get to have her in my arms any second.

I grasp her small palm in mine, curling my fingers around it and tugging her to me. She twirls into the movement, winding up until she's nestled against my chest, her sweet scent overwhelming my senses.

"Everyone, grab your partners and hold them close. We're going to have a little change of pace for the last few minutes of class," she says with a sly smile aimed at me. "My *husband* is going to help give you a better idea of how to mesh the steps we've been learning."

God, it still feels so good to hear her call me that.

"*Dos Locos*" filters through the speakers, a few people whistling when they recognize the upbeat song. Lola presses her chest against mine, bringing her arms up in an arc over her head as she twists her hips, bringing her arms down to wrap around my shoulders.

"This one is fast-paced, with a 4/4-time signature, so if you miss a beat, just count out loud until you and your partner fall back into it, okay?" she asks, and I dig my fingers into her hips, loving the feel of her body against mine and simultaneously willing my dick to remember where we're at. "Who's ready?!" she shouts over the music, dancing backward and away from me for a moment, clapping her hands to the rhythm.

She rolls her shoulders, bending her elbows and shimmying toward me, her feet continuing the fast pace the song has set. It's as if her body has a mind of its own, reacting in time to the pulse of the music around us. When she's back in my arms, I allow myself to let go the same way she's been teaching me to.

I pull her into me, rolling my hips as she brackets my thigh with hers, our bodies moving as a single unit, playing off the other. Our hands roam, my fingertips trailing over her smooth, bare arms, her waist, over the curve of her ass for just a beat before she spins out of my grasp.

At the part of the song where the singers' voices clang together in short, abrupt bursts with the words, *"Que tontos, que somos tu y yo,"* Lola wraps an arm around my neck, turning her side into my chest with one hand on her hip. I keep an arm wrapped around her, the other on her abdomen, pressing into each of the sharp movements she makes, her body punctuating each word the same way the singers seem to.

Her skin glistens with a sheen of sweat, our breaths tangling. My heart races with each movement as we become one. By the time the song is over, I'm completely out of breath, with Lola's body wrapped around mine, our noses brushing, parted lips barely a breath away, chests heaving. Her eyes bore into mine, heavy lids telling me she wants me to take her mouth just as badly as I d—

"This is a family-friendly function, folks. I'm not surprised I have to remind my brother of that, but Lola? I'm disappointed in you," Zeke's mocking voice chimes over the speakers, effectively breaking the spell. Lola and I pull apart, gasping for breath and overcome with laughter as the whole room whistles.

"Kiss him! Kiss him!" they chant, their shouts growing louder and more determined.

Lola tilts her head at me, her eyes leaving mine only for a second to assess the room before finding mine again. The next thing I know, she's catapulting herself into my arms, fingers twining in my hair as she tugs my mouth to hers, branding my lips. The roar of the crowd gets drowned out by this single moment in time, the entire world stopping as Lola Lima, my childhood crush, my best friend, and now, my *wife*, claims me for everyone to see.

My pulse slows, my tongue slipping between her kiss-swollen lips for a quick taste before I pull away. The cheers hit me all at once in the way sound returns after you've been momentarily deafened by a speed train. Our quiet moment in the madness ceases, replaced by something bigger than us, something profoundly beautiful and uplifting, the product of a lifetime of love and devotion to this town, and my heart swells with gratitude.

Lola claps her hands, shaking her head as she laughs at our town's antics. "Alright, alright. Let's get back to work," she says, rolling her eyes playfully.

When everyone is back with their partners, Lola nods at Zeke where he stands in the corner over the small DJ setup he insisted the studio needed. Apparently, he's decided this is his new calling, but I think he just wanted an excuse to buy new gadgets and mess around with installation.

"Nothing in dance has to be technically perfect," she says, addressing the room as our bodies carry us through the movements. "The style of dance lays the groundwork, but how you choose to move your body and engage with your partner is up to you. If this song is too fast, slow it down. If you want to add some big flourishes, go ahead and give it a try. Since this is the last song before we close out the class, just give it everything you've got and enjoy yourself!"

The crowd cheers, and Zeke presses play, "Stand by Me" by Prince Royce surrounding us.

Everyone takes hold of their partners, twirling them around the smooth dance floors, their movements already so much more put together than they had been during that first class in June.

Lola turns her attention fully on me, gripping my hands and taking a step back, swiveling her hips and lowering her body before returning to her full height, allowing me to pull her into me.

I slide my palms down her sides, spinning her so her back is flush to my chest. I wind my arms around her front, and she grinds her ass against my groin. I nip at the soft flesh below her ear and whisper, "Are you tryin' to kill your husband, darlin'?"

She places her hands over mine, chuckling lightly as she smooths my palms over her body before turning to face me, wrapping her arms around my neck. We lock eyes, singing along to the song, enjoying the last moments of tonight with simple movements, embracing each other.

The room starts to grow louder, people joining in, singing to each other and pointing at the nearest neighbor every time we sing the words, "Stand by me." There's a light feeling spreading through the room, as if we're floating, suspended in time. I glance around to find most everyone has broken away from their partners, no longer dancing but pulling each other in for hugs. There's not a dry eye in the room.

Lola stares up at me with tears pooling in her eyes, and I tug her close, resting my forehead on hers as I blink away my own tears.

"I bet this isn't how you expected your birthday to go, huh?" I whisper when the song ends, my voice hoarse.

"It's everything and more," she whispers back as the room erupts in cheers and shouts once more, the class coming to an end.

"I'm so proud of you, Lola," I whisper, reluctantly pulling away so she can address her adoring fans.

"I just want to thank you all for showing up," she starts, and several people laugh. She waves a hand in front of her face, rolling her eyes jokingly. "No, no. I don't mean tonight." Her tone shifts from playful to serious, swiping tears from her cheeks with the backs of her hands. The room quiets down, all eyes and ears on Lola. "Thank you for making me feel safe and loved, free to be completely myself, even as a child. For allowing me to make mistakes and learn from them without the fear that my entire life would be riding on one mess up. You've all shown up for me since the very first day I arrived in Hidden Valley, and you've all continued to do so, even after I'd lost myself for a while. You've helped me rebuild my life, sometimes twice," she says, chuckling lightly at the insinuation. "I recognize that for the gift it is because most people don't have the kind of community we do. And I just—" she peers up at the ceiling, blinking away tears, "I love you all so much. *Los amo, mi familia.*"

Clapping, whistling, and a chorus of "We love you too!" envelop us, and as I tug her close for another hug, I whisper against the shell of her ear, "What's it gonna be, darlin'? Have you finally picked a name for this place?"

"*Lola's,*" she breathes out. "I want it to be completely, utterly *mine.* Just like you, Ryder Lockhart."

If there's one thing for certain in this ever-changing world, it's that *I am irrevocably, undeniably, and eternally Lola Lima's.*

The end.

Lola

Epilogue Part One
BREEDING & FEEDING

THREE MONTHS LATER

"I KNOW you said you've never ridden a horse, but look at you now! You're a natural," Ryder tells Keeva, helping her dismount Penny.

She lands on her feet, dust kicking up around her boots. She unclips her helmet, and long tendrils of deep red frame her face. "Thanks, Ryder," she says with a smile. Her eyes grow wide when she sees me, hurrying to my side and throwing her arms out for a hug. I pull her close to me, rocking side to side a bit as we laugh into the embrace. "When did you get back?" she asks, breaking away from me.

"You act as if I've been gone for a month." I chuckle. "It's been three days, and you saw me last week!" Keeva and I met at one of my dance lessons, and after watching her flail her body unnaturally across the dance floor, I knew I had to help. She was a bit embarrassed at first, having grown up with a Latina stepmom, but she's just an all-around uncoordinated person, and living with dysautonomia doesn't help.

Once Ryder got his equine therapy lessons set up with a licensed animal therapist, he was ready for anyone willing to give it a shot. Keeva was one of many, utilizing riding lessons to strengthen her muscles and lessen the pooling of fluid in her legs that leads to her losing consciousness. She swears it's been life-changing for her already, and she has improved tremendously in our weekly dance classes.

"I know, but I missed you! Mayte invited me over to play Uno and Domino with her, keep her company. I got freaking annihilated, Lola! You should've warned me she plays so dirty!"

My shoulders shake with laughter, and my heart feels full knowing Mayte has more than just me to spend time with, though she might be in desperate need of some alone time come next week, when her cousin moves in. "She is the absolute worst," I agree.

Ryder sidles up to us after he's said his goodbyes to everyone. He winds an arm around my waist, tugging me into his side and pressing a soft kiss to my temple. "You about ready to get out of here?" he asks. "I have a little surprise planned for you." He winks, and my insides melt, cheeks flushing.

Keeva glances between us, rolling her lips into her mouth to hide her grin. "*Well*, thank you for a wonderful lesson, Ryder. I'll just be going now," she says, hurrying away and leaving my husband and me alone.

I twist in his arms, planting my hands on his chest. Glittering blue eyes meet mine, and those soft, kissable lips call to me.

I press onto my tiptoes, hovering my lips just over his. "Does this surprise involve your dick in my mouth?"

A growl rips from his throat, and in an instant, his lips meet mine, taking over all my senses. His mouth takes my breath away as he nips at my bottom lip. I open for him, our tongues tangling and heat pooling low in my belly. Sweet mint floods my mouth, his hands skimming over my waist down to my ass. He clutches me tightly against him, his thick length already ready for me, pressing against my belly.

I have to tear my mouth away from his before I climb him

like a tree, right here in the open, with all the squirrels watching. He gives my ass a firm squeeze before turning me around and swatting my bottom. "Come on, Lols. Let's go see that surprise."

I pull my keys out, climbing into the driver's side of the massive, hot-pink GMC Sierra I bought myself two weeks ago. Being able to afford it on my own from the money I've made from the studio feels so freeing—I'll never have to rely on anyone else ever again. Ryder teaching me how to drive has been the icing on the cake, and the sprinkles are the hot-and-heavy make-out sessions after a job well done on my part. Which is apparently pretty easy to do, seeing as a "good job" to Ryder means not running us into a tree.

He slams the door behind him, buckling himself in and checking that I am too before I pull out onto the dirt road, kicking up plumes of dust. "Where should I be driving?"

"To the watering hole," he murmurs, placing his hand on my thigh and trailing his pinky indecently high. The tip of his finger smooths over the seam of my denim shorts, and he can probably feel my wetness through the thick fabric.

"If you want to make it there, you should keep your hands to yourself," I grit out as heat threatens to swallow me whole.

He releases a low rumbling chuckle, but his palm only climbs higher. My thighs part for him, and I accidentally press down on the brake, rocking us forward. "Ry! I'm seriou—" The word breaks off on a moan, and my eyes are rolling. "Is this how men feel about road head?"

More laughter fills the suffocatingly tight space between us, his entire hand cupping me through my shorts.

I tentatively press on the gas, focusing on the road ahead, and the trees starting to turn to beautiful burnt shades of red and orange.

"I'm not sure, Lols. I've never experienced it before but I'd be willing to if you are." He grins at me mischievously, and I catch it from my periphery.

"Maybe later, but only if you don't get us killed because you can't keep your hands to yourself!"

"Okay, okay," he says, removing his hand and putting both up in surrender.

A few minutes later, we're at the furthest edge of the property, parked and walking hand in hand to the watering hole through the thick trees.

"You know I've seen this place before, right?" I tease. "In fact, I've become *well* acquainted with it over the last few months." I waggle my brows at him suggestively, and he snorts a laugh, bringing my knuckles to his lips.

"Hold your horses. You'll find out in just a minute."

We continue walking in silence, nothing but the setting sun glinting through the treetops to keep us from tripping over the roots running along the ground. When we break through the brush, the moon is on our left, the sun setting on the horizon, creating beautiful rainbows over the smooth water.

"Do you trust me, darlin'?"

I answer without hesitation. "Implicitly."

The corner of his mouth lifts, and he places his hands on my hips. "Then close your eyes," he instructs.

I do as I'm told, listening closely for any signs of what the surprise might be. Crickets sing in the distance, and Ryder's warm scent wraps around me in whispers of vanilla and bourbon. He hoists me up, and my legs wrap around his waist instinctively, my arms winding around his neck as he carries me over crunching leaves and closer to the water slowly running over smooth rocks.

A cool breeze whips past us, my hair flying around my face, but my eyes remain closed.

"For this next part, it's probably better if you open your eyes." I blink rapidly to clear my vision as he sets me on unsteady feet. He pushes my hair out of my face, and his surprise comes into view.

I stare at the structure in awe, mouth gaping as I crane my neck back to take in every detail.

A set of steps hangs from the platform base, leading up to a simple rectangular treehouse built into the side of the tall oak. The canopy of leaves hovers over top, casting a large shadow. "Go on up. I'll give you a boost." He steps to the side, giving me space to grip the smooth wooden planks. He's installed silicone grippers to the tops of each rung to make it easier for me to hold onto, I'm sure. His fingers dig into my hips, supporting my weight as I climb to the top.

I wait for him to join me, hanging on to the sturdy railing at the edge of the tiny, uncovered porch. He tugs me inside, ducking his head as we enter through the small doorway. Everything was built to accommodate my full height, but at six-foot-four, Ryder looks like a giant here.

"What is all this?" I ask, my voice small as I take in the fluffy white carpet, full-size mattress, and all of the white, red, pink, and purple decorations littering the small room. He's got electricity running somehow, a small light flush against the ceiling illuminating the space, and a mini fridge so tiny it could probably only hold two or three cans of pop.

"Remember when we went for your appointment to remove the implant last month, and you said you'd need a place to hide away and relax when we have kids if ours turn out to be anything like Isabela?" he asks with a wide grin.

"Yes…"

He pulls me into his body, resting his forehead against mine. "Well, here it is. Your place to escape," he whispers, and my chest heaves, my vision going hazy behind a wall of tears. Rough, calloused hands glide up my sides, over my breasts, causing my nipples to pebble and goosebumps to erupt along my neck as he raises his palms to cup my cheeks.

"How do you keep getting better each day?" I ask, my words sounding water-logged.

"I learn from the best," he answers pointedly. "Now"—he

lowers his mouth to hover over the shell of my ear—"is my gorgeous wife ready for me to breed her pretty pussy?"

White-hot heat flashes through me, and I let out a whimper, immediately sinking to my knees in the cramped space. His eyes grow wide before narrowing on me. He pushes a hand through my hair, grabbing hold of my roots as I make quick work of his belt, tugging his jeans and briefs down his thick thighs, the tattoo he got just for me on full display now.

"I'm not sure your mouth is the right hole, darlin'. I love it all the same, but I think we need to try a little lower if—" He groans when I grip his base, directing his tip to my mouth. I tap his dick on my tongue, then swirl around it and stroke the underside of his length. "You know what? Never mind. I'll take your pussy later," he says, his head falling back, banging against the wall behind him with a loud thud. He reaches up to rub at the spot, grimacing, but I get to work, sucking him all the way into my throat until he's bottoming out, all remnants of pain forgotten.

I release him from my mouth with a pop, my tongue darting out to lick off the salty drop of precum beading from his slit. His eyes never leave me, staring down at me with a feral expression that has my toes curling.

"Spit on it, darlin," he demands, and I do, running my hand from tip to base to coat him as he grunts, his jaw twitching as he grinds his molars. He reaches down to grab me under my arms, tugging me up before pushing me back down onto my back. I fall unceremoniously into the center of the small mattress as he prowls over me, stopping to tug off his shirt.

The last of the sun's rays filter through the corner window, casting my husband in a stunning golden glow. His abdominal muscles ripple, and his corded biceps flex as his arms flank me. He dips his head, catching my lips in a quick kiss, biting on my bottom lip as he pulls away.

He leans back to stare down at me, running his hands under my shirt. His thumbs caress my peaked nipples, and my back arches into the sensation. The corner of his lip twitches with a knowing smirk. "You like that, huh?"

"Mhmm," I answer, whimpering as he repeats the movement.

"What else does my stunning wife like?" he asks, but it's clear he isn't looking for an answer, not with how his hands move over me, tugging my shirt over my head and falling back to the front-closing clasp on my lacy red bra. He undoes it, making quick work of tossing my clothing to the side before sliding down my body and unbuttoning my shorts. "No answer?" he asks, quirking a brow at me, but my mind is a little slow to the draw with lust fogging my synapses. He tugs my shorts down, dragging my thong with it and dropping them beside the mattress.

"Should I spread my legs for you, or did you want to do that yourself?" I rasp.

His smirk widens to a grin, and he lowers himself to the floor, nudging my knees open and wrapping his arms under my thighs to pull my pussy to his face at the edge of the bed. "Just lie back and let me do all the work, darlin'. I've gotta make sure my wife is taken care of properly."

He presses a tender kiss above my pubic bone, lowering his mouth to hover over my clit. "Ry, *please*," I whine. Ryder's come to realize that not only does he love it when I take control, but when I relinquish control to him, that's his absolute favorite. With anyone else, I wouldn't even consider it, but with him, it's so easy to let go and ask for what I want.

"You smell so sweet," he whispers between peppering kisses over my clit, inner thighs, and my slick entrance. "I can't wait to have a taste." He plunges two fingers inside, and my eyes grow wide, head falling back onto the pillowtop mattress. "Eh, eh, eh. Eyes on me, darlin'," he chides.

I sit up, balancing on my elbows as I watch him pump his fingers inside me with languid strokes. "That's better. Now, what was it you wanted?"

I let out a little huff of annoyance, but I know I'll be rewarded for all his teasing. "Ryder Maddox Lockhart, I *need* you to eat my pussy."

He glances up. "What's the magic word?" he teases.

I narrow my eyes on him and grit out the word, *"Please."* That's all it takes for him to duck his head, remove his fingers, and slurp on my pussy like he's been absolutely

starved for it. His tongue swirls and tastes, lapping at my entrance between flicking the tip over my pulsing clit. I buck against his mouth, pleasure searing through me. He adjusts his grip, lifting my left leg up and pressing my knee into my chest to open me for him completely.

The sounds his mouth is making over my wetness, combined with his groans of ecstasy, are intoxicating, as if eating me out is his favorite part of the day and my pussy is a Michelin star restaurant. It's not long before the sparks of pleasure become too much for me, and I'm falling off the edge of ecstasy with Ryder grunting as he wraps his lips around my clit, allowing me to ride the waves of pleasure.

It continues in small, tingling bursts, and when the aftershocks have worn off, I collapse back onto the mattress, my arms splayed out at my sides.

"Whoever said 'absence makes the heart grow fonder' has never been in a relationship with someone who could make their grown ass husband come without even touching their cock. Otherwise, they'd have mentioned that too," he groans, flopping down on his back beside me. His dick is far from flaccid, but his cum paints his thighs.

"I thought you said you were planning to breed my pussy? How are we gonna make that happen now?" I ask, cocking my head to the side in question. I roll toward him, propping my head up on my hand.

"Give me ten minutes, and I'll make good on my promise," he says with a low, tired laugh.

"We have dinner reservations soon, and we need to get

cleaned up," I remind him, rolling my eyes. "You can fill me up later."

A wicked smirk tugs at his lips, and before I know what he's planning, he grips my thigh, pulling it up to rest on his hip. He swipes his fingers through the cum covering his thighs and perfectly sculpted abdominals, bringing two coated fingers to my core and pushing them inside.

I watch with rapt attention, moaning and rocking my hips against him. When he pulls his fingers out, some of our combined arousal spills out, but he's quick to push it back inside, giving me a lazy smile. "Don't even think about showering before dinner, darlin'. I have big plans for the mess I've made."

Ryder

Epilogue Part Two
IN EVERY LIFETIME

THIRTY YEARS LATER

"ARE you sure you're going to be okay, Dad? I don't want you to trip because you can't see through all those tears," Carmen jokes, squeezing my bicep as I swipe away the tears falling mercilessly down my cheeks.

I suck in a deep breath and blink the tears away. "Yes, *mi amor*. I promise, I'll get my shit together for you," I tell her with a raspy chuckle.

The truth is, walking our daughter down the aisle might just kill me. It's not that I don't love her soon-to-be wife, quite the opposite, actually. I *adore* Maribella, and after the first look, where I got to see Carmen wearing Lola's wedding dress, the delicate lace appliqués still beautifully preserved after all these years, it was just too damn much.

I *love* love! I firmly believe that real men cry, but damn, I'm really ruining a lot of family photos with all these tears.

Lola slips beside us, sliding a hand around my back, rubbing soothing circles between my shoulder blades. "Ry, everything okay?" she asks, giggling at my expense. She and Carmen give each other a look so familiar to me after nearly five decades of seeing it on Lola's face. It's the one that reads, "He's being such a sap, isn't he?"

"I can't help it! Our daughter is just so beautiful, and you know how I get at weddings."

"Ryder, you better get your shit together because I'm pressing play on that song in t-minus twenty seconds, whether you're ready or not!" Mayte whisper-screams at me, her voice startling me. I almost drop the giant black umbrella we're using to shield Carmen from the crowd.

"*Ay!*" Lola and Carmen yelp, grabbing hold of the umbrella to steady it in front of us.

"I promise, I'm good now," I assure them, blinking away the last remnants of wetness from my lashes. "Let's do this."

Lola presses up onto her toes, pecking my cheek with a kiss I'm certain left a perfect red imprint of her lips. She licks the pad of her thumb and swipes at it roughly, my skin stinging from all the tugging.

"You ready, *amorcito*?" I ask Carmen as Lola moves to stand on her other side, looping an arm through hers.

"I've never been more ready," Carmen confirms. "I love that woman so damn much, it hurts."

"I know the feeling," I whisper just as "*El Amor*" starts playing, signaling for us to make our way up the aisle.

I pass the umbrella to Mayte, loop my arm through my daughter's, and walk her down the center of the crowd of people—people who adore her and Maribella more than anything, all smiling and dabbing at tears. I keep my eyes trained ahead, doing my best not to trip in the white sand.

Maribella's dark hair is cropped close to her scalp at the sides, a mop of curls hanging over her forehead. She looks incredible in the cream linen suit I helped pick out. She, like Carmen, holds a bouquet of origami flowers surrounded by silk greenery, her dark eyes brimming with unshed tears.

When we make it to the end of the aisle, Carmen steps out of our embrace, turning to face her *Mami* first, hugging her tight and kissing both her cheeks. She spins to face me, blinking tears from her cinnamon-colored eyes, the same as Lola's.

"Who's the one crying now?" I joke, pulling her into my chest for a crushing hug before pressing a kiss to the top of her head, releasing her after a long beat.

"It's usually you, Dad, but if we're going to cry about something, I think today is the perfect excuse," she whispers.

"I think so too. And Carmen?"

"Yeah?"

"*Te amo.*"

She grins up at me, dimples popping. "*Te amo, Papi.*" Maribella reaches for Carmen's hand, helping her up onto the small platform as Lola and I take our seats in the front row.

The sun is setting, wind blowing lightly around us, as Carmen and the newest addition to our family say their vows surrounded by family and friends who love them exactly as they are.

Lola sags against my side, winding an arm through mine and pressing her other palm against my bicep. "You know, I would do it all again if it meant I got you in the end," she whispers into my ear.

I lower my mouth to the shell of hers and whisper back, "I choose you, Lols. In every lifetime. In every circumstance. My soul will *always* find my way back to *you.*"

The end, for real this time. <3

Acknowledgments

There are about a million people I need to thank for getting me to the finish line with this book, but I'll start with the person who was there from the start, long before I'd ever written a single word on the page (Google Doc). To my Mayte, thank you for sharing every piece of yourself and your culture with me, and loving me since we were kids. You're the best friend anyone could ever ask for, and I hope for many more years together, crying while getting our coochies waxed and having near-death experiences that always lend to an excellent story time (if you're at all curious about the near death experience mentioned in chapter one, either head to my Patreon or purchase the special edition copy of Something Tangled Something True to read "The Lost Chapter" aka the original first chapter before I realized it was more for my enjoyment than the good of the story. *Sighs heavily*)

To my Unhinged Romance Slumber Party (Evelyn Leigh, Cynthia A. Rodriguez, and Kath Richards), thank you for dealing with my constant whining about everything that had gone wrong with this book, and for pushing me to take a breather and get my ass into gear. I wanted to quit so many times while writing this one, but you guys were my rock when I needed you most. (Ps. We all write in the same universe… and the next book in the Rosa Ranch series will include some of their characters, so check those out and get acquainted in the meantime!)

And Cyn, I know I mention you above, but truly, this book would not exist without you. I'd have thrown in the towel completely after [redacted] but you put your whole pussy into helping me rework this book, and make it the absolute best it could be. I can't thank you enough for your time, wisdom, energy or love.

A huge shoutout to Marja Graham, who was so unbelievably kind in her feedback, while also being firm in letting me know that no, I could not simply write this book as a small town romance without actually showing the reader the small town… nor should I just have these characters hunching 24/7. Womp womp. Your alpha/dev feedback was incredible and I couldn't have done it without you. Ps. I'm sorry for the constant "Like this?" and "Better?" replies you received for every comment you made as I attempted to apply your feedback.

To everyone who sensitivity read or provided beta feedback for this book, you have all of my gratitude (Yashira, I'm so sorry you had to learn about my anxiety this way, but thank you for seeing me through every change and giving me the push I needed to make the ending right). I could not write the characters that I do without each of you, and I'm eternally grateful for your willingness to share with me and open yourself up to allow me to grow and learn from you.

Of course, I couldn't forget my patrons! I have so much love for each of you who subscribes to my Patreon, allowing me to have some extra income to pay all the wonderful artists that play such a pivotal role in both my creative process and marketing!

And to you, the lovely reader staring at these words, thank YOU for picking up this book and sharing your love of books with me. <3

About the Author

Giuliana Victoria is an author based in Pennsylvania who shares her readers' deep love of all things romance. She's a full-time physician assistant, whose passion lies in being there for her patients during their most vulnerable moments.

When Giuliana isn't writing swoon-worthy book boyfriends, she can be found yelling about human rights on Threads, hiking with her three large breed rescue dogs, and, of course, curled up with a good book beside her husband, the best "book boyfriend" there is.

She hopes you'll love **Something Tangled, Something True** as much as she enjoyed writing it, and she looks forward to sharing all of her future works with her incredible readers.